F DAY
Eve of chaos.
Day, S
817854

EVE of CHAOS

SA APR 2013
EN MAR·14
SU JAN 15
LC MAR 2017

TOR BOOKS BY S. J. DAY

Eve of Darkness
Eve of Destruction
Eve of Chaos

EVE *of* CHAOS

Sylvia Day writing as S. J. Day

A TOM DOHERTY ASSOCIATES BOOK
NEW YORK

This is a work of fiction. All of the characters, organizations, and events portrayed in this novel are either products of the author's imagination or are used fictitiously.

EVE OF CHAOS

Copyright © 2009 by Sylvia Day

All rights reserved.

A Tor Book
Published by Tom Doherty Associates, LLC
175 Fifth Avenue
New York, NY 10010

www.tor-forge.com

Tor® is a registered trademark of Tom Doherty Associates, LLC.

ISBN 978-0-7653-3750-4

First Trade Paperback Edition: February 2013

Printed in the United States of America

0 9 8 7 6 5 4 3 2 1

*To all the readers who've followed Eve on her
adventures so far. Thank you.*

ACKNOWLEDGMENTS

Faren Bachelis, copy editor at Tor, for the attention paid to my books and for all the lovely notes of praise that sprinkled the margins, both of which I deeply appreciate.

Gary Tabke, for making the delicious One-Eyed Jacks that Eve loves in this book.

Everyone at Tor who went the extra mile for this series. You rock! I appreciate all of you.

Kate Duffy, who went above and beyond, as always. Thank you for the patience and support.

And to Patricia Briggs, for her generosity and kind words. There is nothing in the world like receiving compliments from an author whose work you would camp out on a bookseller's doorstep to get to.

God will stretch out over Edom the measuring line
of chaos and the plumb line of desolation.

—ISAIAH 34:11

EVE *of* CHAOS

CHAPTER 1

Evangeline Hollis watched with clenched jaw as a kappa demon served *yakisoba*—Japanese pan-fried noodles—to her mother with a broad smile. Eve guessed that the ratio of mortals to demons at the Orange County Buddhist Church's annual Obon Festival was about fifty-fifty.

After three months of living with the Mark of Cain and her new "job" as celestial bounty hunter, Eve was resigned to the reality of Infernals mingling undetected among mortals. However, she was still surprised by the number of transplanted Japanese demons who had come out to play at the festival. There seemed to be an inordinate amount of them present.

"You want some?" her mother asked, holding out the plate. Miyoko had lived a mostly quintessential American life in the United States for thirty years. She was a naturalized citizen, a converted Baptist, and her husband, Darrel Hollis, was a good ol' boy from Alabama. But she appreciated her roots and made an effort to share the Japanese culture with her two daughters.

Eve shook her head. "I want *yakidango.*"

"Me, too. It's over there." Miyoko set off, leading the way.

The festival was contained within the gated parking lot of the temple. To the right was a large gymnasium. To the left, the temple and school complex. The area was small, but still managed to hold a variety of food and game booths. A *taiko* drum was elevated in a *yagura* tower overlooking a space that would later showcase Bon Odori dancers. Children competed to win prizes ranging from live goldfish to stuffed animals. Adults hovered over displays of trinkets and homemade desserts.

The Southern California weather was perfect, as usual. A balmy seventy-eight degrees with plenty of sunshine and very few clouds. Adjusting her sunglasses, Eve relished the kiss of the sun on her skin and breathed in the scents of her favorite foods.

Then a foul stench wafted by on the afternoon breeze, assaulting her nose and ruining her rare moment of peace.

The putrid smell of rotting soul; it was unmistakable. It was a cross between decaying flesh and fresh shit, and it amazed Eve that the Unmarked—mortals lacking the Mark of Cain—couldn't smell it. She turned her head, seeking out the source.

Her searching gaze halted on a lovely Asian woman standing across the aisle from her. A *yuki-onna*—a Japanese snow demon. Eve noted the Infernal's white kimono with its delicate *sukura* embroidery and the detail on her cheekbone that resembled a tribal tattoo. In truth, the design was the demon's rank and it was invisible to mortals. Like the Mark of Cain on Eve's arm, it was similar to mortal military insignia. All Infernals had them. The details betrayed both which species of damned being they were and what their rank in Hell's hierarchy was.

Contrary to what most theologians believed, the Mark of the Beast wasn't something to be feared as the start of the Apocalypse; it was a caste system that had been in place for centuries.

Eve's mark began to tingle, then burn. A call to arms.

Now? she asked with a mental query, exasperation clear in her dry tone. She was a Mark, one of thousands of "sinners" around the world who'd been drafted into service exterminating demons for God. She was expected to kill at the drop of a hat, but her mother was with her and they were at a house of worship.

Sorry, babe. Reed Abel sounded anything but. *You're in the wrong place at the right time. Her number's up, and you're closest.*

You've been singing that tune all week, she retorted. *I'm not buying it anymore.*

She'd been vanquishing a demon a day—sometimes two—for the last several days. A girl needed more than just Sundays off when her job was killing demons. *Why am I always closest?*

Because you're a disaster magnet?

And you're a riot.

Reed—aka Abel of biblical fame—was a *mal'akh*, an angel. He was a handler, a position that meant he was responsible for assigning hunts to a small group of Marks. It was a lot like skip tracing. The seven earthbound archangels acted as bail bondsmen. Reed was a dispatcher. Eve was a bounty hunter. It was a well-oiled system for most Marks, but to say she was a squeaky wheel would be an understatement.

Dinner tonight? he asked.

After that wisecrack, cocky bastard?

I'll cook.

She followed her mom, keeping an eye on her quarry. *If I'm still alive, sure.*

In the back of her mind, she heard and felt Alec Cain—Reed's brother—growl his disapproval. Alec was her mentor. Once known as Cain of Infamy, he was now Cain the Archangel. She and Alec had a history together, starting ten years ago when she'd given him her virginity. Nowadays, his position as archangel had stripped him of the ability to have an emotional attachment to anything other than God, but Alec held on to her anyway.

What means more? he had asked her. *When someone wants you because he can't help it? Because of hormones or some chemical reaction in the brain? Or when he wants you because he chooses to want you? Because he makes the conscious decision to want you?*

Eve didn't know, so she was drifting along with him, trying to figure it out.

She was certifiably insane for stepping in the middle of the oldest case of sibling rivalry in history, especially since the three of them shared a unique bond that allowed a free flow of thought between them. Eve often asked herself why she played with fire. The only answer she came up with was that she just couldn't help herself.

I'm calling dibs on breakfast tomorrow, Alec insisted gruffly.

One-Eyed Jacks? No one cooked them like Alec. Grilled pieces of bread with a hole in the middle to hold a fried egg. Buttery and crispy, and served with syrup. He also toasted the centers and sprinkled them with cinnamon-sugar to serve on the side. Delicious.

Whatever you want, angel.

It was a given that Reed wouldn't be around for breakfast, since dating two men at once meant that all three of them were sleeping alone at night.

The *yuki-onna* excused herself from her handsome companion and moved toward the gymnasium, taking the tiny steps dictated by the tight fit of her kimono and the *geta* wooden clogs on her feet. Eve was at an advantage with her attire. Her stretchy capris and ribbed cotton tank top didn't impede her range of movement at all. Her Army-issue "jungle boots" were breathable and functional. She was ready to rock. But that didn't mean she wanted to.

"I have to wash my hands," Eve said to her mother, knowing that as a retired registered nurse, Miyoko would appreciate the need for cleanliness.

"I have antibacterial gel in my purse."

Eve wrinkled her nose. "Yuck. That stuff makes my hands sticky."

"You're too fussy. How many dangos you want?"

"Three sticks." The rice cake dumplings were grilled on wooden skewers and coated with sweet syrup. They were a childhood favorite that Eve enjoyed too rarely, which aggravated her disgruntlement. If the demon ruined her appetite, there would be Hell to pay. Seriously.

Eve handed over a twenty-dollar bill, then set off in pursuit of her prey.

She overtook the demon and entered the gym where picnic tables had been arranged to provide seating for diners. Dozens of festival-goers filled the vast space with echoing revelry—laughing, conversing in both English and Japanese, and eating. Mortals mingled with Infernal beings in blissful ignorance, but Eve noted every one of Hell's denizens. In return, they knew what she was and they eyed her with wary hatred. The mark on her deltoid betrayed her, as did her scent. As rotten as they stunk to her, she smelled sickly sweet to them. Ridiculous really, since there was no such thing as a sweet Mark. They were all bitter.

Tucking herself against the wall, she watched through the tinted glass doors as the *yuki-onna* approached. From the forward vantage, Eve could see the demon's feet hovering just above the ground. Backing up slowly, Eve rounded the corner to stay out of sight. A glass case was mounted to the wall at her shoulder, displaying trophies and a lone katana within its lighted interior.

Eve glanced around quickly, noting the distraction of the rest of the gym's occupants. With superhuman speed, she pinched off the round metal lock with thumb and forefinger, and withdrew the sheathed blade. She held it tucked between her thigh and the wall, hoping it was more than a decoration. If not, she could always summon the classic flame-covered sword. But she'd rather not. Buildings had a nasty habit of catching fire around her, and she had greater proficiency with the sleeker, moderately curved "samurai sword" than she did with the heavier glaive.

Her prey entered the gym and turned in the opposite direction, heading toward the restrooms just as Eve had guessed she would. Closing the women's bathroom while food and drink were present in copious quantities was always a bad idea, but Eve didn't have a choice. Her mother was waiting, and she couldn't risk losing her target.

Her present dilemma was one of the many reasons why Marks weren't supposed to have family ties. The sinners who were chosen were usually loners easily transplanted to foreign soil. Relatives were a liability. Eve was the sole exception to the rule. Alec had fought to keep her close to home because he knew how much her parents meant to her. He was also motivated by guilt, since their indiscretion ten years ago was the reason she was marked today.

The wheels of justice didn't turn any faster in Heaven than they did on Earth.

When the bathroom door swung shut behind the demon, Eve followed. The mark throbbed hot and heavy within the skin covering her deltoid, pumping aggression and fury through her veins. Her muscles thickened and her stride altered. Her body's reaction was base and animalistic, the surge of bloodlust brutal and addicting. She had come to crave it like a drug. Too much time between kills, and she became short-tempered and twitchy.

Despite the rush, her heartbeat and hands remained steady. Her body was a temple now, and it ran like a machine. As she entered the bathroom, Eve was calm and focused. When had she become so at ease with her murderous secondary life? She would have to ponder that later, when she had some privacy and time to cry.

All of the stall doors were slightly ajar, except for the handicapped one at the far end of the room. The stench of decaying soul permeated the space. Affixed to the wall near the door was a tube that held a collapsible Wet Floor sign. She tugged it free and set it outside in the hallway, then closed the door and turned the lock. It wasn't quite as useful as an Out of Order cone, but it would have to do.

There was no way to stave off the sudden deluge of memories of another bathroom, one in which she had fought a dragon and paid with her life. She'd been resurrected to kill another day because of a deal Alec had made with someone, somewhere. She didn't know the details, but she knew the cost had to be steep. If she hadn't been in love with him already, his willingness to make that kind of sacrifice would have sealed the deal. She wasn't ready to die just yet, despite demon killing and a crazy love life.

One day she hoped to marry and have children, enjoy a successful career and family vacations. But she would have to shed the mark first—either by manipulating someone in power or by collecting enough indulgences to work off her penance.

Of course, there were loopholes in the indulgence system. She'd killed the teenage son of the Black Diamond Pack Alpha werewolf *twice*, but had only been given credit for the second kill. Bullshit like that really got under her skin. What was a girl supposed to do when even God didn't play fair?

A soft whimper arrested Eve midstride. The sound had a high, trembling note that sounded childlike. She rolled her shoulders back and waited. Hunting was less about the pounce than it was about positioning. She stood dead center in the most open space in the room. The exit was at her back. The Infernal had no way out but through her. Damned if she would move just to hurry things up a bit.

The mark continued to flood her with adrenaline and hostility. Her senses honed in on her prey, flooding her mind with information. Her stance widened.

"Come out, come out wherever you are . . ." she crooned.

The lock on the handicapped stall turned. The door pulled inward. A child's face appeared, wan and tear streaked. A pretty girl of Asian heritage in a light summer dress with a watermelon design around the hem. Maybe six or seven years old. Shaking with fear. A moment later, the lovely visage of the *yuki-onna* appeared above the girl's head.

Eve growled. "A hostage was a bad idea."

When she had kids of her own, she wasn't letting them out of her sight.

"I will walk out of here with the child," the Infernal said in her lilting, accented voice. She stepped out of the stall with her hand on the girl's shoulder. "Then I will release her."

The child's teeth began to chatter and her lips took on a blue tinge. Gooseflesh spread from the point where the demon clutched her.

"You're going to die," Eve said matter-of-factly. The *yuki-onna* had been targeted. Marks would hunt her until she was dead.

"So are you," the demon retorted. "Do you really want to waste your last moments killing me?"

There's a hostage, she told Reed, ignoring the

standard demon intimidation and bargaining tactics. *A little girl. I need you to get her out of here.*

A warm breeze moved over her skin, tangible proof that her handler was always with her. He was forbidden to assist his charges in their hunts, but clearing mortals out of the way fell under his purview. *On your cue,* he murmured.

Eve had no idea where in the world he was, but as a *mal'akh*, he could shift—or teleport—in and out of a location faster than the blink of an eye.

"I was going to take you down fair and square," she told the demon, holding the sheathed katana aloft. "I should have known you would want to fight dirty."

"I have no weapon." A lie. Demons all had certain gifts, like the *yuki-onna*'s ability to create extreme weather. Marks had only their own wits and strength. They were celestially enhanced physically—able to heal and react quickly—but lacked any supernatural "powers."

"I'll give you mine," Eve offered grimly, "if you let the kid go." She ripped the katana free of its sheath and hurled the lacquered wood at the demon's head.

She reached out to Reed. *Now!*

The demon's arms rose to ward off the projectile. The child was snatched by Reed before the *yuki-onna* caught it.

The Infernal's cry of rage was accompanied by an icy gust that burst through the room like an explosion. Eve was thrust backward into a heated-air hand dryer with enough force to hammer it flush to the wall. She held onto the hilt of the katana by stubbornness alone. Her booted feet dropped to the floor with a dull thud, and she hit the ground running.

Arm raised and blade at the ready, Eve rushed forward with a battle cry that curdled her own blood. The child's fear lingered in the air, the acrid scent mingling with the stench of decaying Infernal soul. The combination sent her mark into overdrive. She leaped, slashing down on the diagonal, but the demon spun away in a flurry of snow. The temperature dropped drastically. The mirrors fogged around the edges, and her breath puffed visibly in the chilled air.

Eve pursued her, feinting and parrying against the sharp icicles the demon threw at her. They shattered like glass against her flashing katana, sprinkling the tile with slippery shards.

Crunching across the hazardous floor, she advanced with precision. The beautiful kimono fluttered with the Infernal's retreat, the thick silk shredded by Eve's calculated attacks. Once the sorriest swordswoman in her class, Eve had practiced exhaustively until she stopped embarrassing herself. She still wasn't much beyond passably proficient with the weapon, but she no longer felt hopelessly inept.

She began to hum a merry tune.

As she'd hoped, the demon floundered, caught off guard by the implied boredom. The *yuki-onna*'s next salvo lacked the speed of the previous ones. Eve caught it with her fist, hissing as the ice splintered its way across her palm. Blood flowed, its scent goading the demon into roaring in triumph, a sound audible only to those with enhanced hearing.

Eve lobbed the icicle back, followed immediately with the katana. The Infernal deflected the first projectile with an icy blast, but was left vulnerable to the second. The blade sliced along the demon's right triceps, drawing blood before impaling the wall behind her. A crimson stain began to spread through the pristine white of the kimono.

"Checkmate," Eve taunted. "Your blood for mine."

The Infernal retaliated with an icicle that pierced straight through Eve's right thigh. She cried out and dropped to one knee. Agonized, she sent up a silent request for a sword. She held her palm open to receive the gift . . .

. . . which didn't come.

Shock froze Eve. She'd gambled with the loss of the katana and rolled snake eyes. She always feared this day would come. Formerly agnostic, she didn't show the deference to the Almighty that others did. She wasn't disrespectful per se, but she might be too forthright in voicing her inability to understand the way God handled things.

She asked again, throwing in a "please" for good measure. The result was the same. Nada. Eve growled, furious that she would be denied the tool required to complete the task she was forced to perform.

The *yuki-onna* quickly deduced what had failed to happen. She giggled, a lovely melodic sound. "Perhaps he realizes that saving you is hopeless and not worth the effort."

"Fuck you."

"It is rare that Sammael sets a bounty so high or allows everyone in Hell a chance to claim it." The demon grinned. "But then, this is the first time someone has run over one of his pets."

"What bounty?" Eve hoped she hid the sudden fear she felt. "Is Satan upset that I ran over his *dog*? That's hysterical."

I'm not laughing, Alec snapped.

I know. Eve sighed. *My life sucks.*

She struggled to her feet, favoring her impaled leg. Reaching down, she yanked the ice dagger free and tossed it aside. Blood spurted from the gaping wound, then gushed. She ignored it for now. She had bigger problems.

"What is funny," the *yuki-onna* retorted, "is how you will be ripped apart by everyone in Hell."

"Everyone, huh?" Eve shrugged. "He'll have to do better than that, if he hopes to take me out."

That's my girl, Alec praised. *Never let 'em see you sweat.*

But she heard the unease in his voice. She also felt him poised to leap to her rescue.

I've got this, she said, staying him. She wasn't sure how, but she would figure it out on her own. Damned if some ice bitch in clogs would kick her ass.

"Sammael wants you," the demon taunted. Her disheveled hair and wide eyes only made her more beautiful. "And I will be rewarded for bringing you in."

Laughing through her growing panic, Eve made a third request—not quite a prayer—for a sword. Again, she was ignored.

She deflected the demon's next icicle with her forearm, then darted to the left to catch another. She threw it back. It was knocked off course by a burst of frosty air. All the while, she closed the distance between herself and the wall that held the katana.

"You can take hostages," Eve taunted, "but you can't take me."

Bravado. Sometimes it was all a Mark had.

"I am beginning to think otherwise," the demon retorted with a malicious gleam in her dark eyes.

Pounding came to the locked door, followed by a string of anxious-sounding Japanese. Not for the first time, Eve wished her mother had taught her the language. All she knew was that someone wanted to come in, and the demon she was fighting was no longer eager to get out. In fact, the *yuki-onna* seemed energized by the intrusion.

Eve took another step closer. Her boot slipped on an ice shard and she skidded, her balance compromised by her injured leg. She was inspired by the near fall, her mind seizing on a possible means to the end.

Dependent upon God's willingness to cooperate and give her a damn break, of course.

Kicking hard, she sent up a spray of water and ice. As the *yuki-onna* retaliated with a rapid volley of icicles, Eve shot forward, using the slush on the tile to drop to the floor in a careening, feet-first slide into home plate.

"I could really use that sword now," she yelled skyward, as the white tile rushed past her in a blur. *"Please!"*

Nothing.

Time slowed to a trickle . . .

The demon leaped gracefully and was held aloft by icy air currents. Levitating into a prone position, the Infernal's facade of beauty fell away, revealing the true evil beneath—eyes of blood red, a gaping maw of blackened teeth, and grayish skin with a network of inky veins that spread into her hairline. With arms splayed wide, spears of ice appeared in her hands like ski poles.

Alec and Reed roared in unison, their shouts reverberating in Eve's skull with such volume they drowned out everything else. In slow motion, she watched the demon hovering like a ghostly apparition, her white robes in tatters, her hair a sinuously writhing mane. Eve raised her arms to ward off the coming attack, then jerked in surprise as a heavy weight forced her forearm to drop to her chest . . .

. . . weighted by the miraculous appearance of a glaive in her hand.

Her grip tightened on the hilt and her back arched up. Hurling the blade forward like a javelin, she struck the *yuki-onna* straight in the chest. The glaive pierced deep with a sickening thud.

The demon exploded in a burst of ash.

Eve continued to slide until she slammed into the wall. At impact, the katana dislodged from its mooring, twisting to fall point down toward her head. She jerked to the side, rolling to avoid the blade. It pierced the floor where she'd been an instant before. Behind her, the glaive—no longer embedded in the demon's body—clattered to the tile.

"Holy shit," she breathed.

A pair of steel-toed boots appeared next to her head, then a hand extended into her line of sight. Looking up, her gaze met eyes of rich chocolate brown. Once, Alec had looked at her with a heat so scorching it burned her skin. She missed that look. Then again, she got hot enough for the both of them just checking him out.

At a few inches over six feet, Alec was as ripped as

one would expect a skilled predator to be. He was God's most revered and trusted enforcer, and his body reflected that calling. His hair, as always, was slightly overlong, but she would fight off anyone who approached him with shears.

"Could God have waited any longer to bail me out of the mess he put me in?" she groused.

"Did you note the lack of fire?" His voice—dark and slightly raspy—was pure seduction, even when laced with the resonance unique to archangels. It didn't sound that way when he spoke to her telepathically, which was sadly appropriate. Who he was in reality was far different from who he was in her mind.

She blinked up at him. "*You* bailed me out? What the hell? Was he just going to let me die? *Again?*"

"Obviously not, since you're not dead. It was a lesson in faith."

"More like a lesson in 'I am God, see me fuck with you.' "

"Watch it," he admonished.

Eve accepted his proffered hand. As he pulled her upright, his powerful chest and tautly ridged abdomen flexed noticeably beneath his fitted white T-shirt. She couldn't help noticing stuff like that, even though she couldn't touch what she was looking at.

"What is it with demons and bathrooms?" she asked. "Grimshaw started a trend when he sent that dragon to kill me. I swear I've vanquished at least half a dozen Infernals in bathrooms since then."

The dragon had been a courtier in Asmodeus's court, but he'd killed her for Charles Grimshaw— former Alpha of the Northern California Black Diamond Pack and father of the wolf she'd had to kill twice. Demon retaliation was a bitch.

Alec cursed at the sight of her thigh. Her toes were squishing in the blood soaking her sock and puddling along the sole. She would need a new pair of boots.

He bent to examine her wound more closely. "I would have gotten here sooner, but I had to scare off the crowd of Infernals in the hall first."

"Crowd?"

"I don't think the ice bitch was kidding about the bounty."

"What do you know that I don't? You wouldn't believe an Infernal without some sort of proof."

Alec had assumed control over the day-to-day operation of Gadara Enterprises—the secular front for the North American firm of Marks—since the archangel Raguel had been taken prisoner by Satan a couple of months back. That meant Alec was privy to almost every hellacious and celestial happening that occurred between the top of Alaska to the end of Mexico.

"The number of Infernals in Orange County has tripled in the last two weeks."

Which was when she'd graduated from training. As she was often reminded, nothing was a coincidence. "No wonder it's been so busy around here."

He gave her a resigned look. "It will get busier, if Sammael's set his sights on you."

"With a free-for-all bounty open to all classes of demons? Jeez, you'd think I kicked his puppy or something. Oh wait . . . I did." Eve put weight on her wounded leg and winced at the immediate throb of agony.

Alec tucked his shoulder under her arm to support her. "We need to bandage that leg, smart ass."

"You *like* my ass, and not because of its IQ."

"Love it." He gave her butt an affectionate squeeze. Alec might be restricted from feeling emotional love for her, but lust wasn't a problem. "But I love the rest of your hot body, too, and I'd like to keep it in one piece."

The mark enabled her to heal super fast. In an hour or two, only a pink scar would remain, and by nightfall, the injury would be nothing but a memory. But she could help move things along in the recovery department by closing the hole with some butterfly bandages. She'd have to hurry; her mom was still waiting for her.

I'll take care of Miyoko, he assured her.

"I'll take Eve back to her place to change," a deep voice intruded.

They turned their heads to find Reed by the door. The men's features were similar enough to betray them as siblings, but they were otherwise polar opposites. Reed favored Armani suits and faultless haircuts. Today he wore black slacks and a lavender dress shirt open at the throat and rolled at the wrists. It was a testament to how completely, robustly *male* he was that he could look so damn fine in such a soft color.

Alec's arm at her waist tightened. The two brothers were like oil and kerosene together. Dangerously flammable. They refused to tell her what started their lifelong feud, and they kept the memory so repressed in the darkest corners of their minds that she hadn't yet been able to find it. Whatever the sore spot was, the murderous rage it incited was easily goaded.

They'd been killing each other for years—Cain more so than Abel—but were always resurrected by God to fight some more.

Which was just nasty in her opinion. Why God enabled the two brothers to keep fighting was beyond her comprehension.

"What are we going to do about this mess?" She offered a soothing smile to Alec before stepping away from him. A trail of blood marked her recent kamikaze slide across the floor. The rapidly melting ice was spreading the crimson stain along the grout lines, creating an oddly compelling map.

Stepping into the water, Alec snapped his fingers and the liquid and blood filled the nearest sink, transferred so quickly she hadn't caught the movement even with her enhanced senses. She would go home with Reed in similar fashion.

Thankfully, Marks had handlers to pick up after them. She was luckier than most in that she had Cain, too, although that created some friction with many of the other Marks who thought she had an advantage. They didn't take into consideration how many demons wanted to use her to get to the deadliest Mark of them all. She might as well wear a bull's-eye for cocky and rash Infernals to aim for.

Then again, it looked like Satan had taped the target on for her.

"Come on," Reed said, extending a hand to her. "Before your mother calls in the cavalry."

"Forget the cavalry." Alec winked at Eve. "Miyoko would charge in herself."

She was halted midlaugh by the stench of a sewer. Looking for the demon whose proximity had to be the cause, she found herself staring into an inexplicably lingering puddle at her feet . . . and familiar eyes of malevolent, crystalline blue. A face in the liquid. She stomped instinctively, destroying the visage of the water demon in an explosion of spraying droplets.

"What the hell?" Reed barked, catching her as her wounded thigh caused her to stumble.

In the literal blink of an eye, Eve found herself in the kitchen of her third-floor condo in Huntington Beach. "Did you see him?" she gasped, leaning heavily into his hard body.

Reed's arms tightened around her. "Yeah, I saw him."

He's gone. Alec's tone was grim. *I'm heading out to hold off your mom, but we need to address this when we're done here.*

The demon was a Nix—a Germanic shape-shifting water spirit. He'd targeted her almost from the moment she had been marked, then made a nuisance of himself until she killed him. Correction: She'd *thought* she killed him.

She *would* kill him. This particular Nix had taken the life of her neighbor Mrs. Basso. Sweet, forthright, widowed Mrs. Basso who had been a beloved friend. Eve's need for vengeance was what motivated her when the damned Infernal bounty hunting got tough.

Pulling away from Reed, she limped down the hallway to her master bedroom. The crash of the waves against the shore pulsed in through the living room balcony's open sliding glass door. In her premarked life, she'd been an interior designer. Her condo had been one of her first projects, and the space remained one of her favorites. Even the mistakes she'd made in the layout were fond ones. She wouldn't change a thing. She felt safe here, less like a demon killer and more like herself.

Eve absorbed the calm she found in her home with deep, even breaths.

Reed called after her, his tone both seductive and challenging. "Need help getting naked?"

She sighed inwardly. Outside these walls, the worst of Hell's denizens were converging en masse. She would need to be ready when she ventured out again.

As if her love life wasn't dangerous enough.

CHAPTER 2

E ve climbed onto one of the Shaker-style bar stools at her kitchen island. "You know, I wish the demons I killed would stay dead."

In truth, they usually exploded into ash like the *yuki-onna* had and were returned to Hell where they were punished for blowing their chance to play with mortals. She was the only Mark to have vanquished the same demon more than once.

"Hey," Diego Montevista protested from his seat on the stool beside her. "I'm alive for the same reason they came back to haunt you."

She smiled. "That's right. And you're worth it."

Montevista—previously the archangel Raguel's chief of security and one badass Mark—bumped shoulders with her. "Damn straight."

Mira Sydney frowned from her position at the other end of the island. Like her partner, Montevista, she was dressed in head-to-toe black—parachute pants and cotton T-shirt, with thigh holsters for both a 9mm and a dagger. "I still don't understand how that worked."

Montevista was large and forbidding, but his lieutenant was tiny and sweet-natured. Fair to his dark, Caucasian to his Latino. But it was clear that decades of working together had created a strong affinity between them. Alec had assigned them to Eve's protection detail after the Obon festival. After all, Cain of Infamy didn't need the same protection that the other archangels did. Eve didn't mind. She'd bonded with both Montevista and Sydney during her training—infamous for being the worst Mark training disaster in history. Out of a class of nine, only three survived. And Raguel Gadara had been taken; the first and only successful archangel abduction.

"The world's gone to shit since Eve hit the scene," Reed grumbled from the stove where he was stir-frying homemade Kung Pao chicken. He was clearly unhappy to have company during their date.

"Gee, thanks," Eve said.

His mouth curved in a devilish smile that contrasted sharply with the wings and halo he occasionally sported for shock value. There was very little that could be called angelic about Reed. "At least you're good eye candy."

Eve groaned. He winked.

As gorgeous as Reed was—and he looked especially fine with an apron tied over his usual elegant attire—he had some seriously rough edges. But she didn't want to smooth them away; she wanted to understand them. She knew firsthand that he was the type of man who could lure a woman to sin with just a look. Charm wasn't a necessity. Still, Eve strongly suspected that some of the crudity that spilled from his mouth was due to his nervousness around her. It was oddly endearing that he would be so affected by her. She couldn't resist exploring the attraction further.

Sydney cleared her throat. "Tell me the whole story. From the beginning."

Eve looked at her. "Surely you've heard it too many times already."

"Not from the source. I want to hear it from you."

"All right." Eve leaned into the counter. "When I was a newbie, I stumbled across a tengu who didn't smell like shit and had no details. I told Cain. We told Gadara. Gadara told us to find out where the demon came from. Abel agreed and put the order through."

Sydney shot a quick glance at Reed. "I remember hearing that you were assigned to a hunt before training."

Reed's features took on a stony cast. As Eve's handler, he was the only person who could put her to work. Marks weren't supposed to hunt before they were fully trained.

Eve nodded. "In his defense, no one believed me. They thought I was in transition and my Mark senses hadn't fully kicked in yet."

"How green were you?" Montevista asked.

"A day or two."

Sydney whistled.

"Yeah. Rotten," Eve agreed. "Especially after I proved I wasn't nuts and we *still* had to track down the source of the tengu's abilities."

"The masking agent," Montevista offered. "Stuff that temporarily hides Infernal stench and details."

"That's what they started calling it. Cain and I discovered that they were producing and distributing the mask out of a masonry located less than an hour's drive from here."

"Ah." Sydney grinned. "Upland."

Eve nodded sheepishly. She was never going to live that down. "The masking agent was concocted from blood and bone meal made from Marks, animals, and Infernals. Plus spells and other stuff. Cain came up with the idea to destroy the mask ingredients in the masonry's giant roller kiln. I came up with the idea to toss the Nix in there and evaporate him, too. Abel came up with the idea to lock the Black Diamond Pack's heir in the kiln room. And it was God's idea of a joke to make the masking agent a life preserver when cooked at high heat. It kept the wolf and Nix alive when they should have been blown to smithereens. It's also what saved Montevista a few weeks later."

Sydney shot a concerned glance skyward. When lightning didn't strike Eve for her blasphemy, she said, "I heard the kiln explosion left a crater in the ground the size of a city block."

"At least." Reed snorted. "It was like a mini–atomic bomb."

Montevista grinned. "The stories aren't exaggerations."

"Wow." Sydney looked at Eve. "So, you killed the wolf a second time, but the Nix showed up today at the festival."

"Exactly." Eve's fingertips traced the veins within the granite countertop. "In fact, the police left a message on my voice mail this afternoon. I wish they would have called yesterday or even this morning. Then I would have been prepared for the Nix to pop up."

Pausing his stirring, Reed stared hard at her. "The same detectives who are investigating Mrs. Basso's death?"

"The ones from Anaheim, yes. Jones and Ingram. I haven't heard from the Huntington Beach Police since their initial interview."

"What do they want?"

"To talk to me. They didn't give any specifics. I'm guessing the Nix might be back to his old tricks. He'd already killed a dozen people before Mrs. Basso, so I can't see him stopping now." Her chest ached at the thought of her neighbor. "I don't understand why we weren't hunting him a long time ago. Isn't it our purpose to save lives?"

I'm sorry, babe. The sympathy in Reed's tone elicited a grateful smile from her.

Montevista gave her hand a commiserating squeeze. "No one knows what criteria the seraphim use to target Infernals."

Most demons kept a low profile. Being too obvious not only pissed off God, it pissed off Satan, too. Neither of the two was ready for Armageddon just yet. Satan wasn't powerful enough, and God liked things the way they were.

But the Nix was too cocky. He'd been killing women all over Orange County and leaving distinctive "calling cards" that caught the attention of the police—a water lily floating in a Crate and Barrel punch bowl. The death of Mrs. Basso had brought notice to Eve, too, who'd unfortunately had her own Nix calling card sitting in plain sight on the coffee table. Now, the detectives were looking at her for information she couldn't provide. Replying with, *There's a rogue demon on the loose, but don't worry because I'm a demon slayer for God,* wasn't the way to alleviate their concerns.

Alec suddenly appeared on her left side, shifting into her home without warning. "Let me guess: Kung Pao chicken."

"Good nose." Eve looked back and forth between the two brothers, noting the perpetual tension that filled a room when they were both in it. Alec should have knocked. Since he lived in Mrs. Basso's old condominium next door, it wouldn't have been a hardship. But a traditional entry wouldn't have the same irritate-Reed factor.

Alec set one hand on the countertop and the other on the back of Eve's stool. Leaning in, he pressed his lips to her temple. "If Abel's cooking for a girl," he murmured, "it's always Kung Pao."

"Really?" She looked at Reed with raised brows.

Montevista's dark eyes filled with amusement. Sydney glanced away with a half-smile.

Reed glared. "If you count 'always' as being a one-time thing in nineteenth-century China. We'd get more mileage talking about Cain's 'Hop on, baby, let me take you for a ride' spiel. You think I suck at pickup lines—"

"I've actually got something worth riding on," Alec drawled.

Reed's bamboo spoon hit the side of the wok with a clatter. "Saddle up and fuck off, then, shithead. No one invited you over."

Eve slid off the stool. "Enough. Satan's lackeys are after me and you two want to argue about who's more adept at getting laid?"

"He started it," Reed snapped.

"I'm finishing it." Eve wished a shot of liquor was an option. Unfortunately, mind-altering substances were ineffectual in her mark-enhanced body. She crossed her arms and asked Alec, "Did you come over because you have some news for us?"

He shook his head. "That's the problem. Not a word on the streets about this supposed bounty. We'd expect to hear *something* through an informant or an Infernal seeking shelter, but it's dead quiet."

"You had to barge in on our date to say you don't have anything to say?" Reed growled.

"No." Alec smirked. "I had to barge in because it pisses you off."

Eve snapped her fingers to bring their attention back to her. "The fact that we've been busier than usual can't be a coincidence, since you're always telling me there is no such thing."

Alec nodded. "Right. I'm still digging."

"Also . . . thinking about that night in Upland brings up something important that I forgot until just now."

Four pairs of eyes trained on her.

"The Nix said something to me," she went on, "just before I rolled him into the kiln. I asked, 'Why me?' and he answered, 'I do what I'm told.'"

"You didn't tell me this before," Alec accused.

"I'm sorry." And she meant it. Staying alive meant not dropping the ball. "He was dead and sent back to Hell. I was trying not to join him. The memory got lost in my brain."

"Shit. This is why you're not supposed to be able to shut us out."

Eve didn't know how or why she was sometimes able to circumvent the inherent connection between Marks and their superiors, but she was grateful. A woman had to have her secrets, especially while embroiled in a contentious relationship triangle.

She continued before they got off on a tangent. "I also noticed something new today—his details say he's now one of Asmodeus's lackeys."

Reed turned off the fire on the stove. "The Nix's details were courtesy of a lessor demon."

"They've changed since that first day you and I saw him," she insisted.

"Sammael *and* a king of Hell," Sydney breathed. "Yowza."

Eve could only give a lame nod. And to think she had once thought of herself as a lucky person. "Can I ask why Satan is a prince, but the demons under him are kings?"

"No!" Reed and Alec barked in unison.

She held up her hands in a defensive gesture. "Ooo-kay, then . . ."

Alec stared at her with narrowed eyes. "Damn it, angel."

Evangeline. Eve. Angel. A nickname only Alec had ever used. He still said it with the rumbling seductive purr that had gotten her into this marked mess to begin with.

Montevista gave her a wry look. "Only you would have multiple high-level contracts out on you, Hollis."

"Maybe the Nix and the wolf met after the explosion, and became friends. Maybe Asmodeus and

Grimshaw were friends," Eve said, "and Asmodeus is trying to help his buddy out in the revenge department. Maybe the Nix jumped ship to Asmodeus so that he had a valid excuse to hunt me."

"There's a hell of a lot of 'maybes' in there," Alec bit out. "And friendship is relative to demons. Favors aren't free. Asmodeus would've had to be paying a debt or getting something in kind."

That didn't sound good to Eve.

"That would have to be a huge debt or gain to make Asmodeus go after someone important to Cain," Montevista pointed out. "Grimshaw came after Hollis in vengeance for the death of his son. Asmodeus has no excuse, and he knew he'd piss off Jehovah and Sammael at once."

Eve sighed. The battle between Heaven and Hell wasn't a free-for-all. For the most part, Celestials and Infernals lived alongside each other in a wary truce. Satan's minions were ordered to stay under the radar, so they could do the most damage. Marks were only assigned to take down rogue demons. Montevista was right. Something big had motivated Asmodeus to break the rules in such a major way.

"Unless Sammael told Asmodeus to do it," Sydney suggested quietly. When everyone stared at her, she shrugged.

Montevista broke the silence. "She's got a point."

"I hadn't run over his dog yet," Eve reminded.

Dog. Ha! Since the damn creature had been the size of a bus, Eve's mind could barely connect "dog" to her road kill in the same train of thought.

"This has to be about more than Sammael's damned hellhound," Reed insisted. "He doesn't care about anyone but himself. Everyone and everything else—including pets—is expendable."

"So he wants something? I don't have anything valuable." Her gaze darted between the two brothers. "Except for both of you."

Alec and Reed fell silent, both physically and mentally. They knew she was a liability to them.

Eve refused to stay that way.

Reed turned back to the stove. Alec began routing orders through the mental switchboard system each archangel had to everyone in their firm. She moved into the living room. She was still within seeing/hearing distance, but the space helped to give her mind a break. Tuning the others out, Eve settled onto her down-filled sofa and contemplated the mess that was her life.

The Nix and Grimshaw's kid hadn't been the only Infernals in the kiln room that disastrous night in Upland. There had also been a gaggle of tengu—Japanese gargoyle-type demons. Since the Nix and the wolf had both lived to be killed another day, it was reasonable to wonder if the tengu might have found second lives, too.

Alec shifted over to her and settled into a seated position on the edge of her glass-topped coffee table. The thick denim of his blue jeans did nothing to hide the fine form of his long, muscular legs.

"You're going to get in trouble for using your powers so much," she admonished.

For seven weeks a year, each archangel was given free rein to use his powers to facilitate in training new Marks, a duty they rotated between them. But the rest of the year using their gifts meant facing consequences. *Suggesting* they live secular lives was God's way of fostering empathy for mortals. Eve thought it was a recipe for resentment.

Smiling, Alec said, "I'm not a firm leader yet. The same rules don't apply to me."

"Isn't that always the case?"

He leaned forward and rested his forearms on his knees. "I've double checked the security measures we installed against the Nix the first time around, both in this building and in your parents' house. I've also assigned a security detail to guard the perimeter against any new threats."

"Can they get rid of that nut job on the corner?"

"What nut job?"

"Don't tell me you haven't seen him. The guy who looks like an evil Santa Claus? Preaching fire and brimstone with his acoustic guitar?"

He stared at her.

"The dude with the big sign that says 'You are going to burn in Hell'?" When he continued to gaze at her blankly, she shook her head. "Are you shifting around so much that you haven't checked out the neighborhood in a while?"

Alec was gone in a blink. A split second later he was back in the same spot.

"I see," he said. "He's harmless."

"He's annoying, and he's been there for days." She snapped her fingers. "Hey, maybe God will take a trade between him and me?"

Eve was only partially kidding. The whole marked system was jacked, in her opinion. There were millions of religious zealots around the world who killed in God's name every day, but they didn't get marked.

Instead, the Almighty used the impious. It was like boot camp for sinners and nonbelievers. God seemed to be saying, *See who you shall hang out with if thou shalt not change thy blasphemous ways?*

"Not a fair exchange," he said, with a hint of a smile. "You're worth a hundred of that guy."

"That's your opinion."

"Clearly I'm not the only one who thinks so, since he's out there and you're with me. I'm also going to talk to Abel about lowering your caseload for a while."

Eve's brows rose. "Won't that put a burden on the other Marks in the area?"

"Somewhat."

"You can't ask me to do that and live with the consequences."

"I'm not asking you."

She considered that for a moment, her fingers drumming on the armrest. "Being an archangel suits you, I see."

"Don't," he warned.

"Infernals are swarming into Orange County—possibly because of me—and you want me to sit around while other Marks deal with the mess? They already don't like me."

"They'll get over it."

"Easy for you to say. No one hates you for working with me."

"You wouldn't do anyone any favors by getting yourself killed."

"Oh, I don't know about that." Her smile was grim. "I can think of a few people who want me dead."

"Not funny, angel."

She sighed. "You know me. I'm a big scaredy-cat.

I don't *want* to jump into oncoming traffic, but I can't hang out here watching *Dexter* reruns and eating Ben & Jerry's while other people are facing a horde."

"Argue all you want, it's still not happening."

"Gadara would put me out there."

"He's not here."

"And what's being done about that?" she challenged. "Or are archangels more expendable than I thought?"

Alec reached out and touched her calf with his fingertips. "We're working on that, too."

"It's been two months. I can't imagine it's been a vacation for him in Hell."

"We can't charge in. It would be a suicide mission."

"So what do we do?"

"*You* are going to follow orders. *I'm* going to work on securing leverage."

Eve ignored the first part of his statement and concentrated on the last half. "Leverage. As in . . . something you have that Satan wants more than he wants to keep Gadara?"

"Yes. Sammael has to bring Raguel to us. That's the only way we're going to get him back."

"What does Satan want more than an archangel bargaining chip?"

His mouth twisted wryly. "That's the question, isn't it?"

He ducked without warning. Something small and white flew through the space his head had been occupying. If Eve hadn't been gifted with enhanced sight, she would have missed it.

"Watch it, prick!" he barked at Reed.

"Keep your hands to yourself," Reed shot back.

Eve watched the object hit the balcony screen door and bounce back into the room. It rolled to a stop by the leg of the coffee table. She glanced over her shoulder. "A water chestnut?"

"It was either that or this—" He waved one of her Ginsu knives.

"Thanks for showing a little restraint with your testosterone." Pushing to her bare feet, she set her hands on her hips. "Now knock it off."

"You can't expect us to like this situation," Alec said.

"I'm not liking it either."

When she was alone and contemplative, Eve acknowledged that her feelings of loneliness and separation were goading her to accept a situation she never would have in her normal life. Technically, she wasn't doing anything more than spending private time with both of them, but technicalities weren't much of a buffer against hurt feelings and possessiveness. She felt disloyal to Alec—even though he couldn't return her affections—and she was concerned for Reed, who was so edgy about the whole thing.

"Maybe sticking strictly to business is the only option," she said.

Both men quieted, their jaws taking on stubborn cants. Montevista and Sydney looked at each other with raised brows.

"This isn't working," Eve persisted, her foot tapping on the hardwood.

Reed went back to chopping vegetables.

Alec leaned forward again. "Are you going to stay put like I'm ordering you to?"

Eve crossed her arms. "What do you think?"

"Right." He stood. "So, starting with breakfast tomorrow, you're back to having a full-time mentor. No more of this shifting in only when you need me."

"You're going to be my baby-sitter?"

His dark gaze raked her from head to toe. "Only if I can take you over my knee when you're naughty."

I'm still holding the knife, dickhead, Reed bit out.

Eve dropped back onto the couch with a silent groan. The two brothers were going to be the death of her.

If the demons didn't kill her first.

CHAPTER 3

E ve held a protein shake aloft. "Want one?"

Alec eyed the green beverage with obvious wariness. Dressed in long shorts and a white sleeveless T-shirt with steel-toed boots, he had the bad-boy look down to a science. His shades were hung backward and rested against his nape, tangling with the overlong mane of dark hair that she loved to run her fingers through.

Behind him, early morning sunlight filtered into her living room. Sydney was asleep in the guest room after an all-night watch, and Montevista was outside getting reports from the guards on the street. Beyond her balcony, surfers called out to each other as they hit the waves before the workday.

"You've got that look in your eyes," Alec said, grinning. "You want me."

She turned her back to him. "I'll take that as a no."

"Yes. I want it." He approached. "I want whatever you're dishing out. Enough that if you don't hurry up and give it to me, I just might have to take it."

There was a dark undertone to his voice that set off alarms. The old, prearchangel Alec would never say such a threat to her, but the new Alec . . . Not only did he say things that were out of character, she half feared he wasn't entirely kidding when he said them.

Eve reached behind her and proffered the glass. His fingers curled around hers, warm compared to the chill of the shake. He kept coming until his every exhale disturbed the loose tendrils of hair that always escaped her ponytail. Through their connection, she sensed his pleasure in the smell of her shampoo and the way their bodies fit so well together. The sharing of information worked in reverse, too, so he knew damn well what he was doing to her. When he stepped back, she missed his body heat, but she didn't miss the darkness in him that chilled her.

There's something . . . in me, he'd told her recently, and she believed him. She sometimes felt it. It was ruthless and cold, and it took every opportunity to slither against her.

She poured another glass from the remains in the blender. Her hands shook slightly in response to his proximity. Desire—for sex and/or violence—was the only emotion that affected a Mark's nervous system. "Let's go back to the construction site where we first learned about Gehenna Masonry."

There was a pause, then he said, "Shit. I forgot about the tengu."

"Me, too, until last night." In the process of hunting down the initial masked tengu, she and Alec had ended up at a construction site for a new Gadara Enterprises building—Olivet Place. They'd killed the two tengu they found there, but . . . "The building has four corners. Since they like to pack together, I figure they'd want to regroup."

"Why not go back to Upland where they were created?"

Facing him, Eve leaned back into the edge of the counter. "Because we blew it up?"

"You know what I mean. Why Raguel's building? Why not one of the others on Gehenna Masonry's list?"

"Because I was invited to this one. Remember?"

"Right," he murmured. "The invitation."

"One of many dangling threads in my life."

She'd stumbled upon the building by accident in her search for the tengu, but later found an opening-day invite in her mailbox. It had been a mock-up of the final invitation and not yet ready for publication, but someone had addressed it to her and mailed it. Someone had wanted her to check it out.

"I looked into it," he told her. "You were invited because all local interior designers and architects were. I checked it out myself. Your name was definitely on the list. All of your old colleagues at the Weisenberg Group were."

"Were the other invitations going to be shipped to home addresses?"

He leaned into the island. The casual pose did nothing to hide his alertness. "Good point. It should have been mailed to your office."

"At the time, I asked you what the chances were that I would be lured to a demon-infested building at the exact same time I was marked. And you said—"

"—slim to none."

Eve nodded. "So what changed your mind?"

"My thoughts went along these lines: the invitations were ordered by Raguel, the infestation was in one of his buildings, and we eradicated the two tengu we found when we got here."

"So you thought it was the work of a divine hand?"

"Could be. The good guys benefited. Anyway, why would an Infernal deliberately set up something that could potentially expose the mask? Makes no sense."

"Is it possible that Gadara set it all up?" She wouldn't put it past him. The archangel had been making her job as difficult as possible from the very beginning. As a mentor and Mark pair, Alec and she were a package deal. Gadara was relishing the novel opportunity to have Cain—and Cain's prestige—attached to his firm. However, his coup didn't stop him from using Eve to assert his authority over Alec. By moving her around like a pawn, he forced Alec to toe the line or risk her paying the consequences.

"He's more direct, you know that."

"But if you believe the invitation was celestially motivated, someone had to know about the tengu. Who?"

"Angel, it could go as high as the seraphim."

"Why not use the established chain of command? Send the order to Gadara, he would assign it to a handler, a handler would assign it to a trained and capable Mark. Bringing it straight to me is ridiculous."

"Is it? You got the job done."

"Flattery will get you nowhere in this. Other times, maybe. But not this time."

He gave her an exasperated look. "I take it you're thinking this is part of a plot of some sort?"

"I don't know. That's why we're heading over there."

His dark eyes were amused. "You know, your brain turns me on."

"Everything turns you on."

"Everything about *you*."

"You're feeling punchy this morning."

"I like being out in the field. Especially with you. Your ability to attract disasters definitely keeps things interesting."

"Not funny." Eve drank deeply and tried to picture him at a desk job. After a minute, she gave up.

"This shake isn't bad," Alec noted, licking his lips.

"What a compliment." The shake was orange juice and banana with green tea protein powder. She thought it was delicious, plus it would keep her fueled for a few hours at least. Marks burned calories like mad. As Reed said, *Highly efficient machines use superior fuel.* Translation: she ate like a sumo wrestler.

"I thought I was making you One-Eyed Jacks."

"When we get back. I'm eager to get moving."

"To face a possible horde of tengu? Why?"

"Can't you read my mind?" she challenged, even as she shut a mental door in his face.

His gaze narrowed with concentration, then one dark brow rose. "We have to figure out how you do that."

"What's to figure out? My acclimation has been out of whack from the beginning." She rinsed her glass out in the sink. He came up beside her and shoved his under the running water. At the same moment, the thought of the Nix entered both of their heads. As one, they pushed the thought away. One demon at a time.

"I'm serious, angel. Our connection can save your life."

"Not my fault. My Novium happened way too soon. Let's face it: the mark and I don't mesh well."

The Novium was a physical and mental transition Marks suffered through to progress from trainee to full-fledged. Like puberty, it altered a Mark's physical makeup, enhancing already keen senses and instilling a devil-may-care confidence. Side effects were edginess and lowered inhibitions. It created a fever that strengthened a Mark's tie to her handler while cauterizing the connection to her mentor. In Eve's case, it had created a triumvirate communication pathway that she was pretty sure would drive her crazy one day.

"Don't blame this on the mark," he chastised. "You're closing me off on purpose."

"You don't need to know everything."

He caught her around the waist when she tried to pass and tugged her close. "I *want* to know you, inside and out."

"So figure me out the old-fashioned way. It's more interesting that way."

She'd been in love with him since she was eighteen years old. It sucked that while he was back in her life now, he could never stay in it permanently. Alec was a killer by nature. He didn't just excel at it, he loved it. Not the kind of guy a woman settled down and had kids with. Of course, Marks were physically incapable of bearing children, but that wasn't the point.

Alec pressed a kiss to the tip of her nose. "You ready to go?"

"Don't shift!" she said quickly. "Let's take the bike."

"Ha! Make you a moving target? No way."

"It's less than ten minutes away! Besides, you don't even know if the bounty is real."

"I'm not using you as bait to find out."

Eve reached around and cupped his ass, giving him a slow, firm squeeze.

"Not fair," he rumbled.

"Did you forget how to ride after all that shifting around you've been doing?"

"Hardly."

"I can drive," she purred, looking up at him from beneath heavy-lidded eyes. "You can shield my back. No Infernal is going to mess with badass Cain of Infamy."

"*You* better not mess with me either," he warned, his eyes dark, "unless you're prepared to deliver."

"Hanging on while I drive is a guaranteed way to cop a feel."

"With our clothes on," he retorted. "Not nearly as fun."

Despite his protests, he shifted them into the carport next to his Heritage Softail. It was a black and chrome beauty, boasting custom saddlebags and a well-worn seat.

"Well, look at that." Eve whistled. "I was half expecting it to be covered in dust."

Alec tossed her the keys. "Shut up and hop on, before I change my mind."

Five minutes later, they were roaring out of the subterranean garage. When the Bible-thumping Evil Santa on the corner screamed *"Jezebel!"* after her, she stuck her tongue out at him. Alec gave her a playful swat to the hip.

Told you, she muttered.

Behave.

Taking Hamilton to Magnolia, Eve weaved confidently among the massive sport utility vehicles, sleek Porsches, and hybrids. A variety of music filled the air from open windows—thumping bass, twanging guitars, and soulful ballads. For the first time in far too long, she didn't wonder how many of the drivers around her were lower-ranking demons. She forcibly shut out the world and concentrated on the joy of driving a Harley with the hottest man on the planet wrapped around her. As far as Heaven went, this was pretty close.

They reached the Gothic-inspired office building before she was ready. Eve considered driving on and circling back later, but a Jeep Liberty was pulling away from the metered curb just as they pulled up. Recognizing the celestial hint, Eve steered the hog into the spot and cut the engine.

"Got you here in one piece," she teased, pulling off her helmet.

The heated thoughts in his mind slipped into hers, telling her bluntly that the feel of her body so close to his was something he craved to a dangerous degree. She slid off the bike and kept her gaze on the building, her breathing altered by the depths of his arousal. There was nothing tender about it. It was pure ferocious lust.

"You can run . . ." he warned.

But she couldn't hide. Her head turned, her senses perking up and searching out any possible threats. The scent of rotting soul drifted on the balmy breeze, but not in a quantity that would alarm her. Infernals were everywhere, working every sort of job, living in every community. Their presence alone wasn't concerning, only the number, which seemed to be under control.

Unless some were masked.

"It wears off, remember?" Alec said, securing the helmets to the bike.

"There could be more."

"Doubtful, since we killed the creators. Regardless, Hank is working on an antidote."

Eve looked over her shoulder at him. "Really?"

"Would I lie to you?"

"Are you sure you want to go there?"

He held up both hands in a gesture of surrender, but the wicked curve of his lips ruined the image.

Shaking her head, she started toward the front door. The building wasn't yet fully operational, but the lobby area was completed and an office for the sales team and property manager was open for business. A perky blonde in a sleek gray suit rushed out when they entered, then laughed when Eve pulled out her Gadara Enterprises badge. "I was ready to give you my sales pitch."

"I'm already sold," Eve said. "Hostile takeover."

Angel . . .

There were two guards at the security desk, one mortal and one Mark. The mortal took her badge and ran it through a scanner to record their entry time.

Gadara's security measures weren't any more rigorous than the majority of corporations, but they were certainly monitored more closely. Instead of keeping watch on things with a celestially enhanced eye, the archangels were forced by the empathy-for-mortals rule to rely on modern mortal technology. They could choose to do otherwise, but there were consequences. That was one of many things that drove Eve nuts about the Almighty. He claimed to give people a "choice," but usually the ramifications of making the wrong choice ensured it wasn't much of a contest.

"Great bike," the mortal guard said to Eve.

"It's his." She gestured toward Alec with a tilt of her head.

"I should let my girl drive."

Alec raked Eve with a heated glance. "It definitely has its benefits."

She pushed the sign-in sheet back over. "Elevators working yet?"

"Yes. Finally." The relief in the guard's voice made her smile. Patrolling the three stories without a lift would be a breeze for the Mark, but for the mortal it was probably more of a workout than he wanted from his job.

"Thanks."

As Eve headed toward the elevators, she noted the limestone floors and pointed arch facades that surrounded the brass elevator doors. A rose window took prominence at the rear of the building just above the exit. She made a mental note to look into the identity of the architect. The building's style was incongruous among its modern glass-hulled neighbors, but not in a garish way. It provided an elegance that the surrounding area had been lacking.

The moment the elevator doors shut, Alec's presence overwhelmed the enclosed space. He stood opposite her with his hands wrapped around the handrail behind him, his biceps and pectorals prominently displayed by his stance. His dark gaze was slightly mocking and more than a little insolent in his appraisal. It turned her on, and she shifted her weight from one foot to the other.

The Novium was a pain in the ass.

It didn't help that sex was like breathing to Marks. The constant near-death experiences created tension that was best alleviated with extended hot sex. The need was designed to force Marks to seek out companionship and comfort from others, rather than retreating into themselves. Eve's platonic double-dating meant she didn't have the stress outlet she needed. Even if that wasn't the case, Alec was different. The softer emotions he used to have in his eyes when he looked at her were gone. He wanted her, and she believed him when he said that he would always want her, but great sex wasn't enough for her. Not after knowing what it was like to have more.

"What's the best thing about being an archangel?" she asked in an attempt to keep her mind out of the bedroom.

"Relief from the rising cost of transportation."

"Be serious."

"You want the Hallmark card answer? Making a difference." He straightened as the car came to a stop. "No one knows better than me how difficult it is to be a Mark. There are aspects of Gadara Enterprises that I can tweak to make things easier on those in the field."

There was no inflection in his voice, no passion. She wondered how he could function that way. God felt it was necessary for the archangels to be emotionally neutral, but Eve called 'em like she saw them—they were unfeeling—and she couldn't imagine that being anything but miserable.

I feel what you feel, Alec said, watching her intensely. *I feel what Abel feels, as well as echoes from every Mark under me.*

So he knew what it was like for her to love him and he knew what it was like for Abel to want her. Maybe that's where his uncustomary sexual aggression was coming from.

Or maybe it was coming from that dark place inside him . . .

Regardless, the whole thing was screwed six ways to Sunday.

Eve sighed and turned her attention to the opening elevator doors.

The third floor was a notable change from the lobby. Ceiling fixtures had yet to be installed, the walls needed paint, and the industrial pile burgundy carpet had yet to be trimmed along the missing baseboards.

"So," she began, leading the way to the roof staircase, "you wanted to know why I was eager to come here."

"Shoot."

"When I went through this building the first time, I had no idea what I was doing. I didn't know what to look for, where the threats were, what was out of place. I need to see it again. Retrace my steps. I feel like I missed something and it's driving me nuts."

Alec's hand wrapped around her elbow. She'd dressed in a pale pink sleeveless shell and well-worn jeans. The outfit was comfortable, feminine, and allowed for ease of movement.

"We don't get to decide when it's time for things to happen, angel. We just roll with the punches and have faith that everything happens for a reason."

"I don't have faith in a divine plan, you know that. I think life is what we make of it and God throws curve-balls on a whim just to keep his days interesting."

"Watch it," he admonished, as if lightning might strike her in the enclosed space. Eve wouldn't be surprised. The Lord had yet to do her any favors.

They stepped into the stairwell. Warm, stagnant air rushed around them, in stark contrast to the cooler air-conditioning of the occupied areas. The heavy metal door thudded shut and images of Reed flooded her mind. He'd branded her with the Mark of Cain in the stairwell of Gadara Tower, a raw and violent coupling that would forever be burned in her memory.

If you don't stop thinking about that, Alec warned roughly, *I'll replace that memory with another one. Right now.*

She blanked her mind quickly.

The Alec she had once known would never have made such a threat. Seduce her, yes. Make love to her until she couldn't move or think, yes. But primal fucking was Reed's style. Alec had been a lover. Eve didn't know how to deal with the new version of him. He was more aggressive, less patient. More like the biblical Cain, she supposed. The side of him she had never seen. She knew she would enjoy whatever he did to her—he wouldn't tolerate otherwise—but she couldn't risk sinking deeper. She was already neck-deep as it was.

The roof door opened above them.

"Pretty Mark came back," a tengu singsonged,

followed by a frenzied thumping as it jumped for joy. "And Cain, too. Time to play."

Tengu were mischievous creatures. They lacked initiative and ambition, so they fell pretty low on the "must-vanquish" scale. Reed likened them to mosquitoes—annoying and you wished they didn't exist, but not as disgusting as rats. They infiltrated establishments as decorations, then worked to cause distress and anxiety in the inhabitants. Buildings with tengu had higher suicide rates than those that didn't. Higher rates of business failures, extortion, eviction, embezzlement, and adultery. Tengu infestation was the cause of community decline, dead malls, and ghost towns. In packs, they could be deadly, or at the very least, seriously destructive.

The door slammed shut and a riotous banging resounded on the roof, the sound of little stone feet dancing. Lots of feet. Lots of dancing.

"Damn, you're good," Alec said.

Eve sighed. Sometimes, she hated being right.

CHAPTER 4

"What are you doing, *mon chéri?*"
Reed stiffened at the sound of the familiar purring voice. Glancing over his shoulder, he met the calculated gaze of Sarakiel, one of the seven earthbound archangels. She walked into Cain's office as if she owned it.

"That's none of your business," he drawled.

"I hear Cain has returned to the field with Evangeline. Perhaps that is why you are rummaging through his office? 'While the cat is away . . .' as they say."

The manner in which Sara said Eve's name spoke volumes. She still coveted Reed, even though they had split ages before Eve was born. The head of the European firm of Marks was often assumed by theologians to be a male. Their mistake was laughable. Sarakiel was a woman in every sense of the word, one who shared his penchant for rough sex and designer clothing.

He pushed the top drawer of Cain's filing cabinet

shut. The archangels usually stayed within their own territory. They didn't like to defer to each other, which was expected when entering another firm's boundaries. It was also dangerous to have archangels in close proximity to one another. Infernals would love to cripple multiple firms with a single blow. But Sara was here because she had requested to assist Cain with his assumption of Raguel's firm. She'd been given her desire because it was her personal guards who had assisted Cain and Eve in Upland. She was lauded for being proactive, when the only reason she'd lent her team was because Reed had paid her with the use of his body. Now, her mentorship of his brother kept her uncomfortably near his business.

"What do you want, Sara?"

"What do I always want when I see you?"

A ripple of disquiet moved through him. "Not today, darling. I have a headache."

Her lips thinned at the blatant lie. *Mal'akhs* were impervious to mortal maladies. Still, the beauty of her features was unaffected by her anger. Tall, willowy yet fully curved, Sara was physically perfect in a way mortal women spent thousands of dollars to replicate. Her pale blonde hair and angelic features were so compelling, they were the impetus that funded her firm. Sara Kiel Cosmetics was a worldwide phenomenon, with sales inspired by the unequaled face of its owner. There had been a time when the mere sight of her could make Reed's blood heat dangerously, but no longer. Now his focus was narrowed to one particular brunette.

Sara stepped farther into the room with her dis-

tinctive sashay, her red silk pantsuit whispering se-
ductively as she approached. She reminded him of a
tigress—golden, lithe, predatory. "You have a dread-
ful way of showing gratitude."

"You haven't done a damn thing for me, Sara, aside
from the occasional orgasm." Reed shrugged. "I can
get that anywhere."

"You used to only want them from me."

"That was a long time ago." Knowing that appear-
ances spoke volumes to her, he sank into Cain's large
leather office chair and forced his frame to relax into
the plush back.

"You want what he has," she taunted, sinking into
the visitor's seat on the other side of the desk. A wave
of her hand encompassed the entire room, a corner office that boasted two walls of windows, a private bathroom with closet and shower, and a glass and chrome
desk with industrial styling. Leaning forward, she ran
her fingertips over the silver picture frame that held a
black and white photo of Evangeline. "You always
have."

"I want what I deserve, what I've proven myself
capable of handling."

"And Cain keeps getting it first."

"That works in my favor. He always fucks things
up and makes me look good."

All of his life, Reed had been the one to follow the
rules and surpass expectations. He was perfect, damn
it. Perfect for advancement, perfect for heading a firm.
It made no sense that his brother was the one promoted. Cain didn't want responsibility of any kind and
he'd been a nomad for too long. He had never learned
to play well with others.

Sara pouted. "I am trying to help you, and you are not giving me any credit. I sent Izzie here, did I not?"

"I'm supposed to thank you for that?" He had been indiscreet with the blonde and Eve had caught him at it. Now, every time she saw Izzie, the memory stung her and caused him to lose what little ground he gained in his attempts to win her.

"You should have stayed away from her."

"You knew what would happen," he bit out. "And you told Izzie to be around when it did."

"As a firm leader, it is my responsibility to prepare for every eventuality. There was a chance that desire for your brother's lover would drive you elsewhere. I had to make accommodations for that event, just in case." Her crimson-painted fingertips drummed atop the armrests. "Do you think I wanted Cain's woman to affect you so strongly?"

Iselda Seiler had been one of Eve's classmates. A woman whose Goth sensibilities were manifested in pale skin, kohl-rimmed eyes, and a fondness for purple lipstick. Izzie also had the distinction of having fucked Cain at some point in his past. One of thousands who'd serviced him over the centuries. His brother didn't remember her, but Izzie didn't care. She just wanted another go-round, both for the sex and because it was guaranteed to stir up trouble. She had lain in wait to sabotage Eve in any way she could, and she'd been ready and more than willing when Eve had pushed Reed too far to think clearly.

But why Sara would claim to want him in the same breath as she admitted sending another woman to service him made no sense.

"You're a real piece of work," he said. "I wonder, do you make Father proud?"

Sara gripped the ends of the chair arms with white-knuckled force, but her voice came with its customary whiskey smoothness. "You malign me without cause, *mon chéri*. You and I are two of a kind."

"Except you're an archangel, and I'm not." There had been a time when he'd been foolish enough to hope that she might help him achieve his own firm. Then he realized that she would never see him as equal to her. He provided stud service and nothing more. "You could have helped me, but you didn't."

"Obviously Jehovah is in agreement with me, since he has yet to promote you."

"Fuck you."

"Finally, a crack in your composure." Sara smiled. "Let me give you a tip: Evangeline is waiting for one of you to make the decision for her. She does not want to bear the responsibility of choosing one of you. With the right push, she will tumble from the tree like a ripe apple."

The allusion to temptation wasn't lost on him. Reed yawned, feigning boredom. "How would you know?"

"I am a woman. I know how women think." When silence stretched out between them, she asked, "Are you snooping in here because of her or not?"

"I want to know what we're doing about Raguel."

"Nothing."

"That's what I thought." What Eve thought, too, and it was niggling at her in a way that concerned him. When she focused on something, she was like a dog with a bone. She wouldn't let it go. And he had his own reasons for feeling similarly about Raguel.

"It is best to move when the time is right," Sara explained. "The seven firms are intact for the present. We can afford to move wisely and not rashly."

"Bullshit."

"What can we do, *mon chéri*? We have nothing with which to entice Sammael to start bargaining."

"You're not even trying."

"Cain is." Sara licked her lips. "Do you hope to win Evangeline's favor by playing the hero? Is your brother one step ahead of you again?"

"You know, Sara," he steepled his fingertips, "Cain isn't the only one who's accumulated favors over the years. If I wanted to, I could make your life far more difficult than it is."

The rage of angels gave her blue eyes a golden tinge. Her voice resonated with an archangel's command, "Do not threaten me, Abel."

"I won't." His mouth curved. "Just reminding you that I have teeth, and they do bite."

As quickly as it came, her rage was gone and in its place was arousal. Despite her claws, or maybe because of them, she craved a firm hand. His hand was firmer than most. But while Sara liked rough sex— regardless of who her partner was—Eve had been shocked by her enjoyment of his handling. She'd responded with complete abandon, in a way that Sara never could because the archangel was devoid of the ability to care deeply for anyone but God. Eve's helpless pleasure had added an edge to their encounter that he craved like a junkie.

But no one could ever know that, or how much he needed her now that Cain was an archangel. Through his connection to her, Reed could conceivably tap into his brother's knowledge and power. He could learn along with Cain, then surpass his brother as he always did.

If his tie to Eve was strong enough.

If she trusted him enough to let her guard down.

If they were lovers.

"Abel." Sara stood and rounded the desk. Her fingers went to the button of her coat and slipped it free, exposing a black camisole and hard nipples. "You look so lovesick when you are thinking of her, you know. But I would be happy to play surrogate . . . for now."

He lunged for her, vaulting from the chair and tackling her to the carpeted floor. Her cry was tinged with both pain and excitement. Bright-eyed and panting, she writhed beneath him. He settled between her spread legs and ground lewdly against her.

"You want it?" he whispered, his mouth hovering just above hers.

"No."

Reed smiled grimly at the familiar game. "Good. Because you're not going to get it until you help me get Raguel."

Sara stilled. "What?"

"You heard me." Shoving off of her, he pushed to his feet. "I get what I want, you get what you want."

She laughed, but it was a mirthless, bitter sound. "As you said earlier, you have nothing I cannot get elsewhere."

"Then get it elsewhere and leave me alone." He straightened his tie and ran a hand through his hair.

Sprawled on the floor and disheveled, she remained undiminished. "I can destroy you."

"Do it," he taunted. "It would benefit both of us. It's so clichéd, you know. This vixenish, sex-starved, femme fatale role you play. You need a makeover, Sara. Perhaps if I'm gone, you'll get one."

For a moment, Reed thought she might shred him to pieces. She could, if she desired. She was far more powerful than he was in every way. Then the moment passed. Her expressive face showed the transformation from furious indignation to sly consideration. She held her hand out to him for assistance. Catching her wrist, he pulled her to standing.

"Why such concern for Raguel?" she asked, righting her clothing.

Reed shook his head. What he wanted from Raguel was for him alone to know.

"I underestimated you." Her tone was thoughtful. She thrust her fingers into her shoulder-length tresses and shook them out. "Trust me on this point: Evangeline cannot be pulled to you. She must be pushed. Rescuing Raguel will not be enough to win her from Cain."

"Why are you so fixated on Eve? Get over it."

"I want *you* to get over *her,*" Sara said without inflection. "And the surest way to do that is to let you have your fill."

He watched the way her gaze darted around the room. Cain's room. The seat of his new power. Understanding dawned. "Ah, I see. Clever girl. This doesn't have anything to do with me. Or sex. This is about my brother."

For once he wasn't needled by Cain's prominence. He was, instead, relieved Eve was not the focus.

Her chin lifted. "Must everything in your life be about him?"

"Don't put this on me," he admonished, amused by her chagrin. "You have to compete with a new archangel, one who retains Jehovah's favor no matter how fucked up he is. Giving Eve to me means getting her away from Cain. That might make him crazy enough to do something stupid. Maybe prompt a response that might prove him unworthy of the ascension"

"You are obsessed with—"

"I like the way you think, Sara," he interjected. "Don't ruin my moment of admiration with your bitching."

Her mouth snapped shut.

Reed moved to the desk and leaned against it. "I'm surprised you approached me with the Eve angle, though. Why not dangle Cain as the bait? Did you really believe she would be more of a draw than my brother?"

"I have never seen you so focused on a woman. I saw the tape. Of you and her in the stairwell. When you marked her."

A surge of fury moved through him. That was for him and Eve alone. The thought of someone else observing—especially Sara—made his gut and fists clench.

He uncurled his fingers one by one.

"Ah, but she's not just any woman, is she?" he murmured. As Sara's mouth curved in a smile, he knew he had her. "We want the same thing, and we're agreed on how best to get it."

Eyeing him warily, she returned to her seat. "So . . . ?"

"I don't think Izzie's enough to lure him away, or to drive Eve to me."

"Iselda had him once."

"When he thought he couldn't have Eve. That's not the case now."

"You spoke of favors owed. What favor would he have cashed in to be promoted?"

Reed stilled. "Maybe . . ." he murmured, "it's a favor he *promised*."

After a moment of silence, she began to applaud, each measured clap like a gunshot in the room. "Brilliant."

"Find out to whom," he ordered, "and—if you can—what the ante is."

"Well," she drawled, "that will only take me a few decades. I am not even certain how many seraphim and cherubim there are."

He knew she would find a way. She wouldn't be the last female archangel heading a firm, if she wasn't both ruthless and resourceful.

As for Raguel, Reed would have to seek alternate routes to reach him, and he would have to move cautiously and alone. No archangel would initiate an offensive maneuver against Sammael, which ensured that no *mal'akh* or Mark would help him either.

To whom did one turn when he wished to go where angels feared to tread?

He turned away from Sara.

To a demon, of course.

Another horde of tengu.

Alec looked at Eve and groaned inwardly. She attracted disasters. And it had nothing to do with her smelling like a Mark.

"Come here," he beckoned, his voice resonant with an archangel's command but lacking coercion. He wanted her to come freely.

She looked at him with wary eyes, sensing the turmoil within him. He wondered if she heard the stirrings in his head, the needs that hissed like serpents, prodding his temper and making him both irritable and mischievous.

If she only knew what that prim pink shirt of hers did to him. The snug fit made it hard for him to concentrate on the task at hand. He wanted her; the darkness in him pushed him to take her, while another part of him was far more fascinated by the little freckle on her nape and the small section of silky hair that was always falling out of her ponytail. The two halves were fighting all the time, exhausting him and leaving him confused.

Did all archangels suffer a similar duality? Or was he—Cain of Infamy—uniquely evil in a way he'd denied for centuries?

As an archangel, he had been stripped of the ability to love anyone but God, but his need for Eve was more urgent than ever. Malevolent voices had joined him with the ascension. They whispered deep within his breast, fueled by the connection he had to all the Infernals within the firm. As long as Eve was near, his control was tenuous. She was a beacon in the gloom and he craved her in a ferocious way, but he couldn't relinquish her, even for her own benefit. She was a direct line into Abel's head and all the knowledge his brother had gained in the centuries he'd been a handler. As a fledgling archangel, Alec needed that information to run the firm.

He couldn't keep his promise to help free her from the mark. Not yet.

Maybe never.

"I can never read what you're thinking," she said, "when you have that particular expression."

"I can show you what I'm thinking . . ." He was unable to curb the edge to his words.

"You and your brother are more alike than you realize."

"Perhaps we're more alike than *you* realize," he warned. His smile felt cruel. He wouldn't be able to resist having her much longer, and when it happened, he doubted he could be as gentle with her as he'd once been.

A shadow passed over her features and through her mind. A sense of loss and melancholy.

Regret settled heavily over him, his humanity waxing and the recklessness waning in response to her withdrawal.

"Come here," he repeated, gentler this time, his hand extended to her.

With her chin lifted, Eve descended the few steps between them. Frustrated by that hint of reluctance, Alec caught her around the waist and pulled her flush against him. He shifted so quickly that she was still midgasp when they alighted on a nearby rooftop.

She smacked him on the shoulder. "You could have warned me!"

He nipped the end of her nose with a tiny love bite. "I could have. But this was more fun."

"For who?"

"For both of us. I know you, daredevil. You're the

type of girl who'd take off with a stranger on a Harley just for the ride."

Her nose wrinkled. "Where's a stranger on a Harley when I need one?"

"What? And miss this party?" He gestured to the roof of Gadara's unfinished building.

A couple of dozen tengu danced excitedly around the massive ventilation and air-conditioning units dotting the shiny metal top. Each little gray stone beast was the size of a gallon of milk. They sported tiny wings and broad grins. Eve had once called them cute, although they were far from cuddly.

"Right," she said, hands going to her hips. "Figures it would have to be the roof again."

"Tengu were the original inspiration for gargoyles. What better place to hide than in plain sight?"

"I don't care about that. I care about my fear of heights not meshing well with running around on rooftops."

Alec looked at her. He knew she had a phobia about heights, but it didn't affect her decisiveness. Her features were set in her gearing-up-to-brawl look: pursed lips, narrowed eyes, and a stubborn jawline. He didn't like her being in the line of fire, but he sure liked her game face.

"Look at the little bastards," she muttered, sending his gaze back to the tengu. "They're trying to brain us."

Sure enough, the tengu had formed a ladder of sorts by standing on each other's shoulders. Other tengu climbed up the backs of their brethren to reach the top of the stairwell enclosure. They waited there for a chance to jump on whoever stepped onto the roof, their hands clasped over their mouths to stem their incessant giggling.

"Why do you think we're over here?" he said. "I wanted you to see what we're up against before you barreled headfirst out the door and into danger."

"I wouldn't have done that!"

"Would have been the first time you held back."

Eve faced him. "As a warm-up to kicking their asses, I'm about to kick *yours*. Why are you pushing me?"

"Because that's what mentors are supposed to do, angel."

She exhaled harshly. "Did you notice that it didn't stink when the door was open? And look, they don't have any details."

"I noticed."

"The mask is supposed to wear off. Maybe we didn't wipe out everyone who knew about the formula."

"Yep. Could be trouble."

"Or could be they were made with the masking stuff mixed into the cement."

Alec smiled.

She shot him a wry glance. "You already thought of that."

"Yes, but only a second before you did."

"We could also have a leak somewhere in the firm."

"It's possible," he conceded, "but that would be my last guess."

While most firms had Infernals working within their ranks, they were rarely trusted with sensitive information. Demons never fully acclimated to the celestial life and the rules that came with it. Many

considered their "conversion" temporary. They secretly hoped to get their hands on valuable information or an object that would prompt Sammael to take
them back into the fold. However, both Raguel and
Alec trusted Hank—an occultist who specialized in
the magical arts—to oversee the investigation into
the mask. Hank had been with the North American
firm for so long that he was a fixture. He was still in-
herently evil, but he was content to be evil for the
good guys.

"So how do we want to do this?" Eve asked, tight-
ening her ponytail. "I suppose we should keep one of
them to see what they're made of."

"If you can manage it this time." The last time they
fought tengu on Gadara's roof, she'd vanquished both
of them.

Shoving him playfully in the shoulder, Eve said,
"Bring it on. Let's see which one of us can catch one."

"What's the ante?"

"Hmm . . ."

"Sex."

"With me? That's worth more than a tengu."

Alec laughed. "Agreed. But I'm hard up, I had to
try."

"We'll just keep it on retainer."

"Works for me. Gives me time to come up with
something really good."

"Ha! Assuming you'll win, which you won't."

He held out his hand to shake on it. "Bring it on."

Eve accepted the handshake with a mischievous
gleam in her dark eyes. "I'll take the lower left corner."

"Upper right. Meet in the middle?"

She nodded.

He snatched her close and kissed her. A hot, wet, deep kiss that took advantage of her gasp to sneak inside and lick. At the same time, he shifted them to the tengu-infested roof, so it was over the moment it started. But it was great while it lasted. He dropped her off, then shifted to the corner on the diagonal.

"Pretty Mark!" an observant tengu cried, followed by excited squeals from the rest of the mob. The few on the stairwell jumped down, one breaking off a leg in the process. It collected its detached appendage and continued on with a one-legged hop.

"Hey," Alec roared as they all surged toward Eve.

"Cain!" several yelled gleefully, separating from the mass and changing direction toward him.

Eve was already in motion, darting to the side and catching a tengu by the arm. Swinging in a wide arc, she gained velocity. She hurtled the demon into its brethren like a bowling ball into pins. Some crashed into those behind them, some leaped over the tumbling wave. She knocked one back with a roundhouse kick and feinted away from another one. Her grim determination and unwavering focus arrested Alec. When Marks were on a hunt, they were bolstered by the effects of the mark—adrenaline, aggression, increased muscle mass. Fear was held at bay by those things. But Eve wasn't on a hunt, she was on her own. She managed it beautifully.

Two tengu launched a third one at Alec like a missile. He ducked. Like Eve, he used rapid kicks to keep his immediate perimeter clear, but maintenance wasn't the goal. Eradication was. A loud crash and high-pitched shouts of dismay on the other side of the roof told him Eve had just smashed one. Tengu were all for having a little evil fun, but not if it meant getting hurt.

Catching a tengu in each hand, he bashed them together. Debris exploded outward and turned to ash before hitting the ground. "Two down. Ten more to go."

"Cain can't save pretty Mark," a tengu sang, flapping its stone wings. "Sammael gets what Sammael wants."

"Sammael is going to get *me*," he barked back, "if he doesn't keep his minions to himself."

Laughing, the tengu regrouped and rushed him. He waited until the last minute, then shifted away. The converging tengu collided. Two overzealous ones hit each other with enough force to wipe each other out. A cloud of ash plumed upward and dissipated in the gentle breeze.

The sound of thick metal sheeting bending in ways it shouldn't turned his head toward Eve. His gaze found little cement feet protruding from a hole in the air-conditioning unit. They'd already repaired the massive and expensive system once before, due to their last altercation with tengu on this roof.

Hang in there, he said, sensing Eve's strength was strained by the heavy beasts.

Don't worry about me. Take care of yourself.

Alec wondered if she knew that she was the only person in existence who worried over him. He stepped up his pace. He snatched up any tengu unfortunate enough to get too close and used them to crush their friends. As he worked, he crossed the roof, closing the distance between him and Eve. She was still several tengu deep, but seemed to be holding her own.

I'm winning, he taunted.

In response to his challenge, she became more aggressive, lunging and catching the little demons just like he was. Considering her much smaller size, he was impressed with her ability to keep up.

They should have backed off by now, she grunted.

Eve was right. Tengu liked to play, but when the tide turned against them, they ran.

They want you, he explained.

Huh?

I'm thinking the ice bitch wasn't kidding.

Fucking fabulous, she muttered, hefting a tengu overhead and braining another with it. Both burst into ash.

Alec grabbed two tengu by the backs of their skulls and pounded them together. Then he moved toward Eve.

Back off, hero, she said, kicking another into a ventilation turbine. *I've got this.*

Grinning, he stepped back and crossed his arms. *There's one to your left. Right. Left. Behind you. Ooh, great shot. Kick it again. Duck!*

I'm going to kill you next, she bit out, struggling to shake off a tengu clinging to her back.

You'd miss me. He rubbed at his chest and the swelling pride that made it ache.

Not right now. She snatched at the demon and yanked it over her head. She swung it like a golf club into the one wrapped around her leg, knocking both free and sending them flying. With arms splayed, Alec caught them in each hand and launched them discus-style into the heavy stairwell door. Stumbling from the blow to her leg, Eve faced the last tengu standing.

"Sammael wants you, pretty Mark," the Infernal said, hopping.

Eve regained her balance and pushed a few stray stands of hair back from her face. "He'll have to take a number."

"You can't run, you can't hide."

"You can't scare me," she sang back with a humorless smile.

"Sammael will."

He dashed toward her with a growl. Alec straightened abruptly, prepared to leap in. Eve feinted to the side, catching the demon's arm as he passed. She swung him up, then hammered him down into the rooftop. Ash mushroomed and hovered for a heartbeat in a pocket of still air, then burst free in a sudden breeze.

Alec applauded. He doubted many novices would have handled multiple opponents with as much aplomb.

It took her a moment to shake off the bloodlust brought on by the lingering effects of the Novium. But when she did, she smiled sheepishly and sketched a quick, exaggerated bow. He loved the bow and the strength of character that made it possible for her to dust herself off so quickly.

He glanced at the kicking feet of the tengu stuck in the side of the van-sized AC unit. "You win."

"Damn straight."

"Of course, you have a great mentor."

The wry look she shot him made him laugh, something he only ever did around her.

"That—" she pointed a finger at the writhing tengu, "—isn't going to fit on your bike."

"Right. Do you want to go back for the car? Or have me do it?" He could shift with mortals and Marks, but not with demons. "I'll have to drive back, so it won't be quick."

"Quicker than me. You can shift to the garage. I have to drive both ways."

"You sure?"

"Sure." Her gaze narrowed on the wriggling cement buttocks. "If it acts up, I'll spank it."

"Lucky tengu."

With a wink, he shifted away.

CHAPTER 5

Less than half an hour later, Eve and Alec were exiting the elevators on the lobby level of Olivet Place with the tengu tucked under Alec's arm. To mortal eyes the little beast appeared as rigid as its stone imitators, but it was in fact wriggling madly.

"Keep it up," Eve warned, "and we'll drop you to the bottom of the Mariana Trench and you'll have to hike back."

The tengu gasped, then stilled.

"Where are you going with that?" the mortal guard asked, but the Mark next to him touched his arm and shook his head.

"You won't miss him," Eve said, waving good-bye. "Trust me."

They stepped outside. She moved directly to the Harley and pulled her Oakley shades out of the leather pouch on the gas tank. "Where's the car?"

"Around the corner."

She gestured ahead with a wave of her hand. "I'll follow you."

Alec took the lead, shortening his long-legged stride to keep her close. Eve walked behind him and slightly to the left, allowing the tengu to be carried along the curb and away from other pedestrians. Her nose wrinkled as the scent of rotting soul roiled in the wind. She held her breath, but a hard bump to her shoulder by a passing pedestrian knocked her back and made her turn her head. She caught the culprit leering back at her. With fangs. His face was covered in writhing black details and his eyes glowed laser-green. With a chopping motion of his hand, he mouthed, *Head will roll.*

Despite an inner shiver, Eve flipped him the bird . . . and crashed into something rock solid.

"Watch it," Alec bit out.

When she looked up at him to explain, she found him staring down the fleeing vampire with the look of death. Coming from Cain of Infamy, it scared even Eve. Then his head turned, raking their surroundings with an examining gaze. She followed suit and froze. Infernals littered the sidewalks in unusually high concentration for the area, far more than had been present when they'd arrived. Having the headquarters of the North American firm here in Orange County discouraged Infernals from playing in the vicinity, but apparently not today.

Alec's growing fury filtered through her, chilling her with his cold aggression. A low, resonant snarl rumbled up from his chest and throbbed outward, visibly pushing every demon back. The power he exuded was dizzying for Eve, who felt it like a phantom limb. An archangel's power alone would be too much for her, but Alec's outburst contained an iciness that seized her lungs.

Alec . . .

The surge ebbed. She reached out to the nearby light post and sucked in deep breaths. That had been an act of possession and claiming, like a dog pissing on a hydrant. And every Infernal within a half-mile radius got the message loud and clear.

Eve studied Alec closely, slightly frightened by the look of mayhem in his dark eyes. "What the hell was that?"

"We need to get you out of here." He gripped her elbow and pulled her down the adjacent street.

The weight of dozens of eyes goaded her into faster steps. She had to jog to keep up, but it wasn't a struggle. Several feet away from her Chrysler 300, Alec hit the trunk release on the remote. He put the tengu in the back and tossed the keys to her. "Wait until I bring the bike around, and we'll head back together."

She nodded.

He shifted away. A moment later she heard the Harley rumble to life around the corner.

Eve closed the trunk, revealing a man standing directly beside her car. She jumped back with a squeak.

"Yeesh." She shook her head. "You scared me, Father."

"Sorry." Father Riesgo's smiling green eyes softened his rugged features. He looked so out of place in the priest's collar that it almost had the look of a costume. Frankly, he looked more renegade than missionary. His cheek was marred by a knife scar and his dark hair was overlong and slicked back in a short tail. Just shy of six feet and built like a tank, Riesgo wasn't handsome, but he was very charismatic and singularly compelling.

"How are you, Ms. Hollis?"

"I'm good." Thumping came from the trunk and Eve smacked her hand down on it.

Riesgo frowned. "What was that?"

"What was what?"

"That noise."

"I didn't hear anything." She glanced around warily, noting how the Infernals held back. Maybe due to Alec's unspoken threat, maybe due to the presence of a priest. "So . . . how are you?"

His gaze lifted from the trunk to meet hers. "Better now that I've seen you."

For some men, that would have been a pickup line. With Riesgo, it was her soul that interested him, not the package it came in.

"Have you been reading the Bible I gave you?" he asked.

"I did. Thank you. I've been meaning to bring it back to you, but work has been crazy lately."

"Do you have any questions?"

Alec could melt wax with his voice, but Riesgo was no slouch in the alluring department. His voice bore the deep sultriness of a phone sex operator. Not that she'd ever called a sex line, but she imagined that's what the men who worked them would sound like. Eve wondered if he was aware of how many women attended mass at St. Mary's just to hear him talk with that suave Spanish accent.

"No questions," she replied, listening to the rumble of the Harley fade as Alec circled the other side of the block.

"And you don't want to keep it for future reference?"

More pounding came from the trunk.

"No thanks," she said, careful not to raise her voice even though it was competing with the noise from the tengu. "I have a good memory."

"What is in your trunk, Ms. Hollis?" he shouted.

"Excuse me?" Her car was beginning to rock and she pushed down harder on the trunk with her super-strength to keep it still.

He leaned closer. "What. Is. That. *Noise?*"

"I don't hear anything."

A dark brow arched. Reaching out, his long fingers caught the keys held in her free hand and tugged them free of her grip. Not that she offered much resistance. She was too shocked by the way he took over. How could a man so clearly commanding in nature become a Catholic priest?

With his forearm, he pushed her back from the car. When it began to bounce violently, he shot her a challenging glance.

"You're pushy, Father."

Riesgo hit the trunk release and it popped open. The tengu froze. The car settled. With one hand on the lip of the trunk lid and the other holding the keys at his side, he stared down at what was a gargoyle statue to his eyes.

"Do you like it?" she asked.

The tengu's head shook violently.

"It's cute." Riesgo glanced at her. The tengu stuck his tongue out behind the priest's back. "What's the matter with your car?"

"Nothing. Runs like a dream. I recommend the 300 to everyone."

Alec's Harley rumbled to a stop beside them. From

behind the shield of her sunglasses, her eyes ate him up as if he was dessert. Which was a fairly apt description, now that she thought of it. He'd hooked her the same way ten years ago. A hottie on a Harley.

He cut the engine and smiled at Riesgo. "Father."

The two men shook hands.

"You might want to take Ms. Hollis's car to the dealership," Riesgo suggested. "Her rear shocks are bad."

Alec looked at Eve who jerked her chin toward the open trunk.

"I think it's due for regular maintenance," Alec conceded with a big smile, his teeth white against his tanned skin.

Riesgo turned back to Eve and held out the keys. "I look forward to seeing you again."

Beyond his shoulder, she saw the proliferation of demons lying in wait. "Be careful on the way back to the church, Father."

After another long look into the trunk, he shook his head and closed it again. With a wave, Eve hurried to the driver's side and slid behind the wheel. Alec shot off ahead of her and she pulled out behind him. The tengu began kicking the backseat.

"Dumping him in the ocean is a great idea," Reed drawled from the passenger seat.

Eve swerved like a drunk. "Damn it! Don't startle me like that!"

"You're jumpy." She felt his gaze move along the side of her face.

"Hell is breaking loose. Literally. I have good cause."

His hand settled on her knee. The warmth seeped through the worn denim and into the flesh beneath. *I won't let anything happen to you.*

In the enclosed confines of her car, the scent that was distinctly Reed's filled her nostrils—leather and starch, a hint of spice and heated male skin. Comforted by his proximity, she set one hand atop his and squeezed.

The tengu continued to bounce around in the trunk of her car.

"If you dent my car," she yelled over her shoulder, "you'll really piss me off!"

The intensity of the blows reduced, but the frequency didn't slow.

Alec passed through Brookhurst, confirming that he was headed for Gadara Tower. That worked for her. She didn't want the tengu in her house for any reason. The damn things were bad luck.

Sensing Reed's disquiet, she asked, "What's troubling you?"

"I've been looking into our Nix problem."

"Oh?"

"It's been two months since you blew him up, but there have been no new reports of murders with his calling card—until this past week."

"Maybe the police have kept it under wraps. They do that sometimes."

His fingers linked with hers, then he moved their joined hands to his thigh. "You watch too much television. And quit feeling guilty for touching me."

Her lips twisted wryly. "Burning a stick of dynamite at both ends makes me nervous."

An image of him covering a disheveled Sara on the floor entered his head, and subsequently hers. Her breath held as she absorbed the searing flash of jealousy she wasn't expecting.

Reed stared straight ahead. His Ray-Bans hid his gaze and his profile revealed nothing more than a ticcing muscle in his jaw. "It's not what you think," he bit out.

Eve blanked her mind. "You don't know what I think."

"You drive me nuts."

"That's not me. That's all the stuff you have rushing through your brain." There was a tremendous amount of information moving through him—kill orders flowing down from Alec, assignments meted out to the Marks under him, reports coming back in from them. The human mind could never handle such an influx and outpouring of information simultaneously, but *mal'akhs* dealt with it daily. The teeny bit she felt through him was cringe-worthy.

Eve tugged at the hand he held. He released it. "I think we need some distance between the three of us."

His lips thinned. "Why do women always pull this shit when they get jealous?"

"Fuck you, you conceited bastard."

"I'm not the bastard," he bit out.

"I'm a liability and you know it. This dating bullshit isn't worth the risk. Alec can't feel anything for me and you're not there yet. We've only been seeing each other a few weeks. Better sooner than later."

His head turned toward her. "Is Cain getting this little speech, too?"

She nodded. "He will."

"So . . . you're saying Cain is heartless, and you think I don't care enough yet. Where does that leave you? Still pining over him?"

"Not enough to hang on, obviously." Her gaze

went back to the road. She merged into the left-hand turn lane at Harbor Boulevard, one car behind Alec. "Listen, the cons outweigh the pros here. I'm a vulnerability that neither of you can afford. And I feel guilty. I hate that."

Reed's fingers tapped his thigh. Because he was rock-hard muscle, the flesh was like a solid surface beneath his impatient touch.

You're gonna notice shit like that, he scoffed, *in the same breath that you're saying you don't want me?*

"I didn't say I don't want you. I just said this isn't going anywhere."

"Quit worrying about where it's going and focus on where it's at."

"I want to focus on staying alive."

"You need sex to do that. It's the way Marks are wired."

"I know."

The silence that filled the car was heavy enough to block out the cavorting of the trapped tengu.

Reed's voice came dangerously low, "Oh, hell no."

She made the turn onto Harbor, then glanced at him. "Excuse me?"

He pulled off his shades and stared at her with hard eyes. "I've played this game by your rules. Now you're telling me the board's getting put away before I score? Fuck that."

Eve gaped. "Don't tell me I *owe* you a screw."

"Damn straight. And I'm collecting."

"That is the most immature, chauvinistic—"

"Yeah, yeah. Save it."

"Give Sara a booty call if you're hard up enough to blackmail someone for sex," she snapped.

"I've been celibate for *you*. *You* owe me."

Celibate for her.

Didn't make up for him being an asshole. "From what I saw, Sara seems to miss your caveman side."

"So do you." He slipped his shades back on and crossed his arms. "That's where I'm blowing it. I should be listening to your body language and not the crap coming out of your mouth. I should toss your ass over the arm of your couch and nail you. Then you'd know this brush-off shit doesn't work with me."

"I wouldn't fuck you if you were the last man on earth."

Reed held a hand to his ear. "Did you hear that? That was the sound of the gloves coming off."

"Whatever. Grow up."

"I wanted you to make the first move. Now . . ." His heard turned toward the window. "I just want you."

The last was said without the cockiness of the rest. It was softer. Resigned. There was more to his need than the physical. Outwardly, he didn't show it, but she felt it.

While it wasn't particularly common for Marks to connect romantically with their handlers, it wasn't unheard of either. The flow of assignments and field reports between the two created a sense of intimacy that sometimes blossomed into love.

"Even if wanting me is what's setting me up as a target for Satan?" she asked, hoping to goad him into lowering his mental guards.

"Even if."

Eve turned her head toward Reed, only to find that he'd left; shifted off to someplace else in the world. That ability to be here one second and gone the next reminded her of superheroes like Superman or Spider-Man.

"But I'm not playing the role of the always-a-hostage love interest," she insisted aloud. "You hear me?"

If he did, he didn't answer.

From his position at the head of a massive U-shaped table, Sammael relished the view of Raguel, the most arrogant of all the archangels, kneeling on the stone ground before him with head bent and fingers curled with white-knuckled force. The pure brightness of his brother's white wings was incongruous compared to the underlying wanness of his coffee-dark skin and the ragged appearance of his woolen shift.

Sammael leaned back into his chair with a smile. Pain. So beautiful and effective. Of all of Jehovah's creations, pain was his favorite. Terror and depression followed a goodly distance behind.

But pain alone would not be enough to break Raguel.

Despite over a month of hellfire burning, there was a lingering elegance to the set of his brother's shoulders, the sight of which Sammael welcomed. The archangel's display of his gold-tipped wings was an additional act of rebellion designed to inspire fear in the lessor demons. It inspired amusement in Sammael.

"Are you enjoying your accommodations?" he asked solicitously.

Raguel's head lifted, his dark eyes revealing a wealth of hatred and fury. He said nothing.

Perfect. There was no room for love of God when the soul was filled with viler emotions.

"Speechless? Ah, well . . . Are you hungry?" Sammael tossed a hunk of meat onto the floor. "It's quite good."

His brother's eyes never left his. No move was made to reach for the sustenance, despite the obvious signs of emaciation. Raguel wouldn't die of starvation, but he was suffering from it.

Smiling, Sammael raked his gaze over his surroundings. Both the Great Hall and the wooden table that filled it grew in proportion to its occupancy. So while it appeared that every seat was taken, in actuality the space was bereft of the number of minions that usually filled it. He hoped the absent ones were enjoying the lovely Southern California weather. Their vacation would soon be over.

"What do you want?" Raguel's voice was hoarse from endless days of screaming. He was kept suspended over hellfire in a metal cage, his flesh seared with every flare, then rebuilt by his angelic gifts. Drained by the need for constant healing, he lacked the strength to free himself. Even now he kneeled, not because he deferred to the Prince of Hell, but because his legs would not support him. He'd put too much effort into re-creating those magnificent wings.

Suddenly irritated by that display, Sammael stood. His wings snapped outward, blood red and tipped with black. The demons in attendance roared and raised their fists. Raguel's chin lifted. Ever defiant.

"Cain is helming your firm," Sammael purred, his

hands clasped beneath his wings against the small of his back. "Our siblings do not seem to be in any hurry to bargain for you. Perhaps they do not miss you. The Seven is intact without you."

"I am not concerned."

"Cain has implemented some changes which have increased productivity and lowered Mark causalities. He has also exposed flaws within the existing system."

"Is he hitting you where it hurts?" his brother goaded.

Sammael laughed. He began to round the corner to his left, his cloven feet striking the floor in rhythmic clops. The massive ruby chandelier above them followed him as he moved. It was the fate of lessors to live in darkness, except for the light he brought them. "For a time it seemed as if his fascination with Evangeline Hollis had passed, but now he courts her again. What does he see in her? What is it about her that makes him cleave to her as he has not done with any woman since his wife, Awan?"

"I care not."

"Truly? Now I see why they have abandoned you. You have grown lazy." He brushed a hand across a succubus's cheek as he passed by. "After all these years, out of all the females in the world—all the Marks and Infernals, all the nephilim and mortals—he finally recommits to this one unremarkable woman. And you do not ask yourself why?"

Raguel's jaw tightened.

"I ask why," Sammael murmured, having no need to raise his voice since no one would dare to speak over or around him. "What distinguishes her? Would you like to know what I have decided?"

"Not especially, no."

The silence remained unbroken, but the shock of Raguel's disrespect rippled outward. It would spread like a cancer if allowed.

As Sammael passed a berserker, he touched him. A loving, gentle caress that made the demon smile . . . before he dissolved into a rancid puddle that splashed over the bench to pool on the floor. Fear spread through the room and tainted it with an acrid scent.

"I am feeling generous," Sammael said, smiling, "so I will tell you anyway. I think it is her lack of faith that fascinates him. I think he relates to her agnosticism and finds compelling similarities between them."

"Cain is pious," Raguel bit out.

"Is he? Can he be?"

"Has he not proven so?"

"He is God's primary enforcer. He kills as often as he breathes. Can such a creature carry love in his soul?"

"His love for Evangeline Hollis proves that to be true."

"*Does* he love her? Truly? Or does something more base and raw move him? Perhaps he has a hidden purpose. Or perhaps it is simply an incestuous fondness for her name. *Eve.* The Temptress. As fresh in my thoughts now as she was the day I met her."

"I pray her memory festers in your mind like an open sore."

Sammael's fists clenched beneath the concealment of his wings. "Cain running a firm. Who could have conceived of him reaching such heights? It must chafe you terribly."

"Do you have a point, Sammael?"

"I am just conversing, my brother. It has been so long since you and I were last together."

Raguel flapped his mighty wings, using the resulting updraft to push his worn body to its feet. "I have nothing to say. Send me back to my hell."

"Say please."

There was a protracted silence, then a snarled, "Please."

His brother's hatred was a writhing, burning thing. Beautiful.

Pleased with the progressing state of affairs, Sammael sent Raguel back with a snap of his fingers while simultaneously shifting to his receiving room. Azazel appeared a moment later, taking a knee and bowing. Aside from similar height and form, his lieutenant was as different from him as Heaven and Hell. White hair and pale irises showcased skin like ivory, while garments of ice blue and silver emphasized Azazel's frosty demeanor. He could chill a room with his presence and was most useful in cooling Sammael's fiery temper.

"My liege," Azazel murmured.

"What was your impression of Raguel?"

The demon's gaze lifted. "He is unbroken, but soul-weary."

"Good. Exactly the way I want him. Now, tell me you have news."

"The *yuki-onna*, Harumi-san, betrayed us to Evangeline Hollis. Cain has returned to the field. It will be more difficult to reach her now."

Sammael smiled. "She has other vulnerabilities."

"Her best friend is backpacking in Europe, and her sister lives in Kentucky."

"Excellent."

"Her parents are local."

Sammael moved toward his throne. His lower limbs changed as he crossed the mosaic floor, turning from hindquarters to legs. His wings retracted, sinking into his spine as if they had never been. "Leave them."

"My liege, I think—"

"No, you do not." He adjusted his black velvet slacks before sinking into his seat and gesturing for Azazel to rise. "Take away her family, and you take away her reason to live."

"Why would that be a bad thing?"

"Her family keeps her mortal, which makes her weak. Why do you think the seraphim choose the un-encumbered to be Marks? A soul is most dangerous when it has nothing to lose. We want her motivated, not a grief-stricken vigilante. She might even become an ally."

"An *ally*?"

"Why not?" He waved one hand carelessly. "She does not believe. It would seem likely that she wants to be free of the mark. Anyone who could assist her in that endeavor would be a friend."

"You seek to extort *and* befriend her?"

"Or kill her. Whatever purpose suits me best. Dis-cover everyone who means anything to her but whose loss won't break her. Close coworkers. School friends. Neighbors."

Azazel snorted. "Ulrich took care of the neighbor already. She would have been perfect. As close as family."

"Ulrich? The Nix?" Sammael's gaze lifted to the mural of Michelangelo's *Fall of Man* on the domed ceiling. "Asmodeus oversteps his place again."

"He is ambitious."

"He is overzealous. He has already succeeded in killing her once by lending a dragon to Grimshaw." He looked at his lieutenant. "Watch him closely. He and I may soon have things to discuss."

A rare smile curved Azazel's mouth. "Yes, my liege."

Sammael leaned his head against the throne and closed his eyes. "And get someone to clean up the mess that berserker made in the great hall."

CHAPTER 6

Eve steered her car into her assigned spot next to Alec's and cut the engine. The subterranean parking lot of Gadara Tower was darker and cooler than the ground level. The temperature change was enough to silence the tengu in her trunk.

With her fingers wrapped around the steering wheel and her senses achingly aware of how pissed off Reed was, she stared at the single placard that displayed both "A. Cain" and "E. Hollis." Such privileges alienated her from the other Marks.

Her car door opened. Alec's large hand extended into her view. She pulled the keys out of the ignition and accepted his offer of help. She'd barely cleared the roofline when she found herself pinned to the rear door by six-plus feet of hard-bodied male.

"So I've been thinking . . ." Eve began.

The tengu resumed bouncing around in her trunk.

We need to tighten things up, he said, *keep information strictly between me and you. Got it?*

"Gotcha."

Alec's hands gripped her waist, his thumbs sliding across her hipbones, his sunglasses dangling from his fingers. "Did I hurt you?" he asked softly. "Earlier?"

Just the memory of his power surge at the tengu building made her shiver, but she shook her head. "I'm fine. You just took me by surprise."

"I didn't think about how it might hit you."

"Do you hear me complaining? I think you saved us from getting jumped."

His forehead dropped to hers. "You're too good for me."

"Alec . . ." Her throat tightened.

"But that Dear John speech you were talking to Abel about? It won't fly with me either, so save your breath."

Eve shoved at his shoulder. "Eavesdropper."

He backed away, laughing. "I'm ruthless."

Alec reached down through the driver's side door for the trunk release just as her cell phone began ringing from its spot in her cup holder. He tossed it to her. The caller ID said only *California,* so Eve answered with a brisk, "Hollis."

"Ms. Hollis. Detective Jones of the Anaheim Police Department."

She winced at the familiar voice. It held a bit of a twang, as if he had originated in the South, then migrated.

The mantra of California natives entered her mind unbidden, *Welcome to California. Now go home.*

As Alec gestured for her to go to the truck, Eve squeezed his arm and spoke with clear enunciation for his benefit. "Hello, Detective."

Alec paused.

"Did I catch you at a bad time?" Jones asked.

"I have a minute."

"My partner and I stopped by your condo an hour or so ago."

"I'm at work."

"No, you're not."

She rounded the rear of the car. "I'm not?"

As the tengu began pounding on the trunk lid, he asked, "What's that noise?"

"What noise? And why do you think I'm not at work?"

"Because we're sitting in your office right now." His voice rose in volume. "Can you hear me?"

Her gaze moved to Alec. He waited for her signal to open the trunk. "You're here?"

"Where are you, Ms. Hollis?"

"In the garage of Gadara Tower."

"We would like to speak with you, if you have a moment."

"Of course. I'll be up in ten." She disconnected.

Alec rested his forearms on the edge of the open door. "I have someone taking coffee and donuts to your office."

As convenient as the archangels' mental switchboard system was, Eve wasn't sure it was worth the headaches. Information flowed through Alec like a sieve, but not in the same manner as it did through Reed. Handlers were stopgaps designed to alleviate the firm leaders' burdens. They had only twenty-one Marks to concern them; the archangels were responsible for thousands.

"They might find the donuts stereotypical and insulting," she pointed out, shoving her phone into her pocket. She hunkered down in preparation of the trunk opening.

"Good. They should know better than to pick on my girl." He hit the truck release.

The tengu burst free with a squeal. Eve caught him with a grunt, but the force of the little beast's velocity knocked her on her ass.

"Pretty Mark!" he cried, snapping at her with his stone teeth.

She waited until Alec rounded the trunk. Then she threw the demon at him.

As usual, the vast lobby of Gadara Tower was congested with many business-minded Marks and mortals. The industrious whirring of the glass tube elevator motors and the steady hum of numerous conversations were now familiar and soothing to Eve. She felt safe here, cocooned from the world outside where demons ran amok.

Fifty floors above her, a massive skylight allowed natural illumination to flood the atrium. The gentle heat from the sun combined with the multitude of planters created a slight humidity. It emphasized the overwhelming scent of Marks to a near suffocating degree.

Beside her, Alec inhaled deeply, then exhaled in a sigh of pleasure. She felt echoes of the surge of power that hit him whenever he was in close proximity to multiple Marks. That charge was unique to him, the original and most badass Mark of them all. She wondered how he'd managed to remain autonomous for so long, considering how much strength he gained when around other Marks. There was a story there, but Alec wasn't telling it.

As they weaved through the crowd, Marks paused to gape at the tengu. It was their first sighting of a masked Infernal. The ripple of unease that followed in her and Alec's wake was tangible. Eve hoped the advent of the mask didn't foster too much doubt. The last thing they needed was for frightened Marks to target mortals by accident.

They'll be all right, Alec said, shaking the writhing tengu as admonishment to keep still. *I'll see to it.*

Eve knew he would. His strength of conviction was powerful. She glanced at his profile and was struck by thoughts of Batman's nemesis Two-Face and the dual sides of Alec's personality. Alec killed with one hand, but worked to preserve life with the other.

Since his ascension to archangel, the division within him felt soul-deep to her. But maybe he had always been so divided and she just hadn't known it. His promotion had come within hours of her Novium, which first established their connection. She hadn't had time to dig into the brain of the old Cain before he became the new one.

They moved to a hidden bank of elevators that descended into off-limits areas of the building. She rarely saw her office on the forty-fifth floor. The majority of her business in Gadara Tower was conducted in the subterranean labyrinth of floors and corridors that housed Infernals both friendly and not.

"Pretty Mark not so nice," the tengu complained as they stepped into the elevator car.

"You're one to talk," she scoffed. "You tried to brain me, tackle me, bite me—"

"Fun, fun!"

Eve flipped him the bird. He stuck his stone tongue out at her.

"Cut it out, kids," Alec said, his dark eyes laughing.

She glared at the speaker in the corner. "What's with the Barry Manilow? Every time I get in the elevator, it's Manilow."

"You're just lucky. By the way, I'm going up with you."

"The detectives don't know you work here."

"So? It's clear you're coming in off the clock. Tell 'em it's your day off and you forgot something."

She looked down and checked herself out. Her jeans were dirty, her boots were scuffed, and her shirt was torn at the hem.

Alec grinned. "Your hair needs help, too."

Turning, Eve looked at her reflection in the shiny brass of the elevator walls. Her ponytail was askew, odd loops of hair protruded all around the top of her head, and Infernal ash concealed its natural luster.

"Oh my god." She hissed as her mark burned in chastisement. "You let me go around looking like *this*?"

"You're still hot."

She glared at him over her shoulder. "You suck."

"Abel didn't say anything either."

"You both suck," she qualified, pulling out her hair band.

I'd still do you, Reed said.

Gee, you're a class act, she retorted.

The car came to a stop and the elevator doors

opened with a ding. Immediately the stench of multiple Infernals filled her nostrils and made her nose wrinkle. A waiting area to the right was occupied with a dozen demons of various classes, all bitching about the wait. To the left a female werewolf sat at the receptionist's desk. She wore headphones and was busy filing her claws.

As Alec's presence became known, silence descended, but he paid them no mind. Eve, however, was totally aware of those around them. Marks and Infernals alike watched her warily. Sadly, it was her fellow Marks who looked at her with malice, while the Infernals were simply curious.

Following Alec down the hallway, Eve read the gilded lettering on the glass doors as they passed them. There was a thin layer of smoke in the air, which—combined with the overall decor of the place—created an old '50s film noir feel. Only the labels on the doors gave away the otherworldly purpose of the place.

When they paused before a door that read Forensic Wiccanology in gold lettering, Eve stepped up and knocked. The knob turned and the door swung inward, seemingly without assistance, since no one stood at the threshold. Inside the room, the overhead lights were out. Pendant lamps hung over various island stations, spotlighting specific work areas but leaving the rest of the space in deep shadow.

"Eve!" The coarse, raspy voice coming from the back of the room always reminded her of Larry King. Eve waited for the familiar black-clad figure to emerge from the stygian darkness.

"Hi, Hank," she greeted him in return. "We brought a present for you."

But the figure who appeared wasn't Hank. It was a young girl with hair as white as snow and yellow eyes like a wolf's. She was around five and a half feet tall, slender as a reed, and timid in the way she moved.

"Hello." The girl offered a shy smile. "I'm Fred."

Eve bit back a smile at the masculine name. Hank and Fred. She was pretty sure Fred was a girl. No one knew what sex Hank was, but Eve thought of him as a man, since he was always in male form when speaking to her.

"Nice to meet you, Fred," Eve said, extending her hand.

Fred shook hands with Eve, then looked at Alec. "Cain."

Alec acknowledged her with a quick, dismissive nod.

Hank stepped into the illuminated circle created by a hanging fixture. His black-clad form altered as he emerged from the darkness, changing from a hunchbacked crone to a tall, dapper gentleman with flame-red hair. Hank was a chameleon, changing form and sex to suit the client. The only things that were immutable were the red hair, masculine smoker's voice, and black attire.

"My new assistant," Hank explained. "It's been so busy around here lately, I needed the help. Fred is half lili/half werewolf. Gives her great eyes and a nose for research."

Lilin were the offspring of the seductress Lilith—first wife of Alec's father, Adam, and mother of innumerable demons. Eve had yet to run across the blonde she-bitch, and she hoped she never did.

"Her fault it's so hectic," Alec said, nudging Eve's shoulder.

She shoved him back.

Hank laughed. "Can't blame him for being right, my lovely Eve. I hear there are a large number of Infernals in town, possibly gunning for you."

"Because of him," she argued, stabbing a finger in Alec's direction.

"Good point." Hank stepped closer to examine the oddly quiet little demon under Alec's arm. "A tengu? Fascinating. The mask hasn't worn off. Or else they've managed to create more of it."

"That's what I need you to find out," Alec said. "Also why this one's so aggressive."

"Traitors," the tengu hissed, glaring at both Hank and Fred.

Fred snorted. Hank laughed. "My theory is that his behavior is a side effect of the mask. Over the course of my experiments, I've discovered that the infusion of Mark blood and bone doesn't sit well with Infernals over an extended period of time. I'll examine this fellow and see if I can prove it definitively."

"Keep me posted," Alec said.

"Of course." Hank looked at Eve. "It looks like he did a number on you."

"He had friends," she grumbled, dusting off her jeans with her hands.

Hank faced Alec and altered into a Jessica Rabbit look-alike in a Morticia Addams dress. "I have also been playing with reversing the mask."

Eve perked up. "Would it make Marks blend with mortals?"

"It should make Marks smell like demons."

"Eww . . ."

Hank shifted back into his masculine form. "However, so far I've only been able to make demons smell like Marks."

"Yikes."

"Destroy that recipe," Alec ordered.

"Already done."

Fred reached out to the tengu. The little beast hissed at her, but she seemed unconcerned. "I'll take him."

Alec handed him over. The demon snapped at Fred with his teeth. She snarled and bared deadly canines.

"My teeth are bigger," she growled.

The tengu whimpered and curled into a ball.

"Does it bother anyone else," Eve asked, "that the demons are so far ahead of us in regards to experiments and genetic mutations? The correct word is 'genetic,' right? Or is there something else I should call it?"

"Infernals don't lack research subjects," Hank explained. "Marks, on the other hand, are trained to kill. They rarely capture for torture or experimentation."

She looked at Alec. "We should work on that."

"We are."

No elaboration, but she was getting used to that.

"Hank," Alec went on. "Do you still have that punch bowl I brought you? The one the Nix gave to Eve?"

"Yes."

"Did you ever get anything from it?"

Hank frowned. "Nothing definitive. And once the Nix was dead, I put it away."

"I need you to dig it out. He's back."

"Back? Like Montevista? And Grimshaw's kid?"

"Exactly." Alec caught Eve's elbow. "We've got an appointment upstairs."

"I'll holler when I find something." Hank waved his hand along Eve's length and she suddenly felt cleaner.

Glancing down, she found her clothes in pristine condition. "You rock."

"Of course."

Eve yelled into the darkness where Fred had disappeared, "It was nice meeting you, Fred."

The lili shouted back from a seemingly great distance, "Bye, Eve. Bye, Cain."

Not for the first time, Eve wondered how big Hank's office was. She was about to ask Alec when she found herself standing in the reception area of her office.

"I hate when you do that," she complained, blinking past her disorientation.

"Don't want to be late."

Candace, the Mark who was her secretary, stood with a smile. "Good afternoon, Ms. Hollis. Cain. I took coffee in to the detectives, as you requested."

He nodded and pulled Eve toward her frosted glass office door. She took a deep breath while he turned the knob. He was cool and calm while she was neither. She'd only spoken with Jones and Ingram briefly a few months ago, but it had been enough to tell her that they were good men. Men who were fighting the good fight with only mortal skills. And she had to look them in the eyes and lie to them. The mark on her arm burned with the sin, which didn't make sense to her at all. It's not like she could tell them the truth.

Detective Jones pushed to his feet when she entered. He was a nondescript man clad in a dated suit dyed a shade of curry that hadn't been used for clothing in the last thirty years. His partner, Detective Ingram, stood at the window looking at the city below. His taste in garments was better, but the handlebar mustache he sported set him back a few decades, too.

"Nice view," Ingram said, eyeing her carefully. "But I was hoping to get a bird's-eye view of Disneyland."

She smiled. "There's a 2.2-square-mile zone around the amusement park that is designated as a resort district. When you're inside the park, there aren't any tall buildings to ruin the visitors' sight lines. They don't want to ruin the fantasy."

"Ah, well," Jones said. "Some of us have to live in the real world."

Eve moved to her desk and sank into her slim leather chair. "What can I do for you, Detectives?"

Jones glanced at Alec, who stood like a sentinel by the door with his wide-legged stance and crossed arms. The detective seemed prepared to protest Alec's presence, then he shrugged and sat. The way he moved caught Eve's attention. His stocky frame didn't show the stiffness of an older man, like his taller partner's did. With narrowed eyes she studied him and came to the conclusion that he was far younger than he appeared. She suspected the misconception was by design and she grew even more wary. Jones was a hunter, too, and the information she held was his prey.

He went straight to the point. "Do you have any further information regarding the death of your neighbor, Ms. Hollis?"

Eve shook her head. "If I had anything to share, I would call you. I still have your card."

"Do you know an Anthony Wynn? He graduated from your high school the year before you. Chinese American. About five foot—"

"Yes. I know him. We attended the same elementary and junior high, too."

"He's dead."

She froze. They had been no more than acquaintances, but she'd partied with him occasionally and thought fondly of him. "When? How?"

"Drowning. Same as the others," Jones said. "When was the last time you saw him?"

It took her a moment to reply. "A-a few years back. I passed him in a grocery store aisle."

"So you haven't kept in touch?"

"No. We weren't close. The only things I can say about him are that he was quiet at parties and drew really great pictures on napkins."

Ingram stepped up to her desk, taking one of her business cards from its beveled crystal holder. "You've only been with Gadara Enterprises for a short time, is that right?"

"A few months."

"You were hired just prior to the murder of your neighbor, Mrs. Basso."

"That's right." She resisted the urge to look at Alec. *Where is this leading?*

Not sure yet.

Ingram shoved her card into his pocket, then reached down for a briefcase resting against the leg of Jones's chair. He pulled out a photo and set it on her desk. It was a picture of one of her business cards surrounded by an L-square ruler. It had the wrinkled look that paper took on after it had been soaked with liquid, then air-dried.

Alec approached. He looked at the picture, then at Ingram. "You found this at the crime scene?"

Jones settled back into his chair, his forearms resting casually atop the leather armrests. "Do you have any idea why we would find your business card on the corpse of a man you haven't seen in years, Ms. Hollis?"

Eve stared at him, dismayed. The Nix was taunting her. "I have no idea."

Ingram reached into the briefcase again and pulled out an item just as familiar as the last—a photocopy of a sketch artist's uncanny rendering of the Nix. The detectives had shown the image to her before. A florist had described the customer who frequented her shop to purchase water lilies.

"We want you to look at this again," Ingram said, holding the image directly in front of her face.

She looked away, disgusted. "I've never seen him."

The mark heated at the lie.

Jones heaved out a frustrated breath. "Look harder, Ms. Hollis. *Think* harder. He has a German accent. He got his hands on your business card at some point. Did he come here to see you? Did you run into him somewhere?"

"I don't remember him." She rubbed at her burning arm. "I sent out letters that included my new business cards to all of my former associates, clients, college classmates, and friends. I mailed at least a thousand announcements about my move to Gadara Enterprises. I also frequently drop them into those fishbowls on restaurant counters, since you never know when you might get a lead."

"Was Wynn on that mailing list?" Ingram asked.

"No. I don't know where he lives. I told you, I don't know him that well."

"He lived on Beacon Street."

Fear formed a knot in Eve's gut. *That's next to my parents' house . . .*

Alec mentally transmitted orders to subordinates with such velocity, she was dizzied by it. Her fingers lifted to her brow and rubbed.

Jones straightened. "Can we get a copy of that list?"

"Of course." Eve reached for her phone.

"This could be personal."

The detective's low-voiced statement stopped her with her arm extended toward the handset. Her gaze met his. "You think this is about me?"

The detective glanced at Alec, then back at her. "This guy stuck around Anaheim for the last nine months. He stepped out of his comfort zone only once that we know of—"

"Mrs. Basso."

"*Your* neighbor. Then his next victim is an old acquaintance of yours and your business card is found floating in the punch bowl with the lily. Things like that are rarely coincidences."

Eve pushed back from her desk and stood, feeling too restless to sit. Jones rose when she did, then resumed his seat.

"What about the other victims?" She looked back and forth between the two detectives. "Did I know them, too? Were they connected to me in some way?"

Was it possible that the Nix had been circling her since *before* she was marked?

This time it was Jones who reached into the bag of horrors and withdrew a typewritten list of names, birthdates, addresses. She looked the column of information over carefully, wracking her brain.

"None of these names look familiar."

"We can't find a connection either," Ingram said. "Maybe you caught his eye just recently. It could have been something as simple as you cutting him off in traffic. Whatever the reason, we think he's stepping things up a notch by terrorizing both the victims he kills and you."

Eve looked at Alec. *I want him dead.*

He met her gaze. *Me, too.*

She crossed her arms. "Were all the victims found in their homes?"

"Yes."

"Then don't worry about me. Nothing unusual has happened in my life recently. Nothing that concerns me or gives me pause. Since Mrs. Basso's death, our homeowners' association authorized the hiring of an extra security guard in the building, so now we have two. One roaming, and one at the elevator on the lobby level. You just concentrate on finding this guy before he gets to someone else."

"It's our job to worry about you, Ms. Hollis."

"No, it isn't." The last thing she needed was to dodge the police while trying to bounce some bounty hunting demons back to Hell.

"Yes, it is," Ingram said dryly. "You see, Ms. Hollis. For the present, you're our strongest lead."

Jones stood with briefcase in hand. "In other words, get used to seeing us around."

CHAPTER 7

*T**he detectives have left the building.*

"Somehow," Eve said with a wry curve to her lips, "that doesn't have the same ring as Elvis's sign-off."

Alec sent a brief mental acknowledgment to the Marks monitoring the security feeds, then turned his attention to Eve. He knew she wasn't going to like what he had to say, but he hoped she wouldn't get overly pissy about it. He had too much shit on his plate, in addition to a simmering temper and a pressing need for a long, hard screw.

Being in Gadara Tower only made things worse. He'd always gained strength and power from other Marks, always relished the rush he felt when he entered a firm. But now the Mark in him wasn't the only thing that recharged. The dark place inside him responded similarly; it had even absorbed power from the Infernals loitering around Olivet Place. That the resulting explosion had nearly injured Eve terrified him.

"You have to let me handle this," he said grimly. "You need to stay home with Montevista and Sydney until we figure out what the hell is going on."

She gave him the "you're-smoking-crack" look. "You're funny."

"Don't cross me on this," he warned, his voice sharper than he intended. He knew a clusterfuck when he saw one and this one had Eve right in the center. As usual.

Her hands went to her hips. "What the hell did I go through training for?"

"Why do you think you have a mentor?" he shot back. "You can't learn everything you need to know in seven weeks. You're not up to a fight like this yet, Eve, and I can't do what needs to be done when I'm worried about you."

Cain. Sabrael's voice throbbed through his brain with the unalloyed power of a seraph. *You must speak with me.*

Alec was physically jolted by the violence with which the darkness inside him recoiled from Sabrael. *Not a good time,* he snapped.

You owe me. Have you forgotten so quickly?

Have you forgotten that I told you I'd get to you when I get to you?

Eve pressed on, unaware of the silent exchange. "So assign me to another mentor."

Alec's first urge was to hit her, which scared the shit out of him. He clasped his hands behind his back. "No."

"Why not? If you're too busy to do your job, you should assign me to someone else."

Fury battered his control. How had Raguel managed it? Alec was exhausted by the constant struggle.

"You're mine, angel," he said harshly. "Even if you don't act like it."

"This is business we're talking about." Her chin lifted. "Raguel threatened to reassign me, so I know it's possible. The mark system has a backup plan for everything."

"I'll back you up." He stalked forward. He felt himself move as if on autopilot, his mind disconnected from the seething emotions that drove his actions. "Against a wall. Nail you right to it."

Another couple of feet and she'd be cornered. Trapped. Nowhere to run . . .

Eve held her ground. "You sound like your brother."

Alec's brow arched. "You spit that out as if you don't want him. And we both know that you do."

Impatient, he shifted across the distance to her, catching her ponytail in a fist and a belt loop with his fingers. The loop ripped free, the tearing noise sparking a wave of heat between them.

"Alec . . ." Her voice was breathy and tremulous. He wanted it throaty and hoarse. Wanted her nails in his back and her sweat on his skin.

He closed his eyes and breathed deeply, relishing the feel of her slender body trembling against his. He felt the Infernals in the firm tapping into his lust and fury. He cut them off and heard the echoes of their protesting cries. Weakened by the loss of their power, Alec sucked the energy he needed from Eve, taking her mouth with a desperation that crawled over his skin.

She gasped her breath into his lungs, her lithe frame stiff at first, then a surging warmth against him. Her lush breasts pressed into his chest, her fingers tangled in his shirt, her legs intertwined with his.

Eve bit his lip. "Is this what you want? To take me down fighting?"

The taste of blood hardened his cock until it ached. He shook her. "I don't give a shit how I have you. I just want you to stop jerking me around and give up the goods."

Her hand fisted in his hair and yanked. "Who the fuck are you? Because you sure as hell aren't Alec Cain."

Shaking violently, he felt like a drunk in need of booze. The vestiges of Eve's Novium were leaching into his system, spurring his dark needs further. He changed tactics.

"Come on, angel," he coaxed. "You know you want it as bad as I do. You know how good it is between us. How hard you come when I'm fucking you . . . until you're begging me to stop . . ."

Her dark eyes were fever-bright, her lips slick and swollen. "You're pushing me like Robert," she said scornfully. "Remember him? My ex from high school who wanted to pop the cherry I saved for you?"

"Eve—" Bloodlust surged at the memory of the cocky blond kid who'd tried to hard-sell Eve into a screw in the back of a Mustang. Alec had known then that he couldn't allow anyone else to have her.

Don't let the thing inside you have her.

His grip ripped her jeans further. A second more and there would be nothing left.

She yanked his head down to hers, her mouth slanting across his, wet and hot. Fueled by anger and determination, the kiss punished him so thoroughly his throat clenched tight against it. He hated her like this, hated himself for making her like this.

I'm sorry, angel . . . sorry . . .

She changed at the sound of his voice. Gentled. A low moan vibrated in her chest, a sound of longing and surrender. The convulsive flexing of her fingers at his nape and the feel of her hand sliding up beneath his shirt conveyed a wealth of feeling. Her tongue pushed past his lips, licking deep and slow. Savoring. She loved him too much to stay mad at him.

And the part of him that had loved her before the ascension knew if he didn't get her away from his personal demons, they would break her.

He twisted his head away, gasping. *He* didn't want her in rushed brutality. He wanted her slow and long. Soft and pliant. It was the *thing* inside him that wanted to turn what they had into something . . . wrong.

"Alec." Eve pressed her forehead to his. "Something isn't right with you. Isn't right *in* you. I can feel it."

Take her, the voices urged.

"I need to fuck," he said coldly. Deliberately. "Take your clothes off before I rip them off."

She pushed away. The pain in her eyes made him desperate to take the words back. He didn't.

"Alec?"

He ripped open the button fly of his jeans, freeing his cock. "On your knees. I want your mouth first."

"Fuck you."

"I'm going to fuck *you* instead."

Her arms wrapped around her torso. She backed

away a step at a time. He forcibly restrained himself from stalking her further.

A tear slipped down her cheek. "It's like there are two people inside you. The Alec I know, and a monster."

"You're starting to bore me, Eve." His mark burned at the lie.

"You're starting to scare me."

Alec struggled to remain upright, wracked by a pain in his chest that threatened to double him over. But she didn't seem to see it. No, she saw only the darkness inside him that wanted to do things to her Alec couldn't allow.

"I changed my mind." He rebuttoned the fly of his jeans with slow, leisurely movements.

Her gaze was wary, as if she was considering running. He hoped she didn't. He wasn't sure he could fight the urge to hunt her down.

"I've decided to accept your Dear John speech after all."

Her gasp was audible, as if he'd struck her.

"What?" he queried snidely. "Didn't you mean it?"

Alec turned his back to her, walking around her desk to put something substantial between them. "That's one of your problems, Eve. You're a tease. You were fun while we were fucking, but now—"

She reached out to Abel and an instant later was gone, shifted away by his brother before he could say more. Alec leaped over the desk, unable to fight the fury at her loss.

An unseen force restrained his pursuit. His feet were rooted to the carpeted floor, causing him to nearly topple when he attempted to lunge.

Sabrael's amused voice spoke behind him. "You broke her heart with laudable precision. You always did cut to the quick."

Alec stumbled as he was freed. He pivoted, flinching from a blinding brightness that put the sun to shame. Blinking rapidly, he engaged the thick layer of corneal lubrication that enabled him to see through the seraph's glow to the man within. Sabrael sat at Eve's desk, his six wings tucked away, his feet resting atop the edge of her desk. The wicked spikes that lined the outside edges of his black leather boots glinted in the glare of his luminescence. The brutal footwear was a stark contrast to the white, one-shouldered robe he wore. The visual dichotomy was a physical manifestation of the angel's temperament. Outwardly a model of his station, Sabrael hid a razor's edge of cruelty.

"I'm busy, Sabrael. You'll have to wait in line."

The seraph's eyes filled with the purest, bluest of flames and a hint of laughter that made Alec's hackles rise. "Relax. I am not here to cash in my chips, Cain. I am here on behalf of your mother."

"No." Alec shook his head, anticipating the question. "Not now."

"You keep delaying her. She is displeased."

Alec snorted. "Haven't you noticed the world's gone to shit? It's not safe."

"Gabriel disagrees." Sabrael's smile was both beautiful and frightening. "He is weary of her complaints, so you have a week to prepare for her. Besides, you have a home now. Surely this visit will be less hazardous than when you were roaming."

"You're pissing me off." The seraphim regularly

withheld information from God, but the extent of their subterfuge never failed to astound. "Tell Jehovah what's going on down here and he'll settle her. He won't risk her, you know that."

Sabrael crossed his massive arms. "You have everything under control, do you not? If you are incapable of the task you requested, simply let me know and I will relieve you of the burden."

Jaw clenching, Alec fought the urge to attack. With a seraph, it would be suicidal. "I've got a handle on things."

"Excellent. Then there should be no problem with your mother visiting." Sabrael brushed at his immaculate robe, as if he were not intensely focused on Alec like a hawk with its prey in sight. "Does Evangeline know that this promotion is what you wanted? Did you tell her that?"

"Does it matter now?"

Sabrael laughed softly. "I suppose not."

"Sara was with Abel for a long time," Alec said with a shrug, while inside, his discomposure grew. "Relationships aren't impossible."

Yes, he'd suspected he would lose his ability to love Eve—if only subconsciously—but he'd planned on her leaving him first. He'd intended for her to be mortal again and moved on with her life when his advancement came. The loss of his ability to love her would have been welcome then. How else would he survive her loss?

But Eve wouldn't understand. She would see only that his love for her had taken a back seat to his ambition.

"Sarakiel *toyed* with Abel," Sabrael argued, "and

Abel used her in return. God created us to connect physically by design. But sex does not a true partnership make."

"I really don't care about Abel or our anatomy."

"And now, you do not care about Evangeline either. Life must be much simpler for you."

"Go away," Alec dismissed. "You're annoying me."

The seraph burst from the chair like a rocket. In a flaming trail of wings, leather, and spikes, he kicked Alec in the chest and ripped through to the other side. The gaping, smoldering hole Sabrael wrought was so wide it nearly severed Alec's torso in half.

Dropping to his knees with an agonized scream, Alec toppled to the floor, his cheek skinned by the harsh pile of the carpet.

You forget yourself, the seraph roared.

In torment, Alec tapped into the power of his beast and found the strength to extend a middle finger and flip Sabrael off.

There was a moment of terrible silence, when his pained gasps were the only sounds to fill the eerie quiet. Then Sabrael laughed—*laughed*—and hauled Alec to his feet, restoring him.

"You amuse me, Cain." The seraph brushed away Alec's tears with tender swipes of his thumbs. "Because I like you, I will not tell your precious Evangeline about your choice of ascension over her. Your secret is safe with me."

Alec slapped the scorching hands away. "Leave Eve out of this."

The seraph hovered over him with a broad smile. "Might I suggest you purchase new linens for your guest room? Something floral, perhaps? Your mother does love gardens."

As swiftly as he'd come, the seraph was gone.

Alec began to pace, his mind working judiciously. The seraph clearly needed something else to occupy him. But what?

Then there was Eve . . .

The time had passed when he could have laid everything out on the table for her. Now he had to find a way to get his shit together. He refused to believe that his brother had been right all those years ago, when he'd shouted the words that had goaded Alec to kill him.

The darkness in him smiled at the memory and his lips curved in a mirroring movement before he caught himself.

Who the fuck was running the show in his body?

He inhaled and exhaled, restoring a semblance of his usual equanimity.

One thing at a time. Sabrael. Eve. Himself.

Hand to his stomach, Alec still felt the tearing of the seraph's boots through his entrails.

Black leather. Spikes.

An idea formed.

He shifted to another part of the building and paused, eyeing the lone blonde on the indoor shooting range. Tucked away in the bowels of Gadara Tower, the range provided a convenient place for Marks to hone their marksmanship. Silver bullets were still the swiftest way to vanquish werewolves.

Sensing his perusal, Iselda Seiler—Izzie, as the other Marks called her—turned her head and met his gaze. She set her gun down and removed the glasses and hearing protection that was less critical for Marks than mortals, but still necessary. She studied him with a now familiar odd intensity that had taken him some time to become accustomed to. There was an air of expectation about her, a sense that she was searching for something in his speech or expression.

His gaze lowered from the kohl-rimmed blue eyes, to the purple-stained mouth, to the spiked leather collar around her neck.

Malice made him smile. "I have a task for you, Ms. Seiler."

Her eyes glittered. "I'm at your service."

Eve was drawing a supporting column in her preliminary sketch when Montevista shouted from her living room.

"Hey, Hollis! Wanna play?"

She finished the precise line before answering. "No, thanks. You two go ahead."

"Aww, man," Sydney complained. "I'm getting tired of kicking his ass at Wii tennis."

"Try the bowling."

She glanced at the clock on the wall. Staying focused for longer than fifteen minutes was impossible when she felt as if her world was falling apart. In her mortal life, her brain would have overridden everything and allowed her to lose herself in her design work. As a Mark, her body was a machine that no longer listened to her brain. The mark tapped into her roiling emotions and channeled them into a nearly overwhelming desire to run, hunt, kill . . .

Alec dismissed me as if I meant nothing to him.

Eve wished she could cry. As it was, she felt as if her heartbreak was bottled up inside her, building in strength until something exploded.

"Ugh." Abandoning the drawing table, Eve moved to the desk and woke her computer. She logged into the Gadara Enterprises system and opened the file that contained her report of the Upland incident. When she'd been told that the mark system kept secular records as well as celestial ones, she had been shocked at what she considered a security breach waiting to happen. But both Gadara and Alec had assured her that a divine hand protected the information. God liked the status quo.

As she refreshed her recollection of the report, she noted the sidebar with various links that ran along the right side of the main text. There were reports from Reed and Mariel—both handlers who'd lost Marks to the hellhounds—as well as the guards who'd been present, Alec, and Gadara himself. It was the latter she was most interested in, so Eve clicked on it. A password prompt box appeared and she frowned.

What would Gadara use as a password?

Archangel. God. Celestial. Mark. Christ. Jesus. Jehovah. Bounty hunter. Christmas.

Nothing worked. Eve growled. A warm breeze moved over her skin. Her eyes closed.

Reed.

She reached for him, into him, farther than was necessary, running the name "Raguel" through his mind to see what stirred.

He who inflicts punishment upon the world and the luminaries.

"That doesn't help," she muttered.

Quit digging, he admonished, with warm amusement. *I'll be there soon, and you can ask me what you want.*

Breathing deeply, Eve closed her eyes and reached out to Alec. She moved tentatively, furtively, like a blind person searching through an unfamiliar room.

Until she was snatched by thick, talon-tipped fingers and tossed into the darkness.

CHAPTER 8

Alec's mind was like an ocean in the midst of a hurricane. Eve was tossed, battered. Dunked beneath the surface, only to emerge gasping. How would she ever find anything inside him? She couldn't even find Alec.

What do you seek?

She ceased her thrashing. The voice was only vaguely familiar, yet alluring in a way only Alec's could be. Floating among the flotsam of his emotions, she waited with bated breath for another word from him that might reassure her.

Ah, pretty angel. You seek Raguel here?

Alec? she queried, still wary. The voice was Alec's, but the inflection was not.

Who else would it be? You want Raguel. One of the holy angels, who inflicts punishment on the world and the luminaries.

Yeah, I heard that already. Give me something new.

Luminaries, angel. Now come see me. Give me some gratitude.

You kicked me to the curb, she reminded, reaching out to Reed for the leverage to pull herself free.

Makeup sex is the hottest.

We haven't made up.

The sea of madness churning around her rose up like a tsunami, dragging her with it to the very peak.

Eve. Alec's voice at last, furious and frantic.

He threw her out of his mind like a bouncer would a drunk at a bar.

Startled upright, Eve opened her eyes. She punched out *luminaries* on her keyboard.

The computer screen flashed, "Good afternoon, Raguel."

"Luminaries, eh?" she muttered, hating that Gadara's sojourn in Hell was the reason she was able to snoop without fear of repercussion. The report opened and she leaned back in her chair to read, her hands rubbing at the goose bumps on her arms. How awful that Alec—the one man who had always made her hot—now left her cold.

Eve quickly scanned the brief text. It was only a few pages and focused more on Reed's uncustomary behavior than on the actual documentation of the events surrounding the discovery of the mask and tengu.

. . . argued extensively about assigning Evangeline Hollis before training . . .

. . . lack of objectivity . . .

. . . too emotionally attached . . .

. . . overreached his position and approached Sarakiel for use of her personal guards . . .

Eve's fingers dug into the flesh of her thighs. Reed.

He'd made a deal just as Alec had. But for what purpose? For her? Or for Sara, who'd been his lover for many, many years? Sara had benefited from her team's support during the raid that night, with added prestige and expanded duties. Gadara believed Reed had done it for Eve.

The true dilemma in her relationships with both Alec and Reed wasn't monogamy or honesty, although she most often cited those. Really, it was trust. She didn't know how much of their wanting her was ambition and how much of it was desire. As long as the two brothers continued to clash over her, she was a valuable pawn to more than just Gadara.

The feel of firm lips pressed to her nape made Eve jump in her chair. The flick of a tongue sent a shiver along her spine. She hit the key on her keyboard that pulled up her e-mail screen and concealed Gadara's report.

"How are you doing?" Reed murmured, his breath a gentle caress over her moist skin.

"Fine."

"No, you're not." He spun her chair around. "You can't lie to me. I feel you. I'm sorry I bailed on you earlier."

Eve tilted her head back to look up at him. He'd shifted her home, then taken off immediately afterward. "Don't apologize. I know you have twenty other Marks to worry over. I'm just glad you came when you did."

"I'll always be here for you." Reed caught her wrist and tugged her up, pulling her toward the futon she kept against the wall. He sat and gestured for her to take a seat beside him. "Tell me what happened."

"Don't you know?"

"You shut me out."

"Really?" She twisted sideways to face him. "And I wasn't even trying."

He mimicked her pose, tucking his right leg onto the seat and tossing his arm over the back of the futon. Her gaze was caught by his Rolex, because of both the beauty of the white gold against his olive skin and the surprise of an immortal concerned with the passing of mortal time.

"Cain pissed you off." It was a statement, not a question.

She made a careless gesture with her hand. "No. He told me to get lost. Apparently I'm boring when I'm not putting out."

There was a beat of silence, then, "He *broke up* with you?"

"That's a kind way to say it."

Reed's gaze roamed the length of her and paused on her ripped waistband and belt loop. He grew dangerously still. "Did he hurt you?"

"Not in the physical sense, no."

"He breaks things, babe. That's what he's always done."

"There's something wrong with him."

"You're just now figuring that out?"

"Be serious."

Reed's fingertips touched her cheek. "I am."

Eve stared at him for a long moment, waiting for some sign that he was playing with her or being less than serious. There was none. All she saw were warm brown eyes filled with compassion. He wore a graphite gray shirt today, open at the collar with rolled-up sleeves, as usual. He was an impossibly handsome man, physically perfect. But it was his imperfections that really did a number on her.

She leaned into his touch. "What do you know about archangels?"

His hesitation was nearly imperceptible, but she was looking for it. "Are you digging for anything in particular?"

"Is there any part of the change that would make someone more aggressive than usual?"

"Cain. Is. A. Dick. Period."

"Listen to me. Don't judge."

"Fine." He couldn't have sounded more disgruntled.

"I know Alec Cain. But Cain the archangel . . . I don't know him at all. They're not the same guy."

Reed's lips thinned, then he exhaled harshly. "You've known Cain three months total, with a ten-year gap in between. Why won't you consider that he was on his best behavior for a while and now the effort is wearing thin?"

"Time has nothing to do with intimacy. You can be around someone for years but not really know them at all. The reverse is also true."

"I think he's fucked you into believing whatever he wants."

Eve bit back harsh words. Reed wasn't trying to be an asshole, he was simply tactlessly blunt. "You can learn a lot about a person when you're making love to them."

He snorted, and she realized he might not know anything about that.

"Making love is for girls," he said coldly, confirming her suspicions. "Guys fuck. We'll do whatever it takes to get into the pants of a woman we've got a hard-on for. Cain is no exception."

"Then do this for me. Dig into ascensions and see if any possible explanations jump out at you."

He froze, his nostrils flaring. "Damn, you've got balls."

"You can't tell me you don't feel the mess inside him. We're all connected. There's something in him that wasn't there before."

"He's the same as he always was," Reed bit out. "He just has more power and less reason to play nice."

"You talk a good game," she shot back, "but that's all it is. I want to know what's inside him."

"I don't think you do." He held up a hand when she opened her mouth. "Say no more. I'll ask around."

"Thank you." She put every ounce of gratitude she felt into the words, but his face remained impassive.

He stood and looked down at her with disdain. "Think about how screwed up you are, Eve. I'm right here trying to be what you want, and you're asking me to help you with a guy who can't love you."

She opened her mouth to argue, but he disappeared.

Sighing, she said, *Come back.*

Eve waited, hating the feeling that her life was spinning completely out of her control. Pushing to her feet, she reached out to him again. *I would do the same for you, Reed. I wouldn't let it rest, if I knew something was wrong.*

Silence.

"Ugh. I can't win for trying."

Exiting her office, she looked down the length of her hallway to the view of the ocean and sky beyond her living room balcony. She was so damn restless, she felt like she was going to crawl out of her skin.

The Novium was pushing her body to have some fun kicking demon ass. That lust for violence could be channeled into a lust for sex as a delaying tactic, but Eve wasn't getting any, which left her spoiling for a good brawl. Here she'd been bitching about how much hunting she was doing, when it had actually been really damned convenient as far as her Novium was concerned. It took being cooped up at home for a couple of hours to drive that point home.

Now, what to do about it? Playing Wii sports wasn't going to cut it. She'd suggest to Montevista that they go to Gadara Tower and use the gym, but she didn't want to risk seeing Alec right now. She would have to thicken her skin before she exposed herself to his barbs.

Eve turned away from the beckoning beach and headed toward her bedroom instead. The moment she entered, she spotted an unfinished task—the beautifully embroidered, burgundy leather Bible Father Riesgo had lent her.

Perhaps Montevista wouldn't bitch too much about escorting her somewhere, if she was going to church. Not that a church was any safer than other buildings; nothing was sacred to demons. But worst-case scenario would be that they cross paths with some bounty-hunting Infernals and throw down, and she'd welcome that. The demons were in town be-cause of her. They should be fighting her, not making life hell for the other Marks.

She'd rounded the bed and was reaching for the Bible when she heard the door shut and lock behind her. Tensing, she glanced over her shoulder. Her hand fell to her side.

"All right," Reed said gruffly. "I feel it, too. Happy?"

His hands were shoved into the pockets of his black slacks; his face was austere and somber.

Eve sensed how it pained him to make the admission and how hard he fought against his jealousy in order to be honest with her. He would have preferred for her to give up on Alec altogether. Instead, he gave her hope.

"Don't get too excited," he muttered. "He's still a prick. He knew what he was getting himself into when he went after the ascension."

She became very still. "You think he *wanted* this?"

"I think he pursued it." Reed looked at her. "There are many handlers who are better qualified. Cain was chosen because he secured an endorsement somewhere."

It felt so odd to be so composed on the outside when she was breaking into pieces on the inside. "H-he had to know that things would change between us in the process, right?"

His face took on a stony cast. "He knew archangels are incapable of romantic love, yes. But he might not have been thinking about that—or you—at the time."

More honesty, even though keeping that last sentence to himself might have helped his cause with her.

"Thank you," she said quietly, rounding the bed toward him. After Alec's Jekyll and Hyde complex, it was a relief to interact with someone who was bare and genuine. To his possible detriment, no less.

Perhaps Gadara was correct in his assumption

about why Reed had approached Sarakiel for assistance.

For her, Abel gave Cain the benefit of the doubt. It was only fair to give the same to him in return.

When she reached him, Eve didn't think twice. She cupped the back of his neck and pulled his mouth down to hers.

Reed's arms wrapped around her so fast, they felt like a steel trap snapping shut. His head tilted to better fit his mouth to hers. His aggressive hunger stole her breath and melted the chilled place inside her.

His fervor was far different from Alec's. There was lust, yes. Passion in spades. But his desire lacked the bite of fury and shadowy darkness of Alec's. With Reed, she didn't feel as if she was a waterlogged life preserver for a drowning man.

Breaking the connection, he rested his forehead against hers. "Don't use me to punish Cain."

"No." She pressed more tightly against him. "No Cain. Just you."

He cupped her buttocks in his hand and lifted her feet from the floor.

Eve . . . want you . . .

His lips, so firm and sensually curved, were softer than she'd expected. The last time he kissed her, he'd been rough. Angry. This time, his tongue was velvety soft as it licked deep into her mouth. The plunging motion was so deeply sexual she grew hot and wet. Moaning, she rubbed against him.

Want you, Eve, want you . . .

Alec's challenge echoed—*"What's more important? When someone wants you because they can't help it? Or when they want you because they make the conscious decision to want you?"*

But Alec was wrong. He didn't want her—consciously or otherwise. He *needed* her, but this afternoon she'd come to realize that she couldn't keep him afloat. Not in that sea of madness inside him. He would pull her under with him, just as he nearly had when he ascended to archangel. A Mark couldn't survive that Change—Alec, a *mal'akh,* had barely survived it—yet, as his body had altered states, he'd dragged her down into the inky blackness of his agony. It was Reed who'd pulled her free and saved her from certain insanity.

Reed pivoted, pinning her to the door. *Want you.*

Her legs wrapped around his lean hips. Their chests heaved together, the sound of their labored breathing more potent for its rarity. Marks didn't sweat, didn't get winded, didn't have racing hearts . . . except when gripped by lust for blood or sex. Stress didn't affect them, nor did regular exercise. The rarity of physical reactions created a craving for them, part of the way God encouraged Marks to retain their humanity despite a life of killing.

He pulled back and pressed his hot cheek to hers. "Sometimes, I hate you."

Eve felt that resentment occasionally, when he watched her and thought she wasn't aware. *If it's any consolation, sometimes I hate myself.*

"You wanted me before he came back into the picture, then denied me afterward." His hand cupped her breast, his thumb stroking across her nipple. Hot, dark eyes watched her pant and arch into his touch. They challenged her, mocked her.

"You damned me."

Want me back.

His voice in her mind was different from the one that spoke aloud to her. It was rougher, deeper, his half-formed fleeting thoughts pushed away as quickly as they appeared.

"I want to walk away from you." He rolled his hips so his hard length stroked directly against where she ached. "I want to fuck someone else and let you know that I have. I want you to lie in bed at night and wish you were beneath me. But you don't."

"I wish it now."

"I'm here now."

He continued to grind into her. The seam of her jeans became an added stimulation that coaxed a whimper of pleasure from her. She hadn't been able to send him away the last time he had held her like this, that first day when she'd thought he looked so much like Alec Cain they could be brothers. Who knew? She'd trembled in his arms like she was doing now and begged for mercy, even as she craved more.

Want me back, Eve, want me . . .

She nuzzled her check against his. *I do.*

"Then let me stay. Now."

Eve pressed her lips to his ear and breathed, "Yes. Stay."

CHAPTER 9

Izzie's blue eyes were wide. "You want me to seduce a seraph?" she asked in a voice inflected with
a German accent.

If Alec were to guess, he'd say Sabrael might like
it.

"If you can get that far." He smiled at the way she
bristled. "But I'd be happy if you can just keep him
out of my hair for a while."

The Mark clearly thought her charms were irresistible, which was another reason he'd approached
her. In order to manage Sabrael, he needed someone
whose confidence was bulletproof and who wasn't
afraid of a little pain. He suspected Izzie's tough-as-
nails appearance was more than just a fashion style.
The gleam in her eyes when she was exposed to violence was a recognizable one.

"Why?" she asked.

"The 'why' is my part. The 'how' is yours."

Keeping Sabrael busy would keep the seraph away

from Eve and out of the way when Alec approached Jehovah about delaying his mother's visit. Better for her to skip a year, than to be vulnerable at one of the most tumultuous times in history.

With his hand at Izzie's back, Alec led her away from the shooting range.

"Can't he hear you plan this?" Izzie queried.

"He could, if he was listening, but he isn't."

"How do you know?"

"Because he's not here kicking my ass," Alec said dryly.

Her mouth curved.

Alec used to seek out women such as her for sex, women who weren't looking for more than a hot, hard rut. Only with Eve had he taken the time to savor the connection.

And look how messy that was. All that angst and grief . . . not worth the trouble.

Ignoring the voices in his head, he said, "We'll get things rolling after I speak with Mariel about borrowing you for a while."

Assigning the latest class of Marks to handlers had been one of his first archangel responsibilities. He'd placed Izzie with the easygoing Mariel for two reasons: One, Mariel had recently lost one of her Marks to a hellhound. Two, he sensed Izzie would manipulate a male handler.

Like Eve does Abel?

Izzie's breast pressed against his arm. "How will I meet this seraph?"

Unwelcome heat flared across his skin. "I'll arrange it."

"Why do you think I can seduce him?" Her voice

was a throaty invitation to compliment her. Hit on
her.

The part of himself that he was beginning to hate
was considering it when a surge of lust burned through
him.

Eve. She was achy and still aroused from his earlier handling of her. As he and Izzie reached the elevators, he glanced at the clock on the wall. An hour
later and Eve was hotter than ever.

*She's yours. Go get her. She'll give in . . . eventu-
ally. And if she doesn't, you can make her like it anyway . . .*

His fingers stroked Izzie's lower back. "Because
you're hot, Ms. Seiler," he purred.

I might have something that would interest you,
Hank rasped.

The interruption was irritating. Alec had other
things on his mind. *How interesting?*

I think it's significant.

Significant wasn't a word Hank used lightly. Grumbling beneath his breath, Alec punched the button on
the elevator. Eve's desire was goading his, which had
every instinct he possessed urging him to get to her
and put them both out of their misery. She might think
she was scared of him, but he could make her give in.
He knew all the right buttons to push . . .

I'm on my way, Alec told Hank. *But you better
make this quick.*

As the elevator doors closed, Izzie sidled up to
him.

He arched a brow in silent inquiry.

"You are flushed," she noted.

Yeah, he was aroused. He felt Eve as if she were in

his arms, pinned to a wall and writhing against him. He felt her breast in his hand, tasted her flavor on his tongue, smelled the scent of her heated skin. The sensations were so vivid and so completely focused in his viewpoint that they felt like a wet dream.

A slow smile curved Izzie's painted mouth. "You are either very angry, or very horny."

Alec leaned back against the handrail and crossed his arms. "Neither of those things concern you."

"Once, they did." She stepped closer. "In Münster, only a few years ago."

Arrested by surprise, he barely registered the delighted, semimaniacal laughter echoing through him. Sweat dotted his brow and nape. The feel of Eve's nipple rolling between his fingertips was so real he was slow to process what Izzie was saying.

Then the memories came rushing back, bringing with them an acrid taste in his mouth.

It had been only hours before dawn. The stinking blood of an Infernal coated his hands and pictures of hundreds of exploited children filled his mind. *How long had the Ho'ok demon been running the child porn ring? How many kids had suffered? Why had the seraphim waited so long to end it?* Disgusted, disheartened, and raging with bloodlust, he wandered the streets of Münster until a blonde whore with spikes at her throat and wrists stepped out of a shadowy doorway in front of him.

"Wollen Sie einen Begleiter?" she'd asked, licking her lower lip. *Do you want company?*

He'd pushed her back into the alcove, lifted her miniskirt, and fucked her until the thirst to kill had faded to a distant ache. Then he'd shoved a handful

of euros her way and left her—and the memory—
behind.

Take her.

Alec stood frozen as the darkness surged up within
him, curling around the lust inspired by Eve and
hardening the entire length of his body. The elevator
doors opened on Hank's floor, but he remained
rooted in place. The raucous arguments of the many
Infernals in the waiting room intruded into the once
quiet space. Then the doors closed again, leaving him
and Izzie alone with his inner demons and an instru-
mental rendition of "Copacabana" drifting out of the
speakers.

He felt the phantom sensation of Eve arching
against him the same moment Izzie's hand cupped
his erection.

"Is this for me?" she purred, stroking him.

Fuck her.

The gritting of his teeth was audible. "No."

She shrugged and reached for the fly of his jeans
with her other hand. "I will only borrow it, then."

As the first button popped free, the elevator began
to ascend.

*Forget Eve. She wants your brother. She's denied
you for him.*

Alec caught Izzie's wrist, staying her hand. Her
gaze lifted. For a moment he saw almond-shaped eyes
of soft brown. Then he blinked and stared into eyes of
cool Nordic blue.

"You don't want what I'm ready to dish out," he
warned.

"I do. I have for months."

Want you, Eve's voice whispered.

He shifted to his office.

But it was the beast in him that pinned Izzie to the wall.

Reed tossed Eve to the bed. She bounced with a soft cry of surprise, then reached for the fly of her jeans. Her limbs were lithe and perfect, the lines of her body slender yet generously curved.

Temptress, he'd once called her. And she was. A trickle of sweat coursed down his spine.

"Hurry," she urged, kicking free of her pants. A sexy-as-hell black lace thong was wriggled off next.

He remembered the one time he'd had her. Sent to mark her, he'd expected to merely toy with the woman his brother had spent a decade pining for. Then he'd passed her in the Gadara Tower atrium and found himself wanting her regardless of Cain.

Her gaze had followed him, filled with such hunger he felt it lick across his skin. That look had made him so eager to fuck her, he'd ripped the clothes from her body. *Hurry,* he had growled. The encounter had been over almost as soon as it began, yet it haunted him to this day.

Shifting out of his clothes, he left them puddled on the floor. He loomed over her. Eve paused in the act of pulling up her shirt, staring at his body with a mixture of awe and desire that swelled his dick further. She licked her lower lip and he groaned, fisting himself to buy a little time.

Did she see Cain in him? He almost probed her thoughts to find out, but resisted the urge. How she viewed him now wouldn't be the way she viewed him when he was done with her.

Eve reclined, half dressed, her pupils dilated from

the Novium. She'd been scorching hot as a mortal. How much more intense would it be with her mark-enhanced body?

Reed's lips twitched, incapable of a true smile with his mouth so dry. She was impatient to have him, to the point that she couldn't be bothered to finish undressing.

"I won't fuck you until you're naked," he warned.

With two hands, she caught the rounded collar of her pretty pink shirt and ripped it straight down the middle.

That single act hit him straight in the gut. His breath hissed out between clenched teeth. He cupped her knees and widened the spread of her legs, wanting to see what he'd coveted for the last few months. She trembled under his gaze, her lower lip caught nervously between her teeth as if fearing he would find fault with her.

He wished he could.

"Slide back," he said roughly, following her retreat with one knee on the mattress, then the other. He pursued her across the California king until she reached the headboard and had nowhere left to go.

"Reed." Her breathless voice dragged his gaze up to meet hers. "Don't wait."

She was panting, and he hadn't even begun. Pressing his lips to her thigh, he hummed in chastisement. "Relax. This is going to take awhile."

"I have people here!"

He licked at the back of her knee. She shivered. "I wouldn't care if all the archangels were here. I'm going to get my fill."

Hurry up, damn you. She sounded winded in his

thoughts, which told him how hot for it she was. Hot for him.

He pushed his hands beneath her buttocks. *I'm going to do everything to you. Everything.* As he lifted her to his mouth, her back bowed. *I'm going to push so deep into you that you'll miss me when I'm not there.*

Her legs fell open, offering herself to him. His first lick was slow and soft. Deliberately teasing. She was slick and burning with need, writhing within his grasp.

She keened softly as he pierced her hard and fast. *Don't stop . . . don't stop . . .*

A quick flutter over her, then he stiffened his tongue and worked the tiny bundle of nerves at the apex, relishing her throaty pleas for more. *Don't stop . . .*

He groaned and ground his hips into the mattress, knowing that he had to get her off now, fearing that he was too far gone to be able to bring her to orgasm later. He was spurred by the knowledge that this was Eve, the woman he wanted for reasons unrelated to sex. Now she was right where he wanted her—spread and willing, mewling with helpless pleasure. They were in the moment together, connected body and mind. He hadn't known he was alone—an angel who stood apart—until he wasn't alone any longer.

Reed grew more fervent, fueled by gratitude and an odd . . . joy. Afraid to be too rough with her, he siphoned the surfeit of lust through Eve and out to Cain, where it could be disbursed to the others in the firm. The tactic bought him some control, allowing him to be gentle with her as he hadn't been before.

Eve climaxed with her hands fisted in her comforter, her thighs shaking, the tender pink flesh beneath his lips spasming with a greed that might equal his own.

He rose to his knees, grasping her legs when they threatened to fall to the bed. He wiped his wet mouth against a perfect calf and the feel of her skin stirred the need he'd denied for months. Denied for her.

"My turn," he bit out, shifting both of her legs to one shoulder and taking himself in hand.

Pliant and drowsy-eyed, she touched his thigh with gentle fingers. He froze, wondering if she'd changed her mind now that the Novium was appeased, and whether he could stop if she had.

The look on Reed's face made Eve's eyes sting with unshed tears. The hand gripping her ankles was flexing convulsively and his throat worked as if he wanted to speak, but couldn't.

"I want you," she whispered. *Inside me . . . with me.*

Take me, then. He lunged forward with a snarl.

Her resultant cry was both pained and pleasured. She had forgotten how he felt inside her, so thick and long, nearly too much. Before she could catch her breath, he launched into a pounding rhythm, surging into her with a force that shoved her into the headboard. Placing her hands above her head, she pushed back when he pumped, shoving him so deep it ached in just the way she needed.

Today, she was as greedy for him as he'd always been for her. He was raw, without artifice, with none of the steely control Alec usually displayed. Reed climaxed immediately and unabashedly—his head thrown back, his neck taut, his abdomen rippling with working muscles. He roared as he came, his wings bursting free in an explosion of white, his thighs straining as he took his pleasure in her willing body.

Eventually he slowed, his chest heaving. He spread her legs, wrapping them around his hips and settling over her. His mouth moved over her face, kissing her, his gusting breaths a separate caress over her damp skin. One arm slid beneath her shoulder, anchoring her. The other hand cupped her breast, kneading. Beneath her calves, she felt his steely buttocks clench and release as he propelled himself into her. Slow, steady, and deep.

Reed—the ferocious one, a man known for his penchant for rough sex—was making love to her. The relief and . . . *joy* of being connected to someone brought tears to her eyes, but she blinked them back.

"Mmm . . ." He purred like a contented panther. A drop of sweat dripped from his brow to her cheek and he licked it away, then nuzzled against her. "That was worth waiting for."

His luxuriant, leisurely thrusts made her moan and arch upward. "Reed," she gasped, shivering into a violent orgasm beneath him.

His smile held a hint of male triumph. His eyes were dark and intent, his biceps flexing as he rolled her nipple between talented fingertips. Against the backdrop of white feathers, Reed's skin was golden, glistening with a fine sheen of perspiration that told her just how aroused she'd made him.

He pressed his lips to hers and whispered, "Now we can get started."

* * *

Alec stood before the wall of windows in his office and ran an agitated hand through his sweat-soaked hair. The air smelled of sex and fury, as did his skin. His shirt was torn and wet. He yanked it over his head and tossed it aside, then shoved down the boxer briefs he'd lowered only enough to free his erection.

His stomach roiled and he found himself wishing he could vomit. He felt violated, as if he'd raped his own body.

Want you inside me . . . with me. Eve's breathless voice combined with the dark ones in his head to goad him into an act he regretted more than the first time he'd killed his brother.

He could barely stomach looking at the woman sprawled on the floor behind him, knowing he'd betrayed Eve with her. Izzie had started out by goading him, spurring his lust and anger, relishing his single-minded focus on rutting. She might have thought it similar to the way he'd been with her before.

That changed as the darkness overtook him. He'd merely been the vessel used to carry out the act and at some point, she realized that. Surprise had hit her first, then fear, followed by anger. In the end, the pleasure overwhelmed the rest, but Alec doubted she would seek him out for sex again. He prayed to God that he would be able to resist her if she did.

I have to gain control of whatever the ascension awakened in me.

Naked, he moved to where Izzie lay sleeping and bent to pick her up. She whimpered and rolled away from him, exhausted by the demands made on her body. He had the strength of an archangel and the needs of a multitude of voices in his head. For all intents and purposes, she'd been fucked by a dozen insatiable appetites. Her clothes were in tatters, her eye makeup and lipstick smeared.

Alec deposited her gently on the black leather sofa that rested against one wall, then moved to the bathroom and the shower that waited there. He'd practically lived in this office after his promotion. Knowing immediately that something was wrong with him, he had been determined to keep away from Eve. But the thought of her with Abel—or any another man—had been unbearable. He'd given in to the need to see her. He didn't have to be in love with her to want to keep her. Affection, admiration, respect, and desire . . . some marriages had far less.

Want you . . .

He was so exhausted that even Eve's voice couldn't rouse him, but he felt a soft humming in his gut that signaled an eventual recharge. He had to get out of the tower and away from the other Marks who made him so powerful.

What have I done?

As the scorching water beat down upon his head and the odor of sweat and sex dissipated in the steam, Alec placed his hand against the cool tile and stared at the water swirling down the drain. Just like his life—and his relationship with Eve.

The things he'd said to her . . . Now that he could think clearly, he knew the full extent of what he had done. His intentions had been right, but the approach was hideously wrong.

He thought of Izzie's exhaustion and his own

stamina. He winced. While he didn't like the means, he was grateful the thing in him hadn't used Eve that way.

Cleaned and dressed in new clothes, Alec moved back into the main part of his office and collected Izzie. He shifted to her apartment and tucked her into bed.

He loathed himself in the brief moments that he hovered over her unmoving form. She had started out a willing participant and he'd pleasured her well, but too much of anything was too much. He'd been rougher with her than he had ever been with another female in his life.

He was exhausted when he shifted back to the hallway outside of Hank's office. So tired that knocking on the door was a chore, but an invitation was the only way to breach the occultist's inner sanctum. As it had earlier in the day when he'd come with Eve and the tengu, the door opened without tangible assistance and Alec entered the shadowy space.

"Took you long enough," Hank rasped, appearing out of the shadows in the familiar crone guise before altering into a voluptuous and lovely red-haired female. Alec used to wonder if the haggard witch guise was really a glamour at all, but later decided it was just a quirk. A ritual Hank performed to get in the mood to work his—or her—magic.

"Sorry." The simple word was incapable of relating the full depth of Alec's remorse.

Hank came to a stop just a few inches away. "You look like shit."

He felt like it, too. "What have you got for me?"

"Some advice." Hank crossed her arms beneath an

ample bosom. "End whatever sort of relationship you have with Eve. You are weakening each other at a time when you both need to be the strongest."

"I've already broken it off with her."

"Ah . . ." Hank studied him with narrowed eyes. "You seem more affected by the loss than you should be as an archangel."

Alec almost snapped back—his temper was still sharp—but the last couple of hours had afforded him just enough control to fight the impulse. "What do you know about the ascension to archangel?"

"I know I've always believed that archangels were born, not made."

Hank turned and gestured for Alec to follow. As they moved, a circle of light, like a spotlight, moved with them. Alec got the sense that the room extended infinitely beyond the shadows, which wasn't possible according to the limitations of mortal structures. But he'd learned to just accept that Hank was a demon of unknown power and origins, and to appreciate the fact that the Infernal was on his side and not on Sammael's.

"Any guess as to why more haven't been created?" Alec asked.

"Because the Seven have remained intact."

"The Seven. You say that as if it were an entity and not just a number."

A small, rough-hewn wooden table came into view and Hank settled daintily into a matching chair, gesturing for Alec to do the same. In all of the years he'd worked with Hank, this was the first time he'd ventured more than a few feet inside the occultist's domain. The air was hotter back here and smelled of sulfur.

Alec sat. The tengu waddled out of the darkness carrying a tray, as docile as a well-trained butler. He set a pitcher of amber-colored liquid and two crystal tumblers on the table, then bowed and scampered away. The stench of his rotting soul lingered.

"What the hell?" Alec barked. "It stinks. And it's . . . well behaved."

"We'll get to that in a minute. Of the many other archangels, only Michael, Raphael, and Gabriel have retained their foothold. Metatron, Ariel, Izidkiel . . . and all the others, where are they now?"

"With God."

"Because they were not able to manage firms and a secular life as well as the others?" Hank queried, referencing the widely spread belief. "With all the power and knowledge at an archangel's disposal, only *seven* were able to remain on Earth? God didn't want to create more in the hopes that they might be able to handle it? And no *mal'akh* has proven capable of taking on the task in the interim? Until you?"

Lifting his glass, Alec sniffed the contents and asked, "What is this?"

"Iced chamomile tea."

Alec set the glass back down. "I was promoted because Raguel was taken." And because he'd promised Sabrael an as-yet-unknown favor, but that was a matter best kept between him and Sabrael.

Hank filled her glass to the rim and downed the contents in one audible gulp. "Which effectively kept the number of archangels on earth at seven."

"You think the number is deliberate? Like a cap?"

"That, or the change is so difficult it is the very rare

mal'akh who can manage it. I like you quite well, Cain, but you and I both know that there are others who are better qualified for the advancement than you are."

Exhaling harshly, Alec leaned into the seat despite its creaking protests. Hank had a generous expense account and could easily afford to upgrade the furnishings, but appearance was everything to the occultist. The rickety table and chairs were meant to convey something that Alec didn't yet grasp. And he couldn't waste time thinking about it now. "No one is more knowledgeable than I am about saving Mark lives."

Hank flicked a lock of long red hair back over her shoulder. "Since when is that an archangel's purpose?"

The subtle challenge caused Alec's lips to pull back from his teeth in a snarl.

"Look at you," Hank rasped. "Like a rabid dog on the edge of attack. Yet you found the will to break up with Eve, when I'm certain that's the last thing you wanted to do. You're not supposed to be able to love her."

"It's not the same as before."

"Diminished, but not gone. Why isn't it gone? Is it because you were in love when the ascension happened?"

"I don't need more questions," Alec bit out. "I need answers."

Hank shrugged. "I'm a scientist. It's in my nature to question things."

"Find the damn answers! What the hell is wrong with me?"

"What's wrong is your belief that something is wrong."

Alec's fists clenched. "I don't like hitting women, but you're pushing me."

The occultist altered shape into a young girl of around six or seven years old, but spoke in the eternally present gruff voice. "Every celestial believes that demons choose to be evil. None will consider that we're created the way we are. We couldn't see the world as you do, even if we wanted to. Just like you can't see our point of view."

But Alec could now. That was the problem. He saw the appeal. Worse, the urges he felt seemed an inherent part of him, not an addition. "So you think I'm supposed to be this way? That I've always been this way. Is that what you're saying?"

"Perhaps you're fighting the change." Hank picked up Alec's untouched glass and downed the contents. "Perhaps the ambitious part of your soul, the part that yearns to be closer to God, is what's rebelling in you. It's becoming feral because it isn't getting what it wants."

"Maybe it's the part of me that wants Eve," he said, just to be contrary.

"Personally, I think it might be that other, darker part of your soul asserting itself. That part you ignore and everyone pretends doesn't exist."

Alec growled at Hank's perceptiveness, the sound more animal than angel. "It doesn't exist. It's a myth."

"A lie from an archangel, instead of mere evasion. That has to be a first." Hank smiled. "Regardless, my concern was for Eve and you've seen to that. Cain of Infamy can take care of himself. I suggest you ask one of the other archangels what to expect. Why come to an Infernal when Sarakiel is here to assist you?"

"Because I'm in competition with the other archangels now."

Similar to children, archangels curried the favor of their Father. They competed with their siblings in the hopes of outshining them. He was now a threat. They'd be sabotaging themselves in order to help him. No archangel was that selfless.

Altering back into the sex kitten form, Hank stood and gestured for Alec to follow suit. "Come on. Let me show you why I called you down here. It might cheer you up."

CHAPTER 10

The soft trill of an incoming text message pulled
Reed from a doze. "Can I smash your phone?"
he murmured, nuzzling his lips against the crown of
Eve's head. "I'll buy you a new one."

She wriggled against his side, her body a warm
weight he was reluctant to lose. "Some of us have to
communicate the hard way," she teased. As she
pushed up on one elbow, the thick curtain of her hair
tickled his chest.

He felt a shadow of unease cross her mind, followed quickly by a stab of guilt. Rolling, he pinned
her beneath him and took her mouth in a hard, hot
kiss. She softened, her hands sliding into his hair to
hold him close.

Pulling back, he touched his nose to hers, somewhat bemused by his need to be tender. "If you start
thinking of this as a mistake, I'll bend you over my
knee and spank you."

Eve laughed, but her gaze was somber. "You're
going to have to be patient with me. I'm not in the

best shape to jump into something serious. I told you that before."

"I'm not in any shape to jump into anything. You know that. I have no idea what the hell I'm doing."

"Or if you're going to want to keep doing it," she added.

Reed winked. "I definitely want to keep doing it."

"Fine. We'll keep it sexual."

"That's not what I meant."

"Yes, it is." She wrapped a leg around his, rolled him back over, and kept on going. She continued alone until she rolled to the edge of the mattress, then slid off of it.

"Babe . . ."

She moved over to the dresser and unplugged her cell phone from its charger. A few button pushes later, she said, "Sara is looking for you."

Closing his eyes, he bit back a frustrated groan. He had a cell phone, but he kept it off 90 percent of the time for just this reason. Anyone he wanted to talk to could do so without secular means. Everyone else could damn well wait until he got to them.

"How bad is it that she knew she'd find you with me?" As she talked, Eve's voice grew distant.

Slitting his eyes open, Reed caught her hot little ass disappearing into the bathroom. Shamelessly naked, which he found very appealing.

She probably contacted all of my Marks, he replied privately, knowing that calling after her would be heard by the two Marks in the living room.

The shower came on. Eve's room was large, with vaulted ceilings and a door-less entry to the bathroom that was several feet wide.

How long were you with her? she asked.

Reed slid out of bed and followed her into the bathroom. "I know what you're thinking, and it wasn't like that."

He found Eve standing with eyes closed and head tilted back beneath a massive showerhead. The shower stall had been built with no door and only a slender floating glass partition, which afforded him an unobstructed view of every inch of her.

What was *it like, then?* she rejoined.

"A waste of time."

Eve straightened and wiped the water from her eyelashes. "Some relationships end with feelings like that, but they rarely begin with them."

"I wouldn't know. I don't do relationships."

"Was she that good in the sack?" She posed the question casually, but he sensed that her interest in the answer was far from it.

"She was convenient. No dating, no wooing, no foreplay. The less I cared about her pleasure, the more she liked it."

"Maybe because she cares about you."

Reed laughed. "She's an archangel, remember? There's barely enough room in her heart for God."

"I'm not kidding. I've seen the way she looks at you."

"She wants my cock. That's not caring by any definition."

Eve squirted apple-scented soap into her palm and shot him a wry glance. "I know some men have fantasies about penis-starved women, but that's a bit much."

He leaned his hip into the counter and crossed his arms, watching her shampooing her long hair with avid interest. "That's not what you were moaning thirty minutes ago."

She paused long enough to throw a loofah at him. Catching it neatly, he straightened and approached her.

"I asked Sara to do something for me," he told her. "She strung me along for years before admitting that she wasn't going to follow through."

"Maybe she *couldn't* follow through."

Reed tossed the loofah back at her, then caught her hips and spun her out of the shower spray.

"Hey!" she protested, as he stepped under the water.

"The point is that she knew she wasn't going to help me. She just led me to believe otherwise." Shaking out his wet hair, he ceded the shower back to her and reached for her shampoo.

"I thought archangels didn't lie."

He paused a second, as if considering that, then began scrubbing his hair. "Why are we talking about this?"

"I want to learn more about you." Shrugging, she began scrubbing at her skin, turning it a lovely shade of soft pink.

"Then why are you asking questions about someone else?"

"Fine. I'll ask a question about you: what did you want her to do for you?"

His hands moved from his chest to hers. The look she gave him said she wouldn't be distracted.

"It's not important now," he said.

Suddenly, she smacked him on the shoulder. "I was right," she crowed. "You *do* want to be an archangel."

Reed growled and tugged her soapy body against

his. "I stayed out of your brain. You have no business digging around in mine."

"*You* thought of it. It just popped into my head."

It hit him that their newfound intimacy might open pathways he'd prefer stay closed.

As if she caught his reluctance, Eve frowned. "What's the big deal anyway?"

He felt her begin to pull back, both physically and emotionally. His fingers flexed into her buttocks.

"It's a lofty ambition," he explained tightly, knowing that he was going to have to open up at least a little if he hoped to keep her. "Not one you want to advertise."

"I can understand that. But you trusted Sara with it. When I asked you about it before, you blew me off."

Bending at the knees, Reed fit his frame more perfectly to hers. "You share thoughts with my brother, babe."

"Why would he care if you want to be promoted?"

His jaw clenched. Talking about himself was one of his least favorite things to do. "In the past," he said carefully, "if Cain knew I wanted something, he would usually get it first."

"Oh." Her arms came around him and the loofah in her hand scratched his back deliciously.

"Scrub my back?" he asked, kissing her forehead.

"Keep talking?" she dickered.

"There are more enjoyable ways to pay you in kind."

"Deal or no deal?"

Grumbling at his inability to tell her no, he altered their positions so that she could stay warm beneath the water while he stood outside of it. As she ran the loofah over his skin, she asked, "Do you think Alec will interfere with your advancement now? He's already been promoted."

"Yes, I think he'd get in the way. He's better at killing things, but that's the only thing he's better at. He knows I'd surpass him."

Eve's movements slowed, then stopped altogether. He waited, then looked over his shoulder.

Her gaze met his. "You said you think he secured the endorsement he needed with a bargain."

"I do. Hasn't he proven that's the way he works? He bargained with God to mentor you. He bargained with Grimshaw to get to you at the masonry. He bargained to resurrect you after Asmodeus's dragon killed you. Cain will break any rule, and he's in demand. Others barter with him to accomplish tasks they're afraid to do themselves."

"The way you bargained with Sara to get her guards to help me in Upland?"

Reed froze. *How much did she know about that transaction?* "Is that what you were digging around for earlier?"

Her gaze lowered. "Did I get it wrong? Did you do it for her?"

He swallowed hard, relieved by her apparent ignorance of his prostitution and terrified by the sudden expectation between them. It felt like a turning point and he wasn't ready for it yet. Didn't know how to get ready for it. "Not for her," he managed, finally.

The grateful kiss she pressed to the wet skin of his biceps made him look away before she saw whatever his face might reveal. She could bring him to his knees with a look. It would be best if she didn't know that.

She cleared her throat. "It would have to be a seraph who helped your brother, right? They're the only ones who have the ear of God."

"Not the only ones, no. The cherubim and thrones are also near Him. But the thrones are humble angels. They lack the ambition to strike a devil's bargain with Cain."

Eve held up both hands in a gesture of surrender. "I'm not in the right frame of mind to have a lesson on the hierarchy of angels."

"Good." He gestured at his back and gave her his best smile. "Please?"

As Eve resumed scrubbing, Reed faced forward.

"I'm really worried about Gadara," she murmured. "It's driving me crazy that everyone seems to have written him off. I want people running around, pushing for answers, hitting the pavement . . . something."

He nodded.

"I have an idea."

Reed tensed at Eve's tone, which held a note of reluctance, as if she knew in advance that what she was going to say would cause an unpleasant reaction. "What?"

"We want Gadara. Satan wants me. Why don't we offer a trade?"

He froze. His chest lifted and fell in normal rhythm, but his heart raced. It shouldn't. He wasn't aroused; he was horrified. "Are you insane?"

"Maybe. Probably."

Facing her, he caught her by the hips. "No fucking way."

"Come on." Her gaze was forthright and earnest. "If we put our heads together we can figure out a way to pull it off without one of us getting killed."

"Helllloooo? Earth to Eve. This is Sammael we're taking about. Aside from Jehovah, nothing exists that can defeat him."

Her jaw took on a stubborn cant. "I'm not talking about defeating him. I'm talking about tricking him."

He shook her. "And what do you think he's going to do when all is said and done? He's already set a bounty on your head!"

"If he really wanted me dead, I'd be dead."

Convoluted logic or not, she had a point. Still, the risk she was willing to take made Reed's gut churn. "He likes to play with his kills," he bit out. "That's all."

"Just think about it."

"No."

"It's the only option we've got!"

"Bullshit." He had a much better trade in mind, but she wasn't going to like the terms. "It's not an option at all."

Eve opened her mouth to argue, but he sealed his lips over hers and shut her up.

"I'll cook dinner tonight," Reed offered. "And no, it won't be Kung Pao chicken."

Eve finished pulling a T-shirt over her head, then glanced at him. His head was down, his eyes on his belt buckle as he fastened it. Perfectly polished, as usual. She took a good long look at him, appreciating his elegance even more for its artlessness. He hadn't primped when he exited the shower; didn't even glance at the mirror. A quick run of his hands through his hair was all that was needed due to the precision of his cut.

This was what she'd once thought her married life would be like. Great sex. Showering together before work. A man she couldn't get enough of looking at. She was turned on by the dichotomy of Reed's present composure contrasted against his fervency in bed and the heat with which he'd rejected her suggestion of a trade for Gadara.

Even knowing that he wanted to advance to archangel and lose whatever feelings he had for her, she still wanted him.

Eve sighed. It had been clear from the beginning that she'd never be able to keep either brother. Their purpose was infinite, hers was finite. She didn't want to hold either of them back and she wasn't willing to give up her own dreams of normalcy, which meant it was up to her to keep her heart out of it.

Reed was reaching for his watch on the nightstand when he caught her staring. He paused, his previously absorbed expression changing to one of bemusement. He really had no idea what to make of her, and that told her that whatever she was to him, it was unique.

She licked her lower lip and watched his breathing quicken.

"Got a minute?" she asked breathlessly.

His slow smile made her toes curl. "I've got all the time you need."

* * *

"What the hell am I looking at?" Alec asked, straightening from the microscope.

Hank smiled. "The reason for your tengu friend's docile behavior."

"Explain."

"The mask suppresses aspects of Infernal genetic makeup, hence the reason for the change in their scent and skin. I just adjusted the spell they used to alter emotions instead. Think of it as Valium for demons."

"But it requires the same materials?"

"Yes."

Alec made an aggravated noise. The masking agent had been made with Mark blood and bone. They had a limited stockpile that they'd confiscated from the masonry in Upland, but once it was gone, there was no way to get more aside from killing Marks. "Does it wear off?"

"Don't know yet, but I would be surprised if it didn't." Hank gestured to the right and a sudden light illuminated a kennel that contained the tengu. "I chipped a piece off his heel and ran some tests. The masking agent was mixed with the cement. That might have been the inspiration for the creation of the hellhounds."

"But even though the mask was built into the tengu, you could still change its purpose?"

"The materials in the tengu are immutable, but the magic isn't. The damned creature was a nuisance, so I cast a spell on it and—" Hank pointed at the tengu, "—that's what happened. So I began playing with the formula to see what variations I could come up with."

A movement by the cage drew Alec's gaze. Fred stood to the side, taking notes.

"It's interesting," Alec conceded, looking back at Hank. "And Valium for demons could come in handy, but considering the limited quantities of supplies, I don't see it being viable."

"It's the first time anyone has subdued an Infernal's base nature," Hank huffed, clearly affronted.

Alec patted her on the shoulder. "Great job. Now . . . can you make me something I can use? An antidote to the mask? A mask for Marks that uses Infernal ash instead of Mark blood? Something along those lines?"

"Those are not the same lines. They are two very different things."

"You know what I mean." Irritation and impatience crawled through him, making him eager to get away. Whatever endorphins his recent orgasms had afforded him were rapidly diminishing. "You've had the masking ingredients for months. I expected more from you by this point."

Fred whistled and sidestepped out of the light.

Hank's beautiful features hardened. "Go away now, Cain," she said with dangerous softness. "Before one of us says or does something that we both regret."

Knowing that Hank was right, Alec shifted away.

"Hey."

Sara smiled at the cocky young man who called out to her. As she passed the volleyball court in the open courtyard of Izzie's apartment complex, he watched her with avid interest. Dressed in only board shorts and a pair of sunglasses, he was handsome enough and boasted a well-muscled physique. She briefly considered dallying with him just for the sport, but the notion quickly soured. His leer told her he lacked the experience to properly satisfy her.

Dismissing him, she climbed the steps to the second floor and knocked. She had to knock again before the door opened and Izzie was revealed. Fresh from a shower and makeup free, the blonde looked impossibly young. Fragile and wary as only a child could be.

Sara pushed her way inside when the door didn't open fast enough for her. The apartment was expansive and bilevel, with vaulted ceilings and steps up to the open dining area and kitchen, as well as a guest bath and bedroom. The master suite was on the same level as the living room and steam from the shower brought humidity into the lower half of the space.

"What happened to you?" Sarakiel demanded, eyeing the Mark critically.

"Cain."

"Really? You look worse for wear. Not that I am surprised. Cain is Cain, after all."

"I am not so sure about that," Izzie said wearily. Bundled inside a thick terry-cloth robe with wet hair hanging around her shoulders and wan face, she padded over to a red velvet sofa and sat.

Sara joined her. "Tell me."

When the tale was finished, Sara settled into the crook of the sofa arm and considered the possibilities. "Did Cain give a name to the seraph?"

"No."

"Can you get it out of him?"

"You don't understand." Izzie's slender fingers played with the loops of cotton. "He was reluctant at first, and later, like a . . . machine. There was nothing in his face . . . in his eyes. Nothing. He spoke in a language I couldn't understand."

"Hmm . . . I will see for myself."

Izzie's head cocked to the side. "How?"

"There are video feeds all over the tower."

"He is not the same man I met before. Something isn't right with him."

Sara pulled out her cell phone. She tried Abel again, knowing she would only reach his voice mail but needing to make the attempt regardless. On a whim, she texted a message to Evangeline.

How would the Mark handle the news of Cain's infidelity? And how far would Cain go to keep the knowledge from her?

A seraph. She hid an inner smile. That limited the scope of her search considerably. Whomever it was, he'd paid a visit to Cain recently enough to spark the ludicrous plan he'd presented to Izzie. Perhaps the meeting had taken place in the tower. While the divine radiance of the seraphim was undetectable to mortal technology such as the video cameras used in Gadara Tower, perhaps Cain had spoken the seraph's name in the course of their discussion. It was a lead, however faint.

"What do you want me to do now?" Izzie asked.

"Mariel will not assign you once Cain speaks with her, so enjoy some time to yourself."

"I'm here if you need me."

Sara brushed the back of her fingers across Izzie's pale cheek. "You will go far, Iselda."

The Mark curled deeper into the couch with a weary sigh. "As long as I go to Heaven. Having seen the alternative, I will do whatever it takes to go the other way."

"Anyone up for tacos?" Eve entered the living room and noted the setting sun just beyond her balcony window. The sky was multihued, telling her that she'd spent hours in bed with Reed. Long enough for Sydney to give up on the Wii and switch to her laptop. Montevista was nowhere to be seen.

"I am." Sydney snapped her computer closed and stood, stretching. "Montevista went to check on the perimeter guards again."

"Great. We can catch him downstairs and save him the trip back up."

Sydney rounded the coffee table. Eve once again marveled at how different the Mark looked in street clothes versus her work attire. Dressed in a dark pink Juicy Couture jogging suit, she didn't look anywhere near her centuries-old age.

"Are you okay?" Sydney looked her over. "You look sad."

Eve was taken aback a moment, then realized that while she might not consciously acknowledge her feelings of loss over Alec, that didn't mean they weren't visible. "I'm fine."

And she would be. Eventually. She didn't regret her afternoon with Reed, even though she'd further complicated her already messy love life.

After grabbing some cash from her purse, Eve followed Sydney out the door and locked the many dead bolts she'd had installed for protection back when she was Unmarked. Then they set off, passing the door to Alec's condo. He'd made it clear on more than one occasion that he would prefer to be living with Eve and not beside her, but the Hollises were Southern Baptists and shacking up before marriage was a serious no-no in her family. Even the next-door neighbor thing was a little too close for comfort.

The ride down to the lobby level was quick and they moved onto the marble-lined entryway with light steps.

"I'd kill for a place like this," Sydney said.

"Don't you?" Eve quipped, glancing at her. "You should check with someone about moving, if you're not happy where you live."

"I'm okay. But I could be happier in a place like this." Sydney smiled. "Not worth it for me to hit up Ishamel about it, though. He freaks me out."

Frowning, Eve asked, "Who's Ishamel?"

They crossed through the parking garage and exited out a self-locking iron gate. Eve glanced to her left, searching out the corner where Evil Santa missionary usually hung out. He was there and talking to Montevista. Luckily, the nut job was facing away from her, while the Mark looked directly at her.

"Heading to El Gordito," she said, in her normal conversational tone, knowing his mark-enhanced ears would easily allow him to hear. He gave a surreptitious thumbs-up.

"Ishamel is Gadara's factotum."

"The secretary?" The man who kept Gadara's office running like clockwork was white-haired and slightly stooped at the shoulders, with a penchant for sleeveless sweater vests and bow ties. Whenever Eve crossed his path, she wondered what he could have done to get marked. Since the mark arrested aging, he'd been old from the get-go.

"No, that's Spencer. He handles everything inside Gadara Tower." Pushing sunglasses onto her face, Sydney turned toward the beach. "Ishamel is the off-site guy. I'm sure you've seen him around. He dresses in gray from head to toe. Rides around in a limousine."

Eve's stride faltered. Gray Man. She'd met him back when she was a brand-spanking-new Mark. He'd picked her up in a limo and driven her to Gadara Tower. "He's creepy."

They hit the sand and turned left. The restaurant was within sight, a casual Mexican cantina with a Plexiglas-framed patio.

Eve considered whether or not it had been a mistake to forget about Ishamel. If he was Gadara's right-hand man, he would know how archangels functioned. Maybe he could help her figure out what was happening to Alec.

"I get the willies just thinking about his grin," Sydney went on.

"It's really more like a constipation-induced grimace." Eve tried to recall other details about him, but without much luck. "What is he? I don't remember him smelling like anything—Mark or Infernal—but I was really green at the time."

"Ishamel is a *mal'akh,* but not a handler like the

others. His sole purpose to make life easier for
Gadara, handling all the pesky little details that are
beneath an archangel but too important for Marks."

"Arranging housing is too important for Marks?"

"Moving into more expensive digs would take
authorization a mere Mark couldn't give. Especially
in this crappy economy. All the firms are taking a
hit."

"I didn't think about that." Eve's nose wrinkled. "I
hate to admit it, but I guess I've come to see the firms
as solid. Invincible. But you're right. We're based in
California—the epicenter of the housing market col-
lapse. And Gadara specializes in real estate."

They reached the patio and took an empty table
with an unimpeded view of the beach. Trays and
trash littered the surface due to an inconsiderate pa-
tron, but they tossed the mess in a nearby trash can
and waited for a busboy to wipe the table down with
a rag.

Montevista walked up just as the waiter approached.

"Three taco plates, please," Eve ordered. "Extra
pico de gallo and sour cream." She looked at her
companions. "What are you having?"

Sydney laughed. "I had no idea interior design
worked up such an appetite."

Eve was grateful the mark prevented blushing.

After the orders were in, drinks were on the table,
and they were relatively alone, Montevista leaned
back in his plastic patio chair and said, "The reverend on the corner is really gunning for you, Hollis."

"Reverend?"

Montevista smiled. "Presbyterian."

Eve reached for her iced tea. "He's a whack job.

Zealots like that should be marked. They're clearly devoted. If the seraphim sent enough of them after Satan, he'd give up quick."

"He thinks you're a call girl."

"What the hell?"

"Because of the number of men you have visiting you."

"Maybe I'm holding Bible study. Did he ever think of that?"

Montevista's eyes twinkled behind his dark shades. "He says you have a body built for sin."

"Gee, thanks. Did you straighten him out?"

"I fought the good fight, but he says I'm bewitched. I don't think anyone short of God will get him to change his mind."

"Great." Eve crossed her arms.

Sydney smiled. "Hey, look on the bright side. I wish someone said I had a body built for sin."

"You do have a body built for sin," Montevista said with a soft purr that made Eve look twice.

Sydney stared at her partner for a long moment, then gulped down her soda. Eve's brows rose. How long had Montevista had the hots for Sydney? And why did Sydney seem so surprised? After working together for decades, any sort of attraction shouldn't have gone unnoticed.

"Anyone short of God, eh?" Eve repeated, considering. "You just gave me an idea."

"Uh-oh." Montevista looked at her with brows raised above the top edge of his sunglasses.

Eve gave him a mock glare. "I have to return a Bible to Father Riesgo. I'll ask him to come over and put in a good word for me."

"Tossing a priest into the line of fire?" Sydney asked dryly.

"Have you seen Riesgo? That man can take care of himself. Besides, he seems determined to save me." Eve sat back as the waiter returned with a tray over-flowing with plastic plates. "He can start with Evil Santa."

CHAPTER 11

A lec sat on the steps of the old Masada fortress for nearly an hour before the power he gained from proximity to the firm waned and he felt remotely like himself again. He breathed slowly and deeply, battling against his new nature until he reestablished enough control to consider associating with others. He needed help, but he wouldn't get it if he kept being an asshole.

Where could he turn? Uriel was his first choice, but if the archangel suspected that Alec was a danger to himself or others, he would tell Michael and Gabriel. They would kill him, Alec had no doubt. But who else had answers? Who would protect him if they discovered his secret?

There was only one place he could go where he would be accepted as he was. Whether that was also the place where he would find answers was something he'd determine when he got there.

Shifting before he could change his mind, Alec

entered Shamayim—the First Heaven, abode of his parents. His booted feet hit the dirt with a thud and he took a deep breath to regain his bearings. The neatly tilled rows stretching out in front of him caused a pang in his chest. There had been a time when he couldn't imagine his life being anything other than that of a farmer.

He wasn't that guy anymore.

So a man will leave his father and mother and be united with his woman . . .

"Cain!"

Alec turned his head and found his father at the far end of the field. Adam dug the plow tip into the dirt and tied the reins of his mule around a handle to keep the beast in place.

Shifting to a spot just a few feet away, Alec offered a wary smile and spoke in Hebrew by habit. *"Shalom, Abba."*

"Your mother has been missing you," Adam said gruffly, pushing his hat back from a sweat-slick forehead. His dark eyes were assessing, watchful.

Alec resisted the urge to bristle at the thinly veiled chastisement. "I miss you both, too," he replied tersely. "It's crazy down there. There's not enough time in the day, even when the days are endless."

He'd learned to include his father in his replies, but Alec resented the fact that Adam couldn't say anything remotely supportive or appreciative. Abel had always accepted their father's distance without issue, but it ate at Alec. When he'd been younger and more hotheaded, he would pick fights to ease some of the sting.

"How is Evangeline?"

The question startled Alec. He hadn't been aware

that his father knew, nor cared, about the details of his life. "She's perfect. I'm the one who's fucking everything up, as usual."

"Something wrong?"

"What do you know about the archangels?"

"I know you're one now. Who would've thought, eh?"

Alec bit back harsh words. Of course his father wouldn't expect him to attain such heights. "Yeah. Would Mom know more about them?"

A fond smile curved Adam's mouth. "She's a woman and a mother, she knows everything. Plus she took a bigger bite of the apple."

"Right." Alec turned to face the large cottage shielded from the sun by a copse of trees. As an afterthought before departing, he tossed over his shoulder, "Good seeing you, Abba."

"Are you staying for dinner?"

"I might. Depends."

"Not enough time in the day," Adam parroted with a mocking tone.

Alec shifted to the cottage, pausing outside of it. Behind him, the bare field was hot. Here in the shade, the temperature was ideal. The home had been built like a fairy-tale cottage, a whimsical request from his mother that his father had spent years seeing to fruition.

A familiar and beloved figure filled the top half of the Dutch front door.

"You just going to stand there gawking?" his mother asked, pulling open the bottom section. She dried her hands on an apron wrapped around her waist and held her arms out to him. "You look like shit."

"While you look beautiful, Ima." He stepped into

her embrace and pulled her close. His nostrils filled with her unique scent and some of the vibrating anxiety inside him calmed.

Withdrawing, he smiled down at her. The phrase "you haven't aged a day" applied to both of his parents. They were arrested in time with the appearance of mortals in their late forties.

"Don't jest," she chided, examining his features with narrowed eyes. "You look sick. You're pale, and the skin around your eyes looks bruised."

A mirror wasn't necessary to confirm her words. He felt wrung out. The fact that it showed was alarming. He was an archangel, damn it. He should be healthier and more powerful than he'd ever been in his life.

Her cool hands brushed over his face, pushing his hair back from his forehead and smoothing his brow. "You need looking after. It's been too long since I visited you."

"I have questions," he said grimly.

She nodded. "Come in and sit."

Alec followed her inside. She untied her apron while moving toward the kitchen in the back. The scent of a cooking meal soothed something inside him. He settled on a sofa in the family room and watched as his mother grabbed a half-filled pitcher from the counter. By the time she reached the seating area, two glasses had materialized on the coffee table in front of him. The darkness within him was irritated by the offering, which made him feel like a visitor rather than a member of the household.

Ridiculous, he knew, but his brain wasn't running the show.

The interior of his parents' home was a mix of primitive and modern. Contemporary sofas rested on a dirt floor and trendy glass tiles decorated the walls of a kitchen that boasted a water pump at the sink. Both his *abba* and his *ima* were blessed with an odd amalgamation of gifts. His mother could chill liquids with a touch and heat them just as easily. Prey came to them willingly, but they skinned and filleted their catch by mortal means. God had made their lives convenient in some ways, while still grounding them in the world they'd known since Creation.

His mother sat across from him, her long dark hair pooling on the seat behind her. She was as lovely as she'd always been, inside and out. Her concern for him was reflected in her brown eyes and the way she worried her bottom lip with her teeth.

"You should have come home sooner," she admonished. "Is there any news about Raguel?"

Alec shook his head. "Nothing. At this point, Sammael hasn't even acknowledged that he has him. Shows how powerful he's become to keep his minions quiet about something of such magnitude."

"He's always been powerful. Don't let mortal gossip cloud your mind. You know better."

Leaning against the overstuffed sofa, he looked out the shaded window at the swaying branches and asked, "Do you know what happened to the other archangels? Sandalphon, Jophiel, and the rest?"

His mother reached for a glass. "No."

"It was suggested to me that there are only seven archangels by design."

"Why? It places an added burden on all of them."

"I wonder if that's the point," he murmured. "Like

mischievous children, if you keep them busy, they don't get into trouble."

"What kind of trouble could they get into?"

Alec exhaled harshly. "They control *mal'akhs* and Marks. If they found a way to work together, think of all they could accomplish."

His mother stilled with her glass to her lips. "Are you talking about a coup against Jehovah?"

"A revolt maybe. A bid for more power. Added privileges."

The glass returned to the table with a sharp click. "You shouldn't say such things. You shouldn't even think them."

"I should have faith," he bit out. "Right?"

Her arms crossed. "When I heard that you'd been promoted, I assumed you must have found a deeper communion with God and this advancement was your reward."

The voices inside him laughed at the notion and prodded him to say bitterly, "Nothing so edifying, I'm afraid. I do the dirty work, Ima. That hasn't changed."

She sighed. Then her shoulders went back, a sign of her determination to ignore his faults and tackle the problems they created. The attitude reminded him so much of Eve that his jaw tightened.

"So someone made you an archangel for a price?" Her fingertips strummed silently atop the padded arm of her wingback chair. "Who?"

"What does it matter?"

"You are now the most powerful weapon ever created." Her dark eyes stared into his. "I want to know who had the balls to pull that off. And why."

* * *

"It's like a ghost town around here," Rosa mumbled around a bite of double-cheeseburger. "Brentwood is boring."

Reed set his soda down and lounged in the restaurant booth they occupied. "Maybe that's the way Grimshaw's Beta is assuming control of the pack, by keeping them tied down until they adjust."

"No. It's because the population of Infernals in the area has dropped considerably in the last couple of weeks. They're all migrating to the southern half of the state."

Hunting Eve. Reed reached out—*Babe?*—and was reassured when she nudged him back.

Don't worry about me, she scolded.

Yeah, right. He returned his attention to his charge. "You did a smokin' job on this latest hunt," he praised. "I think you set a new record for killing a gwyllion."

"I kicked that *corno* back to Hell and I'm ready to roll." She smiled. "Wouldn't mind seeing Disney-land."

"Is that why you wanted to meet with me face-to-face? You want a vacation?"

"I want to be where the action is."

Rosa resumed eating. The burger was almost too big for her to hold. A lovely Venezuelan with snapping hazel eyes and short, spiky black hair, she'd been in her midtwenties when she'd been marked about five years ago and her youth stood her in good stead. She was fast and nimble, with a fiery temper and staunch Catholic faith. Her father had been abusive to both her and her mother. One day, she'd had enough and she put a stop to it. Permanently.

He reached for a french fry, grinning inside at the

cause of his unusual hunger. The second go-round with Eve had taken things between them to a whole nother level. He wondered if she knew that. If not, he planned to bring her up to speed, pronto. "There's plenty of action here."

"Not right now there isn't."

"You know something that's got you fired up," he said, sensing it through the connection between them. "Spill it."

Setting the burger down, Rosa met his gaze. "If this is the start of Armageddon, I want to be in the thick of it."

Reed's brows rose. "Is that what's being said? That it's the end of days?"

Marks gossiped madly. Some of what they made up was entertaining. Some of it was dangerous.

"It's obvious. Satan is breeding hellhounds, Grimshaw was planning a revolt of some sort, and every Infernal within three hundred miles has a hard-on to kill Cain's girl. What the—"

"No." The denial was out before he could censor himself.

"No?" Rosa studied him. "Are you living in a different world than I am?"

Exhaling slowly, he worked to suppress his jealousy. To call his response "possessive" would be an understatement. Eve was no longer Cain's. But for Reed to stake his claim now would only make things more difficult for her. Many of the other Marks resented her for the advantages they assumed she gained from Cain's mentorship. If they learned that she'd moved on and with whom, those resentments might intensify, and right now she needed all the help she could get.

"I meant," he began, "that what is going on now doesn't necessarily signify that it's the beginning of the end. There are signs that would warn us. For one, the Rapture has yet to happen."

"Whatever." She shrugged dismissively. "Just send me down there."

Reed nodded. "All right."

"Yes!" Her eyes lit with both triumph and bloodlust.

"But if I need you somewhere else, don't give me a hard time."

She rolled her eyes and grabbed her burger. "By the way, Sarakiel is trying to get a hold of you."

"I'll touch bases with her when we're done here."

But he didn't.

After he watched Rosa's Prius pull out of the parking lot and head toward the freeway, he went to Charleston Estates. The gated community was the home of the Black Diamond Pack, which had recently suffered the loss of its Alpha, Charles Grimshaw.

Its Beta—now Alpha—was Devon Chaney. If Chaney followed precedent, he would be eager to establish himself as stronger and more powerful than his predecessor. Reed was counting on that impetus to make his plan work.

A guard station stood at the entrance and the exit, and a tall stucco fence surrounded the perimeter. Affluence and privilege were two of the words that came to mind when one saw the exterior. But beyond the crescent moon emblem embedded in the circular cobblestone driveway, there was nothing to betray the fact that every single resident was a werewolf.

He walked up to the guard station with one hand in his pocket and the other twirling his sunglasses. He glanced up casually, a smile curving his mouth as the guard realized what and *who* he was.

"Call your new Alpha," Reed said smoothly, "and tell him I want to chat."

"Repent, Jezebel! Repent or you'll roast in *Hell!*"

Eve fought the urge to roll down her window and sock Evil Santa in the mouth. Instead, she sat impatiently at the stoplight while the zealot stood at her window, strumming his guitar and screaming at her through the glass.

When he didn't get a rise out of her, he moved to the driver's side passenger window and yelled at Sydney. "Save yourself from lust of the flesh and the claws of this heathen woman! Save yourself, before you burn in the lake of fire!"

Montevista cleared his throat, drawing Eve's gaze to where he sat in the front passenger seat. "Okay," he said. "I'm liking your priest idea more and more."

"Yep." Eve hit the gas pedal the moment the light changed. Thankfully, when she'd called the church after dinner, Riesgo had been there, and he had agreed to see her right away. They were heading to Glover Stadium in Anaheim, where he was filling in as a coach for a Little League practice for one of his parishioners.

"Do you think Father Riesgo will help?" Sydney asked. "You're not a member of his congregation."

"I hope he'll play along, but at this point, he could definitely resort to extortion. I'd actually attend one of his services, if it would get that nut out of my hair."

Montevista shook his head. "I've never worked

with a Mark who had no faith. Your parents are pious, right? What happened with you?"

Eve held up a hand. "You and I are friends. That means we can never talk about politics or religion."

He started to retort, then glanced at her. His mouth shut. "All right."

"I know that tone," she said, fingertips tapping against the steering wheel. "You think I'm pissed off at God and irreverence is my retaliation. But I'm not mad. I just think that many of the stories in the Bible show a God who has the same faults we do. He has pride and a temper, and he plays with humans like we're toys. It'll take a damn sight more than the promise of an unseen heaven for me to worship someone like that."

"Yeesh," Sydney breathed.

"Sorry I asked," Montevista agreed.

No one said anything else the rest of the short drive. Not because of the discussion about religion, but because of the number of laser-bright eyes that followed them as they progressed. The sidewalks were only slightly more crowded than usual, but the number of Infernals was clearly elevated by a tremendous degree.

"When we get to the stadium," Montevista said, "just idle by the entrance while I see if the priest has arrived. If shit hits the fan, you punch the gas and get the hell out of there."

Sydney leaned forward. "I can run in. If it comes down to it, you're the best one to protect her."

He made an aggravated noise, then spoke harshly, "No. You stick with Hollis."

In the rearview mirror, Eve watched Sydney's

brows rise. The Mark settled back into the seat and caught Eve's gaze.

PMS? Eve mouthed.

A wry smile curved Sydney's lips, but it didn't reach her eyes. Montevista was a bit off kilter this afternoon.

They pulled into the tiny parking lot adjacent to the stadium. The place was familiar to her. Although her high school was a few miles away, Glover Stadium was the official home of Loara High School football.

Montevista had the door open and was unfolding from the car when Riesgo appeared from between two vehicles. The moment he saw her, a grin lit his blunt but arresting features. He was dressed in black sweats and athletic shoes, and he had a baseball bat bag slung over one shoulder and a mesh bag filled with mitts in his other hand. She hit the button to lower her window.

"Hey," he said.

"Hey to you, too. I brought your Bible back."

Even with the dangerous scar that marred his cheek, the amusement that lit his features made him look boyish. "You could have mailed it."

"Yeah," she conceded, returning his smile, "but I have a favor to ask, too."

"Really." His gaze moved to Sydney, then to Montevista, who stood next to the open passenger door. "Hello. I'm Father Riesgo."

Montevista introduced himself. Sydney stepped out and followed suit.

Riesgo looked back at Eve. "What kind of trouble are you in?"

"Who said I'm in trouble?"

"You have bodyguards."

She blinked, startled by his perceptiveness.

He jerked his head to the left. "I charge for favors. Park your car and come with me."

Eve looked at where he gestured and saw an open parking spot at the end. She glanced at Montevista, who clearly wasn't keen on the idea of her being out in the open. Despite it being a very public place, Infernals would come for her if they thought they could get away with it.

"Close the doors, guys," she said. After a brief pause, both Montevista and Sydney did as she said, joining Riesgo outside. She pulled into the empty spot, exited, and hit the lock button on her remote. She was lucky there'd been a space available. The alternative would have been to park in the larger lot on the other side of La Palma.

Riesgo was waiting nearby. Montevista was saying something to the priest that had both men looking absorbed. Sydney, on the other hand, was scanning the area. Eve followed her lead and noted the stragglers that loitered around the perimeter of the stadium. There were only a few Infernals, for now. They had to be working in packs, reporting her whereabouts in a chain that led from her house to here. She flipped them off, encompassing them all with a wide arc of her hand. One of them flicked his forked tongue at her, reminding her of her first run-in with the Nix.

Another problem to deal with some other time.

As a group, Eve and the others traversed the curving cement path that led from the lot to the stadium bleachers.

Ahead of them, a group of kids played on the dirt

near the pitcher's mound. They appeared to be in the eight to ten year range. Their laughter drifted on the early evening breeze and made Eve tense. They were so young, and innocent of the proliferation of demons she had brought to their doorstep.

"What happened to the coach?" she queried, wondering at the man inside the priest. Physically, he was big and powerful, although not in the way of Alec or Reed. Riesgo was barrel-chested, with thick biceps and thighs. A juggernaut.

"He's having an emergency root canal. So I'm helping out."

"Yuck."

"You're helping out, too," he said. "You can pitch."

"No, I can't."

He glanced at her.

"I'm not kidding," she insisted. "I can't throw worth a damn. I never hit what I'm aiming for."

Of course, Riesgo didn't believe her until he actually saw her in action. Some of her pitches didn't even make the distance to home plate. Others were skewed to the left or right. He thought she was pretending at first.

"Gimme that," he said finally, approaching her from his position as catcher. "You take first base."

She plopped the dusty ball into the palm of his extended hand. "I told you."

"Yeah, yeah."

In short order, Riesgo replaced her with Sydney, who threw like a professional. Montevista took second base. Practice took an hour. The bright field lights came on, turning dusk into day. Like vermin, the Infernals in the area encroached to the edge where light met night. Parents eventually started showing up to reclaim their kids. The team's coach appeared just in time to close shop, mumbling instructions through numbed lips. Montevista and Sydney took opposite positions on the field, staring down the Infernals that the mortals couldn't see in the oppressive darkness.

Riesgo came up beside her. "So, what's with the protection detail?"

She shrugged and told him the truth. "I pissed someone off."

He glanced at the two Marks. "Must be a pretty dangerous someone."

"You could say that."

His mouth tilted up in a mysterious half-smile. "So, how can I help?"

"There's this vagrant on my street. He's a bit of a nut."

As he started toward home base, Riesgo gestured for her to follow him. He picked up discarded mitts and balls as he went along and she helped, finding an odd comfort in his presence. She'd shortchanged him by crediting his charisma and velvet-smooth Spanish accent for the size of his congregation. He had an air of confidence; a rock-solidness that was soothing. He clearly found strength in being devout, yet Eve didn't chalk that up to naïveté as she did with most pious people.

"You want me to find him a shelter?" he asked.

"Uh . . ." She hadn't thought of that. Some days the guy was on the corner, some days he wasn't. He was rarely there past dark. She'd just assumed he had a place to live and chose to haunt her corner for the hell of it. "Well, I'm not really sure he's homeless.

He claims to be a reverend. One of those wrath-of-God, hell-and-damnation types."

Riegso glanced over his shoulder at her. "Does he wear the same clothes every day?"

Eve shoved a mitt into the mesh bag. "I really haven't paid attention. He wears jeans and a T-shirt, but whether or not they're the same daily? Couldn't tell ya. I have a good excuse though. It's hard to pay attention to clothing when you're getting screamed at."

"He screams at you?" The priest stilled.

Explaining the situation only took a moment. The silence that followed lasted longer.

"Why," he said slowly, "does he think you're a jezebel?"

"There's a lot of foot traffic around my place. But I'm not a prostitute."

"The bullet catchers are the traffic." It was a statement, not a question.

"Bullet catchers? Oh, the guards! Yes. They're nice people," Eve defended. "The good guys."

Riesgo caught her elbow and led her to the aluminum bleachers. "Who are the bad guys?"

This was the part where things got tricky. "That really doesn't have anything to do with Evil Santa."

"Sure it does. The guards attracted the zealot to you, you came to me; they're connected."

"In a six-degrees-of-separation kind of way, maybe." She sat next him.

The field was now silent and the sound of numerous cars on Harbor Boulevard was only a distant roar. Above them, the sky was a charcoal blanket with few stars. Metropolitan light pollution vastly reduced the visibility of celestial bodies, which made her feel somber and lonely. Before she could stop herself, she reached out to Alec. Where the warm light of his soul used to be, she felt only roiling darkness. She withdrew, feeling even more melancholy.

Reed.

He touched her briefly, like a quick kiss to the forehead that was distracted and hurried. She pulled back when he did, resenting her own clinginess. Regardless of the numerous Infernal eyes watching her with tangible malevolence, she would take care of herself. This was *her* calling—for now—whether she wanted it or not. Damned if she wouldn't own it while it was hers.

Pivoting at the waist, Eve faced Riesgo. "Do you believe in demons, Father?"

"Yes," he said carefully, warily.

"Do you believe they walk among us? Live among us? Work alongside us?"

His brown eyes were watchful and alert. "Did you hire bodyguards to protect you from demons, Ms. Hollis?"

Eve exhaled audibly. "What would you say if I said yes?"

CHAPTER 12

Alec stared across the small table at his mother and wanted to reach out to her. She had always loved and accepted him just as he was. She had forgiven him when no one else would, and pleaded his case along with his brother Seth to turn his sin into his salvation. But the darkness inside him clenched his throat tight, preventing him from finding solace where he could.

"It doesn't matter who helped me," he managed finally.

"Helped you?" Ima scoffed. "Helped themselves is more like it."

"Whatever." He reached for the juice on the table just to have something to do. He drank it, but tasted nothing.

"What about Evangeline?"

Exhaling harshly, he snapped, "What about her?"

"Oh my." His mother sank back into the chair. "What have you done?"

What had to be done. "I came here to talk about the archangels, not about me."

"Are you no longer together?"

At that moment, he felt Eve gently prodding through the connection between them. Her sadness was a salve, soothing the voices inside him that were irritated by the relief he found by being with his mother. They wanted anarchy and chaos, not peace. He closed his eyes and willed himself to be still inside, a sleeper not yet awakened.

She will turn to Abel, they whispered, fighting his restraint. *Let us have her, before it is too late and she no longer wants you.*

Alec mentally bared his teeth. *Fuck off.*

Eve pulled away. His hands fisted as he held back the part of himself that wanted to snatch her close and use her. Instead, he shut a door between them, a thick barrier that took great energy to erect and maintain. He had no choice but to trust that Abel would keep her safe for now. There was too much inside him that could hurt her, not the least of which were his most recent memories—

"Cain."

His mother's voice brought him back to the world around him. He opened his eyes.

"Your eyes," she breathed, with a hand to her throat. "They're *gold.*"

A prickling chill swept over him, like the shock of jumping into an icy lake.

She stood. "You still live next door to Evangeline, don't you?"

Alec nodded.

"Good. I'll talk with her while I'm staying with you, see if we can salvage things."

"Ima . . ." His tone was a warning. "You are *not* coming to visit now. It's the worst possible time."

"Bullshit." She caught up her hair and twisted it into a knotted bun. "It's the perfect time. Have you considered that things might be so crappy because I haven't visited in a while?"

His brows rose. In every myth and fable, there was a grain of truth. In his mother's case, the tale of Persephone's journey between Hades's underworld and Demeter's Earth had been inspired by his mother. She didn't make flowers bloom or increase crops, but she did seem to have the ability to rejuvenate Marks. For many, her existence established the veracity of the Bible in a way that not even he nor Abel could.

"There are rumors that Sammael has set a bounty on Eve's head," he explained. "Demons from all over the world are flooding the area where we live. You're a prime target. You always have been."

"Like Evangeline is?" she rejoined. "And now she doesn't have you to lean on."

His teeth ground audibly, his temper barely checked. "Abel will keep her safe. That's his job. Not that he's been doing it so far—"

"Then, he can keep me safe, too."

Alec pushed to his feet. "For fuck's sake, Ima! She's a Mark. She is trained to kill demons. You can't compare the two of you."

"Don't use that tone with me!" Her hands went to her hips. "You need me. Evangeline needs me. I'm sure your home is a veritable fortress in order to protect her. It can protect me, too."

"Not like Shamayim. Nothing can get to you here." He ran an aggravated hand through his hair. "I can't deal with worrying about you right now, okay? I can't."

"I'm coming along to worry about *you,* not the other way around." His mother left the room, heading toward the back of the house and her bedroom.

He followed, but stopped when he found his father filling the front doorway with his broad-shouldered frame.

Adam shrugged. "Her mind is hard to change once it's been set. I've never been able to do it."

"She could be killed," Alec bit out. "It's as dangerous now as it's ever been."

"I heard."

Which meant that after Alec had come inside, his father had left the field to make inquiries and get brought up to speed on events. Since Jehovah was probably unaware of the full extent of the story, either Adam still didn't know everything or he had a source of information within the ranks of the seraphim.

The seraphim didn't give anything for free.

Alec was beginning to wonder if his entire family was a pawn in a bigger game he couldn't see because he was in the thick of it.

"How much were you told?" he asked.

As Adam stepped inside, he pulled off his hat and met Alec's gaze squarely. "Enough to know that your mother isn't going anywhere without me. So you better have enough room for both of us."

The new Alpha of the Black Diamond Pack met Reed outside the gates of the Charleston Estates community and together they began walking toward a nearby public park. Although the Alpha appeared to be alone, Reed knew wolves followed them. If

Chaney was an idiot, he'd try an attack. Taking Abel down could be seen as a way to firmly establish his new position. But if Chaney was smart, he would consider a long-term alliance more valuable than a quick strike that would bring the wrath of God upon his pack.

California had three Brentwoods—one in Northern California, where Reed presently was; one near Victorville; and one in Los Angeles. This particular Brentwood had once been a farming community, but it was becoming increasingly residential as the years passed. The sidewalk they traversed framed a wide street. Around them, the youth of the buildings was evidenced by their modern architecture.

As they walked, Reed worked judiciously to keep his connection to Eve at bay. At the moment, the less she knew, the safer she'd be. He had no choice but to trust that Cain and the guards would keep her safe for now. Cain was a prick, but he wasn't idiotic enough to jeopardize her life over personal issues.

"To say I'm surprised you came to see me would be an understatement," Chaney said, after they'd walked a couple of blocks. "Are you here about the breeding operation?"

"No. I'm well aware that Grimshaw's hellhound-whispering days are done." Reed had moved on to the next problem in line.

"So, then," Chaney glanced at him. "What do you want?"

"I think we'd better start off with what *you* want. Are you taking part in the bounty hunt for Evangeline Hollis?"

The Alpha's stride faltered, a mistake Grimshaw

would never have made. "I don't know what you're talking about."

It didn't matter that Reed had no intention of following through with his plan. Just discussing it aloud—especially to an Infernal—scared the shit out of him, but he needed a bargaining chip to get things rolling. Later, he could work on the logistics of the double cross. There were a lot of bigger fish in the pond than Eve, even with her ties to him and Cain.

"Well, you're still up here," Reed continued. "So I could take that as a sign that you're not interested in collecting the prize. But it's such a rare opportunity to participate in the kind of free-for-all we're seeing in Orange County now." Reed kept his gaze straight ahead. "I thought every ambitious demon was pursuing it."

"Like you said," Chaney muttered tightly, "I'm still here and I've got enough on my plate at the moment. Besides, I have no idea what you're talking about."

"Right."

They reached the park and turned into it, taking a winding cement path toward a cluster of sheltered picnic tables. The night air was temperate, the breeze light and pleasant. Around them, Reed could sense wolves watching, moving, even though he couldn't hear them. They kept downwind and he wondered if they thought he was stupid, or if they were just poorly trained.

Stopping abruptly, Reed said, "Then we're done here."

Chaney rounded on him, slightly hunched as if

prepared to pounce. His lip curled back, revealing
pointed canines. "You didn't step out of your comfort
zone for nothing," he growled. "What do you want?"

Reed shoved his hands in his trouser pockets. "I
want Raguel back."

"What the fuck? Since when is he gone?"

It was clear the Alpha was clueless about the
archangel, as evidenced by the strength of his reaction compared to the one he'd had to the mention of
the bounty hunt. Sammael was cunning enough to
know that the knowledge would be more valuable to
upper-level demons when kept a secret; whereas for
lessor demons, sharing would be of greater benefit.

Chaney straightened, his eyes glowing yellow in
the moonlight. "Whatever it is, I want in."

Reed hid his satisfaction behind a bored mien. "It
will take more than enthusiasm to get the job done."

"And it'll take more than vague references to missing archangels to get the rest of what you need from
me."

So . . . the Alpha had a little bite to go along with
his bark.

Rocking back on his heels, Reed asked, "Were you
privy to the discussions Charles had with Asmodeus?"

"I was privy to everything."

"Excellent. Let's get him involved again." The
overly-ambitious king of Hell needed to be dealt with
as well.

Chaney's head cocked to one side. "I take it you're
offering your brother's whore in trade? I'm not sure
that's fair. An archangel for a green Mark."

"Sammael clearly thinks she's valuable."

"But you don't?"

"Like you said, she's Cain's whore," Reed drawled, fists clenching in his pockets.

"You two still haven't gotten over yourselves?" Chaney laughed, the yellow of his eyes softening. "His promotion must really sting."

"You assume I couldn't have prevented it, had I wished."

The narrowing of Chaney's eyes betrayed his renewed unease. It was best if the Alpha didn't get too comfortable around Reed.

Clearing his throat, Chaney said, "Ah, well . . . Works in my favor, doesn't it?"

"I'm also willing to discuss sweetening the deal, but first, I need to know that Raguel is alive."

"I'll get to work on that."

Reed extended his hand to the Alpha. When the gesture was accepted, his mouth curved.

The Alpha began to scream, then howl, his knees giving way so that he kneeled before Reed like a supplicant. As dark forms rushed out of the bushes and leaped over backyard fences, Reed released him. Chaney held his injured hand in the palm of the other, gasping.

"You should memorize that," Reed suggested, gesturing to his cell phone number now seared into the Alpha's palm, "before it heals."

Chaney's head tipped up toward the moon and his true visage shimmered just beneath his mortal guise. As his pack bounded toward them, his mouth widened into a terrible maw, his yellow eyes glowing from pain and the resulting bloodlust.

Reed sketched a quick bow, then shifted to Gadara Tower.

* * *

"You hired bodyguards to protect you from . . . demons?" Riesgo asked carefully.

"Um . . ." Eve's mark heated, even though she hadn't yet voiced the lie.

"Do you believe the reverend is a demon?"

"No! He's a pain in my ass, but he's not a demon."

He shook his head, as if she were a troublesome and frustrating child. "Those two are guarding you like they expect something to run onto the field and tackle you."

"How do you know so much about guards?" She shifted in an effort to get more comfortable on the cold metal bleachers. Mark or not, a hard seat was a hard seat.

He bent forward, putting his forearms to his thighs. "I was born in Inglewood, raised in Compton, and nearly killed in a knife fight when I was fifteen."

"Gangs?"

"Sureño."

"Wow. Is that how . . . ?" Eve touched her cheek in echo of his.

"No. Got the scar in the Rangers."

She nodded to herself. That made sense. Military service explained the confident, capable, yet dangerous vibe he gave off as well as the knowledge hinted at by his comments.

Eve wondered if he'd joined the priesthood as a way to save his life. Most gangs were "blood in, blood out"—you killed someone to get in and you had to be dead to get out. But a priest's robes would be a hard barrier for a would-be killer to get past.

Fact was, the majority of the United States population believed in a higher power.

He steepled his fingertips. "The Army gave me a way out of South Central. God gave me a way out of the Mexican Mafia. Okay, so I've told you mine. Now, you tell me yours."

"It's a long story, and one you wouldn't believe anyway." She reached up and tightened her loosened ponytail.

"Try me." He bumped shoulders with her. "The Lord keeps bringing you back my way. There's a reason for that."

"Father . . . Trust me. If the Lord is deliberately pushing me into your life, that's not a good thing. Not for either one of us."

"We won't know until all is said and done, oh ye of little faith."

"You don't understand me, Father. And I sure as hell don't understand you. Don't you read that Bible you preach from? God isn't perfect. He's just like everyone else. Have you read the Book of Job? First, God brags to Satan about how loyal Job is. Then, when Satan bets him that Job will turn against him if they make him miserable enough, God takes the bet."

Riesgo's gaze was on Montevista as the Mark abandoned his position on the lower right infield to head toward Sydney. "Do you have any idea how many times the Book of Job is tossed out as an argument, Ms. Hollis?"

"Eve," she corrected.

"I expect you to be more original, Eve."

She smiled without humor. "Have you ever considered that Job's story might be a piece of a larger whole? Maybe Job is a construct that represents the entirety of man. Maybe his tale is a parable and not absolute truth. Maybe Satan and God are still trying to win that bet."

The priest turned his head to look at her. "You're attributing mortal qualities to God, like the Greeks did with their gods. The One True God is above those frailties."

"Really? I don't get that from the Bible," she muttered. "What I get out of the Bible is a God so high on himself that he has minions running the show while he lounges around listening to cherubs sing his praises endlessly."

"I can put up with a lot, Eve." There was an edge to Riesgo's voice. "But disrespect and blasphemy aren't on the list."

She blew out her breath in a rush, suddenly feeling very weary. "I'm sorry, Father. I don't mean to belittle your beliefs. It's just that I'm never going to see God the way you do. It's like we're looking at different sides of the same coin. Please don't ask me to come around to your side."

"That's my job," he said gruffly, looking obliquely at her. "I bring God into the lives of others."

"God is in my life, Father." Eve looked him at him squarely, willing him to see the truth of her words in her gaze. "We're working out our issues in our own way. But, in the meantime, that dude on my corner is seriously driving me insane."

"What do you suggest I do about that?"

"You can come and vouch for me."

"Vouch for you." Riesgo's half-smile returned. "For all I know, he could be right about you."

"Ouch." Crossing her arms, she straightened.

"Okay, how about I take you to my office first? Have you been to Gadara Tower? It was voted Anaheim's most beautiful property a couple of years ago."

He reached over and patted her on the knee. It was a grandfatherly gesture, but his touch was so hot it surprised her. The contact was brief, over as soon as it began, but the heat lingered. "Give me directions to your place. I'll run by there in the next couple of days and talk to him."

"Thank you." She returned his earlier bump to the shoulder before standing. "I owe you one."

"Yes, you do." He rose in an economical, yet graceful movement. Power leashed with an iron fist. "We're having a potluck picnic at the church in three weeks. I expect you to come. Bring your boyfriend and those two—" He looked toward the field and frowned. "Where did they go?"

Eve's gaze followed his. Montevista and Sydney were nowhere to be seen. She engaged her mark-enhanced vision, but delving into the darkness beyond the reach of the powerful field lights was impossible without the nictitating lenses that engaged only when she, too, stood in the dark. "I don't know."

She started down the bleacher steps with growing apprehension. The moment her foot hit the dirt, a flash of white caught the periphery of her vision. Too fast to be mortal. Lightning-quick, Eve darted after it. It was faster than she was, feinting to the left and right. Several seconds later, she found herself on the pitcher's mound again. She ran back to Riesgo. The priest was presently rubbing at his eyes with his fists.

"I must be wiped out," he said. "My vision's getting blurry. One second, it looked like you were over there. Then the next, you were right here."

Catching his elbow, she tugged him toward home base. It was rarely good to be cornered, but at least she'd have one less side—their rear—to worry about defending.

"What are you—" He quieted, sensing her preoccupation. Without another word, he bent and picked up a metal baseball bat. Sans the collar and dressed in black sweats, he looked like someone you didn't want to fuck with . . . if you were mortal.

Eve's brows rose, but she put her back to his and tried angling him to face the corner. He, being the chivalrous type, tried to maneuver her the same way.

The flash of white came again, but this time it stopped in front of her. An Infernal such as she'd never seen, with white hair and eyes. He was wearing an ice-blue and silver Halloween costume that included a doublet and bombastic hose.

Her connection with Reed allowed her to recognize the demon inside the getup.

"Azazel," she greeted grimly.

"Hello, Evangeline."

Riesgo positioned himself shoulder to shoulder with her. "Is this the guy that's after you?"

"One of them." Eve sent up a request for a flaming sword. She wasn't too surprised when nothing happened. She widened her stance and raised her fists. The demon laughed, a sound made more maddening for its rich, deep tone.

This Infernal was clearly confident about his skills.

"Stand easy, Evangeline." The unknown voice rumbled through the air from no discernable source.

The ground shook and a fissure opened. Blood

rushed upward from the depths like a geyser before settling into the shape of a man with massive, beautiful crimson wings.

Satan. Eve knew who it was without any help.

"Holy Mary, Mother of God," Riesgo breathed. He made the sign of the cross with his free hand.

"Mary can't save you, priest," Azazel said, with a malicious smile. "God won't save you either."

Fear blossomed in Eve's chest like a spreading stain. The Prince of Hell was impossibly beautiful, far more so than even Sabrael. His skin shimmered as if coated with gold dust. Shiny black hair fell halfway down his back, rippling and writhing with a life of its own. The silky tresses moved sinuously, covetously; caressing him as a lover would, framing a face that could not have been more perfect. His irises flickered like flames, while his mouth curved in a smile that was terrifying for its seductiveness. The urge to undress and spread her legs for him was strong enough to tug Eve forward one step. She jerked herself to a halt by clinging to Reed in her mind, like a snapping flag anchored to a pole.

"Ah," Satan murmured, circling from a distance with a smooth alluring gait. Sex incarnate. "I see why they want you. Looking at you makes a man hard and ready to fuck."

Eve flipped him the bird.

With a careless wave of his hand, he snapped the digit, bending it backward until her knuckle touched the back of her hand. She dropped to her knees, screaming.

Riesgo stepped forward, but she caught him with her left hand around his ankle. As a mortal, she would never have been able to stop him. As a Mark, she nearly toppled him.

"Don't," she ordered in a richly nuanced rumble.

He stilled instantly, frozen.

Persuasion. A gift given to Marks that she likened to the Jedi mind trick. Why it would kick in—for the first time—*now,* when what she really needed was a weapon, was a gripe she would add to her long list . . . later. And while she was bitching, she'd mention the failure of her mark to kick in and give her some ass-whupping mojo.

Where was Reed? Alec? *Anyone?*

She released the priest and reached for her broken finger, groaning through gritted teeth as she wrestled it back into place.

Azazel tsked. "They teach less and less respect as the years pass, my liege."

Satan came to her, looking down at her with gorgeous, emotionless eyes. His clawed fingertips lifted her chin and moved her head from side to side. His touch was cool, almost tender. She was riveted as much by that tenderness as by horror. Deep inside her, something trembled in paralyzing fear.

With proximity, the full effect of the Devil's allure was undeniable. He wore a three-piece suit that reminded her of Reed, but the overlong hair and Dr. Martens were Alec's. Even his features and build resembled her lovers, as did his scent—smoky, exotic, and deeply male. She wondered if he wore a guise to disorient her, or if she and God just had the same idea of what constituted a hot guy.

"Get away from her," Riesgo growled.

Satan shot him a bored but dangerous look.

Eve caught the Devil's wrists, wincing at the throb of her injured hand. It would heal with time, but would hurt like hell in the interim. "It's me you want. I'm the one who ran over your dog. Let the priest go."

The Devil's sleek head turned back to her. He looked amused. "But the priest is the means by which I will force your hand."

She quivered inside. "No. You don't need him. Deal with me."

"You do not yet know what I want," he crooned, cupping her face in his hands. His touch was so invasively cold it seeped into the very marrow of her bones, making her shiver violently. "Perhaps I want to defile you, lovely Evangeline. Perhaps I want to do things to you that will break your mind and spirit. Perhaps I want to watch while others do those same things to you. Listen to the melody of your screams until there is no fight left in you."

She wished she could laugh at his drama, but really, she feared pissing herself instead.

Where were Montevista and Sydney? Were they battling Infernals somewhere? Were they dead?

"Please. L-let him g-go," she managed through chattering teeth. She might as well be dunked in a frozen lake for all the warmth she felt.

Riesgo growled and began to speak. "I command you, unclean spirit, whoever you are, along with all your minions now attacking this servant of God, by the mysteries of the—"

"Shut him up," Satan snapped.

Azazel flew like a bullet across the yardage that separated him from Riesgo. The priest was in the middle of a retaliatory lunge at impact, the crashing of the two bodies thudding violently. The ground opened as they fell, swallowing them whole. As the chasm closed as if it had never existed, the earth shuddered like a child who'd swallowed particularly nasty medicine.

"Oh my god," Eve breathed, so shocked and frozen that she barely felt the burning of her mark. "What the fuck are you doing?"

Satan smiled, his thumbs brushing across her trembling lips. "Such a lovely mouth. You really should be working for me. I would appreciate your cynicism. I certainly appreciate how readily you discount Jehovah's lies."

Somehow she managed to wrench free, tumbling to her side and crawling with what strength she could muster. He followed her with leisurely steps, his hands clasped behind his back.

She stopped after progressing only a few feet. "What d-do you w-want?"

"Poor Evangeline," he murmured, reaching for her. "You are chilled to the bone. Let me warm you."

The moment his hand touched her skin, warmth coursed over her body like a hot summer breeze. So startled was she by the change that it took a moment before the sudden softness of the ground beneath her registered.

Satan straightened. Eve's head turned slowly.

It was now the middle of the day, and they were far from the baseball field. Warm sand cushioned her side and the sun blazed in the cloudless sky above her. It was a desert of some sort, barren except for golden sand and large monolithic outcroppings. The chill in her blood began to fade. She struggled to her feet, ignoring the hand that the Devil held out to assist her.

Eve faced him with shoulders back and chin lifted.

"Some of your mannerisms are so like hers," he murmured, with a mysterious smile.

"So like whom?"

"Your namesake." His gorgeous blood-red feathers fluttered in the oven-hot breeze. "Otherwise known as the ransom you will bring to me in return for the priest. And Raguel."

CHAPTER 13

"What?" Eve hoped she was having a night-mare. "Where are we?"

"Come now," he chastised, "your marked hearing works well enough to have heard me."

He ignored her other question. Was she in Hell? Or some other plane of existence? Her mind whirled with the possibilities.

She turned slowly, keeping pace with him as he circled her so that he never had her back. "You want *Eve?*"

He applauded as if she was slow-witted and finally catching on. "Very good."

Eve hated that he moved so elegantly. Hated that he was so beautiful, so seductive, so much more of both qualities in the light of the desert sun than he'd been under the artificial brightness of the stadium lights. She was mesmerized by him, enough that she sometimes lost touch with how terrified she was. It was a trick of some sort, an illusion.

"She's dead," she managed finally, her voice raspy from the dry air.

"And what is death, Evangeline?" Satan continued his slow, steady walk around her perimeter with hands clasped beneath his wings. "Mortals think of it as the end, like an extinguished flame. But that is not the way of it. The worthy come to me, the unworthy go to Jehovah. They all continue to exist, just in different places."

"Don't you have that 'worthy' thing backward?"

He shook his head. "I expected better of you. You are too intelligent to buy into Jehovah's lies. In fact, I was quite impressed with your argument regarding the wager. How astute you are."

Eve didn't know what to say. In her mind, she imagined that God must be every bit as frightening as Satan. Who was the good guy? Were there any good guys in this mess?

The Devil watched her with a predatory intensity. "I confess, I regret that I was not the first to get my hands on you."

"I don't feel the same," she muttered. "And I don't see how I can help you."

"You have everything you need in that eager flesh between your legs." His words were crude, but his tone was conversational. "Spread them well enough, moan loud enough, beg sweetly enough . . . Cain and Abel will give you whatever you want."

"They're not going to give me their mother!"

Why were they so damn silent? Had Satan cut her off from them? Was he powerful enough to impede a God-given connection?

He gave an offhanded shrug. "They can lead you to her, and you can lead her to me."

"What do you want with her?"

"That is none of your concern."

"You're asking the impossible."

"I will give her back," he said solicitously. "I just want to borrow her for a short time."

Eve's eyes stung. Riesgo had been taken because of her. She couldn't abandon him and she couldn't turn down an opportunity to get close to Gadara. She also couldn't do what Satan wanted in return. Either way, she was seriously fucked. "I can't trust you."

"Can you trust anyone?"

He had a point.

"Evangeline, I have no need for lies. The truth works well enough. Remember that I am not the one who created man and wanted to keep him ignorant. I am not the one who commanded Abraham to kill his only son to prove his devotion. I am not the one who burned, drowned, and buried alive hundreds of thousands of mortals. I am not the one who demanded a man be stoned to death because he collected wood on the day set aside for slavish worship." His head tilted slightly. "Did you know Jehovah almost killed Moses because his son was not circumcised? Yet *I* am the monster?"

Because she was becoming disoriented, she stopped turning. Even after she stilled, the desert around her tipped and tilted. It was too hot now. Arid.

Satan smiled. There was a wealth of promise in the curve of his lips. Temptation. He was infamous for it.

Eve's hand went to her throat, massaging it as if that would create the moisture she craved.

"Jehovah is the original spin doctor," he continued, his voice lifting and falling in a soothing, lulling cadence. "I give him credit for his brilliance. Somehow, he became revered despite his cruelty. I, on the other hand, am reviled for my honesty."

How the hell was she going to spin this to work in her favor? There had to be a way, but it was hard to think. Her mouth and throat were dry. She'd give anything for a drink of water . . .

"Call off your minions," she said gruffly. "They're complicating things."

"Someone must earn the bounty," he reminded, finally drawing to a halt. The spinning stopped along with him. "As I said, I always keep my promises."

"How much am I worth?"

"Immunity. One get-out-of-Hell-free card."

"Hmm . . ." She wouldn't have thought she'd be worth that much. When Infernals were killed, they stayed in Hell a few centuries. A rapid turnaround could make a demon pretty damn cocky and reckless, she'd guess. "Give the credit to Azazel. He's the one who made the first move."

Satan's nose wrinkled slightly, which—insanely enough—humanized him. "Most would find that unfair. Azazel has always moved around freely."

Her hands went to her hips. "I don't give a shit if it's fair or not. I'm a prisoner in my own house right now. Not very conducive to getting things done."

"Fine. I will think of something suitable." He was definitely amused now. She could see it in his eyes. "In return, you will say nothing of our bargain to anyone. You break your word, I am free to break mine . . . including keeping the priest and Raguel. Anything else?"

In hindsight, she realized she'd played right into

his hands. He clearly wanted to keep her off-kilter by confusing everything in her head.

"Yeah, actually." Eve began to circle him in a vain attempt to fight the feeling of a noose circling her neck. She felt manipulated and outmaneuvered. "I also have a Nix problem."

She braced herself for whatever demand he would make in return.

"Ah, yes. You do."

"Suck him back down with you when you go."

"But Ulrich is doing so well." There was a teasing note in the Devil's voice. Again, it softened him.

It's all a trick, she reminded herself.

Eve came to an abrupt stop, frustration riding her hard. "If he kills me, I won't be of any use to you."

Satan grinned. "I would have you full-time, then."

"Cain and Abel would have me no-time," she pointed out while fighting the urge to scream. Why was everyone betting that she'd go to Hell when she died?

"True." He extended one hand to her. Nestled in his palm was a golden chain with a charm—an open circle with various lines and circles within it. "Wear this to protect yourself from the Nix. Put it around him to prevent him from shape-shifting into water."

She stared at the necklace. *Beware of demons bearing gifts.* The thought of having something around her neck that came from Satan gave her the willies. "Isn't there another way? Gold doesn't look good on me."

His brow arched, then he walked toward her. Eve wanted to back away, but was rooted in place by an unseen force. His fingers encircled the wrist of her injured hand and the lingering pain faded. "If you do what I say," he murmured, "we can both get what we want."

Satan released her arm, then draped the charm carefully around her neck. He tucked it inside her shirt with a humming sound of satisfaction. "There. Nix problem solved."

He backed away. Her pent-up breath left her in a rush.

"You will have to kill him yourself, of course," he added. "But without the ability to shift, he should be a much easier target for you. He can be mortally wounded then."

"Gee, thanks," she groused.

Their gazes met and held. Eve wondered if he truly believed that she would hand over Alec and Reed's mother to him. If so, why did he believe that the priest and Gadara were so valuable to her? Worth enough to betray the men she loved.

She had to figure out what Satan was seeing that she was missing. Maybe he thought she'd be grateful to have him call off the bounty and help her with the Nix? He couldn't be that vain. It was more convenient for her, yes. But no matter what, she would have dealt with the Nix and the bounty anyway.

"Are we clear about the terms, Evangeline?"

"Let me get this straight: you want Eve temporarily, in exchange for permanently returning Father Riesgo and Raguel?"

He nodded. "I will call off the bounty and in return, you agree to keep this matter private. I will know if you err. Unlike Jehovah, I keep my finger on the pulse."

"What do you want for giving me the Nix on a silver platter?" she asked, suspicious.

"I will get my reward in the entertainment value. The odds are being evened out, but he may kill you anyway. How can I take recompense for so little?"

With an offhand flick of his wrist, she was back on the baseball field and he was gone.

Eve spun, looking around, finding herself alone.

She set off at a run toward the darkness beyond the athletic field lights, searching for Montevista and Sydney with a sickening feeling of dread.

"Is that where Evangeline lives?"

As Alec pushed his rarely used key into the lock of his front door, his head turned to follow the direction of his mother's finger. It had been awhile since he'd used secular means to enter his condo, but his parents weren't *mal'akhs* and what little gifts they had in Shamayim were stripped from them on Earth. They were mortal in every way but their age. "Yes."

Before he could stop her, his mother was striding down the hall and knocking on Eve's door. He steeled himself to see Eve again. Everything knotted up inside him, except for the voices that relished chaos.

No one answered Eve's door.

His mother frowned at him. "I thought you said it wasn't safe for her to be out."

His father stood at her back, hovering and watchful.

Alec unlocked his dead bolt for his parents, then shifted into Eve's house. It was dark and quiet as a tomb. Standing in her living room, he reached out to her and was met with an eerie silence.

Eve. Where are you?

She hit him in a rush, a full-throttle blindside of fear and worry that knocked him back a step. He growled and shifted to her.

She screamed when he arrived beside her, recoiling from his sudden appearance. Alec caught her by the back of the neck and clasped her to him. "Shh . . . I'm here."

As she trembled against him, a rapid-fire series of images hit his brain. Montevista. Sydney. The priest. Azazel.

Fury churned inside him.

Abel!

His brother's name was a roar. Once again, Abel had left Eve hanging in the wind.

It would be the last time.

Setting Eve away from him, Alec's fingers linked with hers. He pulled her along the length of the chain link fence, searching for any signs of blood, torn clothing, or a scuffle.

Then he felt the Marks. Faint, but nearby. He shifted Eve to the parking lot on the other side of La Palma. The open space was poorly lit, but his enhanced vision picked up two forms crumpled atop each other in the distance.

He shifted again, moving them closer more swiftly. He stabilized Eve when she stumbled from disorientation.

"Oh my god," she breathed. Her hand tightened on his, then she released him and knelt beside the fallen guards.

Montevista sprawled atop his partner, almost as if he'd shielded her body with his own. Eve reached out and brushed her fingers across his cheek. He groaned, then stirred.

"They're alive," she said.

As their firm leader, Alec knew that, but he didn't belabor the point. Instead, he stood behind Eve, wondering why it had taken a few moments for their connection to be reestablished.

Abel appeared on the other side of the two prone figures on the ground. "What the hell happened?"

"If you'd been doing your job," Alec snapped, "you would know."

Eve growled. "If you two start fighting—"

"Where the fuck were *you*?" Abel challenged.

"With Ima and Abba."

His brother's eyes widened. "Why?"

"Don't worry about my business. Worry about hers—" Alec jerked his chin toward Eve, "—and how Azazel snatched the priest right in front of her."

"I can see that." Abel stared at Eve with a frown, getting caught up to speed by sifting through her thoughts.

"You both suck," she groused. "These two are hurt and you're going to stand there bitching at each other?"

Alec ran a hand through his hair. "Get her out of here."

Abel stood and shifted to her side. He glanced at Alec. "You got these two?"

"Yeah. Go."

Eve shook her head. "I'm not going to—"

She was shifted away midsentence by a touch of Abel's fingertips to her crown.

The silence that followed their departure was brief.

Montevista groaned and rolled to his side. Sydney gasped and lifted her head.

"Where's Hollis?" she asked.

Alec knelt beside them. "Safe."

But for how long? The assault on the priest had been too bold. Why not just take Eve?

He placed a hand on both Marks, and shifted with them to Gadara Tower.

"—leave them here like . . . What the hell?" Eve snapped, lurching as Reed returned her to her living room. "I hate when you do that with no warning!"

"Sorry, babe." Reed steadied her with gentle hands. "But you had to know we weren't going to leave you out there."

She glared at him. "And you have to know that I'm going to be worried sick until I know they're all right."

"I'll find out for you." He pressed his lips to her forehead. The moment they connected, the realization of how close he'd come to losing her hit him right between the eyes. His hands tightened on her biceps. She made a soft noise of protest and he released her hastily.

He stepped back, retreating to a safe distance.

"Hey," Eve said softly. "It's okay."

But it wasn't. Not for him.

She tapped her temple with her finger. "Keep me in the loop."

He managed a smile. *Of course,* he assured her. "Get comfortable. When I get back, I'll start that dinner I promised."

Eve opened her mouth to say something, but he

shifted away quickly. He went to the subterranean floors of the tower and leaned heavily against the wall. As Marks and Infernals rushed past him in the busy hallway, he took a moment to pull himself together.

Jerk, she scolded. *I was going to ask if I should get anything ready for you.*

Just yourself. I'll manage the rest.

"Abel."

Reed's gaze lifted to watch Hank—guised in the Jessica Rabbit/Morticia Addams getup—approach with a sex-kittenish sway to her hips. "Hey, Hank."

"How are you?" The note of elation in the occultist's gruff voice was unmistakable.

"Not nearly as good as you, sounds like." Reed straightened. "What's up?"

"I've been experimenting with the mask. I think I'm on to something."

"Oh?"

Hank grinned. "When you're free, stop by and I'll show you."

"Will do."

Shaking off his lingering disquiet, Reed set off toward the main reception area where he could inquire about the location of Montevista and Sydney. He was several feet away from the end of the hallway when Sara rounded the corner. He almost shifted away, but she spotted him and delayed him with an extension of her hand.

"Mon chéri." She smiled. "Do not rush off just yet. I have good news for you."

Reed stood stiffly as she lifted to her tiptoes and pressed her lips to his.

"Take us to my office," she murmured.

He conceded to her request only because he didn't want any interaction between them to be witnessed. As soon as they arrived, he pushed her away. "Make it quick."

"You never answer your cell phone," she complained, with an affected pout. "If you did, I would not have to waylay you in this manner."

The excitement on her face kept him around when he would have shifted. His arms crossed. "You've got my attention now."

"I was right. About Iselda and Cain."

He stilled. "Go on."

As she backed up toward her desk, her smile was wide and girlish. "Let me show you instead."

Picking up the remote that waited there, she activated the screen that lowered over the lone window. Her office was much smaller than Cain's but more elegant. Sara preferred damask over leather and multihued over monochromatic.

The lights dimmed and the show began. Reed looked away halfway through. By the time it was over, he was sitting with his back to the screen in one of the chairs positioned in front of the desk.

Sara took a seat with a rapacious gleam in her blue eyes. She turned off the feed with the remote. The screen retracted and the lights came back on. "I saved a copy on a jump drive for you. All you have to do is find a way for Evangeline to see it. Then sit back and watch the sparks fly."

"I'm not showing that to her," he said tightly.

Her smile faded. "Why not?"

Reed's foot tapped a silent but rapid staccato on

the carpet. If Eve saw that tape . . . His jaw tightened.
It hurt *him* to watch it, and he could give a shit about
Cain or Izzie. Physically, they'd looked to be having
a good time. Mentally . . . the depth of anguish on
his brother's face would be painful for anyone to
watch. Considering how deeply Eve cared for Cain,
it would kill her.

"Damn you," she breathed. "You are protecting
her."

"It would hinder our cause."

Her gaze narrowed. "How so?"

He considered the best way to answer. "She came
to me this afternoon, insisting that something's wrong
with Cain. She asked me to look into it and see if the
ascension is responsible for his behavior. If she gets a
look at that video, she'll be sympathetic and even
more determined. It'll have the opposite affect."

Sara's manicured fingertips drummed atop the
carved wooden chair arms. "You think you know her
so well?"

"She's my charge. Of course I know her. Besides,
it's no longer necessary to split them up. Cain did the
deed himself earlier today."

"*C'est des conneries!* Cain's reactions are separate
from hers. *She* needs to cooperate. He will want her
back eventually and when that happens, we have to
be sure that she will refuse him. That will be his
breaking point. Not this—" she gestured to where the
screen had been "—temporary insanity."

"So," he murmured, "you see it, too."

"He is fine now. I saw him a few moments ago
when he brought the two guards in."

"Did we just watch the same video?"

"Perhaps that is just the way he likes to fuck."

"Now who's talking bullshit? What the hell is wrong with him? Is Eve right? Did the ascension screw him up?"

"How would I know?" she said crossly. "The rest of us were created as we are. Stop worrying about Cain, and give me a better reason for why Evangeline should not see that tape."

"You know . . ." Reed lounged, but stayed watchful. "Despite your animosity toward her, Eve spoke on your behalf today."

"*Vraiment?*" Sara tried to sound nonchalant, but failed.

"I told her you were a lying, self-centered bitch."

Rage shimmered in her eyes. "I have never lied to you."

"You knew I wanted to advance. You let me believe that you would help me do that."

"You used me, too."

He heard the bitterness in her tone and stood, rounding the desk with a deliberate stride. "Eve suggested that maybe you didn't help me not because you *wouldn't,* but because you *couldn't.*"

"I do not need her to speak for me." Sara swiveled her chair to face him and crossed her long legs. The red pantsuit gave her a seductive, wicked edge. The wary look she wore softened the image and reminded him that at one time he'd thought they were perfect for one another.

Placing his hands atop hers, Reed bent over her. She licked her lower lip and stared at his throat.

"At first," he went on, "I thought she was being overly kind by attributing qualities to you that you don't have. But I have considered it a little more, and you know what conclusion I've come to? I think you'd rather lose me than admit there's something you can't do."

Her shoulders pressed more firmly against the seat back. "Did I ever really have you, *mon chéri*?"

"For a while there, you did. Because of that, you owe me the truth, Sara. If you'd wanted to help me ascend . . . could you have? Or was it impossible?"

She swallowed, then answered, "I wanted to help you."

The knot in his gut loosened. "Why didn't you just point me in the right direction? Tell me to go higher?"

"I went higher," she snapped. "I spoke with Jehovah himself. I had to hide the request from the others. If Gabriel or Michael knew, they would stop me. But in the end, it was pointless."

"Why?" Reed straightened. Running his hands through his hair, he asked, "Why was it possible for Cain, but not for me?"

He moved away, needing space, and heard her stand behind him.

"Think of that game," she said softly. "The one where you try and spot the things that are missing from a second picture that were in the first. What is missing now, that was here before?"

"Raguel." Rounding on her, he said, "He's dead, isn't he? That's why none of you are actively pursuing him."

"Look on the bright side," she evaded. "Would you want to suffer like Cain is?"

"Cain's issues might be unique to him and you

know it. And what if you're all wrong? What if Raguel is alive and we can get him back?"

Sara's knuckles whitened. "Then one of us would have to cede territory for the establishment of a new firm."

Reed moved to the window. He stared out at the nocturnal cityscape, but didn't register the view.

Cede territory. For the first time, he wondered if the archangels had cannibalized their numbers. Survival of the fittest, perhaps. Could they be affecting Cain in some way? Corrupting him? Pushing him into madness? Sara was supposed to be mentoring him, yet she was actively working to sabotage him.

Even though Reed had turned away from the screen when the video was on, he'd still heard everything. Cain had spoken in tongues. They both knew every language ever created, so that was not a surprise. It was the words themselves that chilled him.

I command you, unclean spirit, whoever you are, along with all your minions now attacking this servant of God—

The Rite of Exorcism. While *fucking*? It was perverse, and so bizarre Reed couldn't begin to guess why the words were spoken.

Why did Azazel take Riesgo and not Eve? Why would Cain break up with Eve—then turn to Izzie of all people?

Cursing inwardly, Reed knew that he could trust only a handful of people now. They all had something they wanted, and were all ruthless about getting it.

Who could Cain trust since he'd alienated Eve?

Reed smiled grimly. *Their parents.*

He was surprisingly soothed by the thought. If Cain was aware of what was happening to himself, he'd be working to fix it.

Fixing it . . . Alienating Eve . . .

"Shit," he breathed, considering that Cain might have pushed Eve away not because he didn't care about her anymore, but because the reverse was true.

Reed looked over his shoulder and met Sara's gaze dead-on. "Find out who helped Cain ascend. I don't care how you do it, but make it quick."

Sara nodded. "What does this mean for us? You and me? Anything?"

She couldn't love him. He wasn't sure why she bothered to act as if she cared.

"Not now." Withdrawing his cell phone from his pocket, he prepared to shift. "My phone is on. Call me when you know something."

He left to search for his brother.

Sara stared at the spot where Abel had been. There was something different about him, a change profound enough to make a noticeable difference since she'd spoken to him in Cain's office that morning.

Suspecting it was connected to Evangeline Hollis, she woke her computer and tapped out a rapid series of keystrokes, pulling up the recorded feeds from the Mark's home made earlier in the day. She stiffened when she found what she'd been desperately hoping she wouldn't.

"Abel," she whispered, hating him with a passion that equaled her lust for him.

She forwarded the video to Cain's e-mail account.

For good measure, she sent a copy of Cain's video to Evangeline.

Then, smiling, Sara left her office to set her back-up plan in motion. If Abel didn't have balls enough to get things back to normal, she would simply have to do it herself.

CHAPTER 14

Eve flipped through Riesgo's Bible while making a mental list of all the things she needed to accomplish. She was on her couch, legs curled up, a glass of soda on the coffee table in front of her. Gavin Rossdale's gorgeous voice was singing "Love Remains the Same," and the History Channel was muted on the television in the hopes that a biblical documentary might air.

Going through the motions as if everything was normal was one of the ways she'd learned to cope with chaos. It didn't always work—sometimes screaming was better—but in this case, she couldn't risk freaking out and alerting Alec or Reed to her problem. Losing Riesgo and Gadara was too great a price to pay for breaking her deal with the Devil.

She needed answers, but without being able to discuss her problem with anyone, how would she get them? The archives in the Gadara system went back so far it would be like looking for a needle in a *field* of hay. The only solution she could come up with was to visit Hank, who could read her mind. If she managed to let something slip . . .

If she had the means, she would go to Hank now, but her car was still at the stadium, and asking one of the exterior guards for a ride would arouse suspicions she wasn't sure she could deflect. She supposed she could call Hank through a landline and ask for a house call. . . .

Alec's front door opened.

Eve stiffened at the familiar, unmistakable sound. For a moment, déjà vu was so strong it was heartbreaking. She couldn't help but think of her old neighbor, Mrs. Basso, and how much simpler life had been just a few months ago. Eve missed the words of wisdom and support her neighbor used to share with her, and she missed having her best friend Janice— presently on sabbatical—around to commiserate and laugh with.

When the knock came at her door, Eve forcibly tamped down her apprehension. For Alec to come to her the secular way had to mean something. Whether he wanted to talk about Riesgo and the guards or what had happened between them personally, it would be taxing for both of them. She breathed carefully, trying to attain a semblance of composure.

"Evangeline? Are you home?"

The soft, feminine voice froze Eve midstride. Frowning, she became more cautious, sidestepping to avoid being directly in front of the door. She considered grabbing the gun she kept in a padded case in the console drawer—clearly God was done giving her swords when she needed them—but she was concerned about what she might do with it. Jealousy was eating at her, goaded by the volatility of the Novium. What the hell was a woman doing at Alec's place?

"Who is it?" Eve called out.

"I'm safe, I promise."

Eve kept the chain on, but unlocked the series of dead bolts. She pulled the door open and peeked out the opening. The woman on her doorstep was so beautiful, she had to blink a few times to process it.

"Hi," her visitor said with a friendly smile. "I'm Cain's mother."

Her mouth fell open and her grip on the doorknob tightened. *Holy shit.*

Lightning quick, she freed the chain and yanked the original Eve inside. She glanced up and down the hallway, then slammed the door shut and locked it. Spinning around, she faced Alec's mom with her back pressed to the door.

She swallowed hard. "Hi."

"You're just as beautiful as I imagined you would be," Alec's mother said with a warm smile. She approached Eve with arms wide and embraced her. "I'm so happy to meet you, Evangeline."

"It's a p-pleasure to meet you, too . . . Eve," she managed, while alarms were clanging in her mind.

Satan wanted this woman enough to give up Gadara for her. Why? And how had he known she would soon be within reach?

"I would like it if you'd call me Ima," Alec's mother said, stepping back to study her.

They were of a height and similarly colored, but the biblical Eve was more exotic, with almond-shaped brown eyes and a luxuriously voluptuous figure.

She wore a simple linen dress that looked to be handmade, and she appeared to be somewhere in her midforties, which certainly could not be the case. She definitely didn't look old enough to be Alec and Reed's mother.

"Ima," Eve repeated, her brain reeling over the fact that the mother of all humanity was standing in her living room.

"What a lovely place you have." Ima walked deeper into the room, her head tilting back to take in the vaulted ceilings. "Cain says you're an interior designer."

"Yes." Eve followed after her. "Would you like a drink? I have water and tea. Soda, too, if you like that sort of thing."

Eve didn't know whether the woman standing in her living room was a ghost or real. Did she eat and drink? Sleep?

"What are you having?" Ima asked, gesturing at the drinking glass sweating condensation onto the coffee table.

"Diet Dr. Pepper."

"Diet?" Ima smiled over her shoulder. "You don't need to diet."

"Yeah. The whole mark thing . . ."

"Not because of that. You're gorgeous just the way you are."

"Thank you." Eve passed her on the way to the kitchen. She hit the light switch on the wall and grabbed a cup from the cupboard. The barely there weight of the necklace felt like a yoke around her neck.

Alec's mother pulled out a bar stool and sat at the kitchen island. "I'm making you uncomfortable."

Pausing with the cup in hand, Eve sighed and offered a rueful smile. "No, it's not you. I'm just surprised. I'm still getting used to meeting people I always thought were . . . mythological."

"Didn't Cain tell you I'm real?" The grin that accompanied the question had a touch of mischievousness that was endearing. "I saw that you're reading the Bible. Is there anything in particular that you're researching?"

For a moment, the rattling of the ice maker prevented speech. Then, Eve pulled a can of soda out of the fridge and turned to face Ima. She was debating whether she should talk about the whole Garden of Eden, apple, Satan incident so soon after meeting the pivotal figure in the tale, but time was short. Who knew what Father Riesgo and Gadara were going through right now? And how long could the priest be a missing person before his life was irrevocably changed?

Eve set the glass in front of Alec's mom and popped open the can. "I was reading Genesis, actually."

"Don't believe everything you read." Ima picked up the can and poured some soda into the glass. She sat with spine straight and shoulders back, elegant and delicate. Her hair was a deep chestnut curtain that fell to the seat cushion. There was a fine cluster of silver strands at her right temple, almost too faint to be noticed.

"Really?" Eve set her elbow on the island and rested her chin in her hand. "What shouldn't I believe?"

"Well, you won't find it in that version you have there, but that ridiculous story about my husband only liking the missionary position? Ridiculous. He's a man. He'll take it any way he can get it and the less work he has to put into it, the more he enjoys it. Lilith spread that tale because she's bitter."

Eve bit back a smile. Then a knock came at the door and she straightened abruptly.

"Stay here," she said, rounding the back of Ima's chair. "If something happens, run to one of the rooms down the hall and lock the door."

A grip on her biceps stopped her.

"Unless you're expecting someone," Ima said, "it's probably Adam."

Eve blinked. *Adam.* The knock came again, louder and more insistent.

"Isha?" a masculine voice called.

"Isha?" Eve repeated.

"Wife." Ima slid off the chair and moved toward the door. "He'll be so excited to meet you."

Eve's brain took a moment to catch up, then she rushed forward protectively. If something happened to Reed and Alec's mother on her watch . . .

When Adam entered her home a moment later, Eve was dumbstruck. The resemblance to his sons was disconcerting. He was gorgeous. There was a quiet dignity to his bearing, distinguishing him in the way some men achieved with age.

As Eve stood beside the doorway, staring, Adam perused her from head to toe. His face was austere, giving nothing away. Eve squirmed inside, wondering what he thought of her, whether it was good or bad.

She was surprised when he hugged her, so much

so that she stood rigidly for a moment before she hugged him back.

"I can see why Cain thinks she was worth waiting for," Ima said, smiling as Adam straightened and adjusted his rough-hewn vest with an awkward tug. Public displays of affection seemed to be uncomfortable for him.

Eve jumped as Reed appeared beside her with a plastic bag in his hand.

"Don't shoot me, but I brought takeout." He spotted his parents, and his eyes widened. "I didn't know you were visiting!"

"Surprise!" his mother said, dark eyes sparkling.

"Sorry about dinner," he murmured to Eve. "It's almost ten o'clock. I figured it was too late to cook. You didn't eat without me?"

Feeling the heavy weight of his parents' stares, she could only manage to shake her head.

"Good." He pressed a kiss to her forehead, then smiled at his parents. "Luckily, I couldn't make up my mind and bought an excessive amount of food. We can all eat together. Hope you're in the mood for Italian."

He moved toward the kitchen. Eve followed with heavy footsteps.

She heard his mother speak quietly behind her.

"Dear God. Not again."

Reed massaged Eve's shoulders as they stood in the common area hallway and watched his parents disappear into Alec's condo. "Relax. If this place is safe enough for you, it's equally safe for them."

When she heard Alec's dead bolt slide into place,

Eve pulled out of Reed's grip and returned to her own home. She'd spent the last two hours wondering if Alec was going to show up. She was both relieved and disappointed that he hadn't.

"They like you," Reed said, closing her door and locking it.

Eve wasn't so sure about that. They'd had a decent time together once the food had been served, but there was an underlying awkwardness that Reed seemed impervious to.

"How are Montevista and Sydney?" she asked.

"They were sleeping in the infirmary when I got to them, but the witch doctor said they're stable and in no danger."

Frowning, Eve settled onto the sofa.

He sat beside her and tossed one arm over the back of the couch. There was something in his face, a hint of strain.

She reached out and set her hand over his knee. "Is everything all right?"

"No. Everything is far from all right." He laced his fingers with hers. "Obviously Azazel knocked the guards out of commission before going after the priest. The question is: why didn't he come after you instead? He must want something from you in return—guilt, recklessness, anger . . . something. But then why not take your parents? Or your sister? The move was both really bold and too restrained. Makes no sense."

Her grip tightened on his. "I would have lost it if he'd gone after my family."

"Exactly. So he's playing with you. Why? Why not go all the way and hit you where it really hurts?"

Because Satan was clever. He wanted her pushed into a corner where she'd be desperate, but not wild with it. He wanted her levelheaded so that she could do his dirty work. Perhaps he even wanted to seem reasonable. She didn't see how, but then she didn't understand how any of these people worked.

Eve shrugged in reply. "Maybe the bounty isn't for killing me, but for fucking with me? Putting the screws to me because of the whole hellhound thing?"

"Is that what the *yuki-onna* told you?"

"She was under duress at the time," Eve reminded him dryly.

"Why were you out there with the priest to begin with?"

Eve explained the chain of events, wincing inwardly as his face darkened with every sentence.

"So let me get this straight," he said tightly when she finished. "You're supposed to stay in the house. Instead, you left to talk to the priest about a nut job who wouldn't bother you if you stayed in the house like you're supposed to?"

"I guess. But—"

"But nothing. What the hell were you thinking?"

"You know what I was thinking! The demons want me. We want Gadara. Hiding here isn't going to help move things along. I don't need more guilt, Reed. I'm aware that Father Riesgo's abduction is entirely my fault."

Her eyes stung and her vision blurred. She scrubbed at her lashes with impatient fingers. She hated crying in front of other people, but it was worse with Reed, who fidgeted uncomfortably in reaction. Much like his father. So unlike Alec, who felt too much and was open about it.

Reed looked down at their joined hands. "Raguel is probably dead."

Eve froze. It was a good thing her heart worked like a machine, considering how many times she'd been surprised today. "What would make you say that?"

"The impression I got from Sara is that Cain wouldn't have been promoted if Raguel was still alive."

"Do you believe her?"

"I don't know. It makes sense. There have only been seven firms forever. Maybe that number is immutable." His gaze lifted to meet hers. "I have to look into it."

If Gadara was dead, then Riesgo might be, too. She supposed she'd rather take the word of an archangel over Satan. But she had never been a blind-faith sort of person. She couldn't believe anything without proof. Which meant that somehow she had to get Satan to provide some evidence that he had the goods.

She had a long day ahead of her tomorrow.

"I need to crash," she said. The sooner she fell asleep, the sooner she could get up and get to work.

"Yeah." He watched her with dark, slumberous eyes. Waiting.

"I don't want to be alone tonight."

In answer, he stood and pulled her to her feet, then carried her to bed.

A ringing phone woke Eve.

Turning her head, she peeked at the nightstand clock with one eye. It was just before eleven in the morning.

"Oh man . . ." she groaned. "We overslept."

Reed pinned her in place with a heavy leg thrown over hers. "Ignore it."

"The world is going to hell," she argued, "and we're in bed."

"Anywhere else you'd rather be when the world ends?"

He had a point. She lifted the arm he had draped over her torso and kissed the back of his hand. "I have to answer that."

He rolled onto his back with a growl, freeing her. By the time Eve picked up the receiver, voicemail had intercepted, but a quick scan of the caller ID told her the call had originated from Gadara Tower. She was about to dial her office line when the phone started ringing again.

She sat up. "Hello?"

"Ms. Hollis." Her secretary, Candace, spoke in a whisper and sounded slightly panicked. *"The police are here for you."*

Eve brushed her hair back from her forehead. Beneath the oversized T-shirt she wore, Satan's necklace throbbed between her breasts. "Yikes."

"I told them you were out to lunch and that you would call them when you returned, but they insisted they'd wait for you to come back."

"Double yikes."

Reed sat up.

"Okay," Eve said. "I'll get there as fast as I can."

"Thank you."

"No, no. Thank you. You're doing a great job. Be there soon." She hung up and winced at Reed. "Cops."

"I heard," he murmured.

Eve stared at him, unable to look away. As a

mal'akh, he suffered none of the aftereffects of sleep that mortals did. His eyes weren't puffy and he had no morning breath. He was simply gorgeous. Relaxed in a way she'd never seen before, bare-chested with slightly mussed hair that looked as thick and soft as it felt.

Sighing, she tossed the covers back and climbed out of bed. "I have to go."

"I'll take you there."

Right. She had no car. "Forgot about that."

Half an hour later, she was dressed in a pencil skirt and silk blouse with her damp hair restrained in a sleek chignon and three-inch heels on her feet that still left her shorter than Reed.

He'd showered with her, then shifted home to change. While he was gone, she thought about how little she knew of him. She'd never been to where he lived, so she had no idea what his taste in furniture and design was like. As a designer, knowing those things would give her a lot of insight into who he was. As would the selection of books he owned or the lack thereof, his MP3 playlists, DVD collection . . .

"Ready?" he asked.

Eve nodded. "What about your parents?"

"I checked on them on the way back from my place. They're fine. Dad is snoring on Cain's couch. Mom's watching the news and catching up on the soap operas she likes to watch. She says she can miss a year and still not miss anything." Gripping her biceps, he smiled. "Damn, you clean up nice, babe."

"You're never anything *but* dressed up," she said, looking at the perfect knot of his tie. No one wore a three-piece suit like Reed.

"Complaining?"

"No way I could when you look so fine. But you know that."

"Just need you to know it, too. Hang on."

A few minutes later, Eve's heels were tapping out a rapid beat down the hallway to her office. She slowed before entering, grateful that her breathing and heart rate remained steady and even.

"Detectives," she said in greeting as she spotted the two familiar figures waiting in the receptionist's area of her office. "What a surprise."

Ingram and Jones stood, Jones with the dreaded worn briefcase in his hand. "Ms. Hollis."

She gestured for them to follow her into her office. Taking a seat behind the desk, she reached for her phone. "Can I get you something to drink? Coffee or tea, perhaps? Or water?"

"Nothing, thank you," Jones said, with an edge to his tone that told her he was done tiptoeing around her.

"Okay." Eve clasped her hands atop her desk calendar. "Please don't tell me there's been another death."

"Not yet," Ingram answered, stroking the end of one side of his mustache as he studied her. "Do you know Father Miguel Riesgo?"

Eve wished she had a good poker face, but knew that she didn't. The two detectives watched her avidly. Jones leaned forward.

"Yes, I know him," she answered.

Ingram nodded. "When's the last time you saw him?"

"Last night. Why?"

"A missing persons report on Riesgo was filed this morning by a Father Ralph Simmons."

"A little premature, isn't it?" she asked.

"There is no waiting time in the state of California," Jones said. "Father Riesgo didn't show up at the church this morning and his car was found at Glover Stadium here in Anaheim. So was yours."

"Yes. My boyfriend picked me up for an impromptu dinner." She cursed inwardly when her mark burned. *Give me a break,* she thought. *It's pretty damn close to the truth.*

Jones withdrew a notepad from his pocket. "Alec Cain?"

"No. Reed Abel."

"Cain and Abel?" Ingram's brow rose.

She shrugged lamely.

A knock came at the door just before it opened. Gray Man walked in. He was dressed in a three-piece suit of dark gray, his tall and slender frame moving with an easy grace. His hair and eyes were a lighter shade of gray than his garments, and his thin lips were curved in the vaguest hint of a smile that never seemed to reach his eyes. Eve's gaze moved past Ishamel to her secretary. Candace offered a reassuring smile.

"Excuse us," Jones said, pushing heavily to his feet. "Can you please wait outside until we're done here?"

"I represent Ms. Hollis," Ishamel said smoothly, approaching and extending his hand. "Ishamel Abramson."

"Do you feel the need for counsel?" Ingram asked Eve, eyeing her.

"I am here at the request of Gadara Enterprises,"

Ishamel explained, taking a seat on the sofa near the door. "Ms. Hollis is pivotal in the redesign of the Mondego Hotel and Casino in Las Vegas. We want to be certain that nothing interferes with the completion of the project."

Jones stood motionless for a long moment, then he hummed a doubtful sound and sank back into his chair. He proceeded to ignore Ishamel in favor of focusing more heavily on Eve.

She cleared her throat. "I'm confused as to why homicide detectives would take an interest in a missing persons case."

Ingram dug into the briefcase. "Once your name was brought into it, we followed a hunch."

Great. "A hunch?"

Once again, photographs were pushed across her desk toward her. This time, it was a stack half an inch thick. She flipped through the uppermost layer.

The photos were black and white, and very grainy. Eve looked them over, quickly deducing from the quality and angles that they were stills taken from security cameras around the athletic field and nearby traffic lights. She was relieved to see that neither Satan nor Azazel were visible to the cameras, although in some shots she looked ridiculous because it seemed she was talking to dead air.

"See what we see?" Ingram asked, scooting to the edge of his seat and leaning over her desk.

Eve frowned, not sure what he was referring to.

"Here." He pushed the photos around, revealing the ones that sat beneath the few she'd glimpsed on top.

Her breath caught at a blown-up image of the

chain-link fence behind her. The Nix stood there, fingers linked through the chain, an odd smile on his face. She glanced at Ishamel, who stood and came forward.

"That looks like the guy in the drawing you showed me," she said to the detectives, sitting back to put distance between her and the image. "The sketch artist's rendering."

"Right," Jones said. "The man we're looking for in conjunction with the Punch Bowl Murders. We've got him on a traffic light camera a block away. He was standing alone on the sidewalk, but he might have an accomplice who managed the abduction."

"Punch Bowl Murders?" she repeated, finding it horrifying that something so heinous would bear such a ridiculous name.

Ingram's fingers tapped the stack of pictures. "Unfortunately, the quality of the security cameras around the stadium is poor. They have blind spots and record in intervals, so there are times when neither you nor Riesgo are on film, followed by times when you are."

Eve silently thanked whoever had the foresight to take care of that.

"So here's what we've got," Jones said, straightening his tie over straining shirt buttons. "Your neighbor, Mona Basso; your school chum, Anthony Wynn; your priest, Miguel Riesgo; your car at a possible abduction scene, and a serial killer. You're smack dab in the middle of everything, Ms. Hollis. I've been at this long enough to know that you're withholding valuable information. Which doesn't make sense, considering this guy clearly has it out for you. Tell us who he is, before Father Riesgo pays the price.

You don't want the death of a priest on your conscience."

Eve's gaze moved between both detectives. "I have no idea," she said fervently. "Believe me, if there was some way I could help Father Riesgo, I would. Even though he isn't 'my' priest."

"What business did you have with him, then?" Ingram asked.

She explained, leaving out why she wanted a Bible in the first place. "The last time I saw Father Riesgo, he was picking up bats and mitts."

Not exactly the truth, but . . .

"Would you let us take a look at your car?" Jones asked.

"Of course."

"We also need you to come down to the station and give us a statement about last night. We might have your car finished by then."

"Can I come by after work? Say around five o'clock?"

"Fine. We'll send a squad car around to pick you up."

"That won't be necessary," Ishamel assured. "I'll bring her in. Which station?"

"The one on Harbor. By the way," Jones's pen hovered over his notepad. "Which route home did you take with your boyfriend and what does he drive? We'll want to check the cameras and see if this guy was following you home."

"Reed drives a silver Lamborghini Gallardo Spyder. And we took Harbor to Brookhurst." She glanced at Ishamel, who somehow conveyed reassurance without any alteration in his stance. He would find a way to make her fictitious trip home happen for the detectives.

"Lamborghini, eh? Must be nice. Thank you."

The detectives rose to their feet. Ingram collected the photos. His gaze lifted and locked with hers. "Think about what happened last night. Every detail. Every word spoken. Anything that might strike you as odd in hindsight. The smallest detail can sometimes break a case."

"Of course." She stood along with them. "I'm eager to help."

Ishamel walked the detectives out. Eve expected him to return, so she waited for him. But he didn't come back.

Knowing she'd see him on the way to the police station, she set off to find Hank instead.

CHAPTER 15

Raguel smelled the scent of ripe mortal terror before the door to his cell opened. Using what little strength he had left, he altered his appearance, tucking away the wings that kept him warm and altering his features to those of a teenager. He *would* get out of Hell, and when he did, he couldn't risk being recognized as the real estate mogul who was so widely known.

The new arrival was pushed into Raguel's stone enclosure with such force, he stumbled. Shock had already begun to set in. The man's eyes were dilated and his breathing was too quick.

It took a moment before recognition hit Raguel. *Evangeline's priest.* The one to whom she had turned, which had in turn prompted an investigation into the tengu infestation at Olivet Place. She must be the reason why the priest was here.

"Have a seat, Padre," Raguel said, gesturing to the wide expanse of stone floor. "As you can see, there is plenty of room."

Like Jehovah, Sammael employed drama for effect. In this instance the allusion was to the Spanish Inquisition, a time when atrocities had been committed in God's name. Manacles hung from the wall, and distant screams kept nerves on edge and prevented restful slumber.

"Where are we?" the priest asked, sinking to a crouch with unfocused eyes.

"I think you know."

In a rush, the man stood and moved to the door. He gripped the rough iron bars and tried to see outside. There was nothing out there but fire and heat. No ground below, no sky above. Sammael could choose to make it the most gorgeous of spaces, but that would be too kind. This way, the feeling of safety came from their imprisonment.

"There was someone else with me," the priest said roughly. "A young woman."

"Evangeline is fine. For now."

"How do you know?"

Raguel wrapped his arms around his knees. His soul was cold when separated from God. "You would be dead otherwise, or not here at all."

"Who are you?"

"A prisoner like you. Leverage to force those on earth to do a demon's bidding."

"Are you one of them?"

"No. I am a servant of God, just as you are."

"How can I believe you? How do you know Evangeline?"

"You will have to take it on faith, Padre."

The priest's knees lost strength and he dropped to the floor. His lips moved in what was likely a silent prayer. Raguel didn't see the point in telling him that

Jehovah couldn't hear him here. Hope was something neither of them could afford to lose. They had time enough to talk after circumstances sunk in through the shock. There was no point in questioning the man when his brain wasn't running at full speed.

A long time passed. Raguel had begun to doze when the priest spoke again.

"She asked me if I believed in demons."

Raguel scrubbed his hands over his face, hating the smell that coated his skin. "What was your answer?"

"I'm not sure I gave her one."

"Understandable. Even those with faith have their limits."

The priest looked at him. "She claims to have no faith, yet she believed. She even hired bodyguards to protect her."

With narrowed eyes, Raguel asked, "Did you meet these guards?"

"Yes."

"What were their names? Do you recall?"

"Montevista and Sydney. Why do you ask?"

She was in danger. Somehow, Cain or Abel had known she was at risk before the priest's abduction. What was happening? Why would Sammael want Evangeline?

"How long have you been here?" the priest asked. "Are you the reason she believes in demons?"

Raguel leaned forward. "You and I have much to talk about if we are to find a way out of here alive."

"*Can* we get out?"

"We must." *At the very least, I must.*

Cain would have to relinquish the position he'd stolen. Somehow, Raguel would find the tools he needed to make that happen. The priest was all he had to work with and time was short. A prolonged stay in Hell was like a cancer that ate its way in from the outside. The longer the mortal was here, the less of his soul and sanity would remain. Raguel was already feeling the effects and he was far stronger.

"Get comfortable, Padre," Raguel murmured. "I will need you to be as precise in your recollections as possible."

Eve had just raised her hand to knock on Hank's door when it swung open of its own accord. It was dark inside, as usual, with only strategically placed lighting over counters littered with petri dishes and glass tubes. Unlike usual was the racket resounding from the depths of the room. It was the first time she'd visited Hank's domain when it wasn't deathly quiet.

"Hank?" she yelled.

He stepped out of the darkness as a man, dressed in black slacks and dress shirt. The somberness of his garments allowed the brilliant red of his hair to take center stage. Eve was slightly envious of that color.

"Eve." He held out his hands to her. "What brings you to me?"

"What the hell is that noise?"

"Your tengu friend."

In the distance, she could hear Fred cursing and growling.

"What's the problem?" she asked.

"I've been experimenting with the fellow, using him as a guinea pig for my masking agent trials. This most recent test involved a higher Mark-to-Infernal ratio and the demon in him is rebelling."

She winced. "How long will he be like that?"

"Another couple hours, at least."

"I don't think I can shout that long!"

His smile was charming. "Should we go somewhere else?"

"If you don't mind."

They were about to exit when the rapid thudding of cement feet betrayed the approach of the escaped tengu.

"Watch out!" Fred yelled.

"Pretty Mark!" the tengu screeched, before launching like a missile toward Eve.

"Oomph!" She hit the floor on her back, her teeth snapping together painfully.

Her arms wrapped around the heavy beast and she rolled, knowing from experience that it was best to avoid taking the bottom position with a tengu.

They grappled like wrestlers. Eve's stilettos made it difficult to gain purchase on the polished cement floor. The Infernal took advantage, cackling in a manner she'd never heard before. Less mischievous, more maniacal. With a resonance that sounded almost as if there were multiple beings laughing instead of just the one.

Fred bounded out of the darkness in wolf form, barking.

"Enough," Hank roared, reaching down to free Eve.

But the tengu caught a fistful of her chignon and held fast. Eve screamed as he pulled. In the violent jostling, the necklace fell from the V of her neckline. The moment it touched the tengu's forearm, the de-

mon stilled. His mouth opened in a surprised O, then
he blinked as if waking. The hand in her hair loosened and the arm fell to the floor with a heavy thud.

"Pretty Mark," he said in a soft whisper, appearing
dazed.

She yelped as she was hauled upward by Hank.

The occultist grabbed her necklace and stared hard
at it. "Where did you get this?"

Eve blinked as rapidly as the tengu had. She
thought of Satan and hoped that Hank would read her
mind as he often did. Instead he glared at her. When
the tengu began to stir and rumble low in his throat,
Hank pulled the necklace over her head and dropped
it around the tengu's neck. The Infernal quieted, sitting with hands in his lap and his head cocked to the
side. His cement fingers caressed the charm rever-
ently.

"Sammael," Hank murmured, setting Eve on her
feet and straightening her collar.

"I need that," she said, pointing at the necklace.

"I can't read you when you're wearing it."

"Oh."

"And you can't hear me when your friend is having fits. We kill two birds with one stone this way.
You can recover the piece later."

"Gotcha."

Fred altered shape, shifting back into her lili form.
Since she was naked, Eve looked away, but she heard
Fred pick up the tengu and pad back into the dark-
ness.

"You're in deep shit," Hank said, gripping Eve's
elbow and pulling her deeper into the room.

She was startled by the sudden appearance of a

wooden table and chairs. Hank sat and she followed suit, once again wondering at the lack of gentlemanly manners.

He studied her intently. "It's clear that neither Cain nor Abel know. If they did, you'd be locked away. Pointless as that would be."

"I can't say anything."

"And your memories of Sammael are like static on a television." Hank sighed. "Very well, then. I'll do the talking. You just have to ask the right questions."

Eve nodded. She had no idea how old Hank was, but there was no doubt that he held a staggering amount of information inside him. But did that information extend back to the beginning of time?

"Do you know," she began, "exactly how much of the Eve and the apple story is true, and how much of it isn't?"

"Ah, Genesis . . . Interesting." Hank's lips pursed momentarily. "The tale varies depending on who you ask. Some say the Bible is as accurate as can be expected. Others say it's more of a fable, with hidden meanings."

"Such as?"

"Such as Sammael's serpent being a phallic allusion and the Tree of Knowledge referring to female sexual awakening."

She whistled. "Holy shit."

"There are those who go so far as to say that Cain is the son of Sammael and not Adam, and that is why he's so good at killing."

Eve heaved out a shuddering breath. If Satan wanted some reunion nooky, they were all fucked. Talk about disasters.

"He's a good-looking demon," she said. "He wouldn't secretly pine for her, would he? He's got endless choices."

"You have to understand the layers that exist." Hank rubbed the back of his neck, one of very few times that Eve had ever seen signs of stress on him.

"Go on," she coaxed.

"It's a misconception to say that Sammael rules over a place called Hell. Sammael rules the earth. He was banished from Heaven, but given domain here. He isn't roasting in some fiery pit."

"He isn't?"

"No. He can create that visual effect and often does because we've been trained to fear it, but it's just window dressing. There are layers to Heaven and there are layers to earth. Like an onion. Sammael can strip or combine layers in order to create the desired effect."

Fred appeared from the darkness dressed in a lab coat and bearing a slight smile. Carrying a tray with a pitcher and half-filled glasses, she looked more harmless geek than killer demon.

Eve leaned back to make room for the refreshments. "Will you join us?" she asked the lili.

"I can't, but thank you."

Hank's gaze followed his assistant as she retreated. "She's worried that she'll die at any moment. She never relaxes because of it."

One hundred lilin died every day. Eve couldn't imagine living with that hanging over her head.

"Okay, back to the layers," she redirected.

"The layer that you and I occupy most of the time is tricky to navigate for both Jehovah and Sammael.

As you know, they don't play well together. So when they want to function here with the full range of movement that mortals have—to touch, to taste, to lust—they need emissaries."

Understanding hit her right between the eyes. "Like Jesus Christ."

"And the Antichrist. You may feel the hand of God or the claws of Sammael in a figurative sense or through secondary beings such as demons and *mal'akhs,* but you can only feel them literally if they gain access to this earthly layer through an emissary."

"So let's say—hypothetically—that Satan wanted to give me a gift. Not a power, but an actual *thing,* like a necklace, he would have to do so through an emissary?"

Hank wrapped a hand around his drinking glass, but didn't pick it up. "Or he would use an emissary as a gateway to do it himself. If the emissary was strong enough, perhaps Sammael could even manifest separately and the two could occupy the same plane at the same time."

If the emissary was strong enough . . .

Eve wondered why the room didn't spin. She thought it should, considering how shaky she felt on the inside. "Is Cain the gateway?"

How else could Sammael have known that the original Eve would be visiting this layer?

Hank's gaze lifted from watching his thumb draw lines in the condensation on his glass. "Now, you're starting to ask the right questions."

"Why won't anyone give me a straight answer?" Alec rolled his shoulders back, fighting fatigue when he shouldn't be tired to begin with. "You've kept me cooling my heels for hours, then you talk in circles. It's a simple yes-or-no question."

Uriel handed him a bottle of chilled water and sat in the wicker chair opposite him. The head of the Australian firm was shirtless and barefooted. His long, sun-bleached hair fluttered gently in the ocean breeze coming through the open French doors of his office. He was considered one of the foremost yacht builders in the world, but had recently diversified into wine making. The world economy was unhealthy, curtailing luxury purchases.

"Yes, there are only seven of us," the archangel finally answered, after twenty minutes of evasion. "And yes, it might be by design. Is that better?"

Alec snatched up the water and downed the contents in a few greedy gulps. His body grew more feverish by the hour, leaving him with a dry throat and perspiration-damp skin.

"You really don't want to fuck with me now," he growled, returning the empty bottle to the glass-topped wicker coffee table with a hollow thud.

"I hope, for your sake, that you do not think we are evenly matched," Uriel warned. "Or assume that my easygoing nature gives you an edge."

Alec took deep, measured breaths, carefully reining back his temper.

Why can't I feel Eve?

He hadn't been able to feel her since they'd found the two guards. As the archangel responsible for Abel, he could sense that his brother wasn't alarmed, but that only spurred Alec's envy. The damned thing inside him was costing him the only thing that mattered to him anymore.

"Whose design?" he bit out, returning to his previous question. "Did you and the others practice a little sibling winnowing to get to a manageable number?"

Uriel's brilliant blue gaze narrowed. "You tread dangerous ground with your accusations."

"How did you convince Jehovah that seven of you were enough?"

"We have no control over Jehovah. You know that. As with anything, the pros and cons were weighed."

Alec couldn't help but wonder if he was experiencing the cons. Despite the cool evening air gusting in from the balcony, he was sweating. There was no doubt the chaos within him was escalating. "I'm not . . . well."

"I can see that," the archangel murmured, his casual pose unchanged.

"Did the others—the archangels who aren't here anymore—experience similar . . . problems?"

"What problems are you experiencing?"

"Let me rephrase," Alec said tightly. "Have you ever had to put down another archangel because he was out of control?"

Uriel brushed his hair back with a rough swipe of his hand. "No. We seven were created as we are, Cain. You are an aberration. An unknown. Perhaps your once-mortal body is incapable of handling an archangel's power."

"I was *changed,*" he argued. "It felt like I was being ripped apart. The pain was indescribable."

Uriel's mouth quirked on one side. "I bet. That doesn't mean you are now one of us. For Abel to become a *mal'akh,* he had to die. For Christ to achieve his aims, he had to die. It is quite possible that your transformation cannot be completed without shedding every vestige of your former self."

"If I'm an aberration, is it possible that Raguel's still alive and that's why my ascension is fucked up?"

The sudden stillness that gripped the archangel didn't go unnoticed. "I suppose."

Well, that explained why none of them were actively searching for their brother. They assumed he was dead.

Restless, Alec stood and prowled. If there could be only seven archangels, he was in an untenable position. He would first have to ascertain whether or not Raguel was alive. Then, he would have to decide whether to kill, or be killed.

How badly do I want this?

The darkness in him roiled in protest. Power was like a drug, one not easily relinquished.

He moved toward the window and stood on the threshold, his damp skin chilling in the gentle gusts of wind.

Uriel's voice came soft and coaxing behind him. "What ails you?"

"There's something *in* me. It's angry. Violent. Very strong."

"Too strong?"

"Not yet." Alec looked at the ocean. At night, one beach looked like another. He couldn't help but think of nights spent with Eve. The selfish part of him wished he could share this mess he was in with her. "But I want better control over it."

"Perhaps the ascension freed a . . . *repressed* part of your personality?"

"Do you believe everything you hear?"

The wicker creaked as the archangel rose to his feet. Although his approach was silent, Alec sensed Uriel coming. The rush of power he felt around a single archangel was of equal force to the rush he felt when entering a firm.

"Depends on who is doing the talking," Uriel murmured.

Did Jehovah know the truth behind the rumors?

Alec's heart rate kicked up in response to his panic. Something was overriding the safeguards of his mark and the unexpected physical response caused a slight disorientation.

His hand rubbed at his chest through his thin cotton T-shirt. "Who did the talking to you?"

"Does it matter? The point is that perhaps the problem is in your blood." There was a length of silence, then Uriel touched his shoulder. "You should direct your questions to Jehovah."

"And fail my first challenge as an archangel?" Alec scoffed. "No way."

"You think this is a test?"

"Isn't everything? My entire life has been a trial." He faced Uriel. "That isn't a complaint, just a fact."

"I understand. We all face trials, saints and sinners alike. I wish I could help you with this one."

Alec's brow arched. "Are you sure you can't? You haven't offered me much of anything."

Uriel smiled, but the gesture didn't reach his eyes. "The best advice I can give you is to look elsewhere. You speak of anger and violence inside you, yet you do not approach the one of us known for those traits? Why?"

"Michael?"

"Commander of the Lord's army. Who knows darkness better than he? He has defeated Sammael himself."

Alec stepped farther outside. Uriel followed. Together, they stood at the railing and watched the moonlight shimmer over the water.

"You fear him," the archangel noted, still looking forward. "You should. But if anyone can help you, it would be him."

"Thank you."

"Do not thank me yet, Cain." Uriel glanced at him. "If you become a danger, I will hunt you myself."

Inside Alec, the thrill of prospective battle quickened his blood.

Uriel's gaze hardened. "I smell it on you. Perhaps you should go, before I decide not to let you."

Cursing inwardly, Alec shifted away.

Reed was preoccupied with his thoughts. So much so that it took him a moment to register that the beer he'd ordered was sitting in front of him. The waitress who'd brought it was waiting patiently.

"I'm sorry," he murmured. "I missed what you said."

"Would you like anything else?" The pretty brunette smiled wide. Her name tag said she was "Sara," which was an unfortunate moniker but not her fault.

"No. I'm good, thanks." He picked up the bottle, ignoring the frozen glass beside it. For mortals, it was perhaps a bit early in the day for booze. For a *mal'akh*, it wasn't any different from drinking sparkling water.

"I'll check on you in a few minutes," she said. "But if you need anything in the meantime, just gimme a wave."

"Got it."

Sara winked before sashaying back into the restaurant. The invitation to flirt with her was clear and brought Reed some amusement, but he hadn't the time to indulge in such games now. There was far too much at stake.

Alone again, Reed appreciated his status as sole occupant of the House of Blues patio. Music drifted from the interior—of sufficient volume to identify the songs, but not so loud as to impede conversation. Despite the sluggish economy, foot traffic through Downtown Disney was steady. A mixture of trolling teenagers and tourist families window-shopped, ate, and commingled with a large proliferation of Infernals. The mortals had no clue, their open and happy faces betraying their ignorance of the danger. What would they say if they knew the vendor hawking caricature drawings was an incubus? Or that the woman filling popcorn buckets was a *djinni*?

"Abel?"

Turning his head with studious nonchalance, Reed watched as Chaney and Asmodeus approached. The new Alpha was dressed in casual Dockers pants and an oversized polo shirt. His companion, one of the seven kings of Hell, was dressed similarly to Reed— Armani suit, pristinely pressed shirt, and gleaming leather dress shoes. The glamour he wore was impressive. He'd chosen a muscular build and angular features to hide the multiheaded monstrosity he was in reality.

As the demons came around the short metal patio fence and joined him, Reed remained seated. He drank his beer and watched the pedestrians pass.

"Raguel is alive," Asmodeus said without preamble. "Presently enjoying the hospitality of the second level of Hell."

The level that Asmodeus ruled. Of course. The demon must have pleased Sammael in some way to be given such an honor.

"Even better than I expected," Reed returned. "We both have access to what the other wants."

He watched both Infernals through his sunglasses. Neither met his gaze. The Alpha turned his head to people watch and Asmodeus peered into the doorway of the restaurant, making eye contact with Sara.

The two demons ordered food and drink. Reed asked for a second round. When they were settled, Asmodeus pushed up his sunglasses and revealed laser-bright red irises.

"I want more," the demon king said smoothly.

Reed picked at the edge of the beer bottle label, but kept his eyes on his companions. "Do you?"

"I don't see how it benefits me to share a bounty with a lower-level demon. I get a better boon from having Raguel under my watch."

"Ah . . . I see."

"You're not surprised," Chaney noted.

"Of course he's not." Asmodeus laughed. "He knows me well enough."

"I was hoping you would insist," Reed said easily. "I want more, too. I want the priest."

"Done. We don't have any need for him, beyond getting our hands on Cain's woman."

Fingers tensing, Reed drawled, "Right."

The waitress returned with the drinks, promising to be right out with the food. Reed couldn't even imagine eating at this point, and suspected their order was a ruse to appear more in control than they were.

Regardless, they had more control than he did.

"So what more do you want?" he asked, when the silence stretched out.

"What can you get?" Chaney asked.

Reed laughed. "I don't work that way. Let's start with you telling me what I'm bidding against, and I'll see if I can beat it."

The Alpha tried to look innocent. Asmodeus didn't bother. He tossed his head back and laughed.

"I've always liked you, Abel." He grinned. His teeth were a hideous shade of yellow, incongruous within the beauty of his glamour. "How did you know?"

"I didn't," Reed confessed, his mind spinning with the possibilities. "I suspected, you confirmed. I figured someone else besides me would want Raguel back. I couldn't be the only one who'd bargain with a demon to do it."

Cain, maybe? Someone sent by Sabrael? Ishamel?

"I'm under a vow of secrecy," the king said. "Can't tell you who it is."

"I don't care about *who*." He'd tackle that next on his own. "I care about *what*. They're offering you something, but you think you can get more out of me or you wouldn't have shown up today. What are they proposing, and how much more do you want?"

Asmodeus glanced at the Alpha, then back at Reed. "They're offering to widen the Black Diamond

Pack's territory by thinning the ranks of the perimeter packs."

"Okay." Reed waited a moment, then, "Come on. You already said that sharing the spoils with Chaney doesn't work for you. So, what are *you* getting out of it?"

The king slouched in his chair and smiled. "A handler. One who's been a pain in my ass for too long."

Reed staved off his horror and launched into his bid. "I can top that. Easily."

"Oh?" The Infernal smiled. "Whatcha got?"

"An archangel to replace the one you're giving to me."

Chaney whistled. "Which one?"

Asmodeus laughed. "Who do you think?" His eyes brightened to the point that Reed appreciated his sunglasses. "He's going to give us Cain."

CHAPTER 16

Azazel stood with hands clasped behind his back, separate from the mass of celebrants around him. "You gave her the amulet, my liege?"

Sammael shrugged. "Doing so serves many purposes, not the least of which is that she will be marginally safer until news of the successful bounty reaches everyone."

"If you say that I took part in the hunt, it will lower my status. I am above such games."

"Are you?" Reclining more fully on the divan, Sammael watched the revelers through the filmy sheers that surrounded his pallet. Between his spread legs, a succubus worked, her mouth gliding up and down the length of his cock with laudable skill. "How odd. I thought your place was where I put you."

His lieutenant bowed. "I meant no offense, my liege. I simply point out that my ability to perform the tasks you set for me is enhanced when others fear me. That fear is more easily invoked when I am seen as separate from the masses."

Sammael hissed in pleasure at the fervent tongue stroking the underside of his cock. "Worry not, Azazel. I told Evangeline that I would think of something. I did not say I would use her suggestion."

"Thank you."

Sammael turned his gaze back to his subjects who danced and fucked with abandon just beyond the edge of the divan. Unfortunately, his lieutenant's continued agitation affected his enjoyment of the debauchery. "You still have questions."

"Just one."

"Well, spit it out. I resent how readily everyone believes in a divine plan, yet I am always questioned."

"You've given a convenience to someone who is a pawn of our enemies. I just want to understand why."

"Convenience," Sammael repeated slowly. "Yes. I suppose the amulet is convenient. It certainly evens the odds between a powerless Mark and a gifted demon."

"Yes. You could have ended the bounty without making things easy for her."

Lifting his hand in a delaying gesture to his lieutenant, Sammael rolled his hips, screwing into the eager mouth that serviced him. Taking his cue, the succubus increased the pressure and tempo of her suckling. He came with a low groan, shuddering with the welcome release of tension.

"Excellent." He pushed his fingers into the demon's hair and yanked her head back. She stared up at him with heavy-lidded, worshipful eyes. The Asian glamour she wore had been her idea, but he'd taken a perverse enjoyment in it after meeting Cain's woman.

"Azazel is too grim," he murmured, caressing her cheek. "Help him relax."

"With honor, my liege." She crawled over on her hands and knees, the awkward movement made sensual by the leisure with which she crossed the distance.

"I'm not grim," Azazel protested. "Just curious."

Sammael yawned, dangerously bored and only slightly mellowed by his recent orgasm. "Convenience works both ways," he said. "Now loosen up. The priest is our next entertainment, and I want you to enjoy the show."

Eve pushed aside her doubts and trusted her instincts. "I don't believe Cain has anything to do with this. He's not well, but he isn't a portal to a Hell-layer either. He's got too much good inside him."

"He doesn't understand what's happening to him," Hank argued. "How can we rule anything out?"

"He understands enough to push me away." Her head turned to look into the darkened depths of the room. Compared to the racket the tengu had been making before, it was now eerily silent. "I was too hurt to see it at first, but he's trying to protect me from himself. He proved he still cares last night when he showed up at the stadium. The Cain we know is still in there somewhere. He's not completely possessed."

She looked back at Hank. "He would need to be possessed, right?"

"So I assume, but Cain is a loose cannon right now. There's never been anything like him. We're all learning as we go when it comes to him."

As Eve considered the best way to handle the situation, long moments passed. Her fingers drummed atop the wooden table and her lips pursed. Alec hadn't come to her for help and clearly didn't want it, but she wouldn't let that hold her back. If he came apart at the seams, it would be bad for everyone. Especially for him. She had no doubt the other archangels would kill him.

"Hey." She perked up. "You said he doesn't understand what's happening to him. He came to see you, didn't he? He wanted your help."

"Everyone comes to me for help." He shrugged. "I don't always have the answers, but I appreciate being kept in the loop."

"What answers was he looking for today?"

"Actually, I called him down here to talk about your tengu friend. But we also talked about his unsuitability for the position of archangel."

Eve frowned. "Unsuitability? I think he's perfect for the job. He always takes command of the situations he walks into and he knows this job better than anyone."

His mouth curved. "Cain is a hands-on sort of Mark. He's best in the trenches. There are others who would have been better suited to give interviews to the press and sit in an office."

"Maybe that's his problem," she suggested. "Maybe he just can't handle all the periphery stuff. Just listening to the amount of information flowing through Abel's brain makes my head hurt. It's like standing at the base of Niagara Falls. I can't bear more than a few seconds of it. And Cain skipped right over that section of the information superhighway and jumped headfirst into the part where he's getting a gazillion times more info than that. That could drive a person crazy."

"I suppose. Although I've met other archangels who've disliked it and they didn't fall off the deep end."

Eve thought of the archangels—Sarakiel, Raguel, Michael, Gabriel, Raphael, Uriel, and Remiel. They'd all seemed very comfortable with their jobs. "Which ones? How did they get over it?"

"Chamuel had a hell of a time. I don't think he ever got over it. There were others, but their names escape me now."

Leaning over the table, she asked urgently, "There were more than the seven I've met? Abel has a theory about a possible cap on their number. If he's right, we need to know what happened to the others."

"Your guess is as good as mine." Hank's voice remained raspy and steady. "All I know is that shortly after the firms were created the number of archangels rapidly diminished until only seven remained."

"Why? We need to— *Ow!*" Eve caught her head in hands. "Shit . . . migraine."

But she didn't get migraines. Hank stood and came up behind her, touching her shoulders. As the pain bore deep, she curled over the table. Then, as suddenly as it had struck, it disappeared. Leaving behind Alec, who was searching through her brain like a spreading flame, licking along the surfaces of her memories.

Alec.

Where have you been?

He sounded just as angry as he'd been before. It had to be exhausting, carrying around all that fury.

Searching for you, she gasped, still reeling from the force of his entry.

Don't. Not safe.

Let me help you!

He began to withdraw in a rush. Eve caught him with both hands, but it was hopeless. He moved too quickly, like smoke sucked out by a vacuum. In an instant, he was gone.

Eve bolted upright. The back of her head cracked into Hank's chin. He cursed and stumbled back.

"Sorry," she cried, jumping to her feet so quickly the chair fell back and hit the floor. "Jeez, Hank. I'm sorry!"

"Bloody H. Christ!" he snapped, holding his chin. "Don't apologize to me. Are you all right?"

She almost ran a hand over her face, then remembered that she was wearing makeup. "It was Alec— *Cain*—digging around in my brain."

"He hurt you?"

Hank's tone alarmed her, so she quickly explained. "He was trying to share information. The other archangels believe that Raguel is dead, but Cain doesn't. He thinks Raguel is alive and that's why he's so messed up. He believes that the number seven is an absolute when it comes to archangels."

"You were in great pain," he insisted, releasing his chin to grip hers. He turned her head from side to side. He snapped his fingers and a handkerchief appeared. He pressed it to her right nostril. "Your nose is bleeding."

"It was like 'e 'ad to punch 'is way in," she mumbled through the cloth.

"He's your firm leader. He shouldn't have to 'punch his way in' to you . . . Ah!" A look of discovery crossed over his face.

"What?"

"Try reaching him again." Hank rushed into the darkness. He shouted over his shoulder as he retreated. "See if you can make contact."

Eve reached out to Alec. Against her nose, the cloth grew warm with blood. She found him, swirling like a hurricane, furious and destructive.

She reached out to his humanity. *I have so much I want to tell you. I want to . . . lean on you.*

The cyclone slowed marginally, then swayed. Alec didn't say a word, but she could feel him softening.

You owe me, she prodded, *after the shitty way you treated me yesterday.*

I did you a favor.

She snorted. *Bite me.*

Watch out. His voice changed, taking on a singsong note of madness that gave her chills. *I just might.*

"Here." Hank appeared out of nowhere, tossing the necklace at her. It whipped through the air and she ducked, avoiding a lash to the face. But when it neared her, it opened, lassoing her neck in a way that would be impossible without some preternatural means.

And like a dropped cell phone signal, her line to Alec died abruptly.

She blinked at Hank. The mark had done its job and healed the injury to her nose, but the deeper ramifications lingered.

Dropping the hand holding the handkerchief, she asked, "What happened?"

The occultist crossed his arms and looked thoughtful. "That piece of jewelry appears to put a damper on an Infernal's powers."

"I thought it only worked on the Nix."

He shrugged. In the back of the room, the tengu

began to screech and bang against something metallic. A cage perhaps.

"Why would a charm against Infernals work against Cain?"

"We're circling back to my theory now, aren't we?"

"But I don't—"

The tengu continued its tirade.

"Can you shut that thing up?" she yelled. Bending down, Eve righted the fallen chair.

Hank nodded and gestured for her to follow. The spot of illumination followed them, a trick she wished she knew how to pull off herself.

As she'd suspected, the tengu was caged in what looked to be a large dog kennel. He clung from the top with fingers and toes, shaking and shouting violently.

Fred stood nearby, taking notes on a clipboard. She glanced up at Hank and nodded at whatever cue he'd given her. Turning, she set the clipboard on a lab counter, then grabbed a canister that had a nozzle like a fire extinguisher. She aimed it at the tengu and sprayed a reddish cloud of fine mist at him. He sputtered and coughed, causing him to lose his grip and crash to the bottom. He lay there for a spell, shaking his head and appearing nearly as dazed as he had while wearing the necklace. The red liquid was quickly absorbed into his cement shell, leaving him looking the same as always. Hank spoke a lyrical incantation, and the tengu sat up and looked at Eve.

"Pretty Mark," he said, hopping to his feet.

"You're a noisy fellow," she replied.

He moved his gaze to glare at Hank. "Traitor."

Eve leaned toward the occultist and whispered, "What was in the can?"

"Infernal blood."

She almost asked where he got it, but decided she didn't want to know. "Demons find demon blood soothing? We could win the war with that. Kill some, spray the others."

"It wouldn't have any effect on a healthy Infernal. In this case, it's just canceling out the overdose of Mark blood I gave him earlier. I doubt you want to try your scenario with Mark blood."

"Right." Moving closer to the cage, Eve studied the little stone beast. "That was a very ferocious reaction this guy had."

"Oil and water," Fred said. "Infernal and Mark don't mix."

"No kidding."

"About the Nix." Hank walked over to the counter where Fred had set down the clipboard.

"Yes?"

"I dug out that punch bowl you brought me before. I know Cain wanted me to scry for the Nix through any residuals that might be on it, but I'm afraid that isn't possible."

"Oh." Her nose wrinkled. "Would have made things easier, but since he's after me, we'll see him again regardless."

Thanks to the necklace, the Nix was the least of her problems at the moment. She pushed thoughts of him aside for more pressing problems.

"Right, but using a combination of bits and pieces of the mask, I was thinking I could create a repellent of some sort."

Her brows rose. "Unless it's a permanent repellant, I think I'd rather just kill the sucker and be done with it."

"Well, I didn't know about the necklace at the time." Hank leaned into the counter with one hand and set the other on his hip. It was a very feminine pose and made her smile. "Now that I do, I'm thinking I might be able to tweak it in the reverse."

"Reverse?"

"Make you more attractive. Irresistible."

"She doesn't need any help being irresistible."

Alec's low, deep voice hit her ears just before she registered the sound of his boots thudding rhythmically onto the cement floor. He appeared out of the darkness, wild-eyed and dangerous, the veins in his forearms and biceps thick and visible. She might have swooned if she was the type and Unmarked. As it was, she licked her lips. She'd always had a thing for his bad boy vibe, but this . . . yowza.

"You resisted me well enough earlier," she managed.

He kept on coming, a raging force of nature that pinned her against the cage holding the tengu.

His hand caught the back of her neck. "Don't you *ever* hang up on me."

Her shoulders went back. "What are you going to do about it if I do?"

As she'd thought he might, he yanked her closer and kissed her, his lips mashing hers without any semblance of finesse.

His hand at her nape moved, sliding around in a quest for her breast, focused solely on his animal urges despite their audience. Reaching up, she caught the necklace chain. She pulled it up and over her head, then dropped it around his neck.

Alec froze. There was an awkward moment when

they stood like statues with their lips pressed together.

What the hell?

Eve pushed him back and moved away from the
cage where the mischievous tengu had been poking
her in the butt with his stubby fingers. She studied
Alec, noting the drastic change in his eyes and stance.

Sucking in a deep breath, she greeted the Alec she
knew. "Hi."

He frowned at her.

"How do you feel?" she asked.

Hank sidled closer. "Yes. How do you feel, Cain?"

"How the fuck am I supposed to feel?" he barked,
but it lacked bite. He scrubbed both hands over his
face, as he did when first waking up in the morning.

"Not angry?" Eve suggested. "In control?"

Alec lifted the amulet and stared at it. "What is
this?"

"A lucky charm."

"Lucky for whom?" His gaze lifted and met hers.
A pained look crossed his face. Guilt settled like a
heavy stone in her gut. Not hers. His.

"Lucky for us," she said. They'd deal with guilt later.
"We need you on top of your game now. If decking you
out in a pimp chain does the trick, I'm all for it."

"Where did you get this?"

"I tossed it to her," Hank improvised. "It's something I'm working on."

Eve shot him a grateful glance.

"Whatever it is," Alec said, "it's perfect. Glad
something is working out for us in the experimental
department."

His head tilted to the side as if hearing something

she couldn't, then, "Montevista woke up. I need to talk to him."

Hoping the guard would be able to tell Alec what she couldn't, Eve said, "Go check it out."

"You're coming with me." He gave her a stern look. "I need to talk to you, too. Best to get you, Sydney, and Montevista together, and see if we can figure out what happened last night."

"I still have some business with Hank," she protested.

He looked at the occultist. "He's not making you anything to attract the Nix. That's an order."

Hank lifted his hands in a gesture of surrender. "I have no idea if I can pull it off, but if I could, it can help you set the time and place of the showdown to your liking."

"That could come in handy," Eve pointed out.

"Like you don't have enough Infernal trouble with the bounty?" Alec scoffed, tugging her toward the door.

She waved bye to Hank before they moved too far away and he was lost in the darkness.

If I could get Gadara back, she wondered, *what would happen to Alec?*

She'd like to ask whoever endorsed Alec's promotion, but that could run the risk of them killing him. If Alec was the emissary, they wouldn't hesitate.

He's not the emissary, she scolded herself. Besides, she didn't have a clue about who was responsible.

A sudden image of eyes the color of blue flame filled her mind. She almost set the thought aside, telling herself that of course she would think of him. He was the only seraph she'd ever met.

Then, she realized the thought came from Reed.

* * *

Chaney slumped back into the plastic chair, clearly taken aback. "I knew you hated your brother, but this . . . Aren't you going to get in trouble for this?"

"Actually," Reed picked up his beer, "I'm sanctioned."

"Someone gave you the authority to get rid of Cain?" Asmodeus was clearly disbelieving.

Reed considered how much to reveal. "Something went wrong with the ascension. He's a danger to himself and to others."

"We could use a man like him."

"He'll be fatally wounded by the absence of God in his soul, I suspect. Worthless to everyone." Reed looked at the increasing number of tourists as the amount of Infernals grew in proportion. Casting a glance into the dark interior of the restaurant, he regretted his decision to sit outside. The same exposure that gave him a modicum of safety around Asmodeus also bared him to any of the dozens of Marks policing the overabundance of demons in the area. They were too visible out here.

"A fate worse than death for you guys, eh?" Chaney cut into his rare steak and bit into a piece with relish. "Hope I never get on your bad side."

"Then don't fuck up this exchange."

"How do you propose we do this?" Asmodeus asked, poking at his VooDoo Shrimp appetizer with his fork.

"I need you to bring the Nix," Reed murmured, twisting his beer bottle to catch the sunlight. "But rein him in. He needs to be a threat, nothing more. Cain will come to the rescue and I'll make sure there's no one around to get in the way."

"What about Raguel and the priest?" Chaney licked blood off his lips. "Who's going to play the hero? You?"

"No. Let them escape."

"What are you getting out of this, then?"

"The seraph who endorsed Cain wants his mess disposed of," he lied. "That's a favor I can call in later. And without Cain, Evangeline Hollis serves no purpose. Raguel will appreciate both the loss of his replacement and the end of the bounty. Again, another favor to call in at a later date."

"Lose one, save many."

Asmodeus's fork tapped against the edge of his plate. "I'll need help to pull down Cain."

"That's your problem," Reed dismissed. "Not mine. However you go about doing it, just show up the day after tomorrow at Hollis's condominium complex. The Nix knows where she lives, if you don't. Say . . . midafternoon? We'll be out by the pool. I'll open the water lines so the Nix can get in. He can be the distraction while you do whatever you have to do."

"That place is a fortress," Asmodeus growled. "It will be an all-out bloodbath."

"Which is why you better make damn sure that Raguel and the priest are already on the move, if you want to avoid pegging yourself with a Vanquish Me sign."

"Pick a different place," Chaney said.

"Can't," Reed retorted curtly. "After the way the priest was snatched, Hollis is locked up tight. It's either her home or work, and there's no way you're getting into Gadara Tower. We all know that."

"Shit."

"No," Asmodeus said. "I'll wait until things settle down, then I'll go after her when it's more convenient."

Reed's foot tapped silently beneath the table. He'd prefer to wait, too, but the priest wouldn't make it that long. And if the priest died, Eve would never forgive herself. "She and the priest might be dead by then."

"I would rather lose them," Asmodeus snapped, "than me."

"You might lose Cain, too, if he doesn't get his shit together." Standing, Reed pulled his money clip from his pocket and tossed a couple of twenty-dollar bills onto the table. "You know where I'll be, if you change your mind."

"I don't like being played with, Abel."

Reed's mouth curved. "You won't know if I'm playing with you, unless you show up."

"Mariel? Are you all right?"

Mariel pulled her gaze away from the party sitting on the patio of the House of Blues and returned it to her companion. The balcony of Ralph Brennan's Jazz Kitchen was across the busy promenade from the other restaurant, but Mariel's *mal'akh* hearing had no trouble picking up the treasonous conversation taking place there. Even from this distance, she could see the laser brightness of the demon's eyes and hear the malevolence in his voice.

"No," she replied in her Mark's native Zulu. "I'm far from all right."

"What—"

"Don't." She stayed Kobe Denner from turning his head with her hand atop his. "What you don't know can save your life."

Kobe frowned at her, his dark eyes concerned. One of her best Marks, he'd been with her for years. "What can I do?"

"I think we're going to have to end our lunch early."

He pushed his half-finished meal away. "Of course. Go, if you must."

Mariel bunched up the napkin in her lap and set it on the table. "I'm going to shift you out of here. I don't want you to be seen."

Her urgency was conveyed in her tone. He stood quickly. She dug into her purse and left some cash on the table. They gave a quick explanation to the startled waiter before making their way down to the lower floor.

Ducking into the hallway that led to the bathrooms, Mariel quickly shifted them back to the tower.

Alec dragged Eve down the hall and around the corner. There was an alcove with a water fountain and he crowded her into it, pressing her into a corner and cupping her face in his hands.

"I'm fucked up," he said bluntly.

"I'm not exactly prime goods either." Her tone was dry, but her dark eyes glistened in the shadowy hallway.

"We need to talk about the personal stuff later." He

touched his forehead to hers, feeling as thrashed as he did after a particularly nasty vanquishing. "It's ugly and painful, but we have something worth fighting for, if you give me a chance to fix this mess."

He felt her fingers hook into the belt loops of his jeans. "Yes. We need to talk."

Alec sensed a shiver of wariness move across her mind, but he couldn't read the details. Still, that shiver was more than he'd been able to get out of her the last couple of days.

"Are you blocking me?" he asked harshly. "Or is my . . . *condition* causing a poor signal between us?"

"A little of both, maybe," she confessed, tucking the necklace into his shirt. "When I tell you something, I want to do it the mortal way. You and me. Talking out loud. Unhurried and in private."

"Okay. As soon as we get done here." He tugged her out of the alcove with him.

"I have to go to the police station after this."

As they hurried down the hallway, she filled him in.

"Okay." His fingers tightened on hers. "We'll go together."

"Ishamel is going to take me. Part of his lawyer act. It might look weird if you came along."

"Why?"

"Uh . . ." Eve glanced aside at him and winced. "I kinda told them that we broke up."

Alec was grateful his step didn't falter, since he felt like he'd been punched in the gut. He exhaled harshly. "That was quick."

"Cut me some slack. Things are flying at me from all sides. I said what I needed to say at the time."

He didn't have a firm foundation to stand on, since he was the one who'd pushed her away. But that didn't make things easier. "As long as you weren't serious."

She squeezed his hand back. "One thing at a time."

His hand was on the knob to the infirmary when he heard Eve's name being called. He looked around and saw Mariel approaching with an unusually brisk stride.

"Evangeline," the handler called out. "Can you spare a minute of your time?"

Alec released the knob. "What do you need, Mariel?"

"Just Hollis." Her smile was so slight it was more of a grimace. "Girl stuff, Cain. You know?"

"No, I don't." He glanced at Eve. "Come in as soon as you're done."

She nodded. "Of course."

Feeling like something precious was slipping through his fingers, Alec left her in the hallway.

Eve didn't need the ability to read minds to know that the *mal'akh* was terribly upset. The fact that Alec didn't fully pick up on his handler's agitation was further proof that he was still seriously out of whack. Mariel knew it, too. Her gaze remained on the door until it closed with a firm click.

"He's not well," Eve said softly. "I'm guessing you feel it through the connection between handler and firm leader."

"I'm hoping he adjusts soon, but right now, his inability to read us is a blessing in disguise." Mariel turned her attention to Eve. "We have a serious problem. I fear for his safety and Abel's. You're the only one I can trust to find a solution that keeps them both alive."

"What's going on?"

"Something isn't right with Abel. He's not himself. You're not going to believe it when I tell you."

Not himself . . .

Gripping Mariel's elbow, Eve pulled her a short distance down the hall. "Tell me everything . . ."

CHAPTER 17

"I don't remember much of anything," Sydney said with a turned-down mouth and averted gaze. "I was eyeing some movement under the bleachers when Montevista tackled me. I must have been knocked out by the impact. The next thing I knew, you were waking me up, Cain."

Alec turned his attention to Montevista, who looked as miserable as Sydney.

"I've got nothing," the Mark said. "I don't even remember *that* much. I was standing along the fence, mad dogging some Infernals. Then I was here in the tower."

Both guards sat at a metal table dressed in pale blue hospital scrubs. Alec sat across from them, hyperaware of the pendant heating the skin between his pectorals. Something had to give, and fast. Lack of sleep was taking its toll, but he needed to be available to help Eve during the day and he had inquiries to make about his condition when she was sleeping at night.

He glanced at the witch doctor who ran the infirmary. The woman was short, no more than three feet tall, with cropped blonde curls, and a child's features. "Any idea what happened to those two?"

"They both check out," she said. "In Sydney's case, I think she lost consciousness on impact, as she suggested. In Montevista's . . . I'm not sure. I'm inclined to think he jumped in the way of a direct hit. Maybe an energy blast aimed at her. An impact to the back of the head would have knocked him out and caused him to crash into her. Something like that would explain the memory loss, especially if Azazel was the one attacking."

"What are the aftereffects? Are there any?"

"Fatigue. Otherwise, no."

"I'd like to get back to duty," Montevista said.

"Me, too," Sydney concurred.

"Are you sure you don't want some time off?" Alec asked, probing their minds for any traces of trauma.

The search was difficult, mostly because of the suppression of the voices inside his head. Their absence left an odd quiet within him; not a departure, more an anticipation. He knew something wasn't right. He was just waiting for the explosion to prove it.

Montevista nodded and spoke for both of them. "We're sure."

A brief knock came at the door, then it opened and Eve stepped in. She moved straight to the two guards with arms open. They stood, hugging her in return. It was her way. She was so open, so willing to connect to others. Eve let people in from the get-go and hoped they would turn out to be worthy friends. So opposite from him, who had learned to keep people at arm's length until they proved they deserved otherwise.

She asked about their health and how they were feeling. When they requested to resume guarding her, she accepted readily. No recriminations, no guilt trips. The two Marks were clearly relieved.

Looking over her shoulder at Alec, she said, "Is that okay?"

For a second he tensed, expecting the compulsion to say something unkind. He'd begun to feel the way he imagined Tourette's syndrome patients felt, spewing out words before his brain registered them. When the voices remained silent, he grinned.

"Whoa," Sydney murmured.

"Yeah, sucker punches me, too," Eve muttered.

As long as he could still get to her, all wasn't lost.

"I have no objections, if you're all okay with it," he said. "But I want to keep you two out of the field for a couple days, at least."

"Works for me," Eve agreed. "After I hit the police station, I'm going home and staying there. How about they head over there with you now? They can rest in my place while you catch up on some downtime with your folks."

"My folks?" He rose to his feet.

The knowing look in her eyes answered his unspoken question.

Alec looked at the Marks. "Get dressed. I'll be back in a few."

"We'll be ready," Montevista said gruffly.

Heading toward the door, Alec gestured with a jerk of his chin for Eve to come along. He caught her elbow at the threshold and urged her out ahead of him.

They passed neat rows of hospital beds, most of which were empty, and exited back out to the smoky hallway.

"You met my parents."

"Yep. Your mom and dad came over last night."

His jaw clenched. He'd known Ima wouldn't let it go until she'd met Eve face to face. His mother wasn't the type to wait until he was nearby to alleviate her curiosity. "Did you like them?"

He saw the right corner of her mouth lift in a slight smile. "Love them. They're both very charming. I think they might like me, too. They seemed as if they did. It was hard to read your dad. But you've met mine, he's really reserved, too. I didn't take it personally."

She stopped beside the alcove he'd caught her in before, and faced him. He loved her like this, all prim and proper in her business attire. He couldn't help but note the changes the years had wrought in her, turning her into a formidable woman. Freed momentarily from his personal demons, his chest swelled with affection and pride.

"Forgetting you and me for the moment," she began, knocking his ass back into the present, "you need to decide how badly you want this archangel gig."

She pressed her fingers to his lips when he started to speak. "Think about it. Running with the theory that seven archangels is the limit—what's going to happen when we get Gadara back? Are you going to take him on? Step aside? Take out one of the others? How will you feel if God decides he likes things the way they were and knocks you back down to Mark?"

The determined glint in her dark eyes told him that

he'd better keep his silence for now and pretend that he was still undecided. He'd learned long ago that women wanted men to overthink things like they did.

"And," she continued, backing up, "I don't mean to heap added pressure on your decision, but I won't invest myself in a relationship with someone who can't love me."

"Angel—"

"Hey." Her voice was husky. "No hard feelings, if it works out that way. I haven't forgotten that we were always going to be temporary."

As Alec started toward her, a familiar figure rounded the corner behind her. Alec's fists clenched.

"Eve."

She turned around at the sound of Abel's greeting. To Alec's surprise, her fists clenched, too. "What?"

Abel's eyes narrowed at her tone. "You ready to go home?"

"I have to go to the police station and give a report."

"Okay." Abel's gaze lifted to Alec's, but he continued to speak to Eve. "I'll give you a lift."

"That's not necessary. I'm riding with Ishamel."

"Why?"

So . . . Abel couldn't read her either. She was like a radio station with static. A problem they'd have to look into.

The tempo of her walk changed, the click of her heels betraying agitation.

Go home, she told Alec sternly. *Park Montevista and Sydney in front of my Wii and don't let your parents out of your sight for even a minute until I get there.*

And here I thought I was running the show.

After I get back, you can go do whatever you want, she offered.

Whatever I want, huh?

But if you take that necklace off, I'll kick your ass.

What do I get if I keep it on?

She stalked right past Abel. *Keep the necklace on, keep a lid on your parents, and it'll keep you on my good side.*

After yesterday, he couldn't ask for more. But she didn't know about *that* . . . yet. *I've got shit to do, angel.*

After your personality transplant yesterday, I still trust you, she argued. *You owe me a little trust in return.*

I trust you.

Good. Then do as I say. I'll see you later.

He wasn't used to following orders from anyone but Jehovah. But she was right, he owed her. And he was exhausted. He hadn't slept in almost two days. That was too long even for an archangel. He'd take a nap, then track down Sabrael when Eve returned.

Abel pivoted and followed her around the corner. Alec had no idea what his brother had done to piss her off, but he was glad they were both on the outs with her.

He tried to tell her that he'd have dinner waiting, but the connection was static again.

They'd *really* have to talk about that when she got back.

"Let me guess," Reed drawled. "You're mad at me."

Eve reached the elevators and stabbed the call button with her finger. "I don't have time to play games with you now."

He moved in front of her, forcing her to look at him. As with Alec, the sight of him made her a bit weak in the knees, despite what an asshole he could be. "How many times do I have to tell you, Eve? I'm not playing with you."

Her lips pursed. "You know 'The Gift of the Magi'?" Not the biblical story; the one by O. Henry."

"Who doesn't?" His dark eyes narrowed.

"You and I are working at cross purposes now, Reed. I know what I'm doing, you don't. Take my advice and take a trip somewhere. Come back in a few days."

"Eve." He caught her hand. "What are you talking about?"

He had a great game face, but she knew him well enough to sense that his guard was up. Guilty as charged, apparently. But she believed he was trying to do the right thing—to get Gadara and the priest back, and save her from the Nix. However, she didn't doubt for a minute that Reed was willing to let Alec be collateral damage. Fratricide was ingrained in them, but damned if she'd be the cause of either of their deaths.

She felt him trying to probe her mind. She pulled away, breaking the physical contact between them. "I have to run. Think about that story. Tack an unhappy ending onto it and that's what you'll get if you don't back off."

The elevator dinged and the doors opened.

"*Abel.*"

They both turned their heads to see Sara approaching. Eve ducked into the car while Reed was distracted, and hit the button for the lobby.

"Hey." He caught the door before it closed. "What the hell?"

Eve pushed his hand out of the way. "Your brother isn't expendable to me, Reed."

He stared at her with a hard gaze until the doors shut.

Once she reached the lobby, she switched elevators to catch the one that would take her up to her office on the forty-fifth floor. The number of Marks in the tower was declining steadily as the workday winded down, allowing the sickly sweet scent of their souls to settle down to a manageable level.

As Eve entered the reception area, Candace stood and offered a slight wave. Eve smiled in greeting.

"Ishamel said he'd be here at four-thirty," the secretary reported, rounding her desk with message pad in hand.

"Perfect." Eve headed toward her office.

"You have an e-mail from your sister, and also one from Sarakiel that's marked urgent."

Eve paused and Candace almost ran into her from behind. "If it's urgent, why didn't she just call and tell me? She's got my number."

"There's an attachment, so that might be why. Want something to drink?"

"No, thank you. You can go home now."

Eve went to her desk and sat before her computer. She accessed her e-mail and read her sister Sophia's note first. Pictures of Eve's niece and nephew filled the screen and caused her a pang of envy. She was the eldest, but Sophia was years ahead of her when it came to settling down. And as long as Eve had the mark, she would remain behind. Marks were sterile.

She typed out a quick "as soon as I can" reply to Sophie's query about when she'd be coming to visit. Then, she reclined into her chair and took a moment to push past unwelcome feelings of resentment.

As she often did at times like these, she glanced around her office, taking in the mixture of traditional modern and Asian-inspired bamboo pieces that made up the décor. Most of the furnishings had been moved from her previous, much smaller office at the Wiesenberg Group. Part of the effort to blend her old life with her new. That's what she remembered when she felt down—that she'd been allowed to blend her two lives together. None of the other Marks were so lucky.

Refocused, she straightened and clicked open Sara's e-mail. The name of the attachment that came with it gave her pause, since it was clearly a recording of a video feed from "CainOffice" made yesterday. Had Sara become aware of Alec's problems? How much danger was he in if she had?

Eve double-clicked on the video and waited for it to load.

Once the replay began, it took her a minute to comprehend what she was watching. It took a bit longer to break the stillness caused by horror, freeing her to kick the computer's power cord out of the outlet in the floor. The monitor turned black and the computer's cooling fan stopped, leaving behind an empty silence.

Breathing in and out deliberately, Eve leaned into her desk and tried to forget what she'd seen.

"T-that wasn't Alec," she told herself. "That wasn't him. You know it."

It's ugly and painful, but we have something worth fighting for . . .

He meant to tell her. She knew it. Lay it all out there and hope she'd understand. But she was still jealous and pissed off.

Standing, Eve began to pace. Her emotions wanted an outlet and there wasn't one. From the expression on Alec's face, he had been as much of a victim as Izzie. Whatever comeuppance the German bitch deserved for making a play at another woman's man had been served during the act.

Which left only Sara.

Eve stopped at the window and leaned against the console positioned in front of it. What the hell had the archangel hoped to gain by sending that video to her? Sara wanted her away from Reed, so why send her something that was troubling enough to push her right into his arms? Hell hath no fury like a woman scorned, right? Sara had to know that if Eve was pissed at Alec, the best way to pay him back in kind was to hook up with Reed.

"What do you want, Sara?" Eve wondered aloud, her fingers digging into lip of the console. "What do you stand to gain?"

Hell hath no fury—

Her eyes widened, her mind jumping to the conversation she'd had with Mariel . . .

"Are you ready to go, Ms. Hollis?"

Turning her attention to the door, she found Ishamel standing there.

"What are you to Raguel Gadara?" she asked, straightening.

His gray brows rose. "I beg your pardon?"

"You're his lieutenant, right? His right-hand man?"

"Something like that."

Eve nodded. "Is it just a job to you, or do you genuinely care about him?"

There was a slight hesitation, then, "Raguel is a friend to me."

"Is. Present tense." She stopped in front of him. "You think he's alive, too."

He gave a brief nod.

"Do you have access to everything? Can you authorize investigations?"

"What do you want, Ms. Hollis?"

She caught his arm and directed him toward the door. "Call me Eve, please. And don't shift us downstairs. Makes me dizzy. Let's do things the mortal way, if you don't mind."

Again, the terse nod of his head.

"Now," she continued, "I don't know if you'll believe me or not, but I want Gadara back, too."

They moved out to the hallway and turned toward the elevators.

"And how do you plan to get him back . . . Eve?"

"I'm afraid I can't tell you that."

Ishamel stared at her intensely the entire length of the descent to the lobby level. Despite her determination, it still made her squirm. He had the eyes of a shark. Dark and dead.

They exited to the circular driveway. Idling near the center fountain, the requisite limousine waited. At least it was requisite for Ishamel. Eve was more interested in Reed's Lamborghini, which he'd arrogantly left parked directly in front of the entrance. The convertible was a silver beauty, as sleek and dangerous as its owner. She pictured him driving over from his meeting with the demons at Downtown Disney and her jaw clenched. Instead of shifting from location to location, he'd used the car for effect. Maybe as a way to humanize himself, to seem at ease and unconcerned when meeting with a king of Hell. Bravado was a necessary tool of the trade when dealing with demons.

She glanced at the valet booth and pointed to the Lamborghini. "Do you have the keys for this?"

One of the three valets nodded but looked wary.

Ishamel snapped his fingers and the valet kicked into gear, ducking inside the booth to pull keys off one of the many hooks on the wall. He ran over to them and Eve held out her hand.

"Thanks," she said when he dropped the key ring into her palm.

She pulled open the passenger door for Ishamel before running around to the driver's side. Sliding behind the wheel, she adjusted the seat forward, then gripped the steering wheel with both hands.

"Wish I hadn't left my sunglasses at home," she murmured, half afraid to borrow Reed's car without permission. He might find it amusing, or he might be furious.

Ishamel held his hand out and she found her sunglasses clasped between his fingers. With a wry smile, she accepted them. It sure would be handy to be able to shift anywhere and back in the blink of an eye. She pushed the key into the ignition and turned the engine over. It roared to life, then purred deliciously.

"Seat belt," she said, while securing her own.

Then they were off, gliding around the center fountain and exiting onto Harbor Boulevard. The police station was on the same street just a few miles down. Eve told herself that Reed shouldn't get too pissy, since she was just taking a straight shot up the road.

"What do you need from me?" Ishamel asked.

"Can you . . ." She hesitated, then glanced over at him. "Would you be open to spying on an archangel? Do you have people who'd be capable and willing to do it?"

"Cain?"

She sucked in a deep breath and hoped that she wasn't screwing herself royally. "Sarakiel."

"Ah . . ." In the periphery of her vision, she saw his fingertips drum silently on the seat. "And you need this information for use in retrieving Raguel? Are you certain you don't have personal considerations?"

"You don't have to tell me what you find," she said. "Just look into it and if something strikes you as off, deal with it as you see fit."

"An odd request," he murmured.

"Trust me, if you find what I suspect you might, there won't be any doubt that it isn't personal."

He didn't say anything. Eve hoped that he was thinking it over.

A few minutes later they pulled into the parking lot of the police station and she slid the car into a diagonal space that had empty spots on either side. She didn't want to have to explain a door ding to Reed on top of the grand-theft auto.

They entered the station and shortly after, Ingram joined them from somewhere in the back. He led them to a room with a beat-up table and a large two-way mirror. A form and a pen waited there. He directed her to sit and give her statement regarding what she remembered in as much detail as possible.

Eve sat and began to write. Ishamel moved to the far corner and sat in a chair with his eyes closed. He looked as if he was napping, but she suspected he was sending orders to whoever fell under his purview.

She was halfway through her second page when the door opened. The stench of Infernal assaulted her nose and her head snapped up. A uniformed officer entered the room with a bottle of water in his hand. She watched, wide-eyed, as he set it on the table. His mouth curved in a malevolent smile. His detail crawled up from beneath his shirt, coming to rest over his Adam's apple. It was an insignificant design as suited a lessor demon.

"Thought you might like something to drink," the demon said in a friendly voice designed to fool those who might be watching through the glass. Eve got a different show from the front. His lip curled back, revealing the pointed canines of a vampire. "Holler if you'd like anything else. There are plenty of us out there."

Sitting back slowly, she glanced at Ishamel. He hadn't moved, but his eyes were open. The Infernal didn't pay him any mind. Eve didn't know if that was because he was stupid and couldn't pick out a celestial without a Mark's scent, or if he was so cocky he didn't view a *mal'akh* as a threat.

"Thanks," she said aloud. Then, she spoke through her smile. "The bounty's over."

"I ain't heard that," he hissed back. "Lying bitch."

The Infernal departed, but his stench lingered, capping off what had been a brief but crappy day. She set her pen down.

Either the demon was seriously out of the loop, or Sammael had reneged on his end of the deal. She wished she knew which one was true.

"We should go," Ishamel said. His lips moved without sound, *Before too many of his friends arrive.*

I'll finish this later. Eve wrote a quick "to be continued . . ." on the page, then stood.

Ingram was at the door the moment she opened it. "Are you done? Before you leave, I'd like to go over your statement with you."

"No, not done yet," she said, glancing to the left and right, highly conscious of the number of eyes watching her.

It wasn't safe for her to be out anywhere with a price tag stapled to her forehead. Not that she could tell Ingram that. What could be safer than a police station, right?

"We need that report, Ms. Hollis," he said sternly, his mustache twitching in a way that hinted at impatience. "It's vital to our getting a clear picture of what happened."

"I'm sorry. I didn't realize it would take this long." She touched his arm, but pulled back when he tensed. "I borrowed my friend's car—since you have mine— and I have to get it back to him."

"It's only been thirty minutes," he pointed out.

"My client is very busy," Ishamel said smoothly.

"Can you come by the tower for the rest?" Eve asked, regretting that she was taking up the detectives' precious time. They should be working on crimes they could solve, not dicking around with her. "Do I *have* to fill it out here?"

He frowned.

Jones appeared behind him. Shorter and lighter

than his partner, he'd approached stealthily. "I'll give you a call in the morning and set up a time."

"Good. Thanks." Eve shook both their hands quickly. "I'm sorry for the inconvenience."

Ishamel caught her arm and steered her toward the door. "When we get outside the front doors, I'll shift us back to the tower."

"I can't leave another car behind. You'll have to come back and get it."

"I don't drive. Abel will have to do it."

"You *don't*—"

They'd barely put their hands on the handle of the double doors, when they were ambushed. Bold as you please. Shoved outside with hurricane force.

Ishamel sailed into the landscaping on the right side of the door. Eve was sent spinning like a top on the ball of one foot, making a few revolutions before she stumbled to halt.

"Ms. Hollis."

She looked at the door and saw Jones standing on the threshold, holding it open. She brushed flyaway tendrils of hair back from her face. "Yes?"

He looked around her. She did, too, trying to see where Ishamel might have gone. The only evidence of the tackle was some broken branches on one of the bushes and some fine ash that bore witness to the death of an Infernal. The *mal'akh* himself was gone, most likely shifted away to avoid being seen.

"Where did your lawyer go?" the detective asked.

"Bathroom."

Jones frowned, but nodded. "I was wondering. The car you borrowed . . ." He looked beyond her to the parking lot and whistled. "It *is* the Lamborghini."

"Uh . . . yes."

"Mind if I check it out?"

"Uh . . ." Shit. Her gaze darted around the lot again. It looked peaceful enough, but she didn't want to risk the cop, too. Infernals had already proven that they'd take anyone, anywhere, anytime.

The door opened again and Ishamel stepped out, looking none the worse for wear. She breathed a sigh of relief.

Jones was already walking toward Reed's car. Eve rushed to catch up. Ishamel followed at a more discreet pace.

It would be safer to shift, the *mal'akh* said. *But it appears we have no choice.*

She disengaged the car locks and alarm with the remote, and Jones opened the driver's-side door. He glanced over his shoulder at her. "No scissor doors?"

Eve gave a clueless shrug.

The detective stood in the V of the open door and looked at the interior. With the top down, he had an unobstructed view. She glanced at Ishamel, who stood guard on the other side. The feel of Infernal eyes was strong.

If they could just get in the car . . .

"Very nice," Jones said. "How does it drive?"

"Like a dream," she said, with a smile that felt strained. "Detective, I'm sorry. I really do have to run."

"Right." He backed out of the way. "I'll give your office a call tomorrow."

"Great."

Eve hopped into the car and got it started. Ishamel waited until she put the transmission in reverse before climbing in beside her.

Jones stood nearby, watching them with an eagle eye. The detective didn't trust her as far as he could throw her.

Backing out of the spot, she hit the road.

It was hard driving while trying to keep an eye on any possible threats. Eve relaxed slightly when they reached the intersection of Katella and Harbor, feeling somewhat safer in a crowd. The sidewalks were clogged with tourists and business-attired pedestrians leaving the convention center. The excited screams of riders on the various California Adventure amusement park attractions competed with the thumping bass of a nearby car radio. There was a tiny souvenir shop next to the 7-Eleven on the corner; its wares spilling over into its equally tiny parking lot. Customers picked through racks of Disney- and California-themed T-shirts, while a postcard display stand reminded Eve of unfinished business.

"Would you investigate a postcard I received right after I was marked?" she asked, returning her attention to the road. "It came from Gadara Enterprises, so someone there has to be responsible for it."

"What do you want to know?"

The tower was only a short distance away but from the looks of things, Eve was pretty sure Ishamel had already called in reinforcements. There seemed to be an inordinate number of white Chevrolet Suburbans around them.

"Well, for starters," she said, "who sent it. I want to ask them why."

A police car flashed its lights and chirped its sirens until it maneuvered into position directly behind her.

"Jesus," she breathed, wincing at the burn of her mark. "Is he trying to pull me over?"

Ishamel looked over his shoulder. "I sent it."

"*What? Why?*" She eyed the cop through the rearview mirror. The Infernal revved his engine and grinned beneath his shades. The vamp again. Her hands fisted on the wheel.

The Lamborghini was at the light, first one on the line, but in the middle of the multilane road. She was stuck until the signal changed.

"Divine compulsion, perhaps?" Ishamel replied. "I saw the postcard on Raguel's desk and thought it might pique your interest. The building wasn't done and it needed a designer."

"If you're trying to say that it had nothing to do with turning me into a Mark, I don't believe you."

He looked at her, then resumed staring at the squad car behind them. "It had everything to do with the Change. You were agnostic. Appealing to your secular talents was a substitution for appealing to your faith, which is why Raguel scheduled a job interview with you. The postcard was meant to be a follow-up, an added lure. But Raguel was called away and Abel was . . . *impatient*. You were marked before it reached you."

The opposing traffic light changed, turning yellow. Eve prepared to hit the gas. "What about the tengu?"

"I didn't know about the tengu. As I said, perhaps it was a divine compulsion. Not all coincidences are bad, after all."

An eighteen-wheeler barreled west down Katella. As the pedestrian countdown timer began to flash red, the semi's front tires crossed over the line.

The demon revved his engine again. She pretended to run her hand over her chignon to disguise flipping him the bird. He slammed into her, shoving her forward into the middle of the intersection.

The semi hit its horn. Eve saw her reflection in the chrome grill and screamed.

CHAPTER 18

"Look at that car, Adam. There's nothing left of it."
Alec kept his eyes closed and pretended he
was sleeping. His mother's fascination with the news
and daytime drama programming was beyond his understanding. Why couldn't she watch chick flicks or
the action movies Eve favored? Instead, she'd been
surfing through cable news stations since the soap
operas had ended, switching channels whenever a
commercial popped up.

A soft snore from the opposite couch told Alec
that his dad had managed to crash. Alec couldn't, and
not just because his mother insisted he hang out in
the living room with them. His hand kept straying to
his chest, rubbing at the amulet even as his mind
pondered how the thing worked. Good luck charm?
Bullshit. It was designed to repress something, and
he wanted to know what it was. What was in him that
was affected by the amulet, and how did Hank create
the suppressant?

"Those expensive sports cars fall apart when they get hit," his mother continued. "If Abel wasn't a *mal'akh,* I'd make him get rid of that car of his. The one on TV is just like his and look at it now, you can't even tell it used to be car. I can't believe a police office was responsible for such a horrible accident."

Alec opened one eye and glanced at the TV. The reporter stood on the corner, pointing at the vehicle splattered like a bug against the grill of an eighteen-wheeler truck.

". . . there are said to have been several repair requests on file for the police cruiser—a Ford Crown Victoria—involved in this accident. It is not yet known whether the patrol car malfunctioned or if driver error played a part in this tragedy. The name of the officer involved and the identities of the occupants of the Lamborghini convertible have not yet been released."

Alec froze, realizing that the twisted and charred metal on the screen was silver not due to chipped paint, but because silver had been the color of the car.

He bolted upright. *Abel!*

What? his brother snapped in reply.

Leaping out of the recliner, Alec startled his mother into a screech, which in turn caused his dad to roll off the sofa.

Where is your car? he asked carefully.

In the driveway of the tower.

His eyes squeezed shut, along with his throat. *Where is Eve?*

She's at—

The sudden silence was ominous. Broken by a sudden banging on his front door.

"Cain."

Recognizing Ishamel's voice, Alec shifted out to the hallway, pushing the *mal'akh* aside to look left and right. When he didn't see Eve, he set off toward her condo. "Where is she?"

"I don't know."

Alec spun about. "Say that again."

"I had her wrist in my hand before I shifted out of the car." Ishamel's voice had a slight, uncustomary rasp. "But when I reached the tower, she wasn't with me."

Beyond closing his eyes, Raguel hadn't moved since a pair of Infernals had taken the priest out of their cell. He barely had the energy to reopen them when Riesgo was returned. Maintaining the guise of a mortal was draining. Unfortunately, he didn't need his eyesight to see that the priest was badly shaken.

Still, he watched Riesgo retreat to a corner and sit. The priest's arms wrapped around his knees and he curled into a ball. It was alarming to sense such vulnerability in so proud and strong a man. Sammael intended to break them both, and this was a way to accomplish that task with one blow. Raguel was deeply affected by Riesgo's tangible shock and desolation.

"Are you hurt, Padre?" Raguel asked gently, pushing up from his prone position.

There was a drawn-out silence, then, "No."

"You were not gone long."

"Really? It seemed like forever." Riesgo sighed heavily. "I thank God something called him away. I'm not sure I could have borne a moment longer in that place."

"Want to talk about what happened?"

Riesgo set his cheek on his knee. "I'm not sure I know."

Leaning back against the stone wall, Raguel waited patiently. The deeper the silence, the stronger the urge to fill it.

"He wasn't what I expected," the priest said finally. "Satan, I mean."

"He is always what you need him to be. That is his gift."

"He was . . . paternal."

"Because you seek God in this Hell, he tries to fill that role for you. Did he meet with you alone?"

Riesgo stared at him almost blankly. "No. There was some sort of celebration. An orgy. Sex, dancing and . . . other acts that don't bear repeating. There was blood . . . so much . . ."

"He plays the role of an anchor in the storm. A stalwart presence in a world gone mad."

"Like God in the world above, offering peace amid the chaos."

Raguel was impressed by the priest's perceptiveness. "Did that disturb you, Padre? Did it shake your faith as he intended it to?"

"I-I don't know." Riesgo shrugged lamely. "He was reasoned. Quiet. His confidence frightened me more than anything."

"You imagined him to be volatile."

"Yes. Wild and out of control. Someone with a hairtrigger temper. Someone I could see arguing with God enough to get kicked out of Heaven."

"Instead, you found someone cool and calculating. Sammael does not get angry. He gets even."

Riesgo's fingers dug restlessly into his knees. "He had me sit with him on a pallet in the middle of the room. He offered me something to eat and drink. I was so thirsty, but I didn't take anything from him."

"It would not have harmed you if you had," Raguel said, knowing the mortal wouldn't survive long without sustenance. The priest wasn't the only fragile one. After weeks in solitary, Raguel wasn't certain he'd survive the loss of his only companion.

If they could somehow manage to get beyond the void they hovered in, Raguel thought he might be able to get them out. They were in the second level of Hell. He might be able to break into the first, despite his growing weakness, then bargain their way out from that point.

"He had a woman there," Riesgo continued in a whisper. "He told her to m-massage my shoulders."

"A lure, enhanced by powers you cannot expect to resist."

Riesgo stiffened and spoke tightly, "God expects me to resist."

"You did nothing wrong."

"You don't know that!" The priest leaped to his feet. "She changed, while she was touching me. Her appearance . . . *morphed*."

"Did she show you her true face? The rot beneath the glamour?"

"I wish she had." Riesgo ran both hands through his hair and groaned.

The priest's restlessness was so pronounced it penetrated Raguel's weariness and arrested his attention.

"She became Eve," Riesgo bit out. "Evangeline."

Raguel frowned. Then his brows rose as understanding dawned. "It was a cruel trick," he soothed. "It means nothing."

"It means *something*! I was irritated by the woman—until she changed. Then . . ." Riesgo moved to the door and fisted the bars. "Then, my reaction to her changed."

"You are speaking of the Devil himself," Raguel argued, struggling to stand. "He has ways of making you see things that are not there. He can make you believe a lie as if it were gospel. It is no reflection on you or your faith."

"Isn't there a grain of truth in every lie?" Rattling the bars, Riesgo craned his neck to see outside. "I have to get out of here. Now. I have to get out."

Raguel moved carefully over to the priest and touched his shoulder. "You feel drawn to Evangeline because God has a purpose for you in her life. Sammael has twisted that in your mind to circumvent God's will."

"You don't know that." Riesgo looked at Raguel with wild eyes.

A guttural, yet amused voice intruded. "I was going to let you out. But what's the point when you two are so damned loud?"

Turning his head, Raguel found Asmodeus at the door.

Riesgo retreated with a horrified gasp.

Raguel's shoulders went back. He, too, was disgusted by the multiheaded demon, but he would not show it.

Glamourless, Asmodeus was a squat, wide, lumbering monstrosity. A creature both demon and beast.

The king leered with his many mouths and stepped back, gesturing at the cell with a wave of a cloven hand.

The lock bent of its own accord, shrieking as the metal was distorted beyond use. The door fell open.

"Go that way." The king pointed to the left. A cobblestone path appeared, floating over the endless void and seemingly without end. "You'll find a pond a ways down. Swim to the bottom and you'll find a cave. Take that to its end and you'll be back on the surface. The portal won't be open long. You'll have to make a run for it. If you're able."

Raguel hesitated. If Sammael had truly decided to free them, he would do so himself. That way, he could boast of his largesse.

Asmodeus laughed. "Hurry, Raguel. Before the distraction I created runs its course."

"Distraction?" Glancing at Riesgo, Raguel found the priest to be deathly pale but nodding slowly.

"When Satan was called away," Riesgo said. "It seemed urgent."

"That's why they sent you back so soon."

"Yes."

Raguel turned back to Asmodeus, but the king was gone.

"Let's go," he said, gesturing for Riesgo to precede him out.

They didn't look back.

Reed shifted into the hallway outside of Cain's condo. He ignored Ishamel in favor of his brother. "What the hell is going on? Where is my car?"

"*Abel.*"

His mother's voice drew his attention to Cain's open doorway. She stood there wide-eyed, with a trembling mouth. "Is that *your* car on the television? Was Eve in it?"

"My car is on television?" Irritated by the distress everyone was displaying, he brushed past his mother and entered the living room.

He found his father sitting on the couch facing the TV. He turned to look, watching as a camera zoomed in on firemen using the Jaws of Life to pry open what remained of his car.

"Holy shit." He shifted back to the hallway, landing directly in front of Ishamel. "Where. Is. Eve?"

The *mal'akh* met his gaze directly, unresisting yet defiant. "I don't know."

Catching him by the lapels of his gray suit, Reed slammed him into the wall. "Wrong answer."

Cain grabbed him by the shoulder and yanked him around. Ishamel's feet hit the carpet with a thud, but he didn't stumble.

"You are such a monumental fuck-up, Abel. You have one job. *One* fucking job, and you can't get it right."

"Cain . . ." their father warned.

"No, Abba." Cain made a slashing gesture with his hand. "Your precious Abel fucked up, whether you want to hear about it or not. He's supposed to be keeping his charges safe, but in the last two days Eve was ambushed by Azazel and now—"

Cain's voice broke, which nearly broke Reed. Was Eve still in the accordion-like remains of his car? Nothing could survive a collision like that. Nothing.

"*You're* her fucking mentor, asshole," Reed tossed

back, fists clenching at the brutal understanding of his own culpability. He hadn't wanted Rosa in the vicinity, yet he'd allowed Eve free rein because . . . Fuck.

Because she was mad at him and he wanted to pacify her? Because he couldn't read her and took it personally? Because he felt like he was hanging on to her by his fingernails and was afraid to fight with her?

"She was driving *your* car!" Cain bit out.

"I didn't know! I thought she was riding in the limo with Ishamel."

Cain's face took on an ugly, twisted cast. "Betcha left the Lamborghini out front, right? Smack dab in the entryway so everyone would see it. 'Look at my awesome car, which I drive to stroke my massive fucking ego and compensate for my miniscule prick.' "

"Cain!" their mother snapped. "That was completely—"

Reed didn't wait for the rest. He lunged across the space between them, tackling Cain halfway down the hall. They hit the carpet and skid,. grappling. Weeks of frustration, jealousy, and anger poured out through his fists. He didn't feel his brother returning blows. He didn't feel fear at challenging an angel far more powerful than himself. All he felt was good. Really damned good.

Arms and hands intruded too swiftly; his father and Ishamel digging between them to rip them apart. With his wrists restrained behind his back, Reed was pulled off Cain and yanked upright. He continued to kick with his legs—once while his brother was still on the floor and again as Cain managed to regain his footing.

"Enough!" their mother shouted, slapping Reed in the face, then Cain. "Why can't you work together for once? Is your feud more powerful than your feelings for Evangel—"

The sudden halting of her tirade arrested everyone in the hallway.

She moved closer to Cain, her fingers finding and lifting the necklace that had fallen out of his shirt. "W-where did you get this?"

Cain looked down at her hand, his irises still flickering with the lingering rage of angels. "Eve gave it to me."

Reed's teeth ground together. Eve had given a gift to his brother?

Doors opened along the hallway and residents poked their heads out. Sydney, too, appeared from Eve's condo.

"What's going on out there?" one woman asked crossly. "I'm calling the police."

"That won't be necessary." Ishamel released Reed and moved away to address the concerns of the onlookers. Sydney joined him in working damage control.

"Where did Evangeline get it?" their mother persisted, sounding formidable despite her petite stature.

"An Infernal in the firm made it," Cain answered.

Their father stood still and watchful. "No, he didn't."

Tugging at it, she said, "Give it to me."

Cain's head tilted. His gaze narrowed. "I can't. I promised Eve I wouldn't take it off."

"She could be dead!" she snapped, chilling Reed with her callousness. "Give it to me."

Then she gasped and covered her mouth as her

careless words registered. "I'm s-sorry. I didn't mean that."

"What is this, Ima?" Cain asked with dangerous softness, watching her like the predator he was. "What does it do?"

"It doesn't *do* anything."

"How do you know?"

Adam stepped forward and caught her wrist. "Leave it."

"I can't just—"

"Leave it," their father repeated harshly. He pulled her back down the hall to Cain's condo.

Reed turned his attention back to his brother. "What the fuck is going on around here? Where's Eve?"

"Missing." Cain shoved the necklace back inside his T-shirt, then pointed an accusing finger. "Find her. If she was in your car . . ." His throat worked. "Just find her."

Agreeing that Eve came first and killing his brother could come later, Reed shifted to the men's restroom of the 7-Eleven on the corner of Katella and Harbor. As he exited to the street, he saw the crowds and heard the sickening grind of metal being ripped apart. His gut knotted.

Eve.

"You are not wearing the chain I gave you," Satan said smoothly, snapping his fingers and conjuring a throne in the center of the yellow desert. He sank into the seat and stretched out his long legs. His crimson wings were tucked away, leaving behind a frighteningly normal vision of a breathtakingly handsome

man. What was worse was his resemblance to Cain.
And Abel.

Eve would really like to hear the explanation for
that one.

"We really have to stop meeting like this," she
muttered, tugging one of her heels out of a crack in
the hardened ground.

"I just saved your life."

"I'm sure Ishamel would have done the same, if
you hadn't beaten him to it. And by the way, I have to
point out that my life isn't supposed to be in danger.
You agreed to call off the bounty."

As if wounded, he set an elegant hand over his
heart. "I did."

"The vamp that rammed me into traffic didn't
seem to know that!"

"Sometimes it can take awhile for word to spread.
However, you are none the worse for wear."

"The car I was driving can't say the same."

There was something off about the nonchalance
the Devil displayed. If he'd done as he said—and she
believed he spoke at least in half-truths—then he'd
been openly defied. It was hard to believe he would
take such an offense so easily.

"Where is the necklace, Evangeline?"

The way he used her full name gave him a pater-
nalistic air that chilled her blood as surely as his
touch did. She wished that she'd gone to the ladies'
room at the police station. "Somewhere safe."

"Hmm." His head cocked to one side, allowing a
curtain of silky black hair to fall over his shoulder.
"What do you consider *safe,* I wonder? Your parents'?"

"As if I would drag them into this. It's not a big deal, okay? It's fine."

"Maybe I want it back, if it is of no use to you."

"You can have it back once I kill the Nix. That was the deal." Eve had no idea how she sounded so calm and in control when she was far from either, but she was grateful. "Now, why did you bring me here? It's only been one day since we made our little arrangement. You'll have to give me more time."

"Abel?" he persisted. "Sarakiel? Cain?"

Her brow arched, but her fingers were digging into her biceps through her silk shirt. "What. Do. You. *Want*?"

"Perhaps you asked Eve to watch it for you?" he purred.

"No."

One second he was in the chair; the next he was directly in front of her. He gripped her head in his hands, his palms pressing into her temples. He tipped her head back. Looking into her eyes, he held her captive with his icy touch and his burning stare. She couldn't blink, couldn't back away.

His mouth moved, as if he was speaking, but all she could hear was her own blood rushing through her brain at a breakneck pace. Then she realized it was *him* in her mind, sliding in and around everything. Touching Alec. Then Reed. Through her. As if he *was* her.

A smile curved his mouth. His head lowered to hers. Slow. Impossibly slow. When his lips touched hers, she whimpered but couldn't pull away. The kiss he gave her was Alec's. The touch, taste, and texture. The possession and passion; the love and the lust. It was a deep, lush melding of their mouths and she found herself participating with ardor. Tears leaked out of the corners of her eyes and dried in the arid breeze, but whether they were happy or sad tears, she couldn't say.

He groaned softly and pulled away. "You kiss like a woman in love," he murmured, his thumb brushing across her bottom lip in the way Alec's did. "Thank you."

Eve blinked up at him, dazed.

Satan released her and walked away. "That will have to tide me over, I suppose, since you have completed the task I set for myself. Indirectly, of course, and in doing so you have denied me a pleasure I anticipated with relish. But I will consider your part of our agreement met. Regardless of the fact that I was not the messenger, the message was still delivered. You are free."

"Huh?" She kicked herself mentally. If he said she was done, great. Even if it didn't make a damn bit of sense. "What about Riesgo and Raguel? Are they free, too?"

"According to your memories, someone has already made arrangements for their *escape.*" He walked back to his throne. "I cannot release that which I no longer possess."

Settling into the seat, Satan smiled at her. "You will just have to hope that one of those other bargains is successful."

"That's not fair!"

"Why? Because now you have to decide who to save and who to sacrifice? Maybe you will decide to do nothing at all and leave the matter in the hands of Jehovah. I am curious to see which way you lean."

He snapped his fingers.

Eve found herself in the living room of her condo, directly between the television and Montevista. The Mark was sleeping on her couch.

Kicking off her heels, she sat next to him and set her hand on his shoulder. He was cold to the touch, and it took a couple hard shakes to bring him back to the land of the living.

"Hey," he murmured huskily, scrubbing a hand over his face.

"How are you feeling?"

"Like I should have shut the sliding glass door before napping. It's starting to get cold at night." He moved to sit up. "How'd it go?"

"To shit." She slid over to the coffee table. "I'm going to need your help."

"Tell me what you want me to do."

CHAPTER 19

I n search of privacy, Eve took the elevator down to the marble-lined foyer of her condominium complex.

Alec.

She'd barely managed the silent summons before he was in front of her, gripping her by the arms and giving her a not-so-gentle shake.

"Where have you been?" he demanded, before crushing her face into his cotton-covered chest.

She mumbled into his pecs. He fisted her chignon and pulled her head back.

"Not funny." But there was a hint of amusement in his eyes. "You scared the shit out of me."

"Does Abel know?"

"All of Orange County knows. It's on the news."

"Man . . ."

Eve sent a silent apology to Reed. He appeared as swiftly as Alec had, his gaze just as haunted. Poor guys, they'd been worried sick about her. She loved them for that.

Despite Alec's rumbling protest, she pushed away from him, putting equal distance between the three of them so that they formed a V-shaped formation. Through the glass door behind Alec, she could see the nut-job reverend singing on the corner.

She turned her attention back to the two brothers. "We're racing against the clock here."

Both men's brows rose.

Eve pointed at Alec. "You need to figure out what's going to happen to you when Gadara comes back. I'm guessing you have less than twenty-four hours."

His arms crossed. "What have you done?"

She pointed at Reed. "And your secret plan is fucked in so many ways, not the least of which is that it's not a secret anymore. Satan knows about it."

Reed scowled. "I don't know what you're—"

"Yes, you do." She looked back at Alec. "What are you still doing here?"

"Well, *bossy,* I'm waiting for my parents to finish packing so I can escort them back home. After I do that, I'll follow your orders."

Eve's head tilted in concern. "But they just got here."

"Cain caused another fight," Reed said.

"*I* didn't," Alec corrected with a fulminating glare. He pulled the necklace out of his shirt. "*This* did."

Reed nodded. "Ima took one look and lost it."

"Lost what?" Eve asked.

"Her temper. Her mind. Everything."

"Did she say why it bothered her so much?"

"Nope." Alec eyed her suspiciously. "But she did say that Hank didn't make it."

"Actually, Abba said that," Reed amended, eyeing her with the same expression.

"No one said Hank made it," she corrected.

"Where did you get this, angel?"

Eve knew that silky tone all too well. Alec always used it right before she got into trouble. "Would you believe a Cracker Jack box?"

"This is serious, babe," Reed murmured.

What could she say? She didn't want to start shit between Alec and his parents. If their mom hadn't told them about Sammael and the necklace after all these years, Eve wasn't going to be the one to do it.

Something in the periphery of her vision caught her eye. She turned her head to find Evil Santa at the bottom of the steps leading to the locked door of the foyer. He was giving her the death stare from the sidewalk, singing loudly and off-key to the strumming of his guitar. The light of the street lamp circled him in a yellow glow that only made him creepier.

"Can one of you *please* do something about that guy?" she groused.

Alec and Reed looked over their shoulder.

"Do what?" Alec asked.

"I don't know. Take him around the corner and flash your wings. Send him on a mission for God, or at the very least tell him I'm one of the good guys."

Alec gestured toward the door with a flourish. "That's all you, bro."

"Fuck you," Reed shot back. "You do it."

"Somehow, I don't think my black wings will go over well with that guy."

Reed glared at his brother, than glanced at Eve.

You owe me, she reminded, *for bargaining me for Gadara.*

Babe . . . He sounded frustrated. *Do you trust me?*

She did or else she'd have decked him by now and told one of the archangels what he was up to. Still, she wasn't willing to give an inch at this point. As far as she was concerned, he was due for some serious groveling.

Eve set one hand on her hip. *You're kidding right? You're asking me that after you offered me up on a silver platter to a king of Hell?*

Yes, damn you, I am. You owe me, too. You wrecked my car.

Whatever. There's no comparison.

He shot her the dark look that she thought was hot; the one where he looked hard and dangerous, primitive despite the urbanity of his clothing. *You have no idea what I've been through waiting for the fire department to cut open my car . . . waiting to see what they'd find in there.*

She softened. *I'm sorry.*

Then she noticed how rumpled he was. A quick glance at Alec revealed that his T-shirt was stretched in places.

Sighing inwardly, she waved Reed toward the door. *Take care of wacko out there and I'll get back to you about the trust issue.*

He went, but with a clearly aggravated stride.

When she was alone with Alec, she said, "We need answers. Go to the source if you have to, just find them."

He leaned into one of the metal mailboxes built into the wall. "You sound as if you know for a fact that Raguel will be back."

"Maybe I do."

"You need to talk to me, angel."

"I can't. You're connected to everyone in the firm in an unpredictable way. We can't risk a leak like that. You'll just have to hang on for the ride."

He exhaled harshly. "I've been doing that since I met you."

"It's not so bad, is it?"

"Can you at least tell me *why* you have this necklace?"

"To kill the Nix. It, uh, apparently suppresses Infernal tendencies."

Alec grew very still.

"Yes," she answered his silent question. "Something is in you that shouldn't be. But I think you knew that already."

"I didn't know it was Infernal. I thought it was just . . . me." He reached out and caught her hand, his fingers playing with hers. "Angel. I have to tell you something."

"No, you don't."

"Yeah, I do."

"No, really." She squeezed his hand. "I know about Izzie. I know that wasn't you."

He looked shell-shocked, then relieved. His entire frame visibly deflated from the release of tension. "I don't deserve you, you know? I never have."

"Well." The toe of her shoe followed a grout line in the marble. "I have something to tell you, too."

"No, you don't."

"Yeah, I do."

"I don't want to hear it. And when I saw the name of Sarakiel's e-mail attachment, I didn't want to see it either. So I deleted it."

Her shoulders went back. "Because you feel guilty

over something you're not responsible for. You think this makes us even, but it doesn't, Alec. I knew damn well what I was doing; you didn't."

"I don't care," he said stubbornly.

She laid it all out there. "I would do it again; you wouldn't."

"I'm not going to give you a reason to do it again." Alec straightened. "Let's go check on my parents and see if they're ready to go. I need to hit the road."

"Fine." There was no point in talking to him about it now. He wasn't listening. She'd revisit the subject later. She had to. Everything was different. Ignoring those differences wasn't going to help any of them. "But I'll need you back here before noon. You and that necklace. Got it?"

"Got it." Alec shifted them up to his apartment.

His mother sat on the black leather couch in the living room. His father was apparently in one of the back bedrooms. When Eve jerked her chin down the hall, Alec took the hint and joined his dad, leaving her alone with his mom.

Ima looked up at her with reddened eyes and nose. She looked years older than she had the night before, with deep grooves around her pretty mouth and slumped shoulders. Eve took a seat beside her and offered her a commiserating smile.

Setting a hand on Eve's knee, Ima asked in a whisper, "How did you get the necklace?"

"Satan lent it to me."

"Why?"

"It wards off Infernals."

"Does it?" Ima looked away. Her tone grew distant. "I didn't know. It didn't do that for me."

Eve looked down the hall, making sure that Alec was still occupied with helping his father. Then she leaned in and queried softly, "It's yours, isn't it?"

Nodding, Ima explained, "When I married Adam, Jehovah gave it to me, along with twenty-three other pieces of jewelry."

Was the piece around Alec's neck the only one that was charmed? Perhaps they all had a unique gift. "How did Satan get his hands on it?"

"I gave it to him. In a way, it's fitting that you would give it to Cain."

A sentimental gesture. A gift of some meaning, apparently. *A message delivered,* as Satan had said.

"You shouldn't say any more," Eve murmured. "Cain shares my thoughts and memories. Whatever I know, he eventually finds out about."

"Ah, I see." Ima gave her knee a gentle squeeze. "Thank you for the warning."

"Will you be okay?"

"Adam and I have been together forever. That's not going to change now."

"I hope I see you again. A longer visit, perhaps."

"I would like that."

Ima hugged her. A few moments later, Adam did the same, albeit with some awkwardness. Then Alec shifted away with them. The parting was bittersweet for Eve. She'd spent only enough time with them to learn that she wanted to spend more.

Knowing there was much to be done before the morning dawned, Eve returned to her condo. Sydney was cooking chili in the kitchen, Reed was on the phone with his insurance company, and Montevista was in the shower. Once again, Eve kicked off her heels, hoping it would be for the last time tonight. She was beat. She pushed them under the console table by the front door and padded down the hallway to her office.

Ishamel was there, sitting at her desk and staring intently at the computer monitor. He leaned back when she entered and sighed. That sound softened him in her eyes, as did the sight of him sans jacket and waistcoat.

"Hi," she said.

"How are you?"

She hummed a noncommittal sound. "I've been better."

"I found what I think you were looking for."

"Oh?"

The *mal'akh* gestured at her monitor. She rounded the desk to see what he was referring to.

Frozen on the screen was a grainy image of Sarakiel in sunglasses, sitting at a picnic table in what looked to be a public park. Across from her sat another blonde woman and a large dark-haired man.

Eve asked, "What am I looking at?"

"Sarakiel." Ishamel pointed at the familiar figure. "This is Asmodeus. And this is Lilith."

Eve's mouth formed an O. She leaned in closer. Unfortunately, not much was distinguishable aside from body type and hair color. She couldn't get a good idea of what Adam's first wife looked like, much to her disappointment. "That can't be good. How did you get this?"

"Raguel is gone. Two archangels are on his turf. I thought it'd be wise to keep a close eye on things in his absence."

She straightened. "You rock."

"Now it's your turn," he said. "Tell me what this means."

Moving over to the futon, Eve sat with her legs tucked beneath her and explained what Mariel had told her.

She finished with, "Trading a handler would knock twenty-one Marks off their game, but only temporarily. I can't see that being worth trading Gadara for. Unless the handler was Abel."

"That ups the ante considerably," Ishamel agreed.

"Exactly. And leave it to a demon to tell Abel to his face that he was being traded."

"How did you narrow the culprit down to Sarakiel?"

Eve shrugged. "It's a woman thing, I guess. We can be vindictive when slighted."

"You're taking a risk telling me this," he pointed out. "You are all expendable to me, if that's what it takes to get Raguel back."

"Right."

"So you must have a plan."

"I guess you could call it that." She smiled. "Clusterfuck also works."

Ishamel nodded. "Count me in. What do you need from me?"

"An odd location for a meet, Cain," Sabrael murmured. "The most popular place to commit suicide in the United States. Is this a message of some sort?"

"Nothing so morbid." Alec blinked and engaged thick tears, protecting his eyes from the seraph's brilliance. "Eve pointed it out while watching a television show about witches."

"Far from morbid," the seraph said wryly, "I think that qualifies as romantic."

The view from the top of a Golden Gate Bridge tower was unrivaled. The waters of San Francisco Bay shimmered with the city lights and the sea breeze was cold, damp, and brisk. It kept Alec's head clear, which he appreciated.

Sabrael took a seat beside him, his powerful legs dangling over the edge. "Are you enjoying your ascension?"

"For the most part."

"Am I here to be thanked?"

Alec's mouth curved. "I have a few questions, if you don't mind."

"Hmm."

"What would happen to me if Raguel came back?"

"Ah . . . Excellent question." Sabrael turned his flame-blue gaze on Alec. "I was not expecting something so thoughtful."

"Glad I could surprise you."

"What do you think will happen?"

"I don't know. Will I die?"

Sabrael laughed. It was a gorgeous, heavenly sound. Unique to the seraphim. "My dear Cain. I doubt Jehovah could afford to lose a Mark of your talents. You are irreplaceable, I would say."

"Good to know."

"However, you would lose the North American firm and all that comes with it."

"Everything, then," Alec clarified. "Would I return to the way I was before? Would I at least be restored to a full *mal'akh*?"

"You misunderstand me. I would see to it that you retained your archangel gifts, despite the lack of responsibilities that usually accompany them." The seraph's voice took on a biting edge. "Do not forget that you owe me, Cain. No matter what task I decide upon, having you as an archangel is of greater benefit to me."

"I've never failed you, and that was while I had no gifts beyond those of an average Mark."

"What are you saying? Have you decided that the life of an archangel is not to your liking?"

"I haven't gotten that far yet. But my goal was to head a firm, not acquire more gifts. Without the one, I have no need for the other."

"*I* have need of it, and I will not give it up simply because you miss your Evangeline."

"She isn't gone." Alec's fingers curled around the red-painted ironwork. Despite the chilly temperature and the soothing necklace, his skin was growing as hot as his rising temper. "If I can get my shit together, her and I will be okay."

"You have come to the wrong place to ask for sympathy." The seraph's tone lacked all inflection. "She weakens you, and Abel. She is a mediocre Mark, barely sufficient in the practical applications, and prone to blasphemy and irreverence. You are a fool if you think I will sacrifice *you*—the greatest killing machine ever created—for *her*."

Alec's grip tightened to the point of pain.

I won't invest in a relationship with someone who can't love me, she'd said, and he knew it was true.

Which made Abel a greater threat now than ever before. He'd become the go-to guy when she couldn't turn to Alec.

Sabrael levitated until his feet were once again

level with the top of the tower. "You will remain an archangel until I decide you are no longer useful in that capacity. I find that possibility very slim indeed."

The seraph left.

Alec lingered, hoping that time would present the solution he searched for.

Once Sydney and Montevista were settled for the night—Sydney in the guest room and Montevista on the couch in the living room—Eve had Ishamel shift with her to the subterranean floors of the tower. Together they knocked on Hank's door.

"It's late," Eve said. "Are you sure he's still here?"

"He lives here." Ishamel set a hand at the small of her back and urged her through the opening door.

"Welcome back," Hank said, appearing out of the darkness. "You've had an interesting afternoon since you left me."

"You could call it that," she agreed dryly.

He must have noted Eve's velour jogging suit and Ishamel's casual state, because he changed from dress slacks and shirt to a black sweat suit that reminded Eve of Riesgo's, although the priest was considerably more muscular.

Her resolve strengthened further. A lot of people were depending on her to not screw everything up. "I have a couple of questions for you."

"Let's sit." Hank led the way to the now-familiar rough-hewn table. Immediately afterward, Fred approached in a tight patent leather and metal bodysuit. Her face was heavily made-up and her long white hair was teased big. She set a tray down bearing a pitcher of Hank's favored iced tea and three glasses, then sashayed away, revealing a horsetail-thing swaying from the rear of her outfit.

Eve stared. Ishamel looked away.

"Hot damn, Fred," Eve called after her.

Hank gave an elegant shrug. "Note that the tengu is quiet. Seems he's become enamored with Fred. The dominatrix guise keeps him distracted."

Since Eve herself had been rendered speechless for a moment, she could see how well the getup worked. She returned her attention to Hank. "Do you have something or some way to keep Infernals from disintegrating when killed?"

One red brow rose. "Why?"

"I need a body."

"The masking agent seems to preserve bodies."

"It also restores them." She shook her head. "I don't need any more recurring kills. I want the vanquished to stay dead, but I need some remains. At least until cremation."

"Hmm. The necklace might do the trick."

Eve sat back. "You think?"

"It's a possibility."

"Okay, next question. What happens to mortals who see things they shouldn't?"

Hank's fingertips rubbed back and forth along a deep groove in the table. "Depends on how credible the witness is and what proof they have, if any. It's impossible to say until it happens. You'll have to take your chances."

Ishamel picked up a glass and swallowed tea in great big gulps. When he finished, he wiped his mouth with the back of his hand and asked, "It just so happens that I might have a use for a Nix attractant. You wouldn't happen to have one, would you?"

"Why, yes." Hank smiled wide. "I have one. Glad you can use it, since our firm leader ordered me not to give it to Evangeline."

Fred reappeared with a lovely green glass atomizer bottle, which she set down in front of Ishamel. Eve studied the lili while she was close, looking beneath the cosmetics to the delicate features beneath. Eve wondered how closely Fred resembled her mother. She was a very pretty girl, with a delicate deportment that effectively hid the nature of the beast within.

"Thank you," Ishamel said.

Eve's lips pursed.

"What troubles you?" Hank asked.

"Would Lilith have a reason for wanting to get her hands on Abel?"

Ishamel stared hard at her. "You assume she is interested in him. Why not assume her motivation is the resulting gain? I see him as a means to an end."

"Perhaps it's *you* she wants," Hank suggested, catching up on the conversation by reading Eve's thoughts. "Perhaps she views you as a surrogate Eve, beloved wife of Adam. She hates both of them with a passion."

"Let's skip that avenue for now," Eve said. "It's a dead end. Lilith would either kill me or torture me. Either way, end of story. But if she had Abel, what would she do with him? Keep him or trade him, right? If she kept him, why? And if she traded him, what would she trade him for? What does Satan have that she might want?"

Ishamel laughed, a rusty unused sound. "Lilith wants everything. And she's had pretty much everything in Hell in her bed at some point or another. The earth is a playground to her."

Eve looked at Hank, who tossed up his hands in a clueless gesture. "Ishamel's right. Lilith wants everything."

"My mother," Fred said, lingering at the edge of the circle of light that hung over the table, "is motivated by boredom. She does things for odd reasons and oftentimes for no reason at all. I gave up trying to figure her out."

"All right." Eve stood and yawned. "Thank you both for your help."

Ishamel stood along with her. Hank remained seated.

"You're determined to jump the gun and set this off tomorrow?" the occultist asked.

"I'm just setting the stage." Her smile was grim. "Whether the show starts or not . . . We'll have to wait and see."

"Don't get yourself killed. I want to see you again."

Eve gave him a mock salute.

"Good luck," Fred said.

"Thanks. We're going to need it."

CHAPTER 20

It was a little past seven in the morning when Eve left her bedroom and moved down the hallway to the living room. She checked on Montevista, usually the first one awake while on watch, but presently the last one still sleeping. Sydney sat at the kitchen island in a pale blue bathrobe and red slippers reading the newspaper report of the Lamborghini wreck.

"Coffee?" Eve asked, as she opened the freezer to grab the beans.

"Sure." The Mark smiled. "I love how normal you are."

Eve snorted. "This is normal? Shoot me now."

Sydney abandoned the newspaper. "When I was first marked, I didn't know how to take it. It seemed like such a huge responsibility to be a warrior for God. And everything was so different. I used to love coffee. I drank it all day. But I gave it up, thinking there was no point anymore since I couldn't feel the buzz from the caffeine. Because I changed so many things about my life, I felt like a stranger in my own skin for a long time."

Knowing that feeling all too well, Eve nodded. "Look on the bright side, that dedication makes you a much better Mark than I am. I want to be you when I grow up."

Sydney slid off the stool and moved to the cupboard. She grabbed three mugs. "I'm hoping to be more like you."

"Bad with a sword and accident prone?"

"Shut up. Killing things is just *part* of the job, not *all* of it. I actually think your agnosticism gives you an advantage. You don't take anything at face value, so you see things the rest of us don't. Since I met you, I've been trying to reconnect with the things that used to define me. I bought bookshelves last weekend and an outrageously expensive coffee station the week before that. Sounds like nothing, I know—"

"No, I get it. You're building a future instead of living day to day. And you're letting yourself have fun with your life. Good for you."

"Thanks." Sydney set the mugs on the counter. "I'm much happier now that you've rubbed off on me."

Eve bumped shoulders with her. "Here's to hoping some of your kick-ass qualities rub off on *me*."

There was a beat of silence as Eve poured the beans into the grinder, then Sydney whispered, "I guess the new me is more attractive, too. I've been working with Diego a long time and he's never paid any attention to me as a woman. In fact, he once said I wasn't his type."

"I'd say that's changed."

"You noticed it, too?" Sydney's eyes had a sparkle

that warmed Eve's heart. She liked both Marks, and wanted them to be happy.

"Totally. He's got it bad." Eve decided it was as good a time as any to broach a sensitive topic. "Hey, do me a favor. Keep an especially close eye on him. I think he's too proud to admit that he's not up to full speed yet."

"Already on it."

"Of course you would be. You rock."

Pressing on the lid of the grinder, Eve turned the beans into fresh grounds. When she let go and the racket died down, Montevista was clearly heard stirring on the couch.

"Time to get up, sleepyhead," Sydney called out, moving toward the living room. "We have to clear the residents out of the building."

Eve turned the coffeepot on and washed her hands. Part of the plan she'd passed on to Montevista included informing all the condo residents of a suspected (and fictitious) gas leak. The Marks who'd been running guard duty around the perimeter were gearing up to pose as local utility inspectors and firemen. In order to keep the complaints down, Ishamel had arranged for Gadara Enterprises to foot the bill for a local hotel stay and two-hour gondola rides. The last thing any of them wanted was to catch some mortals in the crosshairs. Better to be safe than sorry.

Moving to her office, Eve sent an e-mail to her secretary, telling Candace that she wouldn't be coming in today. She would wait another hour, then call the detectives and let them know. With her schedule set, she leaned back in her chair and stared up at the ceiling.

What would Gadara be like when he returned? He'd been gone so long . . . And Riesgo. How would he be? Her heart ached for the both of them and what they must have endured.

"So . . ."

Eve lifted her head and discovered Reed in the doorway. "Hi."

"I'm still trying to decide how I should feel about sleeping alone last night."

"We don't live together."

He entered and took a seat on the futon. His shirt was a deep red, perfectly pressed and left open at the throat. Paired with black slacks and his dark hair, it was edgy in a way that made her toes curl.

"So Cain calms down a bit," he said tightly, "and you throw me over, is that it?"

"No. That's not it."

"Am I your dirty little secret now, babe?" His dark eyes were hard and cold. "Are you going to pretend that we didn't happen?"

"I'm going to pretend that you're not insulting me now. I'm going to convince myself that it's because you like me so much that you're being an asshole."

"Are you going to tell Cain about us?"

"I already did. Well, I tried to," she amended. "He didn't want to hear it, but he knows."

Reed's entire mien changed, softening to the point that it made her breath catch. He was as vulnerable in that moment as he'd been with her in bed. It was somehow more intimate with them both fully clothed and a room's length away from each other.

"Is it over between you?" he asked.

"Honestly?" She rubbed her palms over the arms

of her chair. "I don't think it'll ever be over. I'm in love with him. I've been in love with him forever."

Nodding slowly, Reed's gaze remained on her but it was distant. Unfocused.

"Thing is," she continued, "I'm pretty sure that I'm halfway in love with you, too."

He stiffened, now tensely alert. "Go on."

"I have no idea how that's even possible, but there it is. I know you're not good for me. You're needy and self-centered—"

"Eve . . ."

"—but I crave you like chocolate."

"And what do you think Cain is?" he snapped. "Healthy for you? Gimme a fucking break."

"He's *healthier*, but I have a sweet tooth. That doesn't mean you're my guilty pleasure, so don't take it that way."

"You don't know what you're doing."

"I know I can't have both of you. And I can't choose between you. I guess that leaves me with having neither of you."

"Fuck that," he retorted without heat. "I've got you right where I want you now."

"Is that so?" Eve tried to hold back a smile, but felt her lips twitching anyway.

"Oh, yeah." Standing, Reed came toward her. He leaned over her and pressed his lips to her forehead. "Thank you."

"For what?"

He retreated enough to meet her gaze. "For everything, really. Most especially for not castrating me for offering to send you to Hell. You say you don't trust me, but you couldn't prove more clearly that you do."

"What's your plan anyway? Get everyone here to-morrow, then what? The way I understand it, you'd have to go into the trade assuming they let Riesgo and Gadara escape. You know better than to trust a demon."

Reed's mouth curved in a slow, smug smile. "Ah, but they don't know better than to trust me. That's the beauty of it. Asmodeus is worth a lot to Sammael. He's one of only seven kings in Hell. Once Asmodeus makes sure you and Cain are here on the premises, he won't be able to resist trying to nab you. He can only see things from his perspective, and to him it must be a potent temptation to get rid of Cain. It won't even enter his head to think I'll double-cross him and take him prisoner instead."

"And if things go to shit, then what?"

"Cain would be with you to protect you. For all his fuck-ups, I'm sure that when push comes to shove, he's got your back. And I'm confident that Sammael won't kill him."

"That is *not* what you were thinking when you offered him."

Reed winked. "Prove it."

"Well, if Sarakiel has her way, you'll be there to protect me, too."

He straightened abruptly. "Sara?"

Eve explained about the tape of Sarakiel's meeting with Asmodeus. "My guess is, Asmodeus is gambling that he can take all three of us at once. With Sara's help, why not?"

"One day, you're telling me you think she loves me. The next, you say she wants me burning in Hell."

"It's because she loves you that she wants you to burn in Hell."

Snorting, he said, "That's female logic if I ever heard it."

"What can I say? We're twisted."

"Don't lump yourself in with Sara." He licked the tip of her nose. "I'm going to deal with her today. Right now, actually."

"Then I need you to round up Asmodeus."

His gaze narrowed. "Tomorrow. I need time to get things together."

"I've already got things together. Ishamel helped. You know how thorough he is."

"Do you have any idea of what kind of manpower we're going to need to nab Asmodeus?"

"We're not going to nab him. We just want him here."

Reed sank to a crouch in front of her, leveling their gazes. "Spit it out. All of it."

"You're right, Asmodeus is valuable to Satan, but not for the reason you think. Satan knows your plan. He tried to act nonchalant about it, but I read between the lines. He's pissed, and he's going to take Asmodeus down."

"Good. Let him."

"Sure," Eve agreed. She opened her mind to him, allowing him to see her conversations with the Devil. "But not now. You've been bargaining with Asmodeus but really, the deal is between me and Satan."

"Babe . . ." He made an exasperated sound and dropped his head into her lap. "You're a walking disaster," he mumbled.

"Listen." She lifted his head with her hands. "He promised me something, then reneged."

"And that's a surprise to you? Come on, Eve—"

"He wouldn't renege with me, Reed," she insisted. "For whatever reason, he wants me to trust him. He's going to fulfill his end of our agreement."

"That's not what he said to you!"

"What he said was that I'll have to let the moves you and Sara made play out."

"What he said," he retorted, "was that he can't release what he doesn't possess. A melodramatic way to say he got what he wanted, and you're on your own."

"Or it's a roundabout way of saying someone stole from him." Eve shot him a wry glance. "Do you really think he's just going to let that go?"

"He doesn't need *you* to put Asmodeus in line."

"Right. He just needs to fulfill his end of the bargain. He gave me two choices—help you or Sara with your plans, or leave the whole thing in the hands of God. But—" she wagged a finger at him "—he knows I'm not a believer. He made a big deal out of my agnosticism being one of the reasons he likes me. He appreciates my cynicism."

"He's always trying to lure Marks to the dark side. He doesn't *like* you. He doesn't give a shit about you, other than the fact that fucking with you fucks with a lot of other people, too."

She pressed on. "I think his question was incomplete. I think what he was really saying is, 'Will you leave it in the hands of God . . . or *me*.' That was the basis of our previous conversations. He says God isn't going to give me what I need, but *he* will. This is his chance to prove it. I think he's going to take it, if only because he wants to knock Asmodeus down a notch in a major way."

He gripped her hands painfully tight. "You know . . . Marks spend their entire careers hoping they never meet Sammael. But not you. No, you lack the self-preservation gene."

She could feel his fear for her in the connection between them. She was freaked out, too, but things were getting out of hand—Gadara, the priest, Cain, the Nix, and Satan running around as he pleased. It was time to set the world to rights.

Eve squeezed his fingers. "Hank told me Satan's using an emissary to be able to meet with me face-to-face. We need to know who it is. I have a theory, and this is the way to prove it."

"What theory?"

"It's too dangerous to share until I know for sure."

Reed's jaw tensed. "It's Cain, isn't it?"

"Just trust me, okay. You get Asmodeus to show up, and we'll see if the emissary passes the news onto Satan so that *he* can show up."

"You're not going to rest until I'm insane, right?" Tilting his head, Reed pressed his lips to hers. The kiss started out short and sweet, but swiftly heated. When he straightened, she made a small sound of protest.

"You owe me," he said. "Dinner. Hot dress. No underwear. High heels."

"You're a pig."

"Can't help it. I think I'm in love. Why else would I agree to this shit?"

He shifted away before she could reply. She sat

there for a moment, considering. Another tall, dark figure filled the doorway to her office.

Alec came in with a mug of hot coffee and set it on her desk. From the café au lait appearance, she knew he'd fixed it perfectly. From the look on his face, she knew he'd heard Reed's declaration.

"Good morning," he said.

"To you, too." She lifted the mug. "Thank you."

"Anytime." He managed a ghost of a smile. "I thought I'd come over early. Get the day started."

"You're always welcome here."

He moved to the futon. "I followed your orders. Looks like I'm too valuable to kill."

"I could have told you that." She smiled against the rim of her cup.

"But I would lose the firm."

Eve swallowed a mouthful of perfectly creamed coffee, then set her mug down. "I'm sorry. I know how much you wanted it."

Alec sat back and crossed his arms. "I want you, too. Can't have both, so something's got to give."

She knew what that was like.

He sat with widespread legs, his booted feet resting flat on the carpeted floor. His jeans were worn in all the right places and the arms of his T-shirt stretched around gorgeous biceps. He hadn't aged a day in the ten years since she'd first seen him.

"You're not upset?" She studied him for hints of underlying disappointment or frustration.

"You know I'm not doing well with it," he said gruffly. "I have to be collared like a dog to get a grip on myself."

"Did you talk about that to whoever you went to see last night?"

Alec shook his head.

"Why not?"

"I thought he might change his mind and decide to knock me out of commission after all."

Eve stood and moved to sit beside him. She set her hand on his thigh. "What is it with men not wanting to ask for help?"

"I've been asking for years, angel. No one's talking." His foot tapped restlessly atop the carpet. "For a long time there's been speculation that my mother was unfaithful and the result was me."

"Do you believe that?"

He glanced aside at her. "You won't tell me about the necklace, and I couldn't get anything out of my parents either. It's never good when you can't get answers. If there was nothing to worry about, there'd be nothing to hide."

"Alec." She squeezed his leg, which was like stone beneath her hand. "What are you thinking?"

"You said this necklace suppresses Infernal traits, and the ugliness inside me shuts up when I wear it. What does that tell you?"

"That you think you're half-demon?"

"It's not like my mom had a lot of choice in men back then," he said dryly. He leaned into her. "Maybe the ascension triggered some repressed asshole genetics. What if they can't be locked up again? Like Pandora's Box or something. I'd be too great a threat to keep around."

Wrapping her arms around him, Eve pressed her lips to his forehead. The scent of his skin and the feel of him beside her was familiar and beloved. "I don't know the answer to your question."

"I can see that," he said, reminding her that if she

didn't work actively to keep him out of her mind he had free access to everything.

She pushed him out, gently but firmly. "If there's a story there, it's not mine to tell. And I don't want secrets like that between us."

Alec slid an arm between her and the futon, then tugged her into his lap. "I don't want *anything* between us. I want to fix us. You and me."

"Are we broken?"

"Abel slipped into a crack, so we must be."

"You wanted this promotion. My understanding is that you had to bargain for it, probably with unfavorable terms for you. Don't give it up for me. I want you to be happy."

"I'm unhappy without you. We'll get Raguel back, and life will return to the way it was before and I'll be okay with that. More than okay."

"Are you sure?"

"Completely."

The phone rang. Eve scrambled off his lap and returned to her desk, picking up the cordless handset. "Hello?"

"Ms. Hollis. Detective Ingram here."

"Good morning, Detective."

"Your secretary told me you wouldn't be in the office today. It was your boyfriend's car that was in that big wreck yesterday on Harbor, right? Shortly after you left the station?"

"His car was in a wreck, yes. Fortunately, neither of us was in it and he has good insurance." She rushed forward, waylaying any further questions on the matter. "I know you need the rest of my statement, but you still have my car."

"If you're up to it, we'll come to you. The first forty-eight hours after a disappearance are crucial, Ms. Hollis. You might have information we can use and not realize it."

"When would be a good time for you?"

"My partner and I could come by in about an hour and a half, if that's okay."

"That's fine. See you then." She hung up and returned the receiver to its base. She looked at Alec. "Visitors in ninety minutes."

"You couldn't put them off?"

"They're all over me. If I delay any longer, it might get ugly."

Asmodeus had already stated his desire for the cleanest extraction possible. If he was coming, he'd wait until the coast was clear.

"Angel—"

Eve stood. "You'll know what to do when the time comes."

"I hate this," he growled, rising in a fluid ripple of power. "I hate not knowing when to duck."

"You love it," she retorted, stepping close enough to set one hand on the taut muscles of his abdomen. "Unpredictability is your forte."

"I've had enough of that the last few weeks." Alec caught her hand and moved it over his heart. "I'm ready for stability."

"Haven't you noticed that I'm normalcy-challenged? Chaos reigns in my life. If I'm your best shot at stability, you're in trouble."

He grinned. "Don't I know it."

* * *

The police arrived before an hour had passed. Eve suspected they'd done so as a way to keep her unnerved.

Montevista and Sydney rode the elevator down with her and Alec, but they separated on the ground floor. The guards headed toward the open-air courtyard where the pool was. Eve and Alec went to the glass entrance door and let the detectives in.

"I hope you don't mind that we're early," Jones said as they stepped into the foyer. He was sporting an avocado green suit and the grimly assessing gaze she was getting too familiar with. "We were in the neighborhood."

Ingram shook Eve's hand with a palm made cold and wet by the chilled water bottle he carried. He shot a sidelong glance at her when he greeted Alec the same way, betraying his dubious view of her dual boyfriend situation.

"I see firemen around the building," Jones noted. "What's going on?"

"Suspected gas leak on one of the floors," she lied, becoming irritated when her mark burned.

Is that really necessary? she complained, with a glare sent skyward. *It's a white lie.*

"Should we go somewhere else?" Ingram asked.

"My floor is clear, but we can sit in the courtyard." She gestured in that direction and they moved ahead of her. She and Alec exchanged glances.

They gathered around a circular glass patio table, one of the few that lacked an umbrella since the temperature was cool and the sun warm. The pool was being topped off. A small spigot released a stream of tap water, raising the water level. The tinkling sound created a tranquil atmosphere. Eve deliberately chose a seat that kept her back to a planter bordering a wall. Montevista and Sydney, professionals that they were, were inconspicuous.

Jones was lugging around the briefcase Eve had come to dread. He set it on the pebbled cement and withdrew her unfinished statement. After pushing it across the table toward her, he leaned back in the cushioned metal chair.

"I've been going over our previous discussions," he said.

Eve picked up the pen he provided. "Yes?"

"And I think—"

A burst of crimson. A scattering of black feathers. Alec's chair rocked back onto its rear legs before toppling him completely. The gun's report echoed.

He was sprawled across the patio before anyone registered the ambush.

Reed was waiting at Sara's desk when she came in. Her dangerously short pinstriped skirt was paired with a fitted white dress shirt and four-inch stilettos that matched her red lipstick. The length of leg exposed and the lack of a bra weren't lost on him, but neither did they impress.

She paused just inside the threshold, eyeing him warily. "Abel. What are you doing?"

He smiled. The chair he occupied was angled parallel to the length of the desk. His right arm draped along it, his fingers drumming into the stained walnut top. "Didn't I tell you that showing that video to Evangeline would be counterproductive?"

She stepped closer, her gaze moving to the computer monitor. She saw that the "sent" folder of her e-mail client was on display and murmured, "You go too far."

"You think so? But I haven't gone nearly as far as you have. For example, I haven't yet offered to trade you to a king of Hell to be rid of you."

Reed had to give her credit, she didn't even blink.

"We match today, *mon chéri*. We look so good together. Perfect for one another." Sara reached him and settled into his lap, her slim arms encircling his shoulders. "I would never wish to be rid of you."

He caught her close and whispered, "I can't say the same about you."

An instant later, they occupied a sofa in Michael's office. It was after six in the evening in Jerusalem, and the head of the Asian firm was literally on his way out the door when he spotted his visitors.

"Abel. Sarakiel." The archangel paused and pushed his hands into the pockets of his Western business slacks. His voice was deeply resonant, powerful in a way even some seraphs never achieved. "I suggest you find another place to play your games."

Reed pushed Sara unceremoniously onto the couch beside him and stood. He withdrew the jump drive he'd brought with him and tossed it. "Sara's latest game is one you may not want her to continue playing."

Michael caught the drive with a fluid outstretching of his arm. He looked at the item in his palm, then back at Reed. One dark brow arched in silent inquiry.

"It seems," Reed explained, "that our lovely Sarakiel has taken to making deals with demons."

Michael's eyes shimmered with blue flame. He looked at Sara, who tilted her chin defiantly while tugging her skirt back into place.

Reed crossed his arms and prepared to enjoy the show. Then Eve hit him like a freight train. He stumbled from the blow.

"Gotta run," he said.

Sara straightened. "You cannot leave me here! It will take at least a day to get back—"

He shifted away before she finished her sentence.

As Alec rolled out of his chair, Ingram yelled and reached into his jacket for his holstered gun. A bullet caught him in the back, exploding through his right shoulder in a shower of flesh and blood. His chair tumbled to the left. His arms flailed, then his skull hit the edge of a stucco planter with a sickening thud. He crumpled to the ground, still as death.

Eve slid under the table in a limbolike glide. Arching over the metal legs, she scrambled for Ingram's gun. Her hand circled the grip and she yanked the weapon free of its shoulder holster. Another shot rang out and Jones jerked violently. He crashed headfirst into the tabletop, shattering the glass on impact. The slivers rained down on her, prickling across her bare arms and skittering along the patio.

A battle cry preceded the snapping deployment of Alec's wings. He launched from the courtyard floor in a streak of ebony, his ascent propelled with such force that the downdraft shoved Eve into the planter.

As he targeted a marksman in an open third-floor

window, she struggled to her knees. He disappeared into the building and a moment later, a horrendous scream cut off abruptly.

Sydney appeared at the end of the courtyard. She darted toward Eve, weaving around the obstacles between them. Bursts of green hellfire dotted the ground behind her, mimicking her footsteps and urging her to a faster pace. Montevista shouted and ran the length of the opposite side of the pool, deliberately drawing fire away from both Eve and his partner.

Eve scrambled out and upright, slipping in the blood pooling beneath Detective Jones. His body hung over the broken table, folded at the waist with his arms, torso, and head inverted inside the empty frame.

She hopped into the planter behind her and took cover behind a mature palm tree. Hugging the trunk, she aimed Ingram's gun around it. Windows along the upper floor were dotted with demons. She and the two Mark guards were in a fishbowl, with enemies positioned all around the rim.

By clearing out the building to protect the mortals, they'd opened the entire complex to an Infernal infestation. Eve didn't wonder how they'd gotten past the perimeter guards. She'd made it possible, after all.

Sydney jumped into the planter behind Eve, shielding her back with a flame-covered sword. Montevista was pinned behind a trash can, crouched low and holding two flameless daggers in his hands. He popped up occasionally, hurtling the weapons at strategic windows, then ducking to summon replacements for the next salvo.

"He's covering us," Eve bit out. "So we can get to the lobby."

"On your count," Sydney said. "We'll make a run for it."

Eve fought off the emotions she didn't have time to feel and revealed the whole of her plan to her handler in one powerful surge of thought.

A massive shadow swept over the courtyard. *Alec.* Flying across the expanse from one window to another. Another scream rent the morning calm, followed by another trail of black as he darted back to the other side. Creating a canopy of sorts with his body, a barrier between her and the Infernals above.

As the Marks who'd been on watch on the street joined the fray, flickers of flame could be seen behind many of the windows. Eve's mark began to burn, pumping adrenaline and aggression like a cocktail through her veins. Her gaze met Sydney's. On the silent count of three, they leaped out of the planter in unison.

"Not so fast."

Eve turned. A three-headed . . . *thing* galloped toward her on mismatched animal limbs. She aimed and squeezed the trigger. It feinted fast as lightning, dodging the bullet before lunging. Eve was propelled into the pool, striking the water on her back. The massive demon pushed her beneath the surface, weighting her down in a rapid descent to the bottom.

The shock of the water caused Eve to drop the gun. The weapon hit the bottom with a muffled thud and skittered away. She couldn't retrieve it while pinned nine feet down.

The necklace.

The moment the thought entered her mind, a shadow blotted the sun. An object struck the water and sank quickly. As Alec moved out of the way of the light, the gold chain glittered, catching a ray of sunshine. The necklace arrowed its way toward Eve as if she were a magnet.

The demon released her in a panicked scramble that tore flesh from her thigh, bolting from the pool like a missile. The amulet settled around her neck and she clawed her way upward, breaking through the surface with great, burning gasps.

"Hollis!"

Sydney stood at the pool edge, one shirt sleeve bloodied but the other arm extended. With a mark-fueled kick, Eve surged up and toward her, catching Sydney's hand and gripping it tightly. The Mark hauled her out with a violent yank, dropping her on the ground in a bleeding, sputtering pile.

Eve gained her hands and knees, then ducked as a flame-covered dagger flew over her head. Her gaze lifted to Sydney's, but the Mark was looking beyond her, tossing blades in a barrage.

Eve looked over her shoulder. A massive man stalked toward her, wet and naked, with dripping black hair and laser-bright red eyes.

One by one, he gripped the dagger hilts from where they protruded from his chest and ripped them free, stomping forward with a ferocious, relentless stride.

Alec swept down in a potent gust of wind, alighting on the path between them and roaring like a beast. Many beasts. A sound so fearsome the walls shook with it and the pool water sloshed up and over the rim in a wave.

She had the necklace. There was nothing reining him back now.

His thirty-foot wingspan refolded into his back as if it had never been. The demon hunkered down before quickening into a full-bore run, fisting bloodied daggers with upraised arms, blades leading the way.

His forward momentum was awesome, each footfall shaking the ground like aftershocks. Alec crouched, visibly braced for the impact.

"Cain!" the demon bellowed, leaping high and hurtling downward.

He was directly above Alec when he stopped abruptly, momentarily hovering before snapping backward as if retrieved by a rubber band.

The demon's flight was halted by a brutal collision with something on the walkway. His body slid down, revealing Satan standing rigidly behind him. Claws formed from the Devil's hands and dug deep into the demon's torso, arresting the downward slide in a vicious semblance of an embrace.

Eve glanced at the detectives, but they lay unmoving. Were they both dead? Casualties of a war they didn't know was being waged?

She looked back at Satan and found him staring at her.

"Took you long enough to step in," she muttered.

Alec backed up in deliberate steps, forcing Eve to clamber to her feet to get out of his way. She was behind him one second, then tossed over Reed's shoulder the next. "*This* was your plan?" he bit out.

He shifted her near a body lying prone on the ground.

Montevista. Felled like a cut tree with his eyes open and sightless. The whites swallowed by black.

"Damn it," she breathed, hating that she'd been right. She grabbed the Mark's shoulder and rolled him into her lap on his back. She brushed his dark hair back from his forehead and hunched over him protectively, linking her fingers with his and holding his hand to her chest. Alec shifted Sydney over a split-second later.

From their position on the opposite side of the pool, she watched in horror as Satan reaffirmed his dominance.

"You want what's mine, Asmodeus?" the Devil hissed. His claws rent through the demon's torso, eliciting screams so agonized tears came to Eve's eyes. Through the lacerations in his mortal skin, Asmodeus's true shape could be seen. The monstrous many-limbed body writhed and sizzled within the torn flesh. Smoke poured from the widening cavity and filled the air with the stench of rotten soul.

"It will cost you," Satan crooned with his lips to the demon's ear as if they were lovers.

The Prince of Hell threw the decimated body into the swimming pool like rubbish. The water shuddered in response, bubbling red and churning, boiling and hissing steam. A geyser erupted from the center, spewing into the air in a twenty-foot tower.

Eve looked at Satan, who smiled his gorgeous smile. Dressed in black velvet vest and pants, he was classically and elegantly beautiful.

Something flitted across his features. A wince, then widened eyes. He clutched at his chest, hunching over with a groan.

Montevista's hand tightened on hers with a pained gasp. *"Eve."*

She jolted in surprise, then looked down at her friend. Montevista's powerful body began to shudder. His eyes were his own, no longer black.

"Only way," he wheezed.

The necklace draped inadvertently over their clasped hands, awakening the Mark in him and freeing him to summon the dagger now impaling his heart.

"No!" Reaching up, Eve caught Reed's wrist.

His gaze moved from Satan and settled on Montevista. "Oh shit . . ."

"Take him to the tower. Hurry."

Reed hefted the Mark into his arms and shifted, disappearing in the blink of an eye.

"Eve," Satan snarled. His arm snapped out toward the pool, the veins bulging along the rigid muscles.

The earth shuddered and groaned. The water in the center of the pool twisted into rope and arced onto the cement, forming the outline of a man whose endless arms extended in a desperate grasp for Alec.

The Devil's form flickered, his face contorting with savage rage and frustration. Then he faded completely. There one moment, gone the next.

Eve lunged into the Nix's path. He caught her, laughing, hauling her across the pool and up against his chest.

"Fuck you," she bit out, ripping the amulet from her neck and shoving it fist first into his torso. He instantly gained form, materializing into a man as nude as the others had been. Her hand pulled free of the closing flesh, leaving the necklace behind inside him.

He fell on her, writhing. She drew back her fist and decked him, sending him rearing upward with a violent arching of his back.

"Freeze! Police!"

The Nix clawed wildly into his mortal chest, struggling to excise the necklace.

A gunshot reverberated in the semienclosed space. Followed by another. The Nix jerked with each impact, screaming an inhuman sound as two holes appeared in his torso. Blood spurted onto Eve. He fell to his side, convulsing before shuddering into stillness.

Eve twisted to look behind her.

Detective Ingram kneeled beside his fallen partner with Jones's gun in hand. As his gaze met hers, his pistol arm fell to his side. A trail of blood marred his temple and the side of his neck.

"Are you okay?" he asked, swaying.

"Detective . . ."

His eyes rolled back in his head. He slipped into unconsciousness, slumping to the ground before she could reply.

"Holy shit." Eve rolled painfully to her stomach.

As she regained her feet, the pool continued its roiling boil. She stared at it, unblinking.

When Gadara burst from the depths in a flurry of dirty and tattered wings with Riesgo cradled in his arms, she was too numb to be surprised. The archangel landed on both feet, then fell to one knee. Riesgo lay in his embrace with arms splayed wide and head lolled back, breathing shallowly. The picture they presented—that of wounded angel protecting frail humanity—struck her with a message of faith and benevolence as nothing else in her life had ever done.

"Alec," she croaked.

He shifted beside her and caught her close.

CHAPTER 21

Eve tried not to look disgruntled as Reed pushed her through the hospital room doorway in a wheelchair.

I feel ridiculous in this thing, she muttered.

You looked ridiculous trying to maneuver on crutches, he retorted, softening the sting of his words with a squeeze of her shoulder. "Good afternoon, Detective."

Ingram offered a slight wave that jostled the IV tube connected to the back of his hand. The detective's other arm was in a cast. He looked soul-weary, the pale blue of the hospital gown only emphasizing how wan he was. The other bed in the room was closed off by a curtain, leaving the detective alone with a uniformed female officer who he introduced as his daughter.

"Nice to meet you," Eve said, extending her hand as Officer Ingram stood. The younger Ingram was trim and fit, with pretty features and dishwater blonde hair cropped super short.

"Are you okay?" the officer asked.

"Yes. I'm fine. Healing nicely, they tell me."

Eve didn't really need the wheelchair. The mark had healed the deep gash to her thigh over the last forty-eight hours and only a little redness remained. Still, the subterfuge was necessary since the wound had been nasty enough to take weeks for an Unmarked body to heal.

"You're a popular guy, Detective." She gestured at the profusion of flowers and balloons.

"They should be sending these flowers to the funeral home," Ingram said bitterly.

Reed's fingers caressed the side of her neck in a silent offer of comfort.

"I'm sorry for your loss," she said quietly.

"We all lost." Ingram sighed heavily. "Jones was a great cop. I was honored to w-work with him."

Her eyes stung when the detective's voice broke. "I need to thank you, Detective. You saved my life."

He flushed. "I was just doing my job."

"You're a great cop, too, something I'm profoundly grateful for." Changing the subject, as she'd learned to do when her dad became uncomfortable with sentimentality, she asked, "How long will you be in the hospital?"

"I'll be released tomorrow. Thank God."

She nodded and managed a smile. "I'm going to check on Father Riesgo now, but I'll stop back by before I go home."

Ingram looked at his daughter. "The priest is back?"

"Popped up yesterday," she confirmed. "Said he decided to walk home."

"From Anaheim to Huntington Beach?" Ingram was clearly dubious. "What's he doing in the hospital?"

"Severe dehydration."

"From the trek home? No, don't answer." Ingram heaved out a sigh. "I swear this world is going to hell in a handbasket."

Reed turned Eve's wheelchair around and pushed her back out to the hallway. As he steered her in the direction of Riesgo's room, he murmured, "Well, they'll be out of your hair now."

"See? It all worked out."

"Oh, no, babe. You're not getting off the hook that easily. Your plan was more fucked up than mine."

"No way," she argued, tilting her head back to look up at him. "Everything's wrapped up perfectly—the mask is contained, the wolf and Nix are finally dead, so are the hellhounds, the police are off my back, and the tengu are eradicated from Olivet Place. I finally feel like I can get started with a clean slate, like every other Mark does."

"If the way this shit has gone down is your idea of perfect," he said dryly, "we have a lot to talk about."

Reed slowed, then turned into a room. There were two beds—one occupied, the other freshly made. The patient in the far bed was sleeping. And he wasn't Riesgo.

"Wrong room," Eve said.

Backing up, Reed looked at the number by the door. "No. This is the number they gave us at the desk."

He hailed a passing nurse and asked, "Do you know which room Miguel Riesgo is in?"

"I believe he was discharged," she said briskly. "Just a short while ago."

Eve frowned. "Thank you."

The nurse moved away.

Reed's hand settled on her shoulder. "Didn't you leave a message that you were coming?"

"Yes, this morning." She reached up to link her fingers with his. "I'm really worried about him."

Riesgo had looked so broken when he'd returned. Half-dead. She could only hope that his emotional state was better than his physical one. She wouldn't relax until she saw for herself.

"We'll track him down when we leave here," Reed promised, giving her hand a reassuring squeeze. "We'll make sure he's okay."

Eve wished it was possible to fade into the woodwork while staring straight into a satellite feed. Alas, there was no way to hide from the many eyes that rested heavily on her.

"How is it that no one recognized what happened to Diego Montevista?" Gabriel asked. "He worked directly with all of you. You saw him every day."

Five beautiful faces frowned in unison from the massive LCD screen hanging on the wall directly opposite Eve. The feed was divided into six equal sized boxes, with one box left blank because Sarakiel was present at one end of the table. Gadara sat across from her, separated by several feet. Hank, Alec, Reed, Sydney, and Eve rounded out the room's occupants. A shade had been lowered over the wall of windows, dimming the light from the midmorning sun.

Hank leaned forward and all eyes moved to him. "It appears that Montevista could be left dormant at times and activated at others."

"But you suspected him, Evangeline?" Remiel

asked. Like most of the other archangels, he was dark-haired. Unlike the others, his eyes were almond shaped and his features tinged with a decidedly Asian cast.

Eve cleared her throat. "I didn't at first, no. But when Hank told me about his experiments with the tengu and I saw how violently it reacted to the mask mixture, I started thinking about Montevista and his resurrection from the hellhound blood. The only other known . . . *resurrectees*—is that a word?—were the wolf and the Nix, both of whom acted erratically after they came back to life. It seemed reasonable to assume Montevista wouldn't be the only one unaffected."

"That is a considerable leap," Michael said, in a voice that was both deeply seductive and highly terrifying. There was power in that voice. It underlined every word he said with a threat. The fact that he was gorgeous only made him more frightening. "To decide that he was Sammael's emissary because of the behavior of two lessor demons."

"I *guessed*," she corrected. "And it wasn't just because the wolf and Nix seemed to have lost all sense of self-preservation after cooking in the masking agent." She looked at Alec. "Cain became erratic, too. He wasn't himself. Since all of you have the same setup at your firms that he had—the connection to Marks and Infernals working beneath you—I looked at the differences between his situation and yours."

"Everything about his situation is unique," Uriel said.

"Including Montevista," she finished. "I figured that

if he was connected to Sammael by the mask, some of that evil would filter into Cain. It would explain a lot of Cain's behavior if that was the case."

"There were other possible explanations for that."

She met the archangel's gaze directly, understanding that he was referring to the paternity gossip that pained Alec so greatly. "I'm not one to rule anything out. The mask, Cain's problems, the way Montevista would lose consciousness every time Satan manifested—there were a lot of considerations involved. But since I didn't know for sure, I wasn't going to accuse him outright. It was too dangerous for Montevista. I hoped that if I turned out to be right, Hank could save him somehow."

"I am concerned," Remiel said, "at how often you work alone. You have a mentor for a reason. We cannot afford to have these types of large-scale battles waged in public places."

"And I," Gadara said dryly, "cannot afford to replace every luxury car that has the misfortune of crossing paths with her."

"I didn't have much choice," Eve protested. "In this case, Montevista was a wild card. I guessed he was involved in some way, so how could I share information with Cain, knowing it might leak to Montevista? If Satan knew we were on to him, what would he do? That was my concern."

"You should have approached your handler."

"She did." Reed leaned forward to set his elbows on the table. "She asked me to touch base with Asmodeus, and when everything blew up, she called me in to keep one eye on Montevista. When he blacked out, it proved her theory. She also kept Ishamel and

Hank in the loop. She doesn't have a savior complex, if that's what you're inferring. She knows her limits."

Don't piss them off, she protested, knowing he was already taking heat for his deal with Asmodeus.

They're pissing me off, he shot back.

Raphael rocked back in his office chair. "And Sarakiel made herself a threat with her association with Asmodeus, so you could not turn to her. But you must understand, Ms. Hollis. You are consorting and conspiring with Sammael by your own admission. You say that he deliberately summoned the Nix for you to vanquish before he lost contact with Montevista. His offering to you concerns us, of course."

Okay, they're pissing me off, too, Eve groused.

"Is there news of the priest?" Uriel asked.

Gadara leaned forward. There was nothing about his posture or features that bore witness to his ordeal, but it was there in his eyes. Especially when he looked at Alec. "Nothing," he replied. "He has not been seen nor heard from since he recovered enough to leave the tower. He has left the church and broken his residential lease. I *will* find him. It is only a matter of time."

There was a length of silence as the archangels flipped through copies of the various reports in search of unasked questions. Eve waited for queries about Ima or the necklace, but they didn't come.

Sydney raised her hand, which raised one of Gadara's brows.

"Yes, Ms. Sydney?"

She cleared her throat. "Montevista . . . Did he get in?"

"He committed suicide," Sarakiel said.

"I *know* that. What does that mean?" Sydney's gaze darted across the screen, then shot to Gadara. "Diego did it for us. To save us. To save us all."

"I testified highly for him, Ms. Sydney," Gadara murmured.

"As did I," Alec said.

"That's it?" She looked at Eve and tears welled. "That's all?"

"I think we are finished here," Michael said. "If we have further questions, we can revisit this discussion."

Eve quickly found herself in the hallway outside the conference room. Sydney hurried off, her shoulders tight and her posture defensive. Sarakiel, Gadara, and Reed lingered behind, speaking in harsh tones.

Hank was walking up to Eve when Alec appeared beside her. He caught her elbow and asked, "Can it wait, Hank?"

"Certainly." The occultist smiled. "Good to have you back, Cain."

Alec grinned. One blink later, Eve found herself standing in the midst of a city at night. The sights, sounds, and smells were foreign and exotic. Her disorientation lasted a moment, then she tugged free of Alec's grip and smacked him in the arm. "Don't do that without telling me first!"

He caught her about the waist. "Have you ever been to Cairo before?"

"Cairo," she repeated. "No, I can't say I have."

"There's a first time for everything." The glint in his eyes told her he was thinking of a more intimate first time between them. "Are you hungry?"

"When am I not these days?"

"Good." He held her hand and tugged her out of the shadows. "There's a great restaurant up the street I've been dying to take you to . . ."

Lilith stood in front of the window with her back to him, dressed in white from head to toe—turtleneck, slacks, and high-heeled boots. Her waist-length hair was so pale that it blended in with the rest. As a whole, her sleek alabaster form was a stark contrast to the greens and blues Sammael had determined would showcase her to perfection.

The same snap of his fingers that had wrought the instantaneous change in the color palette also urged her to turn around. She spotted him and her entire demeanor changed. Her shoulders went back and her stance widened. Defensively aggressive.

"Lilith," Sammael murmured. "How good of you to come so quickly."

"As if I had a choice," she retorted, but her breathless tone gave her away.

He terrified her. He could make her tremble and cry, cower and beg. And she loved it, which gave him power she'd rather not cede. She'd been grateful when he tired of her so many, many centuries ago.

Which begged the question: what had possessed her to incite his wrath, when even his amusement was a horror to her?

"You did have a choice." He moved to the chaise by the fire and sprawled across it. "You chose to barter something of mine for your own gain. Which is why you are here now. Had you chosen to barter something of your own, you would not be."

Her chin lifted. "You have something that belongs to me. I needed something of yours to entice you to give it back."

"Hmm." His mouth curved. "You speak in near riddle. I need to punish you soon, so hurry up and tell me what you wanted."

Lilith hesitated, her gaze darting about as if she was trapped, which she was. He couldn't allow anyone to steal from him. Such offenses had to be dealt with harshly and swiftly, as he'd proven to Asmodeus.

"I want Awan."

Surprise reverberated through him, followed by a growing delight. "I had forgotten about her."

"I haven't."

"You could have just asked me."

She clasped her hands behind her back. "I knew you wouldn't give her to me."

"Did you? And you reached that conclusion how?"

"Because," she pouted. "You've always made certain that I never get what I want."

Sammael propped his head on one hand and looked into the fire. "You think too highly of yourself, if you believe I deny you for the simple pleasure of it."

"Prove me wrong."

He raked her with an insolent glance. "Nothing about you gives me pleasure . . . except this request."

Lilith stood frozen, then a look of wonder crossed her beautiful face. "You'll recycle her?"

"Yes, but you will not be seeing her for a while." He breathed on his claws, then buffed them across the settee's velvet. "You see, a prison cell that has recently become vacant must be filled."

She inhaled sharply.

"Come now," Sammael crooned. "You have been missed around here. You should have many visitors. Most will be very eager to reacquaint themselves with you. And have no fear, I will not be one of them."

He waved her away. Two demons emerged from the shadows to take her by the arms.

"I hate you," she spat.

"My dear Lilith." Sammael laughed. "I really would not have it any other way."

"Are you okay?"

Eve glanced up as Reed straddled the picnic bench beside her. The ocean breeze ruffled his hair, giving him the deliciously disarrayed look of a man fresh out of bed. She'd only seen that look on him a few times, but it was a look she loved.

"I miss Montevista," she admitted. "And I'm angry about it. It's not fair."

"Babe . . ." The frown on display above his Armani sunglasses betrayed his concern. "He's in a better place. Trust me."

"Look at Sydney." She jerked her chin toward the sullen Mark who sat at a table near the grill where Alec flipped burgers. "She was just starting to get her mojo back. Now she's back to square one."

"This job is rough." Reed surreptitiously stroked the side of her pinky finger. "I worry about what it'll do to you."

Eve worried, too, which was why she'd brought her parents along today. They kept her grounded. Her dad sat at a table with Kobe Denner and Ken Callaghan, one of her marked training classmates. Her mom was working her way through the gathering with a tray of mini sushi and her shockingly naughty sense of humor. If some of the Marks were jealous that Eve still had her folks in her life, they weren't showing it today. Montevista was on everyone's mind and grief trumped envy every time.

"I'm going to go sit with her," Eve said, climbing off the bench. Reed came with her.

Sydney was accepting a plate from Alec when they joined her. The grill he manned was massive; large enough to cook hamburgers for a dozen oversized Mark appetites at a time. It had taken a trailer to get it out here—a tailgate party done on a Gadara Enterprises scale. Eve had mentioned her desire to do something for the Marks who'd come under fire because of the bounty, and Ishamel had swiftly taken it to the next level.

"Hey, you." Alec leaned over and gave her a quick peck on the forehead. "You feeling medium, or medium-well today?"

She was about to reply when the distant rumble of a Harley gave her pause. Pulling tendrils of wind-blown hair out of her lip gloss, she watched through her sunglasses as a platinum blonde on a hog maneuvered into the parking lot. Dressed in a black leather halter vest and chaps, the rider drew every eye except for Alec's.

The bike rolled to a halt beside the trailer as Alec turned his head. The pretty blonde winked at Eve, then blew a kiss at Alec.

The spatula in his hand clattered onto the cement.

Eve looked at Reed. "Who's that?"

"Awan." He grinned like the Cheshire Cat. "Cain's wife."

"Ex-wife," Alec correctly swiftly.

Awan licked her lips and purred, "Hi, honey. I'm home."

She was a lili. The demonic green eyes gave her away. They were laser-bright and filled with mischief.

Eve stood. This was the mother of Alec's children; the only progeny he would ever have. She had a piece of him that no one else ever would.

Eve's turmoil must have reached Alec, because his fists clenched. Awan laughed. With a saucy wave, the lili roared off as quickly as she'd appeared.

For a long moment, no one said a word.

Then, Sydney broke the tense silence. "Uh . . . I thought your wife was your sister."

Alec snatched the spatula off the ground and threw it into the back of the trailer. "My father kicked Lilith to the curb long before I was born. There's no relation between me and her kids."

Eve cleared her throat. "Your c-children were half demon?"

His shoved his hands through his thick hair. "One quarter demon."

What could she say to that?

Her mom walked up with an empty tray and a bright smile. "What a great party!"

Reed tapped his steepled fingertips together and kept on grinning.

Tossing her bath towel over the hamper, Eve left her bathroom. A quick glance at the clock told her it was nearing eight o'clock in the evening. She pulled on her favorite pajamas and shook out her damp hair, contemplating how best to spend her evening. A feel-good movie while curled up on the couch sounded like heaven to her. She usually preferred blow-'em-up action flicks, but she'd had enough explosions for a while. Maybe *Becoming Jane* would do the trick or something stupidly funny like *Blades of Glory*.

She moved down the hallway toward the kitchen, seeking comfort food. Hot coffee, maybe. And something sweet. She deserved it after today.

Straight ahead, the balcony door was closed. It was starting to get cold at night. Summer slowly turning into autumn. What a year it had been so far. Last Christmas she'd grumbled at RSVPing to the Weisenberg Group's company party without a date. Now, she had her dream job at Gadara Enterprises and two determined men she couldn't resist.

Admittedly, the dream job was more of a nightmare and the two men were both in the off stage of the on-and-off relationships she had with each of them, but she wasn't going to think about that now.

Eve was turning into the kitchen when Stevie Nicks's beautiful "Crystal" replaced the silence. She stopped midstride. Then cautiously started forward again, continuing to where the hall emptied into the living room.

On the coffee table, a silver champagne bucket held a napkin-wrapped bottle next to two half-full flutes. The man at her entertainment center felt her gaze and turned to face her. Although he appeared casual and relaxed, his dark gaze was avid. "Hi."

"Hi, yourself."

He approached, picking up the glasses along the way. "I hope you don't mind that I popped in."

"You're always welcome. Nothing is going to change that."

A cool flute was pressed into her hand. She looked down, catching sight of something circular glittering at the bottom. Her breath caught.

"I'm glad to hear that," he murmured with his warm fingers wrapped around hers. "Because I have a question to ask you . . ."

APPENDIX

The Seven Archangels

1 These are the names of the angels who watch.

2 Uriel, one of the holy angels, who presides over clamor and terror.

3 Raphael, one of the holy angels, who presides over the spirits of men.

4 Raguel, one of the holy angels, who takes vengeance on the world of the luminaries.

5 Michael, one of the holy angels, to wit, he that is set over the best part of mankind and over chaos.

6 Sarakiel, one of the holy angels, who is set over the spirits, who sin in the spirit.

7 Gabriel, one of the holy angels, who is over Paradise and the serpents and the Cherubim.

8 Remiel, one of the holy angels, whom God set over those who rise.

—The Book of Enoch 20:1–8

The Christian Hierarchy of Angels

First Sphere: Angels who function as guardians of God's throne.

- Seraphim
- Cherubim
- Ophanim/Thrones/Wheels *(Erelim)*

Second Sphere: Angels who function as governors.
- Dominions/Leaders *(Hashmallim)*
- Virtues
- Powers/Authorities

Third Sphere: Angels who function as messengers and soldiers.
- Principalities/Rules
- Archangels
- Angels *(Malakhim)*

ABBREVIATED PLAYLIST *(in no particular order)*

"The Judas Kiss"—Metallica
"Dare You to Move"—Switchfoot
"Love Remains the Same"—Gavin Rossdale
"Broken, Beat & Scarred"—Metallica
"Crystal"—Stevie Nicks

More extras at www.sjday.net

Sylvia Day is the #1 *New York Times* and #1 international bestselling author of more than a dozen award-winning novels translated into over three dozen languages. She has been nominated for the Goodreads Choice Award for Best Author and her work has been honored as Amazon's Best of the Year in Romance. She has won the *RT Book Reviews* Reviewers' Choice Award and been nominated for Romance Writers of America's prestigious RITA award twice. Visit the author at www.sylviaday .com, facebook.com/authorsylviaday, and twitter.com/sylday.

3 3132 03435 5257